NIGHTWATCH

NIGHTWATCH

JON HENDERSON

Tyndale House Publishers, Inc.
Wheaton, Illinois

**FOR
THE PIPS,
WITH LOVE**

Library of Congress Cataloging-in-Publication Data

Henderson, Jon, date
    Nightwatch / Jon Henderson.
       p.   cm.
    ISBN 0-8423-4251-6 (sc : alk. paper)
    I. Title.
PS3558.E4853N53   1995
813'.54—dc20   95-19799

Printed in the United States of America

00 99 98 97 96 95
7   6   5   4   3   2   1

On my bed I remember you;
I think of you through the watches of the night.
Because you are my help,
I sing in the shadow of your wings.

Psalm 63:6-7

PART I

1

"So, tell me *all* about him." Rebecca Keefe tucked her legs beneath her and settled more comfortably into the corner of the porch swing. "We've got a few minutes yet before they get here from Bangor."

Anne Dryden brushed an errant wisp of hair from her eyes. She let her gaze wander over the tree-lined greensward that swept from the back of her cousin's home down to the shore of Moosehead Lake in central Maine. It was a beautiful setting—a perfectly romantic place for her little vacation with Jake.

"You've shown me his picture," Rebecca continued, "so I already know he's tall, dark, and handsome."

Anne gazed with mock innocence at Rebecca. "Isn't that enough? What else do you need to know?" Anne kept a straight face until her cousin frowned at her incredulously. Then Anne smiled, and the two women laughed comfortably together. "Jake's smart," Anne bragged, "and strong, and—"

Anne's characterization was interrupted by the flailing of chubby arms. Six-month-old Lauren Keefe, nestled in the crook of Anne's arm, had knocked her now-empty bottle aside and was glaring impatiently at her. Anne smiled indulgently, draped Lauren over her shoulder, and began patting her back. When Anne looked up, Rebecca was staring intently out at the lake.

"What is it?" Anne asked.

"It's that man again," Rebecca replied tersely. "See him? There—just off the dock."

Anne looked out at the island-dotted expanse of water. A battered aluminum skiff bobbed beyond the end of the Keefe dock. In it stood a man wearing a blaze orange hunting cap and an olive green poncho. He was facing them. The skiff twisted slightly in the water, and the sun glinted from the binoculars the man was holding to his eyes.

"This is the fourth day in a row he's been here," Rebecca whispered.

"What's he doing?"

"Bird-watching. At least that's what he said when I asked him the other day."

"In front of a house?" Anne asked skeptically. "And into the sun?" She held Lauren more tightly as she watched the stranger. "Bird-watcher or not, he gives me the creeps."

"Me too," Rebecca agreed. As the skiff drifted northward with the current, the man kept the binoculars pointed in their direction. "I wish Brian were here."

The drone of an airplane drifted in from the south end of the lake. Rebecca looked hopefully in its direction. "That should be them now," she said, relief evident in her voice.

Anne watched as the man in the boat jerked his head toward the sound of the plane. Quickly he sat down, started the skiff's small outboard motor, and sped away. Almost instantly the boat disappeared around one of the outcroppings of weathered granite that jutted from Moosehead Lake's shoreline.

Rebecca relaxed. "If that man shows up tomorrow," she

said grimly, "I'm going to have Brian chase him away—with the floatplane."

Anne pointed. "There they are!"

Still bright in the setting sun, a Cessna 185 Skywagon floatplane buzzed along above the now shadowed lake. As it passed the house, the plane swooped into a tight, descending left turn and skimmed along just over the lake's surface. The Skywagon touched down, plumes of water rising up on either side of its floats. A pair of frightened loons whistled irately as the plane's pontoons made long Vs in the water, then drew up alongside the dock. As the engine sputtered and died, Jake MacIntyre stepped out onto a pontoon, grabbed one of the lines, and secured the plane snugly against the dock pilings.

"You didn't tell me he was so tall," Rebecca said as she and Anne walked down to the dock. "Your picture doesn't do him justice."

"That's because *I* took it," Anne replied. "Jake's the photographer, not me."

Brian Keefe stepped onto the dock next to Jake. "And he likes fly-fishing, too, doesn't he?" Rebecca added.

Anne stared at her cousin. "Jake's nuts about it. How did you know?"

Rebecca laughed. "Look at Brian. The only time my husband grins like that is when he finds out he's picked up someone as addicted to fly-fishing as he is."

Anne eyed Rebecca. "That's the *only* time he grins that way? You haven't been married *that* long." Rebecca Keefe laughed and shook her head. "Still," Anne continued, "I have this sinking feeling that—"

"That we're not going to see too much of them in the next few days?" Rebecca finished. "If the salmon are running, you can count on it."

Anne waved hello to Jake, then watched Brian as the two men unloaded Jake's gear. He was an inch or two shorter than

Jake's six-foot-four, but Brian obviously carried as much muscle. When he lifted a crate from the fuselage of the Skywagon, his brawny shoulders stretched tight against his faded denim shirt. Anne continued to observe him as he sat down on the crate and grinned at his wife and daughter. His bright blue eyes gleamed, and his broad smile showed a flash of white teeth behind an enormous mustache that was as black as his unruly shock of hair.

Anne and Rebecca joined the men on the dock. Rebecca bent over and gave her husband a kiss as Anne tilted her face up toward Jake. When the expected kiss didn't materialize, Anne opened her eyes. Jake stood in front of her, wide-eyed, staring at a point below her chin. Anne followed his gaze. She smiled at Lauren, who had fallen asleep.

"Who's that?" Jake asked.

"This is Lauren Keefe," Anne replied, "Rebecca and Brian's daughter."

"You know, Jake," Brian added cheerfully, "the daughter I told you *all about* on the way up here." Brian slipped Jake an exaggerated wink. "As much as you wanted me to tell you about the fly-fishing around here, I insisted on talking about *nothing* but Lauri." Brian smiled benignly up at his wife. Rebecca rolled her eyes, then pulled the bill of Brian's cap down over his eyes.

With a mischievous smile in Rebecca's direction, Anne held Lauren out to Jake. "Why don't you hold her?" Anne suggested. Jake backed up a step. From the corner of her eye, Anne saw Rebecca's smile broaden. "She's asleep, so she won't bite," Anne pointed out with feigned sweetness. "And we just changed her, so you don't have to worry about *that.*" Jake held up his hands, shaking his head mutely.

Brian came to Jake's rescue. "Smart move," he told Jake. "The women don't tell us this, but babies are contagious. On my first date with Becky she conned me into holding her infant nephew, and look what's happened to me."

Anne handed Lauren to her mother. "Am I safe now?" she asked Jake.

Jake put his arms around Anne, then abruptly picked her up. Stepping over to the edge of the dock, he held her out over the water. "Not quite. Need to wash the baby residue off first."

"Jake MacIntyre, don't you dare!"

"Too late, Jake," Brian called. "The stuff doesn't come off. It's as indelible as the ink they make sure you sign the marriage license with."

Jake put Anne down and kissed her soundly. He and Brian gathered up his gear, then followed Anne and Rebecca up to the house.

A squad car pulled up in front of the Piscataquis County sheriff's office. The square brick building on the corner of Pritham Avenue and State Route 15 had a fine view of both Moosehead Lake and downtown Greenville. Recently purchased from a failed savings and loan, the building was still affixed with a sign on its front reading only Greenville Branch.

Sheriff Roy Barnard switched off the television as Bill Estes came in. The deputy sheriff had disappeared an hour ago, lights flashing, in response to 911 calls reporting both a prowler and shots fired.

"Anything?" Barnard asked.

Estes snorted. "The 'prowler' was a moose in Widow Humphrey's turnip patch. Third time this week."

Barnard grinned. "And the shots?"

"Old Man Petersen, across the road from Widow Humphrey. When I got there, he was blazing away with that antique Remington of his, trying to scare off the moose. Came closer to hitting Widow Humphrey than he ever did to the moose." Estes grinned. "You know, I think Petersen's sweet on her." He looked at the silent television. "What did I miss on this week's *True American Crime Stories?*"

"Three car chases, a bigamist, and an update on the 'Hula Hoop' serial killer."

"Shoot. We never get that kinda stuff. Some people have all the fun."

Sheriff Barnard got up. "Speaking of fun, let's close up shop. Time to go over to the Lakeview and mooch some pie."

Five minutes later, with a wave to Sandy at the front desk, Roy Barnard and Bill Estes crossed the lobby of the venerable Lakeview Inn. Built by a timber baron more than a century ago, the green-and-white gabled mansion sat imposingly on a hillside above Moosehead Lake. From its spacious, shaded porches, decades of visitors had contemplated the lake's waters and islands.

No sooner had the pair taken their usual booth by the coffee stand than two pieces of coconut cream pie appeared. "Back in a sec with the coffee, guys," Doris Rodgers said as she vanished in a rustle of pink polyester.

Estes looked around the dining room. "Pretty slow tonight, even for after Labor Day." Barnard nodded agreement. The only other diner was at a table across the room. As they watched, he glanced at his check, tossed a bill on the table, and got up to leave. Halfway across the dining room, the dark, impeccably groomed man noticed the two lawmen. He started slightly, looked at his watch, and walked rapidly into the lobby.

"Don't get many suits around here," Estes remarked. "Lots of parkas and gum boots, but not too many suits and wing tips."

Doris collected the money and rang up the man's check. She brought Barnard and Estes their coffee, then poured herself a cup and sat down with them.

"Is the man who just left a guest?" Barnard asked her.

"Haven't seen him before tonight," Doris replied, "but I sure hope he is. Left a five-dollar tip on a fifteen-dollar tab. So long as he keeps tipping like that, he can stay until Christmas."

8

✧ ✧ ✧

Rebecca Keefe came into the kitchen, where Jake, Anne, and Brian sat around a massive oak table. Through the French windows behind them, the tip of Harford's Point glowed with the indigo hues of a late-summer twilight.

Rebecca dropped into a chair. "With all this excitement, I thought Lauri would never get to sleep."

Jake shook his head as Rebecca poured herself a glass of iced tea. "Even now that I've met you both, I still can't figure out how a Boston society girl like you fell head over heels for a country boy from the thriving metropolis of Caribou, Maine."

Rebecca laughed. "*Fell* is the right word. The summer before my last year of graduate work at Bowdoin, some girlfriends and I decided to take a rafting trip on the West Fork of the Penobscot River. Everyone else wanted to go on what Brian calls a 'float and bloat'—maximum eating and sunning broken up by short, easy floats down the river. But *I* insisted that we run the Ripogenus Gorge, some of the toughest white water in the country." Rebecca grimaced. "Naturally, I was the one who fell out of the raft. Right in the middle of the gorge. I was terrified. After floating downstream for what seemed to be forever, I managed to crawl onto a rock sticking up out of the water. There I sat, huddled up and miserable. The raft company must've had a walkie-talkie because a little while later, a raft with Rescue on its side showed up. They stopped upstream, and one of the men in the raft hooked a line to his belt and jumped in."

"Brian?" Jake asked.

Rebecca nodded. "He floated easily down to the rock and braced his feet against it. Then he grinned at me, trying hard not to laugh, while I sat there like a drowned rat." Rebecca glanced at her grinning husband. "I could've killed him. Then he held out his arms and told me to jump. I was so scared and embarrassed, all I could do was shake my head. He finally had to reach up and pull me into his arms. I held onto him for dear life as he pushed off into the river and his friends lined us over to shore. Then, when he tried to put me down, I wouldn't let him." Rebecca smiled at Anne's quiet laughter. "I guess I was afraid of falling into the river again. Anyway, Brian held me all the way out of the gorge. We dated all through my last year at Bowdoin, and you know the rest," Rebecca finished with a glance toward Lauren's bedroom.

"Once we got to shore and I had a chance to size her up, I almost threw her back," Brian said, taking his wife's hand. Rebecca snatched her hand away from his and shoved Brian playfully.

Then she frowned. "Brian, that man was here again today."

"Which man is that?" Brian asked. He looked at Jake. "So many men are chasing my wife that it's hard to keep track."

"The bird-watcher," Rebecca replied. "Drifted by this afternoon, staring right at Anne and me through his field glasses. Just like the other times."

Brian shrugged. "It's a public lake, hon."

"But he gives me the heebie-jeebies. Anne too." Rebecca looked at Anne, who nodded.

"And he took off in a hurry when he heard you coming," Anne added.

Brian reached out and ran his finger along his wife's cheek. "Tell you what. I'll mention it to Roy Barnard when I go into town tomorrow. *True American Crime Stories* was on tonight, so he's probably chomping at the bit for something that will get him on the show."

Rebecca stuck her tongue out at her husband, then looked at Jake. "By the way, you have my undying gratitude."

Jake peered at her over his glass of iced tea. "For?"

"For providing a reason for Anne to come visit that she couldn't refuse. Until you came along, it was easier to pry a limpet off a rock than it was to dislodge my cousin from her classroom." Rebecca smiled warmly at Anne, knowing how much Anne loved teaching first grade in Portland.

"You aren't easy to visit, Cousin," Anne replied. "Disappearing as you did right after your wedding on a yearlong honeymoon."

"Honeymoon?" Brian snorted. "You call spending a year in Assyria while she finished her postdoctoral research a honeymoon? No beer, no baseball, and I turned out to be allergic to camels."

"How was the fishing?" Jake asked jokingly.

"Rotten." Brian leered cheerfully at his wife. "Speaking of honeymoons, maybe we could leave Lauri with Jake and Anne while you and I sneak off to the Greenville Inn. . . ."

Rebecca ignored him. "What brings you to Greenville?" she asked Jake.

"Trees."

"No shortage of those, but why here?".

"Ever hear of an outfit called the Nature Conservancy?"

"Sure," Rebecca replied. "They own land all over the state. Do a good job of taking care of it, too. We send them some money each year."

"And," Brian added, "they're a lot easier for a Maine Guide like me to work with than some of those tree-hugging outfits."

"But what do they want with you?" Rebecca asked. "Anne says you're a photojournalist. News photos, that sort of thing."

"I used to do a lot of work for *National Geographic*," Jake explained. "Back in the days when I traveled a lot more than I get to now."

Rebecca glanced at Anne and saw her cousin's face cloud up briefly.

"The Conservancy's art director remembered my work," Jake continued, "and she's commissioned me to photograph a preserve of theirs called Big Reed Pond for next year's calendar.

The preserve's not too far from here, so when Anne told me Brian ran a flying service, I figured he could help me get around."

"Air express service," Brian promised. "Where do you want to go first?"

"Kokadjo."

Brian nodded understandingly. "The Roach River at dawn. Can't do a decent job of photographing any place in Maine without seeing it first."

"Makes sense," Jake agreed. "Are they hitting Black Ghosts?"

Brian shook his head emphatically. "Gray Ghosts are much hotter. But it's spawning season, so I'd use an attractor pattern or a Kennebago smelt."

Anne turned to Rebecca. "I didn't know Brian was a photographer." She frowned. "But what's a Kokadjo? And what's all this about ghosts?"

"Brian can't tell one end of a camera from the other," Rebecca replied sardonically. "We have exactly four pictures of Lauren. Kokadjo just happens to be the fly-fishing capital of Maine, and a Gray Ghost is a kind of dry fly. I know because I reached into the washer one day and came out with one stuck in the end of my finger." She stood and picked up her mug. "C'mon, let's go somewhere else. If Jake knows as much about fly-fishing as it sounds like he does, they'll be here all night."

❖ ❖ ❖

Baghdad

The clamor of the disco faded as the heavy glass doors swung shut behind them. Potted palms dotted the balcony. Off to one side a tuxedoed drunk, one eye covered by a silken black patch, lay sprawled on a chaise longue.

Hafez Adid leaned on the tiled balustrade. The city below him stretched eastward toward the impending dawn, the blue shimmer of lighted swimming pools contrasting with the fires that burned throughout the city's overflowing slums.

Adid surveyed his companion critically. "We cannot stay," he said emphatically. "Not here."

"But we must," his partner replied. "There is still so much to do."

"It is too dangerous." Adid set down his frosted glass. "The Americans can extract us. It is time to leave."

"Not until my vengeance is complete."

Adid's angry gesture swept the tumbler from the balcony rail. "A thirst for revenge as boundless as yours will *never* be satisfied! You know that as well as I do. And when they catch you—not *if*, mind you, but *when*, if you keep this up—they will either parade you around the Presidential Palace and then chop off your head or simply take you out into the desert and shoot you. Whose vengeance will be complete then?" His tone softened. "Listen to me. You have always trusted me with the business end of our little venture. So trust me now—it is time to go."

A spasm of indecision furrowed his companion's face, then dissolved into resolution. "Very well. We will leave." Adid's relief was checked by his partner's upraised hand. "After one more operation."

Adid shook his head. "We have done enough."

"I disagree, but that is not the point. As you say, the Americans have offered to extract us. But we both know that in America, as anywhere else, the more currency one has the better one lives."

"The Americans have promised us money!" Adid replied vehemently.

"I'm not talking about dollars. I'm talking about the currency the Americans value most—information, and the power which derives from it. This one last effort will provide us with the information we'll need to ensure ourselves of a rich, full life in America." A smile crept into the husky voice. "Besides, it will afford me a final modicum of peace."

His chin cupped in his hand, Adid watched the dawn for a long time. Then he turned back to his partner. "Very well. Just once more. Besides," he added with a grin, "when have I ever been able to refuse you? Now let's go back inside—we have been out here far too long."

When the balcony was deserted, the man on the chaise sat up, suddenly awake and alert. He adjusted his eye patch, then reached inside his tuxedo jacket and shut off the small tape recorder in his pocket.

2

A flotilla of loons, their breakfast interrupted, watched Roy Barnard as he strode through the rising mist. The hollow clunk of his boots on the wooden dock sent them skittering away over the waters of Moosehead Lake.

A sign on the building squatting precariously at the end of the dock read Carver Marine. Barnard threw open the building's door and wasn't surprised to find no one behind the battered formica counter. He walked around to the top of a rickety staircase tacked onto the building's far end. Six feet below him, a man stood on a floating dock, pumping gas into the tank of an outboard motor.

"Hey, Jack!" Barnard shouted.

Jack Carver looked up and waved. He capped the tank, wiped his hands on his pants, and came up the stairs.

"Mornin', Roy," Carver said affably. "The togue are hittin' over in Doughnut Cove. Troll a shiner at about thirty feet."

Barnard smiled. "Don't tempt me. Here on business, I'm afraid. Brian Keefe came by the station house this morning. Seems someone's been spying on his house from one of your boats." The sheriff explained about Rebecca and the bird-watcher. "So," Barnard finished, "I'm trying to track this guy down so I can have a little chat with him."

Carver scratched his head. "I'm doing lots of business, what with the lake trout running. Did Brian say what this fella looked like?"

"Just what Rebecca told him. The clown was wearing an orange hunting hat and drab poncho."

The fishing guide snapped his fingers. "Yeah, I've seen him. Came in five, maybe six days ago. Said he wanted to rent a boat for a week—to go bird-watching. Struck me as kinda funny."

"Funny how?" Barnard asked.

"Normally, the Kennebunkport bird-watching types I get look like they just cleaned out L. L. Bean. Not this guy. He looked like a refugee from a garage sale. International-orange deerstalker hat, moldy-green poncho, and—get this—underneath the hat he was wearing some kinda bandage! Funniest lookin' thing I ever seen. But he had the cash, so I rented him a boat for a week."

"What does he look like?"

Carver shrugged. "Nothing special. Tall, kinda skinny. Black hair, and a real big nose. He was wearing sunglasses, so I couldn't see much else."

"Did you get some ID?"

"Do I look stupid?" The boatman turned. "Got it written down. Up in the boathouse."

Barnard followed Carver into the building perched on the end of the dock. Carver riffled through a ledger. "Lessee. Funny kind of name." With a forefinger he stabbed the ledger triumphantly. "Ali Hassad!" Carver swung the ledger around. Barnard took out his notebook and began copying the entry.

"How did Mr. Hassad pay for the rental?" the sheriff asked as he copied.

"Cash on the barrelhead." Carver grinned. "Cash deposit,

too. Two hundred-dollar bills." The grin widened. "Didn't tell him the boat's only worth one-twenty, tops."

"Did you get a look at the picture on his license?"

Carver frowned. "Nope. Couldn't."

Barnard looked up. "Why not?"

"It was one of those temporary licenses. You know, a little piece of paper all typed up and stamped. I asked him about it, and he said he had just moved. Looked OK, though."

The sheriff slipped the notebook back into his breast pocket. "Did you ask where he's staying?"

"Nope. Didn't care. Not with a two-hundred-dollar deposit."

"When you see him," Barnard said as they walked up the dock, "tell him to come by the station house, will you?"

"Sure thing." Carver watched the loons as they scattered again. "That reminds me. This Hassad character pointed at the loons and asked me what they were."

Barnard nodded. "Understandable, I guess, if he's from away. . . . But a bird-watcher?"

"Yeah. When I told him they were loons and said, 'That's another for your life list,' he looked at me like I was crazy. Does that make sense? Any birder serious enough to rent a boat keeps a life list." Carver shook his head. "If that guy's a bird-watcher, I'm Betty Crocker."

❖ ❖ ❖

"You frosted over last night," Rebecca told Anne.

Shadows from the ash tree's expansive canopy of leaves dappled the quilt spread out on the grass. In the middle of the quilt, Lauren Keefe held on to her mother's fingers as she practiced standing.

"I did?" Anne asked. "When?"

"When Jake mentioned that he used to travel a lot more than he does now."

Anne shook her head. "I feel so . . . stuck," she said at last.

"Actually, I feel like *we're* stuck, Jake and I. We don't seem to be going anywhere."

Anne followed Rebecca's gaze as her cousin looked at the emerald-and-gold ring that graced Anne's left hand. "Really?" Rebecca asked. "I remember when you wrote me about Jake giving you that ring. You were *thrilled.*"

"That was almost a year ago. And he still hasn't asked me to marry him." Rebecca nodded her understanding. "He acts like we're going to get married," Anne explained, "and everyone assumes we're going to, but I still haven't heard 'Anne, will you marry me?'" Anne reached out and smoothed a stray wisp of Lauren's chestnut hair. "Sometimes, I wish he'd ask just so I could tell him no. Not that I'd really mean it, of course, but it wouldn't hurt him to stew for a while."

"Have you asked him about it?" Rebecca asked.

"You sound just like Mama," Anne said with a sigh. "Not really. I've tried to find out about him, hoping he'll open up to me more. When I asked him about his family, he told me about how his parents used to fight all the time. When I ask him about his married friends, he tells me that all his friends in New York are getting divorced." Anne hesitated. "I know Jake's had some . . . some girlfriends before me, some relationships that didn't turn out too well." Anne looked away. "I think he's scared."

"I think you are, too," Rebecca said softly.

Without looking back, Anne nodded.

Bill Estes looked up as the two men approached.

"Mind if we join you?" Brian asked.

At the deputy's invitation, Brian and Jake slid into the booth in the Lakeview's dining room. Brian introduced Jake. "Jake's chartered me out for a week," Brian explained to Estes. "On business, but first we're going to do some fishing."

Estes grinned at Jake. "You're in for a treat. Brian can take you to spots only he and God know about."

Brian waved Doris Rodgers off. "Two of today's specials, Doris," he called.

She returned shortly. Jake smiled appreciatively at the platter of roast pork with gravy, baked beans, steamed broccoli and cauliflower, and glazed carrots. Macaroni salad and fresh baked bread completed the meal.

After a simple, heartfelt grace, Jake looked at Brian. "Sure beats the takeout from the Italian place across the street from my apartment," he commented, gesturing at his plate.

"Whereabouts you from, Jake?" Estes asked.

"New York. I've got an apartment in Soho."

The deputy shook his head. "Been to New York once. Police convention. Took us out into the subway at three A.M. Never seen *anything* like that."

Jake shrugged. "You get used to it after a while."

Brian turned to Estes. "I need a hand, Bill. Something's come up. I dropped by the station house this morning and mentioned it to Roy, but I think you should know about it, too."

Estes looked up from his French dip. "You need a hand, you got it. What's going on?"

"Some jerk's been cruising past our dock the past few days. Becky says he's been checking out our place with binoculars. When she asked the guy what he was doing, he said he was a bird-watcher, but Becky doesn't believe it." Brian paused. "I don't, either."

"Has he said anything threatening to you or Rebecca?" Estes asked. When Brian shook his head, the deputy grinned. "I didn't think so, or *he'd* be the one asking for police protection—from his hospital bed. But," Estes added with a shrug, "if he hasn't said or done anything overtly threatening, there's not much I can do. You're a Maine Guide; you know as well as I do that the lake is public property. This joker can cruise past all he wants, as long as he doesn't trespass. He hasn't tried to tie up to your dock or anything, has he?" Estes added hopefully.

"Not that I know of," Brian replied. He shrugged. "Becky's probably just overreacting. I've been gone a lot this season, and she's been nervous being alone with Lauren. What you *can* do for me is check in on them while I'm gone this next week with Jake."

"You got it," Estes promised. "Your place is on the road to my house. I'll stop by on my way to and from work."

Brian nodded his thanks. "I wish I didn't have to be gone so much," he admitted. "But it's a good thing I've been chartered out this season—babies are expensive!"

"Tell me about it," Estes agreed with a smile. "But I got bad news for you: It only gets worse. My oldest just started college, and there's three more where he came from." He paused to take another bite. "You got kids, Jake?"

Jake shook his head. "Not married."

"That's good to know," Doris told Jake as she slid their desserts onto the table. "At least *one* of the three best-looking men in town is single. Name's Doris, honey. Brian's got my number if you're interested." She winked at Jake as she sauntered away.

Jake looked at Brian. "Why do you have her number? Did you used to date her?"

"We dated some back in high school," Brian confessed. "As a matter of fact, we still see a lot of each other."

"And Becky doesn't mind?"

"Not at all." Brian looked at Jake, then grinned. "Doris baby-sits for us," he explained.

Their dessert was interrupted by the approach of a tall, well-groomed man. "Mr. Keefe?" the man asked in slightly accented English.

Brian stood up. "I'm Brian Keefe. Do I know you, Mr. . . . ?" Brian's voice trailed off questioningly.

The man smiled. "I have not had the pleasure of your

acquaintance. Allow me to introduce myself." A business card appeared in the man's hand.

"What may I do for you—" Brian glanced at the card as he took it—"Mr. Marduk?"

Marduk's smile was both charming and debonair. "When I told the front desk that I wished to hire a plane, they referred me to you. They also told me you were lunching here in the dining room."

"I've got a floatplane, but I'm afraid I'm booked this week," Brian said.

Marduk nodded. "I am not yet certain of my requirements, as I am awaiting the arrival of my associates. Is there a number where I might reach you?"

Brian fished around in his wallet, then handed the man his card in return. "Will you join us for lunch?" Brian asked.

"Thank you, Mr. Keefe," Marduk demurred, "but I have another engagement. Forgive me for interrupting. Now, please, continue your luncheon."

"Whew," Estes sighed after Marduk had left. "He was wearing a suit last night, too. Guy like that sort of makes you feel like you should be dressed up."

"Seemed nice enough," Brian replied.

"What'd he say his name was?" Estes asked.

Brian read the card.

Professor Darius Marduk
Department of Cultural Anthropology
al-Azhar University

"Wonder where that is," Estes said. "And I wonder what he's doing here in Greenville."

The White House

The president rose from his chair as a tall, regal woman

was ushered into the Oval Office. "It's good of you to come, Mrs. Doral."

Lydia Doral nodded. "My pleasure. And allow me to congratulate you on your election."

The president smiled winningly. "I was told, correctly, that you are ever the diplomat." He motioned toward a sideboard. "Coffee? I'm sure you know where everything is—you and everyone else around here have been in this office far more often than I have."

Cup of coffee in hand, Doral settled gracefully into a Hepplewhite chair. Gazing coolly at the president, she took a long sip before continuing. "And what may I do for you, Mr. President?" she asked. "Calling in a previous administration's ambassador is a rather unusual step."

"Unusual times require unusual measures. I need a special envoy, and from what I've been told, no one's better qualified for the job than you."

Doral did not rise to the flattery-baited hook. "And to where is this mission?"

"Iraq." Despite his close scrutiny, the president could detect no change in Doral's fabled imperturbability. *She's as good as they say she is,* he decided. "Few people in the world know as much about the Middle East as you do," he added, "and you've a proven track record as a career ambassador."

Doral set her cup aside. "As a result of the Gulf War, diplomatic relations with Iraq are, as the State Department puts it, 'temporarily suspended.' Are you considering reestablishing them?"

The president shook his head firmly. "Not even close. What we need is someone to spearhead a mission that will conduct a brief, onetime round of negotiations with the Iraqis. You'll be our plenipotentiary, backed up by a team of top-flight people."

The former ambassador smiled knowingly. "And will anyone on this top-flight team be from the diplomatic corps, or will they *all* be CIA agents?"

The president laughed and shook his head. "I was also told—correctly again, it would seem—not to try and pull the wool over your eyes. Yes, several members of your mission will be CIA field agents."

"And the nature of the mission?"

"I'd prefer to wait until we're joined by my staff before answering that question. I wanted a chance to get to know you personally . . . and to find out if you'd be interested in a chance to further the cause of international relations."

Doral smiled. "A noble phrase, Mr. President, and one which rarely coincides with the motives of diplomacy." She leaned back in her chair. "By the way, who, if I may ask, is this so-accurate biographer of mine?"

The president grinned. "A mutual acquaintance of ours. Joel Dryden."

3

Lieutenant Mark Sewell poked his finger at a page of the information manual he was holding. "I'm right, Chief. It's 'Hor-muze,' not 'Hor-moose.'" The young officer swung around in his swivel chair and smiled triumphantly at the grizzled old sailor. The two were seated at consoles in the Combat Information Center of the Ticonderoga-class cruiser USS *Alameda.*

"Lieutenant," Master Chief Petty Officer Shiloh Turk replied cheerfully, "unless one of the countries around here starts making beer, I couldn't care less how you pronounce it." Turk didn't take his eyes from the radar screen that glowed in front of him. "But you know what I miss even more than beer? I miss—" The chief sat up. "Radar contact. Possible bandits, eleven o'clock."

Lieutenant Sewell strode over to a lucite rectangle glowing gold in the deep-red lighting of the CIC, the display panel for the cruiser's Mark 7 Aegis fire-control computer. On it was projected a computer-generated map of their position, updated every thirty seconds by the *Alameda*'s navigation computers.

Fed with data from the ship's global position sensing system, the display was accurate to within fifty feet.

The lieutenant tapped a key on the keyboard mounted below the board, activating the SPS-52 three-dimensional planar radar atop the cruiser's mainmast. Two red dots appeared in the display's upper left corner. Another keypress displayed a ring of green dots, centered on the *Alameda*, representing the F-18 Hornets and F-14 Tomcats flying Barrier Combat Air Patrol for the 233d.

The two red dots stretched into short lines as the radar provided course and speed information to the Aegis. As Turk watched, the lines bent slightly to point straight at the flotilla of which the *Alameda* was a part.

"Looks like they're coming to call," Sewell decided. "Got any ID on them?"

"Not a peep," Turk replied. "IFF negative." Following standard operating procedure, Turk had sent the intruding aircraft a radar-based identification, friend or foe, message on both military and civilian frequencies. When so queried, the transponder of a friendly aircraft would automatically respond with a positive identification.

Sewell, new to the Combat Information Center, looked at Turk. "Think we should light 'em up with the SPY?" Illuminating the approaching aircraft with the *Alameda*'s RCA SPY 3B phased-array tracking radar was the first step in preparing to fire the ship's surface-to-air missiles.

Turk shook his head. "No way. You're too young to remember the *Vincennes* foul-up. Upgraded or not, I don't trust that beast." In 1988 the USS *Vincennes*, an older version of the *Alameda*, mistook an Iranian Airbus airliner for an attacking aircraft. It shot down the Airbus, killing all aboard.

"OK, then," Sewell agreed, "we'll check 'em out first. Let's make them feel welcome." The lieutenant picked up a phone. "Bridge, CIC. Bogies, bearing three-three-five." He tapped a sequence of keys. Numbers appeared at the bottom of the plotting board. They were at angels four—forty thousand feet. "Altitude angels four, range one-eight-three true, closing at Mach point-eight-five."

With the phone to his ear, Sewell watched the plotting board. When two of the green dots had broken out of the circle and sped northward, he hung up and sat back down. "Now, Chief, what could you possibly miss more than beer?"

"You've met Robin Hawkes, my chief of staff," the president said to Lydia Doral as two men entered the Oval Office. "And this is Elliot French, the CIA's director of operations."

Smiling her hello, Doral extended a long-fingered hand to French. "How's Chris doing?" she inquired. "I imagine she's ready for the baby to make its debut."

Grinning, French nodded. "*Their* debut," he corrected. "Twins. And you can bet that she's doubly anxious for next week to get here. I'll tell her you asked."

The president and his chief of staff exchanged a glance. *Even if we don't seem to be old friends like everyone else around here,* he thought, *at least Robin and I know each other.*

"Before I met you," the president told Doral, "I was going to have Elliot give you a big sell job to try and get you to do this for us. But now—" The president shrugged. "Elliot, just see if you can tell Mrs. Doral something she doesn't already know."

The CIA director leaned against the back of a red leather, hobnailed chair. "With the fall of the Soviet Union, the new world order we so eagerly pursued is presenting us with some interesting new forms of crisis.

"Today's hot spot has Russia—a high-tech, no-money country—hopping in bed with the no-tech, high-money country of Iraq. The object of their coupling being, of course, to bear fruit. Fruit in the form of lots of Iraqi petrodollars for

Russia and lots of shiny-new, Russian-made nuke-thy-neighbor weaponry for our friends the Iraqis."

"But Russia has signed the Nuclear Nonproliferation Treaty," Robin Hawkes protested.

"True," French agreed. "And so far, they've adhered to it. But suppose all they sell to the Iraqis are the delivery systems for nuclear warheads. All legal, on the up-and-up, and not subject to international sanction."

"But just how much use can the Iraqis make of this stuff?" the president asked. "How much nuclear capability do they really have?"

"You haven't had time to be completely briefed yet," French replied, "but it's a lot worse than we're letting on to the public. Reconnaissance flyovers by our INDIGO-LACROSSE and KEYHOLE satellites are confirming just how little damage Desert Storm really did to their fissionable-material-generating capabilities. Plus, any equipment which was destroyed in the war is quickly being replaced by the nuclear-flea-market types—like our old enemies the Pakistanis and our old friends the Chinese." French grimaced. "We estimate that within six months, Iraq will be able to generate weapons-grade plutonium in quantities sufficient to create warheads in the hundred-kiloton range."

"So the Russians keep their plutonium," the president concluded, "enabling them to swear piously by the NPT while selling the Iraqis everything but the bang." He looked at French. "What kind of hardware are we talking about?"

"Big money for big iron. We figure around ten billion over the next five years for goodies like Tu-22 Blinder medium bombers and MiG-29 Fulcrum all-weather strike fighters. New stuff, hot stuff—the real cream of the Russian crop."

"Maybe they'll use it all on Iran," Hawkes suggested hopefully.

"We should be so lucky," French replied. "But even if they

glazed Iran into one giant serving dish, they'd still have lots left over for places like Riyadh and Cairo."

"Not to mention Tel Aviv and Jerusalem," Doral added.

"What really makes this so much fun," French went on, "is that Iraq is dickering with the Russians to buy a Kilo-class submarine." The director of operations smiled at Doral's disbelieving stare. "A frontline, Russian-made attack sub," he added, "cruising around with a bunch of terrorists aboard. Reassuring idea, isn't it?"

Doral frowned as she realized the implications. "Of course," she added, "the Russians will offer to supply a crew until the Iraqis are trained. And that training could be arranged to take a *very* long time."

French nodded grimly. "Giving the Russians the Persian Gulf port they've lusted after for so long. Combine that with the 'technical advisors' they'll offer to supply along with the aircraft and the sub, and we've got ourselves one *big* problem."

"How much of this arsenal do they already have?" the president asked.

"That's where the ambassador comes in," French answered. He smiled at Doral. "You really will be going on a trade mission. Your job will be to distract them with the offer of gobs of American money in the form of agricultural grants. Meanwhile my boys—your staff, that is—will go snooping around. Feel up to it?"

The ambassador recrossed her long legs. She gazed at the president over steepled fingertips. "Is this how you wish me to 'further the cause of international relations'?" she asked pointedly.

The president, making a mental note to meet Mr. Doral sometime, nodded.

"Do I know any of my staff?" Doral asked French.

The DO shook his head. "They're all young hotshots, headed up by a guy they consider positively elderly at the ripe old age of thirty-two. Based on some work he did for me last year in Tibet, I promoted him to Mike Force, our elite counterterrorism unit. Name's Randy Cavanaugh."

"Counterterrorism?" Doral questioned. "This sounds more like a military affair."

"Right both times," French agreed. "World-class military hardware in the hands of a terrorist state. Cavanaugh's well versed on both fronts: He's spent time in the former Soviet Union, and since joining Mike Force, he's become more than a little familiar with the tactics of the boys in Baghdad."

The ambassador nodded. "And the code name of this little escapade?"

"Operation Plowshare."

Doral laughed. "In light of our supposed 'trade mission,' that seems appropriately agrarian."

"And also appropriate because," French added with a grim smile, "whether they like it or not, that's what we're going to beat their swords into."

✧ ✧ ✧

Doris Rodgers sank into a chair in the small office behind the lobby of the Lakeview Inn and wearily hauled her feet onto another chair. Arms hanging limply, she let her head flop loosely over the back of her chair.

Seeing that the lobby was unoccupied, Sandy Neill, the Lakeview's day manager, came into the office and sat down beside Doris. She surveyed her old friend critically. "Lunch wasn't all that crowded, so it must be your new boyfriend." Sandy waited expectantly.

Doris stretched. "He's fun, generous with his money, and a great dancer. He also refuses to believe that no is part of the English language."

"How long did it take you to remind him of that last night?"

"Until two-thirty." Doris quickly changed the subject. "Know anything about our star guest?"

"Which one's that?"

"The one who looks like Omar Sharif's handsome brother."

Sandy smiled. "You mean room ten—the professor?" The manager paused. "He hasn't asked me out, if that's what you mean."

"Then consider yourself lucky. He'd be a *weird* date. Three times I've served him salad with his meals, and each time he's picked through them."

"So? Lots of people do that."

"Yeah, but how many people carefully cut the skin off the cucumber slices and then eat the rest? Or eat the slices of red and yellow pepper, but not the bell pepper? Or shove all the lettuce onto the butter plate?" Warming to her gossip, Doris sat up. "Not only that, but today at lunch he went through the butter sauce on his fish, picked out all the bits of parsley, and set them aside." She shook her head. "Like I said, *weird.*"

"Food isn't all he's finicky about," Sandy replied archly. "I originally had him in room twelve. You know—the one with the royal blue carpet and the pretty cornflower damask curtains? Well, I had no sooner opened the door than I thought the man was going to have a stroke. He backed away and demanded another room. When I asked what was wrong, he said that he'd prefer a room on the first floor. I told him that all our rooms were upstairs and showed him room ten. Suddenly, he was all smiles and everything was fine." The manager shrugged. "Go figure."

Doris's eyes narrowed. "Room twelve doesn't have twin beds, does it?"

"In a bed-and-breakfast?" Sandy replied disparagingly. "No twin beds in a B-and-B. Not if you want to stay in business." The bell at the front desk rang, and she stood up. "You're right, he's an odd duck. But I'd still go out with him if he asked."

Doris stared at her friend. "You would?"

"Sure. He's really handsome, and he's got a platinum American Express card. With a combo like that, I can overlook a *lot.*"

31

As Mark Sewell came up onto the deck of the USS *Alameda*, it seemed to him that the rising sun was dyeing the waters of the Strait of Hormuz a bloody red. The navy lieutenant stretched, tired after an eight-hour shift in the CIC, then turned toward the rear of the ship. He found Shiloh Turk just where he expected him to be. The master chief was leaning on the *Alameda*'s fantail, puffing contentedly on one of the vile cigars he favored, its smoke trailing away in the breeze behind him.

"Under orders to lay down a smoke screen, Chief?" Mark asked as he leaned on the rail next to Turk.

"No, sir," Turk replied between puffs. "Not with *this* stogie. This here's chemical warfare."

Mark looked out at the vista stretched behind them. Only thirty miles wide, the Strait of Hormuz was the choke point through which the majority of the free world's oil passed. A line of giant supertankers stretched out behind them, gray steel football fields disappearing into the haze. Skittering about their feet were dozens of the tiny fishing boats called dhows, each sporting a tattered triangular sail. In each boat's stern, a flickering fire served as a running light, a small protection against being swamped by one of the supertankers or warships that were the dhow's competition for space on the waterway.

Mark watched the six-man crew of the dhow closest to the *Alameda*. With the precision born of long practice, each man hauled in a line, removed the wriggling red snapper, tossed it into a basket, then rebaited the hook and threw it overboard.

"Ever do any fishing, Turk?" Mark asked the older man.

"Nope, not me. The way I figure it, I spend my life hoping to stay *on top* of the water. Why should I spend my free time trying to catch something that would rather stay *under* the water? Seems like a colossal waste of time to me—though I don't mind eating what some other fellow has caught."

"My sister Rebecca's husband is crazy about fishing—he's

32

a guide up in the backwoods of Maine. But he actually lets the big ones go. Talks on and on about the thrill of the catch, says there's not a prettier sight than a trout breaking water at dawn."

"Talk about a sight, you gotta see this one." Turk pointed to where two dolphins were surfing in the cruiser's wake. "Check this out."

Turk shouted in Arabic to the crew of the dhow. One of the men looked up and smiled, then held out his hand. Turk reached into his pocket, took out a quarter, and tossed it to the man. The next time the fisherman hauled in a snapper, Turk nudged Mark. "Watch this."

The fisherman leaned over the dhow's gunwale and slapped the water with the fish several times. Then he threw the fish high into the air. As the fish descended, one of the dolphins came out of the water, a silvery rainbow trailing behind it. At the top of its arc, the dolphin grabbed the fish, then nosed over and disappeared gracefully beneath the surface of the strait.

"Pretty slick, eh?" Turk asked as he waved to the fisherman. "First saw that trick back in '87 during Operation Earnest Will, when we were escorting reflagged tankers through here. They used to do it for free until they caught on that we'd pay for it." The master chief flicked the stub of his cigar over the fantail. "Good investment, too. Those dhows are the best protection we've got."

Mark looked out over the calm waters. "Against what?" he asked. It seemed impossible that any threat could lurk in so tranquil a scene.

"This is your first tour through here, ain't it? Then you probably don't know that the regulars call this place Silkworm Alley. Named after the Chinese antiship missile. We don't know how many our Chinese friends have sold to the Iranians, but it's a bunch." Mark looked eastward, where the Iranian coastline lay shrouded in the morning mist. "They pop off one o' them babies," Turk went on, "and you got about thirty seconds to do something *real* clever before you're on the bottom. That's why I keep the dhow crews happy. If they think you're a soft touch, they'll keep close to you. Lots of dhows means lots of targets, which makes for one confused antiship missile. They're better cover against a Silkworm than all the F-14s we can muster."

Suddenly, the scene didn't look nearly as peaceful to Mark. *I was right,* he thought. *The water does look like blood.*

❖ ❖ ❖

"*Brian!*" Rebecca's whisper sliced through the darkness, jolting him to wakefulness. "Did you hear that?"

Brian turned over. "Hear what?"

"*That!*"

"I hear a storm coming in, the last of this year's bumper crop of mosquitoes, and Old Man Petersen's darn dog." Brian patted his wife's hip. "Go to sleep, City Girl."

"There's someone outside!"

Brian sat up and rubbed his face. "Last time you heard prowlers was outside our tent in Assyria. You thought it was cobras; it turned out to be a hungry camel." He peered suspiciously into the darkness. "You're not pregnant again, are you?"

"Hush. Someone's outside."

With a sigh he shoved his feet into a pair of battered hunting boots and grabbed a flashlight from his dresser. "OK, but you'd better be awake when I get back."

She wasn't.

❖ ❖ ❖

"Sorry about the ruckus last night," Brian apologized as Anne came into the kitchen. "Hope you got back to sleep after it was all over."

Anne frowned. "Ruckus? What ruckus?" She looked at Jake, who shrugged.

"Makes sense that you wouldn't have heard it, Anne," Brian agreed, "since your bedroom's across the hall." He looked toward his wife, who was making sandwiches at the counter.

"Last night, about oh-dark-thirty, Becky thought she heard a prowler."

Brian paused and made sure Rebecca was listening. "Turns out she was right." Brian grinned at Anne's startled frown. "I jumped him outside Lauri's bedroom window," he explained, "and that's when all the screaming and cussing started. Must've taken me twenty, maybe thirty minutes to wrestle him to the ground and hog-tie him." He peered at Anne. "I'm surprised you didn't wake up, what with Jake hollering out his window asking if I needed help and the sirens and helicopters and all."

Rebecca stuffed the sandwiches into a paper bag. *"Here,"* she said, turning around and holding out the bag. "Take your sandwiches and *go*. Anne, Lauren, and I will do just *fine* without you, thank-you-very-much."

Brian finished his coffee, rose, and strode across the kitchen. Stepping past the proffered bag, he folded his wife's arms around him. "I know you will," he said with a smile. "Jake and I will be at my camp. We'll be back late tomorrow or early Saturday morning. Call Roy Barnard or Bill Estes if you need me—we'll be within radio range of their repeater." With a fingertip, Brian tilted Rebecca's face toward his. "And before we go, Jake and I will move the trash cans from under Lauri's window so old Mr. Raccoon doesn't wake you when he tips them over again."

Rebecca Keefe smiled up at her husband. "Thank you."

"Remind me to call Roy Barnard," Brian said to Jake as they made their way down to the dock. "I'll ask him to come out and set some of my traps. Roy'll get a free hunting trip out of it, and I'll get some peace of mind."

Darius Marduk walked into the dining room of the Lakeview Inn just as it opened for breakfast. Through the picture window at the end of the dining room, the rising sun ignited the tops of trees lining the ridge above a still-dark Moosehead Lake.

"Take any table you like, Mr. Marduk," Doris Rodgers called. "I'll be right with you." Marduk seated himself in a small booth near the window. He idly stroked his neatly clipped mustache as he watched a floatplane, serene in the morning calm, glide off the surface of the lake. The spume thrown up by its takeoff formed a white streak in the dissipating darkness.

"Coffee, Mr. Marduk?" Doris asked.

The olive-skinned man opened the menu Doris handed him. "Please."

Doris returned with a steaming cup of coffee. "The corned beef hash looks really good this morning," she suggested helpfully, wishing to cultivate this proven source of big tips. "And since you don't appear to like green food, I'll hold the melon that comes on the side."

The sharp glance Marduk gave her made the waitress shiver. Then he broke into a charming smile. "Thank you, Miss Rodgers. That is most kind of you. It is a . . . how do you say it . . . an *allergy* of mine." Marduk handed her the menu. "The hash will do quite nicely."

After placing his order, Doris brought him a basket of muffins and butter. It was still early, and Marduk was the only diner, so Doris paused by his table. She was intrigued by this urbane, educated foreigner, so different from the guides and foresters who constituted the male population of Greenville. "Will you be in America long?" she ventured.

Marduk turned from the window. "That is difficult to say."

"What brings you to our country?" Doris asked in the stilted fashion of those unused to talking with foreigners.

"Research," Marduk said. "I am an anthropologist."

"Are you Saudi Arabian?" Doris asked hopefully, remembering vaguely a *60 Minutes* piece she had seen on the Saudis' fabulous wealth.

Marduk transfixed her with another icy glance. "No," he replied curtly. "I am—Egyptian."

Doris sighed. "I'd love to visit Egypt someday. The Pyramids, and King Tut, and Cleopatra sailing on her barge on the Nile . . ." She stopped abruptly when she noticed Marduk staring uncomprehendingly at her.

"Tell me, Miss Rodgers," Marduk asked. "Are there many children in Greenville? As an anthropologist, I am in your country to study American children."

Doris winced as the raw nerve of her own childlessness was scraped. "Unfortunately, not as many as there used to be," she replied. "Most of the kids around here move away before they start having kids of their own." She brightened. "There's still a few, though. Like Lauren, Brian and Rebecca Keefe's daughter. She's a real cutie."

The anthropologist looked interested. "And how old is this Lauren Keefe?"

"Six, maybe eight months by now," Doris replied. She smiled. "Brian and Lauren come for breakfast sometimes in order to let Rebecca sleep in. Lauren trashes the place, but she's so cute, it's worth it." A lighted number appeared above the door to the kitchen. "Your breakfast is ready," Doris told Marduk.

Doris paused at the door to the kitchen and looked back just as Professor Marduk took a business card out of his coat pocket. He stared at it for a long time before putting it away.

❖ ❖ ❖

"There she is," Brian said as the Skywagon broke through the thin layer of clouds. "Munsungan Lake. You'll find no better fishing in all of the North Maine Woods."

Jake looked down at the glassy, finger-shaped lake. Clumps of sugar maple trees, their leaves already scarlet, formed brilliant clusters along its dark-green shore. "Nice day," he observed, "not a ripple."

"Yeah, I know," Brian muttered. "Darn it."

Jake looked over at his pilot. "Huh? I thought a smooth surface would be ideal for landing."

"It is," Brian replied. The whine of the Skywagon's engine deepened as Brian adjusted the pitch of the three-bladed prop. He pointed the nose of the plane at the water. "The problem is getting down onto that glassy surface."

Through the windshield, Jake watched the lake rush up toward them. "We seem to be doing just fine so far."

"When you land on a runway," Brian explained, seemingly oblivious to their rapidly diminishing altitude, "you have all sorts of visual clues as to how far you are above the runway—the runway markings, the ground on either side of you, and so on. Not so with a glassy surface. You can't pick up any clues from the water, and trying to judge your altitude from a shore half a mile away is *really* tricky." Brian pulled down on the switch that lowered the flaps. "If I've got the room, I'll just set up a descent rate and fly it onto the surface. Or when it's like this, we make our own markings."

At the last moment, Brian pulled back sharply on the controls. The Skywagon flashed along, inches above the surface of Munsungan Lake. He then brought the plane into a steep, climbing turn. As they doubled back, Jake could see that the propwash had churned up a long stretch of water.

"Presto!" Brian said with satisfaction as he set the plane down in the middle of the swath of ripples. "Instant runway."

Steering with the small rudders mounted on the back of each of the floatplane's pontoons, Brian brought them up to a floating dock on the lake's eastern shore. A line of four well-kept log cabins stretched northward along the pebbled shoreline, separated by copses of cedar and pine. The camp lodge, with its stone chimney and long windows, waited for them at the head of the dock.

The Skywagon's engine died with a sputtering growl. "I'll button her up while you start unloading our gear," Brian said as they climbed out. "As befits such a distinguished guest as yourself," he added with a grin, "we'll be sleeping behind the kitchen."

✧ ✧ ✧

As he waited with the others in the Oval Office for the Iraqi special envoy to be ushered in, Randy Cavanaugh ran a finger inside his collar. He hated both neckties and diplomats, and just now he felt as if both were tightening around his neck.

Cavanaugh, the president, and Robin Hawkes stood as the door opened. Randy noted with envy the authoritative ease that Lydia Doral radiated, even though she remained seated. A small, oily man and a large, muscular type were shown in by a White House usher. Introductions were made, excluding Cavanaugh and the large Iraqi.

Ybrahim Ibn smiled effusively at the president. "My government welcomes your overture," the special envoy began. "And after the unfortunate bellicosities which have strained relations between our sovereign nations—" none of the Americans missed the slight emphasis on *sovereign*—"we look forward eagerly to a mutually fruitful resumption of trade." Ibn paused, his eyes flicking from the president to his chief of staff.

"As do I, *Wallah* Ibn," Lydia Doral said, using the correct Arabic honorific.

"Allow me to introduce *my* special envoy," the president added, "Mrs. Lydia Doral." The Iraqi stared at Doral, who casually extended her hand.

Gotta hand it to her, Randy thought as he watched the first round of battle. *She's making him look up to her even though she's sitting down.*

Doral gestured to a chair. "Now that the introductions have been made, we can get down to business."

Ibn's eyes slid to, and over, Randy. "Your aide, Mrs. Doral?"

"Mr. Cavanaugh is my *cawal*, Mr. Ibn." Doral smiled as Ibn's eyebrows shot up. "Now," she added, "shall we start by discussing the size of the mission?"

"Impressions?" the president asked after the Iraqis had left.

"Hope we're in need of snake oil," Robin Hawkes commented acerbically, "because that seems to be all we're going to get out of them."

The president looked at Doral. "Lydia?"

"I'm afraid I must agree with Robin," the ambassador replied, "if not in tenor, then at least in tone." She looked at the president. "I hope you're not expecting any substantive results from this mission."

"Not from your end of it, I'm not."

The ambassador turned to Cavanaugh. "Randy?"

"Wouldn't trust him with my worst enemy's three-legged dog." Randy smiled at Doral. "Nice job euchring him into agreeing to a twelve-man 'security squad.' That'll let me bring all my boys along." He paused. "By the way, what was that you called me? Did you say I was AWOL?"

Doral laughed. "I called you a *cawal*. It's a term left over from the days when Iraq was ruled by the sheiks. Each town in a sheikdom had its *cawal*, a head man appointed by the sheik to maintain law and order—his security chief. Even today, outside of the major cities, *cawals* still carry a good deal of weight and dispense a brutal form of Islamic frontier justice."

The president nodded admiringly. "So in one fell swoop, you reminded Ibn of his country's backwater reputation, set yourself up as a sheik in his eyes, and established Randy as your head goon. Nicely done."

Randy grinned. "Sounds more like I'm your personal enforcer." He looked at Doral and scratched his chin thoughtfully. "Never thought I'd be working for the God*mother*."

4

After a quick glance up and down the Boulevard of the Martyrs, Hafez Adid stepped into the Good Time Café. He carefully shut the postered-over door behind him, cutting off the blare of Baghdad's traffic. Two old men sat at a table in the corner of the small, dingy room, arguing over glasses of mint tea. The counterman, his feet propped up on a drum of palm oil, inspected Adid briefly before returning his attention to the thundering TV. Adid strode past the end of the counter, brushed aside a filthy curtain, and turned left into a dim storage area. At the end of the closet, Adid opened the door marked Dry Goods, stepped into a narrow passageway, and closed the door firmly behind him.

As he hung his overcoat on one of the many pegs lining the wall, a woman swathed in the floor-length, veiled garment called a chador came in behind him. Adid tensed, waiting, until it was clear she was ignoring him. In a swirl of black, the woman pulled the garment off, revealing a sheer silk blouse tucked tightly into red stirrup pants. Adid smiled appreciatively as he held the inner door for her.

A mirrored ball suspended above the café's dance floor

41

spun slowly, bathing the couples dancing below it in streaks of multicolored light. A three-piece band played a recent pop tune. Behind the bar, one bartender polished a glass while another pulled vigorously on the handle of an enormous espresso machine. At the tiny round tables scattered across the floor, young men in silk suits laughed with young women in short skirts and sequins.

Adid weaved between the tables, brushing aside the stubby antenna of a cellular phone. In one of the secluded alcoves that lined the room's perimeter, he slid onto a vinyl seat, ignoring the couple embracing in the next booth. Dots of light from the punched-tin lamp dangling over the table spangled his partner's face.

"Well?" he asked. "Do you have what we need?"

The other occupant of the booth shoved a copy of the *International Herald-Tribune* across the scarred tabletop. "Judge for yourself."

Adid opened the newspaper and began leafing through it. Three pages into the first section was a sheaf of paper. Leaning slightly to bring the sheets into the light, the young Iraqi pored over them. Adid swore quietly, then looked at his partner in astonishment. "How did you get this?"

A confident smile was followed by an elegant gesture. "They are such fools that it was almost too easy. Now, do you have any doubts that this will suffice as our passport to America?"

"None," Adid stammered. "But how—"

"You leave for Ankara tomorrow?"

"Yes, but what about—"

"Good. It is essential that this be delivered, too." Adid's partner slid an envelope across the table.

"Very well," Adid replied. He slid the envelope in behind the papers and refolded the newspaper. "But what is in the envelope?"

"It is my—"

Screams and the staccato bark of automatic rifles erupted in the same instant. "No one move!" an amplified voice brayed. "You are all under arrest!" Adid slid beneath the table, pulling his partner down beside him. From the table's shadow he watched as six men dressed in black uniforms began making their way through the cabaret, roughly hauling each woman to her feet. Behind them another black-clad man, a patch over one eye, carefully scrutinized each woman. Each time he shook his head, then more men dragged the struggling woman away.

The men worked their way methodically through the room, accosting one table of terrified revelers after another. "They must not get those papers!" Adid's partner hissed.

Adid nodded. Just as he began to stuff the newspaper under the booth cushion, a young man at one of the tables came to his feet, cursing drunkenly. The man grabbed a chair and flung it at the invaders. Tongues of fire exploded from rifle muzzles, hurling the man backward. As he crashed to the dance floor, the screams began anew.

"Now!" Adid rapped. "This way!" He stuffed the newspaper into his shirt as he ran.

Crouched low, the pair scurried along behind the last row of tables. Adid ducked behind the bar, ignored completely by the paralyzed bartenders. His foot lashed out, caving in a kick panel built low into the wall behind the bar. The shrill screams mingled with the raspy blare of the bullhorn, masking the sound of breaking wood.

Come! Adid gestured frantically. After his partner dashed past him, Adid scuttled crablike through the opening. He stopped, turned, and hurriedly pushed the panel back into place.

"Where are we?" Adid's partner asked.

"In a vacant warehouse behind the café storefront," Adid replied. Street light filtered dimly through flyspecked windows, revealing packing cases mounded with dust. He pointed toward the far corner of the warehouse. "Quickly now."

The two trotted through the warehouse, plumes of dust settling slowly to the floor behind them. Light glinted off metal, and Adid grinned. "We might make it yet," he whispered. "I'll go up the ladder first and get the trapdoor at the top open."

"How did you know about this?" his partner asked.

Adid grinned again. "You have your specialty, and I have mine." Grabbing the rusted iron rungs, he started up the ladder.

Thirty feet above the floor, Adid shoved the iron hatchway with one hand. Nothing. Sweating, the young man looked down at his partner, a few rungs below him. "It's stuck!" he whispered. Holding on to the top rung with both hands, Adid slammed his shoulder against the hatch.

A square of white light flooded the warehouse as the kick panel exploded inward. Adid's partner gasped. Flashlights began to rake the gloom. "Hurry!" his partner hissed. "*Hurry!*"

Adid pulled his legs up beneath him and braced himself against a rung. Frantically, he hurled himself against the hatch. Muffled footsteps grew louder as the men followed the trail of footprints in the dust.

The young Iraqi threw himself against the trapdoor one final time. It burst open, the scream of tortured metal filling the warehouse. The force of Adid's effort sent him sprawling onto the warehouse roof. As he turned back to the hatchway, gunfire erupted beneath him. His partner surged up the ladder.

Adid knelt beside the opening. "Grab my hand!" A ricochet grazed his temple, flooding one eye with blood. Black shapes appeared at the base of the ladder.

Shots tore through the roof as his groping fingers closed on a wrist. Adid stood, hauling his partner up through the trapdoor. They tumbled away from the fusillade of bullets.

"Do you still have it?" Adid's partner gasped.

Adid anxiously patted his shirt until he found the lump of paper. "This way!" he ordered.

The two ran across the roof, stumbling over debris. As they reached the far side of the building, the first of the black-suited men poured through the hatchway. Flashlight beams began sweeping the darkness.

"I will distract them," Adid's partner declared, "while you escape."

"You will do no such thing!" Adid replied heatedly. "We both escape, or we both surrender!" A movement in the street three stories below caught his eye.

"That information *must* get out!" Adid's partner demanded. "My life will be merely another of the many expended to obtain it. Now *go!*" Adid's partner turned to run toward their pursuers.

Adid glanced at the street, then began to gesture broadly as if in protest. As the sweep of his arm passed his partner's chest, Adid shoved violently. With a terrified shriek, Adid's companion disappeared backward over the edge of the warehouse. Crouched low, Adid watched as his partner landed in the middle of the rags piled high in the back of a donkey-drawn cart.

Bullets crashed into the rooftop around him, and Adid hurled himself sideways. Speared by flashlights, the young Iraqi ran pell-mell across the roof. When he reached the edge, Adid hurled himself headlong into space.

Adid hit feetfirst. He threw himself forward, falling, letting his momentum expend itself as he tumbled down the steep hillside that bordered this side of the warehouse. Briars ripped at him as he careened past. At last he rolled to a stop, faceup. Panting, Adid waited until the stars in his field of view stopped their crazy dance. Pulling himself up on one elbow, the young Iraqi carefully checked that the paper was still inside his shirt. Flashlights were sweeping the base of the warehouse, working

45

their way down the hillside. A machine gun began systematically raking the slope, the lethal stream of bullets inching its way toward him. Gasping raggedly, Adid crawled into the beckoning darkness of a corrugated-iron culvert that ran under the road at the bottom of the hill.

Can't stop now, he told himself as he fought the overwhelming desire to lie down. *What you are carrying is too important. And if it has cost the life of yet another tonight, that makes it all the more dear.* Adid stumbled toward the dim, blue circle of light at the far end of the culvert. *But I must know*, he realized. *I will not be able to rest if do not at least check.*

Once out of the culvert, Adid crept along the far side of the road. When he judged he had gone far enough, he crept cautiously up to the edge of the road. Eyes level with the pavement, Adid searched the length of the street that ran alongside the warehouse. There was no sign of either the rag cart or its occupant. Suddenly very tired, Hafez Adid slid down the embankment and disappeared into the weeds and the night.

✧ ✧ ✧

"Thanks for letting Lauri trash the place again," Rebecca told Doris Rodgers as she scrubbed her daughter's face. "And thanks for the endless supply of wipes."

The waitress waved dismissively. "It's no worse than when I baby-sit, and at least here we've got a busboy!" She turned to Anne. "It was so nice meeting you. Staying long?"

"Only until Brian can browbeat her boyfriend, Jake, into proposing to her," Rebecca interjected. Blushing, Anne made a face at her cousin, then joined in the laughter.

"What a lovely child," a masculine voice rumbled.

Rebecca looked up to find a handsome, well-dressed man smiling down at Lauren.

"Hello, Professor Marduk," Doris said. She tucked a stray wisp of hair behind her ear. "Did you enjoy your lunch?"

46

Marduk smiled. "Very much so. Are you related to this lovely little girl?"

Doris shook her head. "No, but this is her mother."

"Then perhaps you would introduce us."

"Of course. Becky, this is Professor Darius Marduk. He's a . . . , a . . . " Flustered, Doris threw up her hands. "I'm sorry," she apologized to Marduk.

Marduk smiled charmingly. "It is no matter. I wonder myself sometimes what it is that I do." He introduced himself to Rebecca and Anne. "I am a cultural anthropologist, here in the United States to study American methods of child rearing. Hence my interest in your lovely daughter."

Rebecca nodded. "I'm Rebecca Keefe. This is my daughter, Lauren. And this is my cousin Anne Dryden."

Marduk's eyes widened. "There is a Dr. Rebecca Keefe of whom I have heard, a paleolinguist of the first order? . . ." His voice trailed off inquiringly.

Rebecca smiled self-consciously. "I'm Dr. Keefe. But as to the 'first order' part of it—"

Marduk beamed. "This is wonderful! To think I find myself in acquaintance with the translator of the Haradi Document! Dr. Keefe," he added earnestly, "perhaps we could talk sometime? To be able to confer with a colleague of your reputation . . . "

Now it was Rebecca's turn to blush. "I've been semiretired from academic life for some time, Professor Marduk," Rebecca explained, clearly flattered. "But if there's any way I can help your research, I'd be glad to."

Marduk bowed. "Time spent merely in your presence will be the highlight of my visit to your lovely country." He took a business card from an expensive leather case. "My card. I am working with Professor Richard Collins of the University of Maine. Please, call him to verify my credentials."

Rebecca smiled. "I'm sure that won't be necessary, Professor. Why don't you come over today at four."

"You are too kind, dear lady. Four it is, then. Now, if you will excuse me." With another crisp bow, Marduk left the dining room.

"Boy!" Doris said indignantly. "Some people!"

Rebecca frowned. "What's wrong? Professor Marduk was perfectly charming."

"Not him!" Doris replied. "You!"

Rebecca stared at Doris. "Me? What did I do?"

Doris frowned with mock ferocity at Rebecca. "First, you go and marry the best-looking hunk in Piscataquis County. Now, you've got a sheik begging you for a date!" She directed her glare at the doorway through which Marduk had departed. "He didn't ask me out even after I gave him an extra helping of lamb chops last night!" The waitress shook her head. "Some girls have all the fun."

Doris leaned over to Anne. "Speaking of fun, honey, tell this reluctant boyfriend of yours that you're being called on by an Egyptian sheik. See if *that* doesn't get him moving!"

"They're rising just over there," Brian whispered. "That riffle—where the brook empties into the lake." He dipped his paddle into the water, and the canoe drifted silently toward shore.

Jake flicked his left wrist, and the tip of his fly rod whipped back and forth in an arc over his head. Each time the rod tip came forward, Jake let some more lime green dry-fly line slip out of his right hand and through the rod's stripping guides. When his series of false casts had released thirty feet of line, Jake made his final cast. The line arched out gracefully in front of him, settling on the water and bringing the fly in a perfectly straight line to the target. Brian nodded approvingly. Both men watched as the dry fly dropped onto the surface and drifted toward the riffle.

The water exploded. Jake brought the rod's tip up sharply, and the fly rod curved into an arc as the line tightened. Near the shore an enormous brook trout rocketed out of the water, trailing droplets of water as it shook its head violently. Then the line went slack, and the trout disappeared beneath the surface.

Jake winced, and Brian grinned in commiseration. "You set the hook too early," he explained as Jake reeled in his line. "The brookies around here are wily, and they'll roll a fly around in their mouths before they clamp down on it. If it doesn't taste right, they'll spit it out. Go for it an instant too soon or too late, and you're sunk." Brian brought the bow of the canoe around. "Let's go get some lunch and unpack. Then we'll hit it again around sunset."

"Well, since it was a royal decree, I knew the Haradi Document had to be written in Emegir Sumerian," Rebecca was explaining from her perch on the window seat in her study. "But it took me the longest time to realize that I had to agglutinate the infixes rather than inflect them. Once I figured that out, the rest was mere translation." She reached for a pitcher. "More iced tea, Professor?"

Darius Marduk held out his glass. "You are much too modest, Dr. Keefe. I know little of paleolinguistic theory, but I do know that your fundamental discovery has unleashed a torrent of translations of heretofore cryptic works." Rebecca smiled and reached down to Lauren, who was playing at her feet. With a fingertip she combed her daughter's hair.

Marduk smiled at the gesture. "I hope you did not think me inattentive during your lecture because I was paying so much attention to your little girl. As you know, I am here to study American children. Specifically, I am trying to determine which aspects of your wonderful prenatal-care system may be most effectively exported to Egypt." Marduk's face fell. "Especially in the rural areas of my country, such care is almost unknown."

Rebecca nodded. "We have our own such areas here in America, only they're located in the hearts of our largest cities." She hoisted Lauren onto her lap, then laughed. "Actually, Professor, I'm afraid Lauri will be something of an anomaly in your statistics."

Marduk took out a small notebook. "Really? Why do you say that?"

"Because as perfect as she is, she received none of that American prenatal care you admire so much." When Marduk motioned for her to go on, Rebecca settled back against the cushions piled in the corner of the window seat.

"Soon after my husband, Brian, and I were married," Rebecca explained, "we moved to that part of Asia that, three thousand years ago, used to be Assyria. As part of the ongoing excavation of the ancient Assyrian city of Nineveh, a team from Oxford had uncovered the library collected by King Ashurbanipal during his reign in the seventh century B.C." Marduk smiled at Rebecca's excitement.

"Ashurbanipal was one of the few ancient Middle Eastern rulers who was literate," Rebecca went on, "and his scribes amassed the first systematically collected library in that region. Archaeologists had been looking for that library ever since A. H. Layard discovered Nineveh in 1845. The Oxford team asked me to consult with them, and my Guggenheim grant was to help them begin to decipher and translate the scrolls coming out of the library."

"Fascinating," Marduk replied. "What type of material was it?"

"We haven't cataloged it all yet, but the library seems to have emphasized scholarly and literary texts and works on magic. Quite a bit of what I worked on concerned itself with descriptions of the pantheon of Assyrian gods, including the Scorpion Man, the god Ea, who was half goat and half fish, and the demon Pazuzu." Rebecca made a face. "Some of it was pretty gruesome."

"And you finished so immense a job in so little time? I am impressed."

Rebecca shook her head. "Don't be. Three months after Brian and I arrived in Assyria, I discovered I was pregnant." A long-suppressed anger flared up in Rebecca. "After a quick trip to the American hospital in Cairo to make sure everything was all right, I went back to Nineveh. Since I did my work with a PC and a magnifying glass rather than a pick and shovel, I figured I could stay until just before my due date." Rebecca winced. "Unfortunately, the hospital was a little off on their predicted due date, and I was a little too insistent about staying until a particularly crucial piece of translation was finished. Hence, I went into labor one night in a tent in the middle of the North Arabian desert.

"Blessedly, there was an American missionary field hospital in a nearby small town called Ain Sifni." Rebecca looked up, startled at Marduk's sudden, intense glance. His interest in her story was flattering, however, and she continued. "The archaeological team from Oxford I was working with turned out in their nightshirts to see us off, waving their stocking caps and shouting 'Godspeed!' Brian whisked me to the hospital, and thirteen hours later, Lauren came into our lives."

"Fascinating," Marduk replied. "How very fortunate for you that the hospital was nearby. Where did you say it was?"

"Ain Sifni," Rebecca repeated. "It's a small town near Jebel Maklub."

Marduk nodded, wrote in his notebook, then peered at Lauren. "She certainly seems normal in all respects."

Rebecca nodded thankfully. "We're very grateful that she is. And we came home as soon as I was able to travel."

"And how long after she was born was that?"

"About two weeks," Rebecca replied. "Why do you ask?"

The professor smiled. "Many rural Egyptian women are confined to their homes for a month or more after the birth of a child. Since frequently these days the father has gone to Cairo to work and it is the mother who must tend their fields and flocks, this can cause great hardship. I am trying to determine if it is still necessary." He glanced at his watch, then stood. "I have taken more than my share of your valuable time."

When they arrived at Rebecca's front door the tall, courtly scholar smiled. "One more favor of you, Dr. Keefe. I have young friends around the world, and I love to send them birthday cards from my homeland. Might I add Lauren to my list?"

Charmed, Rebecca smiled. "Certainly. Especially since Lauri only has a real birthday every four years." When Marduk frowned, Rebecca added, "She was born on Leap Year Day, the twenty-ninth of February."

Marduk laughed. "In that case, I shall see that she receives a card worthy of Cleopatra herself!" The professor straightened and bowed. "Good day, Dr. Keefe."

After she had closed the door, Rebecca looked at Lauren. "Thank you for being part of Mommy's academic afternoon, my loverducks. Now, let's go see what Cousin Anne has dreamed up for dinner."

✧ ✧ ✧

Darius Marduk's smile glittered as he arose from his chair. "A superb meal, Miss Rodgers. My compliments to your chef. What did you say that wonderful fish was called?"

"Togue," Doris replied, self-consciously wiping her hands on the apron of her uniform. "It's the local name for lake trout. Yours was caught fresh, just this afternoon."

Marduk nodded appreciatively. "It was indeed most delicate. But," he added, catching her eyes with his, "mine seemed to be prepared differently than those I saw you serving to the other patrons." He cocked one sleek eyebrow and peered at her questioningly.

I must be as pink as my uniform, Doris thought as she felt the blush suffuse her cheeks. "The chef was putting a green sauce called pesto on the other orders tonight," she confessed, her eyes downcast. "I remembered how you feel about green food, so I had him sauté yours instead."

The exotic stranger's smile broadened. "In my country, Miss Rodgers, a favor such as yours does not go unreturned." Marduk leaned closer, and Doris reached down and steadied herself against a chair. "After observing you with young Lauren Keefe at lunch, I realize that you know much about children. You are, perhaps, familiar with the concept of the extended family?"

Doris nodded, biting her lip. *When you're thirty-eight and single, "extended" is about as close as you're ever going to get.* Deep within her, the loneliness and fear ignited anew.

"Then," Marduk went on, his eyes consuming her, "perhaps you would let me repay your kindness by allowing me to escort you to someplace where we could talk. You could tell me about being a part of the Keefe family, and I could tell you about life in—in Egypt."

He stood, looming over her. "Is there someplace nearby?"

"We could talk here if you like—," Doris began.

Marduk held up an admonishing finger. "No, not here. It must be an elegant place." He brought his finger down to point at her, and she felt the intensity of his gaze increase. "A place worthy of you."

Doris took a deep breath and smiled her best smile. "There's the Greenville Inn. They have a nice bar with a reading room and a fireplace. . . ."

"Perfect. When are you finished here?"

"We close at nine. I'll need a few minutes to change, so

why don't you come by my room—that's room three—around nine-thirty."

Smiling, Marduk nodded. "Half past nine it is, then." He bowed, turned, and left.

Doris waited until Marduk had left the room, then rushed for the house phone by the coffee station. Praying that Sandy Neill would be in her room, Doris stabbed at the phone's keypad. "Sandy!" she whispered when the day manager answered the phone. "Is that blue cocktail dress of yours clean?"

❖ ❖ ❖

"I don't remember the last time I had champagne," Doris sighed as Marduk refilled her flute. Marduk emptied the bottle into his glass. Then, one arm flung out along the back of his chair, he smiled at her from across the table. Doris sipped from her tall, tulip-shaped glass, wrinkling her nose. "The bubbles tickle," she giggled.

"I've told you all I know about Lauren Keefe and her family," Doris said, gazing over the rim of her glass at the tall, athletic foreigner. "Now, when are you going to do me *my* favor?"

Marduk's luxurious mustache twitched as he laughed. "Very soon now," he replied. "But first, more champagne."

"Oh no, I couldn't—"

Doris's protest was interrupted by an out-thrust palm. Marduk summoned the waiter. When the bottle arrived, he stood, threw a fifty-dollar bill down on the table, and reached out to Doris. "Now," he announced, "we shall stroll back to the Lakeview. Then, in the privacy of my chambers, we shall indulge ourselves while I relate to you stories of the desert never before heard by Western ears."

Marduk picked up the champagne and two fresh glasses. His hand enveloped hers as she rose, face upturned, seeing nothing but his jet black eyes. Marduk drew her close as they disappeared into the night.

5

Aboard the USS Carl Burch, *on patrol in the Strait of Hormuz*

"What've you got, Corky?" the executive officer of the *Burch* asked, leaning over the young sonarman's shoulder. An urgent summons from the sonar room had brought the XO down from the *Burch*'s bridge.

Specialist, Second Class, Micah "Corky" Cochran pointed at the round screen in front of him. Across the screen was painted a jagged pattern, called the "waterfall," which represented the echoes returned by the *Burch*'s sonar. "Right here, sir," Cochran said eagerly. "See this?"

"I see it," the XO replied. "Now, suppose you tell me what it is I'm seeing."

"A sub, sir," the sonarman said proudly. "Probably that Russky sub they said was headed this way. Should we tell the *Mayfield* to scramble the Sea Stallions and do us some sub hunting?"

The executive officer hid his smile at the young seaman's zeal. "We just might do that, Corky," he agreed. "You got a range and bearing for me?"

Cochran's face fell. "Did a minute ago, sir. Had a real good

Doppler." He peered at the waterfall accusingly. "Kinda lost it now, though."

The exec nodded understandingly. "Why don't you print off what you have, and I'll take it to the captain. We'll let him decide what to do. If he needs your advice, we'll call you to the bridge."

The sonarman beamed. "*Yes, sir!*" Thirty seconds later he handed the XO a high-resolution copy of the sonar display.

"Stick around, Corky," the exec advised. "We may need you."

The exec left the sonar room. Instead of going back up to the bridge, he went down two decks and along a short companionway to the ship's infirmary. One of the beds was occupied by a portly, balding man.

"How's it going, Chief?" the XO asked.

Master Chief Red Dowell, senior sonarman and chief of the boat, winced as he rolled over. "Could be better, sir," Dowell admitted. "Heckuva time for these shingles of mine to act up."

"Your depraved life catches up with you at last, Chief," the exec said sternly. Dowell, a church elder and longtime chaplain aboard the *Burch*, grinned back at the younger man. The XO handed Dowell the sonar printout. "Young Cochran's all worked up over this, Chief. You see anything in it that I should tell the old man about?"

The sonar chief studied the waterfall printout. "Let's see," he mumbled. "We've got two herds of dolphins, a lot of bottom shadow on account of the water being so shallow here, and a good deal of surface noise from this miserable storm. Other than that, I don't see much at all."

The exec pointed at the printout. "What about this spot *here*, Chief? Corky's having a litter of kittens over it."

Dowell laughed, then winced again. "The Good Lord will deal out tribulations as he sees fit," he told the exec, "but it just doesn't seem right that an affliction should hurt when you *laugh*." The chief pointed to the spot the XO had indicated. "What you got there, sir, is the wreckage of the *Iaso Maru*, a Japanese supertanker sunk back in '67. A big mass of steel, right on the bottom—just the thing to fool an inexperienced young hotshot's eye into seeing a sub."

The exec looked relieved. "Good thing I didn't take this to the old man. He would *not* have taken kindly to having been responsible for calling in a preemptive strike on a pile of rust." A frown replaced the relief. "But Corky mentioned something about a Doppler showing the target moving."

Dowell shrugged, then grimaced. "That's something I've been working with the boy on. New to the Strait as he is, he hasn't yet learned to factor in the nasty crosscurrents we get around here. When we were directly abeam the *Iaso*, we were being pushed away from it westward at probably five or six knots. That's what gave Cochran his Doppler, and that's why, now that we're past the wreckage, he can't get another. The Doppler effect diminishes according to the sine of the relative angle of attack, sir; but you know that."

"You bet, Chief," the XO replied, blinking. "Get well soon. We need you in the sonar room."

"Aye aye, sir. Now, get out before you make me move again."

✧ ✧ ✧

"Thank you for interrupting your busy schedule for us," the president said as Lydia Doral was ushered into the Oval Office. "They said you were over in Georgetown," he remarked. "Shopping for antiques?"

"Delivering a lecture at the university's School of Foreign Service, actually," she replied, taking the cup of tea Robin Hawkes offered her. Doral smiled, obviously enjoying the president's surprise. "Far less appealing than browsing through the shops on Wisconsin Avenue, now that you mention it." She set the cup aside. "Now, what may I do for you?"

The president handed her the folder Elliot French had given him. "Director French, Secretary Waite, and I all agree that it is vital you see this, since it directly affects both the nature and the purpose of your mission."

They watched as Doral leafed through the folder, turning the pages quickly. Less than a minute later, when she had finished, she looked up expectantly at the president.

"If you need more time to study the documents," the president offered, "I'm sure that can be arranged."

The ambassador shook her head. "No, this one reading will be sufficient."

The president nodded, giving himself time to recoup. *A page-at-a-glance reader, undoubtedly a photographic memory to go with it, and a stare that would make a cobra blink. Glad I'm on* her *side of the negotiating table.* "Any questions?"

"Just one, Mr. President. You said the information in this document directly affects both the nature and the purpose of my mission." She gazed up at him, the look in her dark eyes a velvet-sheathed sword. "How, exactly, does it do that?"

Taken aback, the president stared at her. "For one thing, it greatly increases the danger to you personally. *Physical* danger."

A small smile crept across her lips. "Mr. President, given the driving habits of the students at Georgetown University, I shall most likely be in far greater danger shopping along Wisconsin Avenue than I shall ever be while I am in Baghdad." One long-fingered hand waved dismissively. "The only change to the mission which is specified in this document is an additional task for Mr. Cavanaugh and his people."

"But that is exactly what makes it so much more dangerous," Barbara Waite, the secretary of state, protested.

"Agreed," Doral replied. "But since minimizing the danger is not the mission's objective, the amount of danger is irrelevant. Besides, I fully expect Elliot's people to carry off their assignment with such skill and finesse that the Iraqis will never suspect anything is amiss." Doral smiled. "And don't discount the diplomatic half of the mission, Mr. President. I intend to negotiate both seriously and in good faith. Perhaps both Mr. Cavanaugh and I shall have spoils of war to heap upon your desk when we return home."

The men in the office rose as Doral stood up. "You're sure, Mrs. Doral?" Robin Hawkes asked.

The ambassador smiled charmingly. "Quite sure, Mr. Hawkes. I always try to keep in mind that unless men and women are willing to place a greater good above their own physical, emotional, or spiritual security, very little would be invented, almost nothing artistic would be created, and one of the world's great faiths would never have been born."

Another brilliant smile and she was gone.

"Feel like taking a walk?" Rebecca asked Anne after they had dried the lunch dishes. "Brian said there's a storm coming in, so we might not have that much more good weather. Besides, we need a few things from the store for dinner."

"Sounds like fun," Anne agreed. She gestured at Rebecca's large kitchen. "But what on earth could we possibly need from the store?"

"Lots of things," Rebecca replied archly. "Since the men aren't around, tonight's Make Our Own Pizza Night! So we'll need fresh mozzarella, fresh tomato sauce, fresh mushrooms—"

"Fresh Ben & Jerry's," Anne added, referring to her favorite ice cream.

Rebecca frowned. "Ice cream on pizza? Last time I tried it, it kept the cheese from getting all gooey and stringy."

Anne shrugged. "OK then, we'll save it for after."

"Fresh pepperoni," Rebecca continued. "Fresh—" She

paused. "You like anchovies, don't you?" Anne bit her lip and nodded. Rebecca winced. "Yuck. Well, it can't be helped—no Make Our Own Pizza Night tonight."

"I'll skip the anchovies, if that'll help," Anne offered.

Her cousin shook her head. "Nope. Since you like anchovies, tonight has been officially redesignated We *Each* Make Our Own Pizza Night!" Anne laughed. "Just keep those disgusting fish far away from my masterful creation," Rebecca warned. She handed Anne pencil and paper. "You make the list while I get Lauri ready."

❖ ❖ ❖

A carpet of pine needles and club moss cushioned the path along the rocky, granite shore of Moosehead Lake. Small trout flitted in the shallows while two red squirrels bickered raucously overhead.

"How's Lauri doing?" Rebecca asked.

Anne looked up at the baby girl, snuggled in the carrier on her mother's back. "Sound asleep," Anne replied.

"It's about twenty minutes from here to Greenville Junction. They have a little mom-and-pop store there where I like to shop." Rebecca looked at Anne. "You don't mind walking, do you?"

Anne plucked a sprig of cedar and rubbed it between her palms. "Not at all," she replied, breathing in its fragrance. She looked out over the vast expanse of lake, cloud shadows scudding along over the slate gray waters. "Especially when it's as beautiful as it is here."

Rebecca nodded appreciatively. "I fell in love with this land the first time Brian showed it to me. It was owned by one of Brian's favorite clients. When he found out we were getting married, he practically gave it to us as a wedding present. Said he wanted to make sure it stayed in good hands."

"Jake and I take a lot of walks together," Anne continued. She stuck her hands in her jacket pockets. "Especially now, when the tourists have left Acadia." Rebecca nodded at the mention of the national park near Anne's parents' home. "We'll take lunches and spend all day walking along the carriage roads. Sometimes we'll follow the trail out to Great Head and have a picnic dinner while we watch a harvest moon come up out of the ocean."

Rebecca smiled, warmed by her cousin's obvious happiness. "Sounds romantic."

Anne laughed. "It is *now*. But, at first, Jake was so conscious of his new faith I thought I was going to have to get a note from our pastor telling him it was all right to kiss me."

Rebecca made a face. "Well, Brian certainly didn't have *that* problem when he and I were courting." Her laugh was followed by a sigh. "But nowadays, Brian's idea of romance is to clean the fish he catches *before* he gives them to me to cook." She shook her head in mock despair. "Between Brian's salmon and your anchovies, I'll *never* get the smell out of my kitchen."

They rounded a bend. Just ahead an ancient white pine, silver-gray with age, leaned out precariously over the water. Gnarled and weather beaten, a knot of twisted branches at the tree's crown gave the tree a Medusa-like appearance.

"That tree marks the edge of our property," Rebecca explained.

"It's *huge*," Anne exclaimed. "How come it's so much bigger than the rest of the trees around here?"

"Brian said this area has been logged at least once, and this tree is one of the few original old-growth trees left. They probably left it standing to serve as a landmark for the steamboats that used to haul logs and cargo up and down the lake." Rebecca frowned as they approached the battered giant. "That's odd. Looks like a chunk's been taken out of the trunk."

They stopped at the base of the pine. Seven feet up the smooth sweep of wood, a notch had been cut. Rebecca peered up at it. "Now, who would do a thing like that?" she asked.

Irritation edged her voice. "If it's a trail marker, somebody is going to learn real quick that this is private property."

"Maybe it's a nest," Anne offered.

"Can't be. The edges are too smooth. Most likely it's some boy trying out his birthday hatchet. Well, I hope Brian catches him the next time he decides to chop something."

Anne, who was taller than her cousin, stood on tiptoe. "I still think it's a nest. Looks like there's something inside." She reached up into the "nest," then jerked her hand back. "Eggs!" she told Rebecca.

Rebecca shook her head. "Not at this time of year. Go ahead and fish whatever it is out." *If they* are *eggs*, Rebecca thought belatedly, *by now they're seriously rotten, and Annie will be seriously annoyed.*

Anne's fingers closed around the contents of the notch, and she scooped it out. Both women frowned when she opened her hand. Nestled in her palm were five irregular earthen balls the size of large grapes.

Anne examined them. "I think you're right about a young boy being the culprit. These look like the clay marbles we make in my first-grade class. Except," she added, "we use gray clay and this stuff's reddish."

Rebecca picked one up. "Maybe they use red clay in the schools around here. It had to come from somewhere else, because there's no naturally occurring clay around here that I know of." She squinted at the ball she held. "Is that writing?"

Anne joined her in squinting. "If it is, it's like nothing I've ever seen before." She peered at Rebecca. "You're the paleolinguist; you tell me if that's writing."

Rebecca shrugged. "It looks familiar, but it's probably nothing more than some kid's cache of slingshot ammunition." Rebecca laughed. "I wonder if *Biblical Archaeology Today* would be interested in an article on *that?*" She shaded her eyes and looked out at the sky. "Brian said it was going to storm, and I don't like the looks of those clouds. Let's get a move on." Anne handed her cousin the rest of the balls. Rebecca pocketed them, and they walked on.

Sandy Neill poured herself a cup of coffee before sliding next to Doris in the booth. "Gary called a little while ago," Sandy told her friend. "He claims you stood him up last night." When Doris merely shrugged, Sandy peered at her suspiciously. "You mean you really *did* stand him up?"

Sandy frowned. "Come to think of it, you whipped out of my place with that blue dress so fast, I didn't get to find out who the lucky guy was. I just assumed it was Gary." She took a sip of coffee. "OK, girl, out with it," Sandy demanded. "Who could've possibly sent you into a bigger tizzy than Gary Davis, this week's Mister Right? Gary's got everything you're looking for: He's fairly good looking, single, alive—"

Doris smiled archly. "Can you say, 'Platinum American Express Card'?"

Sandy stopped. "You mean *Marduk* asked you out?" Doris nodded happily. "And you went out with him?" Another nod. "In *my* blue dress?"

The day manager's excited smile vanished. "And that's also why you didn't answer when I called you this morning to borrow some mascara, isn't it?" When Doris shrugged noncommittally, Sandy looked at her. "Are you sure that's wise? I mean, you hardly know him."

"It's no big deal," Doris replied coldly. "You're just jealous!" Sandy held up her hands defensively. "And if you really *must* know," Doris went on, "we just sat around and talked. He told me stories."

The bell on the front desk rang. "I'm glad that's all that happened," Sandy said as she got up. "But you be careful." She looked carefully at her childhood friend. "And just remember how men tell us stories."

Doris frowned. "How's that?"

"One line at a time, hon. One line at a time."

❖ ❖ ❖

National Security Agency Headquarters, Fort Meade, Maryland

The Special Operations Division staff sergeant looked up, then came abruptly around from behind the desk. He stood beside the metal door that led to the NSA's Special Classified Intelligence Facility. *I've got to get a better look at this*, he thought.

The woman approached him purposefully, the hallway lights glinting from her long, coppery hair as it undulated sinuously in response to her walk. She stuck her right hand into a skirt pocket, then frowned. Still rummaging in her pocket, she stopped in front of the guard.

"May I help you—" his eyes darted to her left hand, then lingered on their journey upward before meeting hers—"miss? If you're looking for the data-entry pool, it's one floor down."

"Is it really, Sergeant?" she replied sweetly. She stuck her hand in the other pocket of her skirt, then smiled. "Is that a Purple Heart?" she asked, peering at the rows of ribbons on his chest.

"Yes, miss," he replied proudly. "Won it in Panama. I can tell you all about it on our way down to the typing pool, if you'd like me to escort you."

"No, thank you," she replied. "You see, I'm not lost." From her pocket she pulled a white credit-card-sized piece of plastic. When she held it next to a reader on the desk, a red light switched to green and the metal door unlocked with a click. "Now, if you will excuse me," she told him, all traces of sweetness gone from her voice, "*I* have useful work to do." Blinking in disbelief, the sergeant pulled the heavy vault door open.

"By the way, Sergeant," she added as she passed him, "perhaps you should try working on not being such a good target for the enemy. Then maybe next time they won't have to give you a Purple Heart."

❖ ❖ ❖

When the heavy, metal door slammed shut behind her, Allison Kirstoff found herself at the bottom of a narrow stairway flooded with bloodred light. As her eyes acquired their night vision, she became aware of a green glow emanating from the landing at the top of the stairway. *Feels like I'm in a cheap horror movie*, she decided as she climbed the stairs. Then Allison noticed how the red light turned her blue silk blouse black and her hair silvery white. *For that matter, it looks like I'm in one, too.*

At the top of the stairs, a disembodied head, bathed in the eerie green light, turned and looked at her. Startled, Allison froze. "Access card, please," the head said when she hesitated.

A closer examination revealed that the head was attached to a Special Operations Division officer. Her navy blue uniform, like Allison's blouse, changed to black in the red light. The green glow came from the terminal screen in front of her.

Allison held her card to another reader. The officer glanced down, then back at Allison. "Console 27, Ms. Kirstoff," she said. A door as sturdy as the first unlocked with a click.

Allison reached for the door, then paused. "Will I be able to tell which console is 27?" she asked.

The officer looked up. "Second row from the bottom, third seat in." She smiled understandingly. "New here?"

Allison nodded. "Why the Tunnel of Love?" she asked, gesturing at the stairway.

"Two reasons," the officer replied. "First, it creates a mantrap. If someone we don't like comes along, we let them through the first checkpoint, then we keep them on ice here between two locked doors until the cavalry arrives." The officer pointed at a video camera mounted over the desk. "Second, the SCIF is really a little room suspended at the center of a much bigger room. These stairs bring you up and in, toward the center of the big outside room, to the door of the SCIF. The space between the two rooms is filled with an emission-suppressing foam, completely surrounding the SCIF."

"That way," Allison realized, "no spurious transmissions can get in—"

"And no trace of what happens in there can get out," the officer finished. She leaned forward and beckoned Allison closer with a finger. "You know what I think *really* goes on in there?" she whispered conspiratorially.

Allison bent over. "What?" she whispered back, amused.

"Personally, I think they watch Looney Tunes in there all day." She grinned again. "Let me know, will you?" The officer leaned back and smiled reassuringly. "Second row from the bottom, third seat in, Ms. Kirstoff."

Allison laughed as she opened the door into the heart of the SCIF.

✧ ✧ ✧

An out-of-balance ceiling fan creaked steadily as Hafez Adid inched his way up toward the dented steel counter that served as departure control at Baghdad International Airport.

"Your passport!" the uniformed official standing behind the counter demanded. He thrust out a hand, his face a sweat-sheened scowl.

Adid handed over the document. He waited patiently as the customs officer examined it meticulously.

The small, fat man smiled triumphantly. "You have no exit permit!" he pointed out sternly.

As the officer began to gesture to two policemen lounging behind him with their submachine guns draped across their bellies, Adid held up a hand. "Wait." The official watched suspiciously as Adid reached into the breast pocket of his expensive sharkskin suit and took out a piece of paper. He unfolded it and handed it to the officer. "Here is my travel permit. Issued last night, as you can see, by the Ministry of State."

Determined to let no trace of his nervousness show, Adid

thought again of his partner as the officer scowled at this new complication. *How right you were to insist we keep some of these in case we needed to leave quickly. And how wrong I was to argue with you about the terrible risk you took in smuggling them out of the Palace of Government. Now everything rests on how good a job of forgery I did last night.*

The official beckoned to another uniformed man. Adid tensed, then realized that he might as well relax. Hemmed in by railings as he was, there was nowhere to run. The other man scanned the document, nodded curtly, and walked away. Clearly disappointed, the customs officer turned back to Adid. "Open the briefcase!"

Adid set the briefcase on the table, unlatched it, and pulled it open. The official pulled out a manila folder and opened it. His eyes widened. "These documents are in English! English is forbidden!"

Outwardly unruffled, the young Iraqi smiled. "Allow me to introduce myself, Officer. Suresh Faraz, import-export merchant." Adid pulled a business card from the briefcase. The name on the card matched that on the passport, and Adid again blessed his partner's foresight. He handed the card to the official, making sure the man could see the heavy gold rings which adorned several of his fingers. "Since the infidels with whom I deal do not read our glorious language," Adid went on, "I am forced to deal in their barbaric script. Incomprehensible, isn't it?" Intimidated by Adid's apparent wealth and urbanity, the customs man nodded mutely.

Adid reached into his pocket again. He took out a second piece of paper, which he didn't unfold. "And here is my permit to carry documents in English."

The officer took the paper. He began to open it, then stopped suddenly and glanced around. When he saw that the other customs official was not in sight, he slipped the folded paper and the thousand-dinar note into his jacket pocket.

"All is in order?" Adid asked.

The officer, suddenly obsequious, nodded. "Yes, effendi. All is well. May Allah bless you with a safe and prosperous journey."

As the antique Ilyushin Il-86 climbed out after takeoff, Adid leaned on the armrest of his window seat, peering down through the smoky murk at the tangle of streets, houses, and mosques of Baghdad. *Are you down there somewhere?* he wondered as he thought of his partner. *Are you still alive? And if you are, do you know that I am still alive and very close to achieving your dream?* The plane leveled out, and the city disappeared from view. Adid settled into his seat, staring straight ahead. *And your dream will be realized. It must.*

6

Jake waited, holding the rod tip high to keep tension on the line. Brian dipped the net into the water and expertly scooped out the fat lake trout. The nearly horizontal rays of the setting sun turned the trout's scaly side into glittering, golden chain mail.

"Twenty pounds, I'd say," Brian observed as Jake carefully lifted the trout from the net. "One of the biggest togue I've ever seen come out of this part of the lake." He held up a small camera. "Mind if I take a picture for my next brochure?"

"Sure," Jake replied. "But it might be a good idea to swing the canoe around so the sun's over your shoulder." Jake grinned as he held two feet of plump trout out in front of him. After Brian had taken the picture, Jake gently lowered the fish into the water. The trout, gills working, rested in his hands for a moment before slipping into the darkness of Munsungan Lake.

The warm light of sunset disappeared abruptly. Brian and Jake looked up. A squall line of angry clouds had flung itself over the ridge of mountains bordering the western edge of the lake.

"There it is," Brian said as if introducing the storm he had predicted earlier in the day. "If we really dig, we can get back to the lodge in time to stay dry."

Jake scratched a match along the scrap of sandpaper stapled to a wall of Brian's camp kitchen. Turning on the propane lantern, he held the match to its mantle. With a soft pop the lantern burst into warm, hissing gaslight. Outside, pine boughs whipping in the full-blown storm scratched the cabin's roof.

Across the spacious commercial kitchen, Brian was rolling the last half dozen small trout in cornmeal. He spooned some more bacon grease into the cast-iron skillet, and the fish slid in with an appetizing sizzle. From the oven wafted the mouthwatering aroma of warming bread.

"You're pretty good with a barbless hook," Brian commented as he flipped the fish over. He gestured at them with his spatula. "Most of the so-called sports I get up here couldn't land one of these little guys with a barbless hook, much less the lunker you hauled in today."

Jake shrugged. "Practice." Jake had long ago adopted the common fly-fishing custom of filing the barb off a fly's hook. This minimized the damage to the fish's mouth, thus greatly increasing its chances of survival when released.

"I'd call it skill," Brian countered, "and adaptability. Like how you changed leaders today when the wind came up. Or how well you followed my casting suggestions." He turned off the fire under the skillet. "Practice, adaptability, and skill. All good qualities to develop. Especially when dealing with women in general—" Brian looked pointedly at Jake— "and Anne in particular."

Jake groaned. "You're not going to start in on me, too, are you?"

Brian pulled a platter mounded with trout from the oven. He shoveled the fish in the skillet onto the pile and grabbed a baking sheet of rolls from the ovens. Turning, he kicked the oven door shut, strode the length of the kitchen, and slid the food onto the dining table provided for the camp staff. "You bet

I am," he replied firmly, "because in my humble opinion you're about to let the catch of your life get away." Brian grinned. "Now *you* say grace, 'cause I think you're gonna need it."

✧ ✧ ✧

As Rebecca came in from the kitchen, Anne curled her feet beneath her and tucked her nightgown around her legs. A flash of lightning illuminated the rain sheeting across the window and the trees bending in the wind.

"You OK?" Rebecca asked, seeing Anne jump nervously at the lightning.

Anne smiled. "Never have liked thunderstorms. Especially since I got too big to crawl into my parents' bed with them," she said as she accepted the cup of chamomile tea Rebecca offered her.

Rebecca settled into the other end of the couch. "Getting Jake to pop the question will fix the no-one-to-snuggle-up-to problem. And, if his snoring is anything like Brian's, you'll get used to thunder really fast."

"I hope they're all right," Anne said as real thunder rumbled through the room.

"From what I've seen of Jake, the two of them are probably in hog heaven. Right now they're probably trying to out-macho each other by challenging each other to do some more fishing in the lightning or some equally brain-damaged stunt." Rebecca laughed. "The colder, wetter, and slimier it is, the better Brian likes it."

"Just like Jake and his fishing." Anne wrinkled her nose. "Scales, guts—ugh." She looked at her cousin. "Doesn't Brian ever pester you to come along?"

"Not since the first time he suggested it," Rebecca replied firmly. "We were planning our honeymoon. I told him I'd like someplace with down comforters, a canopy bed, and a big cast-iron bathtub. Much to my surprise, he said he knew just the place."

Anne took a sip of tea. "Was it nice?"

"*Nice* is not the word for it. When he showed me the brochure, it was for a hunting camp up on Eagle Lake! His idea of a 'down comforter' was a sleeping bag, and the 'canopy' on the bed was mosquito netting!"

"What about the big cast-iron bathtub?" Anne asked, laughing.

"The camp had one all right, but it was outside!" Rebecca shook her head. "My beloved learned right then and there that my definition of camping is staying at a place without a telephone in the bathroom." She smiled fondly. "We worked it out eventually—he goes with me to visit my Boston friends, and I *don't* go camping with him."

"At least you were talking honeymoon," Anne replied. "If I even mentioned the word to Jake, he'd be over the horizon in a minute."

"I think I know what your problem is," Rebecca said seriously.

"Oh, what's that?"

Rebecca peered at Anne, surveying her critically. "Yes, that's definitely it."

"*What?*"

"You're nowhere near cold, wet, and slimy enough."

"Anne was a bridesmaid at Becky's and my wedding," Brian said as he speared a flake of trout. "Most of the Boston society crowd was there, the Sewells being who they are, and the male half of that crowd spent the reception practically hanging off Anne's ankles." He broke open a steaming roll and slathered it with butter. "Not that I had eyes for anyone other than my bride, mind you, but even in one of those dumb, fluffy bridesmaid's dresses, Anne was *stunning*. She made every one of those society jerks feel as if he had her undivided attention without really giving any of them so much as the time of day. And you could almost hear the collective mental groan when she left on the arm of the guy she was going home with."

Jake sat up suddenly. "Huh? She went home with somebody? Who?" Brian waited. Jake stared at him over the small Coleman lantern perched in the middle of the table. "Well?" Jake demanded.

"She went home with her father, dimwit," Brian replied. Jake folded his arms and slumped down. Brian grinned. "Gotcha."

Jake laughed, shook his head, and helped himself to another trout. "Now that we've established that you care for her," Brian added, "we can go on." A gust of wind shook the cabin door. "For example, we won't see that big trout you landed today ever again," Brian pointed out.

Jake nodded. "Catching them twice is the real trick," he agreed, reciting the old fishing adage.

"Same thing applies to Anne. You're only going to get one shot at her. But unfortunately, there are no barbless hooks in romance. If you let her go, you'll tear her up. And once she's done hurting, and healing, and hating you for it, you'll never see her again. Just like that big old togue. I know—I almost lost Becky that way. Remind me to tell you about it sometime." Brian stood up. "Let's get these dishes done," he suggested, grinning at Jake's expression, "and then we'll get out the fly tying gear, and I'll see if I can tie you up in a few more knots."

Lightning filled the room as Anne, still laughing, picked up a pillow to toss at her cousin. "Stop!" Rebecca commanded, thrusting out a hand at Anne.

Anne lowered the pillow. "What is it?"

Rebecca didn't turn her face from the picture window. "There's someone outside. On the lawn."

"In this weather?"

Lightning cracked again. The pillow fell from Anne's

hands as she stared at the figure silhouetted sharply against the light. Another bolt showed the figure nearing the trees at the edge of the lawn. A burst of rain rattled against the windows.

Rebecca gasped. "He's headed around the side of the house! Go get Lauri. I'll call the sheriff."

Both women came to their feet. Rebecca crossed the room and picked up the phone. She held it to her ear, then threw it down and flipped the switch on the shortwave radio that sat next to the phone. As Anne rushed into the hall she could hear Rebecca calling, "CZY253, do you read? Over. CZY253, this is LMH347 calling. Do you read? Over. . . ."

Anne flicked on the hall light as she ran into Lauren's bedroom. Outside, lightning arced across the sky behind the wildly whipping treetops. Through the window she glimpsed a shape, dark against the silver-gray grass. Then, just as Anne scooped the sleeping baby into her arms, the room was plunged into darkness.

"That's it," Brian coached. "Palmer the herl around the shank a couple more times. Now tie it down with a few loops of your silk." The knotty pine walls and plank flooring of the cabin glowed in the warm gaslight. Gusts of wind rattled the stovepipe of the Ashley Automatic woodstove, which sat in a corner, radiating warmth. Chairs made from branches, a varnished pine table, and two tiers of bunks completed the rustic decor.

Jake squinted through the magnifying glass mounted on the front of the fly-tying vise. Gingerly he whip-finished the knot he was tying with fine silk thread, forming the head of the fly. Jake clipped off the excess thread, then sealed the knot with a dab of clear nail lacquer. He straightened up and stretched, wincing as his shoulder popped. "So you think they'll go for this?" he asked.

Brian grinned. "Rule Number One that they teach you in Guide School," he explained, "is 'Never laugh out loud at a sport's fly selection.' Instead, say something like, 'Try it; it might work,' or, 'That could be the one.'"

Jake laughed as Brian held his Gray Ghost up to the lantern and examined it closely. "But in this case I can guarantee it," he said approvingly. "After a storm like this the big ones will be coming up to feed. Drift this along that undercut bank just across the lake and *blammo!*"

Rain hammered against the roof of the cabin. With a deafening report, lightning split a huge white pine outside, sending it crashing into Munsungan Lake.

Jake chuckled. "Good thing Annie didn't hear that."

"Thunderstorms make her nervous?"

"Always have, she says. Especially real winners like this one." Jake fished a needle out of his tackle box and began tying a new leader onto the end of his fly line.

Brian shrugged. "Becky's used to weather like this. She'll keep Anne calm. They've probably made some tea and are talking about clothes or something."

Anne stood, disoriented in the darkness, clutching Lauren to her. Breathing hard, Anne fought off panic. "Becky!" Her voice was more scream than shout.

A light appeared at the end of the hall. "Down here," Rebecca called.

Holding the sleeping Lauren to her, Anne rushed toward the light. Rebecca trained the flashlight on her daughter, then on Anne.

"You OK?" Rebecca asked again. Lips pressed together, Anne shook her head mutely. "C'mon," Rebecca said, turning away. Anne followed the bobbing flashlight into the family room. Rebecca took Lauren from her, and Anne collapsed on the couch.

"I saw him," Anne whispered. "Outside Lauri's room."

Rebecca nodded and switched off the flashlight. "Did you get through to the sheriff?" Anne asked.

"No. The power went out before I got an answer." Rebecca took a deep breath. "Lord," Anne heard her pray quietly, "the Bible tells us that you made a decree for the rain and a path for the thunderstorm, but isn't this just a bit much?" Despite herself, Anne smiled into the darkness. She felt Rebecca take her hand, inviting her into the prayer.

Anne's words turned into a gasp as she felt Rebecca's grip tighten. "What?" she whispered.

"*Shh!*"

Anne held her breath and listened. Against the pattering of raindrops she could hear the sound of footsteps making their way across the back porch.

Rebecca thrust Lauren back into Anne's arms. She handed her the flashlight. "I'm going to go see who it is. If anything happens to me, take Lauri and run like mad." The two women got up.

Holding the sleeping baby to her breast, Anne waited by the front door. She watched as Rebecca crept into the kitchen. Outside the footsteps paused, then continued their steady approach.

Through a doorway Anne saw Rebecca silently slide open a drawer. A large mallet appeared in her fist. The young mother crossed her kitchen. Mallet held high, she waited motionless next to the back door.

Anne stifled a scream as the kitchen door shook with a thunderous knocking.

"Who is it?" Rebecca shouted.

"Bill Estes," a muffled voice replied. "Are you all right, Mrs. Keefe?"

Shaking with relief, Rebecca sagged against the doorjamb. "Just a minute, Bill," she gasped. Rebecca pulled a slicker on over her nightgown as Anne stepped into the kitchen doorway.

Rebecca took a rechargeable flashlight out of its socket, flicked it on, and opened the back door.

"Hope I didn't startle you, Mrs. Keefe," Estes said. "Too much, that is," he added as Rebecca set the mallet down on the counter. "Everybody's lights are out up this way," the deputy explained. "Transformer blew down by West Cove. The Power and Light boys say it'll be a few hours before you get your juice back." Water dripped from the brim of Estes's hat. "Since Brian asked me to keep an eye on your place while he's gone, I just thought I'd stop by and let you know."

Rebecca smiled. "Thanks a lot, Bill." *How about that,* she thought. *The big goof* is *thinking of us.*

Estes eyed the mallet. "You got a permit for that thing?"

Rebecca laughed sheepishly. "Anne and I thought we saw somebody outside a while ago."

"Sorry," Estes apologized. "That was me. When I got here, I saw that the door to Brian's boathouse was open, so I went down and closed it. I figured you were asleep so I didn't bother to knock first."

"Quite all right, Bill," Rebecca reassured him. "Thanks for the help."

"Sure thing." Estes lifted his hat, said good-night, and left.

"Whew," Rebecca breathed as she closed the door behind her. "So much for the humdrum existence of a full-time wife and mother. I haven't had this much excitement since the time a scorpion gave birth in my underwear drawer. *And,*" she added with satisfaction, "I get to give Brian grief when he gets back about not locking the door to his precious boathouse." She frowned. "That's not like him." Rebecca retrieved her daughter. "Why don't you make another pot of tea while I put this one back in her crib."

7

Ankara, Turkey

The battered cab pulled up to the curb along Ataurk Bulvar. A young man got out of the back of the cab and retrieved his briefcase. He tossed a bill through the front window, then set out southward along the wide boulevard. To his left, an illuminated fountain gurgled, its glow silhouetting a couple walking their dog. Above him, distorted reflections of a pale half-moon shone down from a glass-fronted office building.

The man reached the end of the park and turned left. Halfway down the block, when a copse of trees blocked him from view, he veered suddenly and trotted across the street. Once safely in the shadow of the Museum of Anatolian Civilizations, the man stopped. Every nerve taut, he listened carefully. The man backed into deeper darkness and waited as a group of drunken carousers, their arms around each other, careened past. When silence descended again, the man resumed his brisk walk. At the end of the street, he disappeared into the warren of twisted lanes and dilapidated hovels that made up Ankara's Old Quarter.

One of the carousers, suddenly sober, watched from the far end of the street. He spoke into something he held against his face. Then he trotted after the man with the briefcase.

Heedless to their imploring cries, the man with the briefcase brushed past the barkers who infested Ankara's souk, the marketplace that forms the heart of any Arab city. He hurried past overflowing stalls laden with bales of mohair and angora in muted contrast to the piles of gauzy cotton blouses.

The man stopped, looked over his shoulder, then turned into a narrow alleyway. A mangy, half-blind cur lunged, snarling at him. The man's well-aimed kick sent the dog shrieking. He emerged from the souk onto the road that encircled the citadel at the center of Old Ankara. The ruined walls of the fortress loomed overhead, brushing against the man's sleeve as he trotted along. Just ahead, the lights of Ankara's business district outlined the ancient citadel. The man with the briefcase picked up his pace. A date vendor watched the man closely, then pulled something from under a pile of fruit and spoke into it rapidly.

The front steps of the American Embassy were brightly lit. Hidden in the scant shadow of a recessed doorway across the street, the man with the briefcase cursed the illumination. He knew nothing could be done about it. Even if all Ankara were plunged into darkness, emergency generators in the embassy's basement would keep the compound's perimeter well lit.

Spurred on by urgency, the man took a deep breath. He looked both ways. A few parked cars sat along the deserted street. The man stepped from the doorway, walked purposefully across the street and up the steps, and disappeared into the embassy.

In one of those parked cars, its windows darkened, another sentinel sat silently, watching. And waiting.

❖ ❖ ❖

The uniformed marine corporal inside the sentry booth looked up from his copy of *Stars & Stripes*. The young man in front of him was well dressed, carried an expensive briefcase, had a large bandage on his forehead, and was sweating profusely. *Big briefcase and lots of sweat equals potential suicide bomber,* the corporal decided. He pressed a button that set off an alarm inside the guardhouse next to the embassy commissary. The corporal eyed the briefcase. *I know this outhouse I'm in is bombproof, but just how bombproof, I don't want to find out.* The sentry toggled his intercom switch. "The embassy is closed, sir. Visa applications are accepted from eight-thirty to four."

The man with the briefcase fought for breath. Out of the corner of his eye, the marine saw the muzzle of a sharpshooter's rifle appear over the railing that ringed the second-floor balcony. *One false move now, buddy, and you're camel-driver purée.*

"I have an appointment," the man said in impeccable English. He started to reach for a handkerchief, then thought better of it.

"The embassy's closed."

The man regained some of his dignity. "My appointment is with Mr. Markham. He is expecting me."

Cripes, the corporal thought sourly. *Only three days at this post, and something like this comes up.* He picked up his phone. "Sarge? It's Curtis. In the booth."

"You OK, Curtis?" the duty sergeant asked from the guardroom.

"Yeah, I think so. Some geek out here says he's got an appointment with Mr. Markham. What should I do?"

"You'll find out, Curtis," the sergeant replied, "that Mr. Markham has odd visitors at odd hours. Call Markham. If he wants to see this bird, he'll let you know. And by the way, Curtis, don't worry about what any of Markham's visitors do to the metal detector. Markham can take care of himself." The sergeant hung up.

Curtis dialed, then listened. "OK," he told the man when he had hung up. "Mr. Markham is expecting you. His office

81

is—" The corporal hesitated, then reached for the embassy directory.

"That's quite all right," the man said. "I know where Mr. Markham's office is."

"Please sign in, sir," the corporal asked as he opened the electronically controlled door.

The man went through the door and stopped at the logbook. The man paused, smiled to himself, then wrote something. "By the way, Corporal," the man said, "before you call a visitor to your embassy a 'geek' you might want to switch off your intercom. Good night." The man with the briefcase walked up the stairs to the second floor.

The duty sergeant walked across the lobby, motioning to the flustered Curtis to meet him outside the booth.

"Look at this, Sarge," the corporal exclaimed. He pointed to the man's entry in the logbook. "It says, 'Mustapha Gilhooley.' What kinda name is that?"

The old sergeant peered at the entry. "Sounds Irish to me, Curtis."

"If that guy was Irish, then I'm Mother Teresa!"

The sergeant snorted. "If one of Mr. Markham's visitors says he's Irish, then he's Irish." The noncom jerked a thumb. "Now get back in the booth, Mother."

The man with the briefcase crossed the landing at the top of the stairs. He paused, framed in an office doorway. "Hello, Mr. Markham."

Seated behind his desk, Gil Markham relaxed. As he stood up to greet his visitor, Markham surreptitiously shut the desk drawer that held his well-used Walther P5. "Hello, Hafez. You have something for me?"

Hafez Adid nodded. The young man crossed the office, shook Markham's hand, and sat down. "But first," he replied, "I hope you have something for me."

Markham grinned. "As always." From a small refrigerator he pulled two frosty bottles of San Miguel beer. He opened them and handed one to Adid. In the four years since he had first met Hafez Adid, the CIA agent had developed a fondness for the earnest young Iraqi. "From the looks of you," Markham observed as he lifted his bottle in a silent toast, "you look like you need this. What happened?"

Adid took a long pull on his bottle, then recounted to Markham his narrow escape.

"And you've heard nothing from your partner since?" Markham asked.

The young Iraqi shook his head. "Nothing." Markham didn't miss the desolation in Adid's voice. "What country did you say this beer is from?" Adid asked after another long drink.

"The Philippines," Markham answered, "an island country north of Australia."

"Is there much sand there?"

"A little. Mostly on white, sandy beaches."

"And, does it rain in the Philippines?"

"All the time," Markham replied. "Why?"

Adid sighed, "Why is it that countries with little sand and much rain produce such wonderful beer, while countries like mine, with much sand and little rain, produce no beer at all?" He set his briefcase on Markham's desk, next to a framed picture of a blonde woman holding identical twin toddlers. Adid opened his briefcase, took out a sheaf of papers, and handed it to Markham.

The CIA station chief leaned back in his chair and started reading. Markham frowned, turned back a page, then whistled softly. Without looking up, Markham reached out, picked up his untouched San Miguel, and handed it to Adid. He finished his reading just as Adid finished his beer.

"Is this reliable?" Markham asked.

"Hasn't everything we've given you turned out to be true?" Adid replied with some indignation.

Markham held up his hands. "Absolutely." He gestured at the document. "But *this* . . ." Markham's eyes held Adid's. "And, as usual, you want nothing for this?"

The young man shook his head. "This time we do want something." He took an envelope from his briefcase. "I am to give you this, too."

Markham slit open the envelope. He took out a single sheet. "So, you want out at last," he said when he had finished reading. "Getting you to the States is no problem, since you're already out. Extracting your partner and the rest of your team will be a bit trickier. How many more are there?" When Adid said nothing, Markham frowned. "Look, Hafez," he barked, "you've got to tell me. If I'm going to need to charter a 747 to get the rest of your people out, I've got to know now."

The young man shook his head. "Just me," he said softly. "And one other."

Markham's eyebrows shot up. "Just one?" Adid nodded solemnly. "Who? And where?" Adid explained the workings of his operation. When he was finished, Markham shook his head. "Amazing, just amazing." He thought for a moment. "How much longer are you in Ankara?"

"Four more days."

"OK. Be back here four days from now. There'll be an American passport waiting for you." Markham smiled at the look in Adid's eyes. "We'll get you on a plane, and there'll be someone waiting for you at Dulles International."

Adid shook his head. "I cannot go alone."

"You'll have to. Obviously, in light of what's happened, we're going to have to extract your partner separately." Markham staved off Adid's protest. "Don't worry—we'll get you back together in the States as soon as we can." *But only*, Markham added mentally, *after separate interviews by our Middle Eastern specialists.* "Do you want to stay here until then?"

"No, thank you. I have business to conduct. It would seem suspicious if I suddenly disappeared."

Adid shut his briefcase, and the two men stood. "I can't thank you enough for this information," Markham said.

"A new life in America is all we ask."

"You'll be treated well. I promise." Markham shook Adid's hand. "Until Thursday."

Adid paused, his hand on the doorknob. "One more thing . . . "

"Yes?"

"Is there San Miguel beer in America?"

Markham laughed. "You ain't seen nothing yet, my friend."

Adid nodded. "Good." The door closed behind him.

Gil Markham picked up the phone on his desk and punched a button.

"Flores," a voice answered.

"Good thing you're still here," Markham told the embassy courier. "Don't leave without seeing me first."

"OK, but I'll need it in half an hour in order to catch the Lufthansa flight to Frankfurt."

"You'll have it."

Markham punched up an outside line, then dialed. "Hi, hon. Are the girls asleep yet?" He chuckled at his wife's reply. "Looks like you get the duty tonight. And do me a favor, will you? Show them that video your sister sent them. . . . Yeah, the one of that miserable singing dinosaur. That way I won't have to sit through it again tomorrow night. . . . Love you, hon. Bye."

Markham powered up his PC. One by one, using a Hewlett-Packard Scanjet IIcx scanner, Markham scanned the sheets Adid had given him into an image file on his PC's hard disk. The PC's high-resolution monitor bathed his face in ghostly light as he surveyed the results. Satisfied, Markham carefully ran the sheets through the shredder that squatted ominously in one corner of his office. Small strips of paper dropped into the burn bag sitting behind the shredder.

Markham inserted an emerald green writable compact disc into the CD-ROM writer attached to his PC. Twenty-five minutes later Markham removed the CD-ROM, just as a soft knock sounded at his door.

"Come," Markham called.

John Flores came in. "You ready?" the embassy courier asked.

"Got it right here." Markham dropped the CD into the case Flores held out. The courier snapped the diplomatic pouch shut.

Using his key, the CIA agent locked the case's two locks. He then pressed an ornately embossed gold-foil seal over each of the locks. "I'll give you a lift to the airport," Markham offered. "It's on my way home."

An hour later, from the airport parking lot, Gil Markham watched the Lufthansa Airbus 330 take off. Only after it had disappeared into the night did he start his car for the trip home.

8

Enveloped in the swirling fog, Jake paddled his canoe silently through the waters of Big Reed Pond. Somewhere a fish jumped, its landing echoed by the soft plop of the paddle as Jake dug it into the water.

An outcropping came into view, its dark outline slowly coalescing against the featureless gray backdrop. Jake brought the canoe up against the shore, stepped onto a mossy embankment, and wrapped the canoe's line around the limb of a fallen tree. When he had set up his cameras, Jake pulled an apple from a pocket of his photographer's vest, sat down on a tree stump, and waited for the fog to lift. Water was all around him, dripping from the Spanish moss garlanding the maple boughs overhead, lapping against the rocks at his feet, forming tiny dewdrops on the hairs on the back of his hand.

As he waited, eating his apple, something inside him twitched impatiently. Jake frowned as it stirred restlessly again. *What's up?* he asked himself. *You've waited like this a thousand times before. Waiting for the light to be just right, for the clouds to come in or go away, or for the expression or gesture that would turn just another ordinary photo into a cover shot. You're used to this—it's no big deal. So what's up?* Tendrils of fog swept suddenly around him as if stirred by a giant, unseen hand. A loon warbled, seeking its mate. Jake paused, listening, then closed his eyes.

You want her with you—that's what's up. Half a state away, much less half a world away, just doesn't cut it anymore. Half a bed away would be nice—waking up to her, all warm and sleepy, and brushing the hair out of her eyes. Jake laughed to himself. *Well, you know what you have to do. Just . . . get . . . married.*

It can be done, Mac, Jake reminded himself sternly. *There are lots of good marriages. Just look at Brian and Becky, or your friends Dave and Stephanie, or Anne's parents, Pat and Joel, for that matter. Her parents have a great marriage. You see it, it's all around you, it's God's truth, but you still refuse to believe it.*

Frustrated, Jake flung his apple core out over the pond. *Because that's not what I saw growing up*, he countered. His thoughts drifted back to his childhood, to growing up in Montana, the only child of unloving, unyielding parents. A home steeped in cautious, distant silence. Three individuals connected by brittle, tenuous relationships; fragile bonds shattered by a word, action, or look. The fearful envy with which he had greeted the rowdy, loving, boisterous play that had been the norm in the homes of his friends. The gradual distancing from his parents, the separation suddenly rendered permanent and complete by their deaths in an automobile accident. The excesses in response to that final abandonment. The damage suffered as a result of those excesses. The attempts to prove himself, over and over again.

What are you trying to prove this time? Jake asked himself. *Who are you trying to impress? You know you're strong, you know you're brave, and you know you're a good photographer. Are you afraid of what you'd have to give up? Sure, you wouldn't be able to take off on assignment as easily or as often as you do now, but you've got to admit that sleeping in some bedbug-infested flophouse has kind of lost its charm recently.* Jake absently massaged the shoulder shattered by a Vietcong machine-gun bullet while he had been rescuing one of his men—an act of heroism for which he had been awarded the Silver Star. *You're old enough to realize you're not going to get everything you want, and you have enough faith to realize that if you accept those good things God chooses to give you, then you've really got it all.* The mist around him stirred, winding itself into coils that began to lift off the water. *"Every good and perfect gift is from above,"* Jake told himself. *Your photography, your fishing, and someone who'd love to be the one to greet you when you come home from them.*

So what's left? Impressing Anne? Impressing God? Anne doesn't want to be impressed—she's told you that enough times in no uncertain terms, and God can't *be impressed! So, now what?* Jake chuckled again. *Time to take Brian's advice. He was all over you yesterday to keep your line tight; you lost a couple of good fish because you didn't. And he was telling you the same thing last night. If you don't keep the connection between you and Annie tight, if you don't help it to grow and strengthen, you're going to lose her.*

The fog rose. Jake got up and went to work.

The president's intercom buzzed. Without taking his eyes from the draft of the speech he was to give that night, he pushed a button. "Yes, Carol?" he said, stifling a yawn as he stretched. Early morning light burnished the Oval Office's mahogany and oak.

"Director French to see you, sir."

The president frowned at the intercom. The fact that Carol Levine, a friend and confidante since high school, would call him sir meant that something was up. The president put the speech into a desk drawer. "Send him in, Mrs. Levine." He frowned again at Robin Hawkes, who was sprawled on a sofa across the Oval Office. Hawkes shrugged. The president shrugged back, finished the coffee in a battered mug that read

Uncle Billy's Southside B-B-Q, and poured himself another cup.

French entered the Oval Office, trailed by two large, grim-faced men. The left side of both their suit coats bulged suggestively.

French paused just inside the doorway. After scanning the room with his eyes, he nodded, and the pair backed out of the room, closing the door behind them.

The president motioned French to a chair. The CIA director of operations sat down, briefcase on his knees. French glanced at Hawkes. "If you'll excuse us, Robin?"

The chief of staff's protest was interrupted by the president. "Robin gets to know everything I get to know, Elliot."

French nodded. "I understand, sir. But 'not quite everything' is more accurate. What I have here is for your eyes only. If you wish, Mr. President," French added urbanely, "we can call in your counsel to explain the applicable law."

Exasperated, the president shook his head. "If you don't mind, Robin." Hawkes rose, his displeasure evident. "Don't worry, Robin," the president added as Hawkes walked toward the door, "we'll get the hang of this. Eventually. Probably just about the time I have to leave office."

After Hawkes left, French unlocked the briefcase, opened it, and took out a heavily sealed folder, which he placed on the president's desk.

"All this cloak-and-dagger stuff had better be worth it, Elliot," the president growled as he peered at the folder through his reading glasses.

"A very necessary inconvenience, Mr. President," French replied. "What you're about to read arrived via special courier from our Ankara station chief, who received it yesterday at approximately three P.M., our time."

The president glanced at the clock on his desk, then stared

at French. "It got from Turkey to here in under eighteen hours?"

"Actually, it was around fourteen."

The president's eyes narrowed. "Should I ask how much this delivery cost the taxpayers?"

French smiled. "It would be extremely helpful if you didn't." He gestured at the folder. "After you read it, I hope you'll agree it was money well spent. By the way, the information in that folder is classified EYES ONLY—OMEGA/TRIAD."

"Which means?"

"Which means that only you, I, and the secretary of state have copies. No other copies may be made, and no one else may see it without the written consent of all three of us."

The president sighed. "Would it do any good, Elliot, if I pounded the desk and shouted, 'Now, hold on just a minute. *I'm* in charge here!'?"

"Not a bit, Mr. President. However, as I said, I'm sure the White House counsel would be able to explain the relevant statutes—"

The president waved him off. He took a small Kershaw knife from his pocket and opened it. "If I slit the seal with this, will it explode in my face?" he asked, only half joking. When French nodded ambiguously, the president stared at him. "Once," he grumbled, "just once during my term of office, I'm going to get a direct, straightforward, unvarnished answer from one of you spooks. I'm not counting on it, mind you, but I'm going to try nonetheless." He slit the seal, closed and pocketed the knife, and began reading.

Five minutes and as many muttered expletives later, the president looked up. "Is this for real? Does this sort of stuff really go on?"

French nodded. "Much more than we let the public know. But this is nothing. Just wait until you get to the next page."

When he finished reading, the president closed the folder slowly. "You're wrong about the security classification, Elliot. Dead wrong."

"Really?"

"Yup. Three of us is two too many to know about this." The president frowned. "Maybe three too many." He peered at the man responsible for all of the CIA's field operations. "So, now what?"

"With all due respect, Mr. President, that's *my* line. You've read the report, and you've read my analysis and recommendation. Now, *you* get to make the call."

"Has Barbara Waite seen this yet?" the president asked. "As secretary of state, she is part of the triad."

"Not yet. As soon as we're finished, I'm going to brief her."

The president grinned. "I'm sure she'll go for it. She loves this kind of covert stuff. She's read everything Clancy and Ludlum have ever written."

Elliot French didn't laugh. "One small difference, Mr. President. This is for real."

The president nodded. "If we decide to do this, who do we send in? This sounds like it calls for a cross between James Bond and Indiana Jones."

French didn't hesitate. "You've already met him. Randy Cavanaugh."

"Lydia Doral's aide? He's more than just a security-chief muscle type?"

French nodded. "Lots more. He's smart, resourceful, speaks five languages, and is sudden death in all directions. Cavanaugh's the best I've got for this sort of mission."

The president glanced at the OMEGA/TRIAD folder. "Hang around," he told French. "I want you to brief Barbara here, instead of in her office. I'm certainly not." He smiled grimly. "I'm certainly going to miss out on seeing the expression on her face when she finds out about *this.*" The president punched his intercom. "Carol, ask Barbara to step in. Also, call Ambassador Doral, and tell her I need to see her at her earliest convenience."

He turned back to Elliot French. "Obviously, this changes the nature of the mission entirely. Is there any way we can pull this off without placing Ambassador Doral and her people in grave danger?"

The CIA chief returned the president's somber gaze. "No, Mr. President, there is not."

Allison Kirstoff took off her headphones, leaned back in her sheepskin-lined chair, and stretched luxuriously. *I've gotten used to this* real *fast,* Allison decided as she looked around.

The Special Classified Intelligence Facility was shaped like a small amphitheater. Five gently curving rows of consoles peered down at a bank of large monitors. One monitor in the center of the array, larger than the rest, showed a Mercator projection map of the earth. Superimposed on the map was the sinuous line of a satellite's orbital track. At various consoles throughout the room, faces peered intently at glowing screens. Allison took a deep breath, drinking it in. The large, flat, square monitor in front of her also displayed the satellite's track. Numbers flickered past in the screen's lower left corner, counting down rapidly.

All right! she thought. *This is it. The big time. The chance to work on live data, not on what some NRO photo jockey thought might be important. The chance to work in real time, not on some fuzzy, days-old photo enhanced by some frustrated Picasso.*

Allison opened her backpack and took out some papers, pencils, and a notebook. She also pulled out a scrunchie, which she wound around her thick hair as she pulled it into a ponytail. Then she turned her attention to the headphones lying on the console desk. *Wow,* Allison thought admiringly as she slipped them back on, *I've never seen any Sennheisers like these in the stereo stores. Bet I won't, either.*

Allison glanced to her left as someone slid into the chair of the console next to her. A short, plump young man grinned at her. His beady eyes peered at Allison from behind high-magnification glasses. *Oh no,* Allison thought, *not another finalist for Nerd of the Year. I wonder which are stronger, those Coke bottles he's using for lenses or the industrial-strength frames that are holding them up.*

The young man punched a button on his console. "Hi," he said through Allison's headphones. "Name's Fred. Fred Meyerdorff. New here?"

Allison surveyed her console, trying to find the button Fred had pushed. "Here, let me help," Fred offered. He leaned over, pressing against her as he did so, and pointed at a button. "It's this one, right here," Fred explained, turning his grinning, pimple-ridden face toward hers. An almost-palpable cloud of halitosis enshrouded her.

Suck it in, girl, Allison told herself sternly. *Throwing up on your second day on the job is* not *a good move.*

Fred pressed the button. He sat back up, oblivious to Allison's none-too-subtle shove. "There," he said cheerfully. "Just punch that button and you can talk to me whenever you want. Now, what'd you say your name was?"

"I didn't. It's Kirstoff. Allison Kirstoff."

"Cool. We hardly ever get girls in here. Anyone call you *Ali?*"

"My *friends* do. Why?"

"Knew a girl named Ali once. Back in high school. She was cool." Fred gestured expansively, forcing Allison to duck. "Anyway, this place is really cool. You'll like it here."

If he'd just make eye contact once. Just once. Allison sighed. *But I have to stay calm. Throttling a coworker, no matter how richly he may deserve it, is probably against policy.*

"I'm doing LANDSAT work," Fred announced proudly. "Statistical analysis on the crop diversity in central Nebraska. It's *so* cool!"

"Do you watch grass grow in your spare time, too, Fred?" Allison inquired sweetly.

Fred blinked rapidly. "Nah. When I get home, I fire up my PC and download GIF files. There's a couple of nodes on the Internet that've got some *really* hot photos!" Fred winked conspiratorially. "I can e-mail you their IP addresses if you want."

Allison shook her head. "No, thanks," she demurred. "I don't think so. I probably wouldn't be too interested, what with my being a *girl* and all."

The young man's head bobbed. "Oh yeah. Right. Cool."

"Nice pants," Allison said, glancing at Fred's slacks, whose chartreuse polyester ended at midshin. "Pick them out yourself?"

"Nah. Mom got them for me for Christmas." Fred grinned. "Mom's cool."

"She must be," Allison agreed, nodding with mock enthusiasm. "You don't see anything like that in *GQ.*"

Ignoring Fred's confused frown, Allison turned back to her console. She stabbed the intercom button and went back to work.

❖ ❖ ❖

Bill Estes finished securing the last of the traps to the ground beside the Keefes' trash cans.

"Check this out," Roy Barnard called to Estes, who came back across the road. Barnard pointed at Lauren's bedroom windowsill. The sill was marred by a series of cuts and gouges. With the toe of his boot, the sheriff stirred up a pile of wood shavings on the ground below the window.

"That coon must've been really hungry to do that sort of damage," Estes observed.

"Either hungry or sick," Barnard replied. "Coons don't normally do that sort of thing." The sheriff frowned. "We haven't had any cases of rabies up here yet, but there's always a first time." He carefully checked the screen covering Lauren's window. "Let's get Brian's tools back to his boathouse," Barnard told Estes, "then we'll go back into town."

As Barnard was putting a hammer away in Brian's toolbox, a fluttering on the back of the boathouse door caught his eye. The sheriff pulled the door partially shut. "What do you think this might be?" he called to Estes. "Doesn't look like the kind of thing a Maine Guide would post in his boathouse."

The deputy examined the piece of parchment fastened to the back of the door with a nail. "Beats me," he replied. "Those wavy lines look like some kind of foreign writing." Estes grinned. "Maybe it's a copy of the fish and game regulations from that Arab country. You know—the one he and Rebecca went to last year."

Barnard laughed and prodded Estes out through the door ahead of him. "Let's go," he said as he closed the boathouse door. "We need to keep moving."

When they got to the patrol car, a red light was blinking on the radio console. The two men listened to the recorded emergency call as Estes started the car. "Carrie Williams wouldn't call unless something really bad has happened," Barnard stated. He looked at Estes. "Punch it, Chewie." Gravel flew as Estes tore down the Keefe driveway.

The town doctor met Barnard and Estes at the entrance to Greenville Seed & Supply. "Other than a headache, George will be OK," Andy Danver told the lawmen, "but it was close. Sure hope you find the nut who walloped him." The doctor left, and the two lawmen went into the store.

George Williams sat behind the counter of his hardware

store, his wife, Carrie, beside him. A bandage covered his right ear.

"Feel up to telling us what happened, George?" Barnard asked.

Williams nodded, then winced. "Fella came in and looked around for a while. Don't know him, but he's been in once, maybe twice before. After a while, he picked up a gallon can of kerosene, then came back to the counter. I figured it was time to get to know him, so I stuck out my hand and introduced myself like I always do. No sooner than I had said, 'Hi, my name's George,' this guy looked at me like I had just insulted his mother. He screamed something, then swung the can at me like he was Willie Mays goin' for the fences." Williams motioned at the dented can lying on the counter. "Fortunately he hit me with the middle of the can instead of the end, or I might not be here." Carrie Williams put her hand on her husband's shoulder, and George reached up and patted it.

"That's all you said to him?" Barnard asked.

"Yup. Just introduced myself. Can't figure it out."

"Got a description for us?"

"Sure. This guy's easy to remember. Foreign looking, with a big nose. Blaze orange hunting hat, green poncho, baggy pants, and canvas tennis shoes. Weird."

Barnard and Estes exchanged a glance. "Sounds like the guy who's been pestering the Keefes," the sheriff told Williams. "We didn't have anything chargeable against him before, but we sure do now." The officers turned to go. "We'll find him," Barnard promised the couple. "And when we do, he's toast."

"Another excellent repast," Marduk told Doris as she refilled his coffee cup. "Never in all my travels have I been as well taken care of as I am here. I attribute that in large measure to you."

Deep within her, Marduk's smile stirred long-abandoned longings. He beckoned with a finger, and Doris leaned close. "I hope," he whispered, "that there were no repercussions from our long chat the other night. I could not bear it if an indiscretion of mine had sullied the virtue of a flower such as yourself."

Doris smiled gratefully, trying to remember the last time a man had considered her virtue as anything but an obstacle to be overcome. "I'm a big girl, Darius," Doris assured him, "and I can take care of myself. Besides, it was fun." She patted his hand, letting her fingers rest for a moment on his. Doris straightened up to find Marduk smiling sheepishly. "What is it?" she asked.

"After all your kindness, I find that I have to ask you for another favor."

"It's no problem," Doris replied. "What can I do?"

"I foolishly lent my rental car to a colleague without remembering that I have an important interview this evening with a family in Millinocket." The urbane foreigner spread his hands helplessly.

"You're working with other people?" Doris asked.

Marduk nodded. "There are five of us from the university. We are spread out over this area. My associate's car broke down, so I lent him mine without thinking." He frowned. "Foolish."

Doris smiled. "I think it was sweet, not foolish. Of course you can borrow my car." She leaned over again. "But that means you've got to do me a favor."

"Your wish is my command."

"Tell me some more stories. Tonight. When you get back."

Marduk grinned up at her. "It might be quite late."

"I'll be waiting."

Thirty minutes later Marduk pulled Doris's Ford Escort into the Rockland public boat ramp. He carefully parked the car behind a screen of bushes, got out, and pulled a large duffel bag from the trunk. Standing on the turf by the water's edge,

Marduk took a flashlight out of the duffel. Using a button built into the flashlight's switch, he semaphored a complicated pattern of flashes out over the lake's expanse.

Listening intently, Marduk grinned into the night when he heard the putter of a small outboard engine. A moment later, a dented aluminum skiff pulled alongside the pilings. The flashlight's glow revealed a thin man with a big nose at the helm of the skiff. Several other shapes, shrouded in darkness, filled the rest of the seats.

Marduk threw the duffel into the skiff's bow and climbed down into the one remaining seat. "Do we have everything, Ali Hassad?" Marduk asked.

The big-nosed man shook his head. "No, *Pir*, we do not. We lack fuel for our torches."

"Was there no fuel to be had?" Marduk wondered.

"There was, *Pir*, but when the infidel blasphemed me, I struck him and ran." Ali Hassad recounted the incident at the hardware store.

Marduk grabbed Ali Hassad's shirt. Effortlessly he pulled the man out of his seat. "You miserable fool!" Marduk raged. "This is America, not our homeland! Here we must put aside our beliefs until we have obtained that which we've come so far to obtain! We *must* have the return of our *Kalifa!*" Marduk shook Ali Hassad until his teeth rattled. "I ordered you to attract no undue attention to yourself, and you do this!" He slammed the flashlight savagely into the side of Ali Hassad's head, then threw him down next to the motor. "If you have in any way jeopardized our mission, I will personally see you fed to *Shaitan* himself!" Marduk sat down and glared at the gibbering man. "Now, we go."

Eyes closed, stockinged feet propped close to the woodstove, Jake lay sprawled on an ancient tartan sofabed that occupied one end of the large cabin. "It can't be that bad, can it?" he asked.

Brian looked up from the spool he was winding fly line onto. "Can what be that bad? Dropping a client's trophy bass over the side of the boat? Yes, *that* can be that bad."

"No, I mean marriage. Just how bad is it?"

Brian squinted suspiciously at Jake. "Wait a minute. Hold everything. You've worked for the CIA, right?"

"Not exactly, but sort of. Why? What does that possibly have to do with marriage?"

"Everything, my friend. That means Becky's hired you to worm your way into my confidence, find out what I really think about being married to her, and then report back." Brian ignored Jake's amused snort. "Whatever she's paying you, I'll double," Brian offered. "Even better, come over to my side, and you can fly out of here instead of having to walk."

"Seriously, what's it like?"

Brian smiled. "If you're looking for someone to bad-mouth being married, my friend, then you're asking the wrong person. I wouldn't trade places with anyone."

"That's easy for you to say now," Jake replied. "Becky's wonderful, and Lauren's a real cutie. Only," Jake added hastily, "don't tell Anne that part about Lauren. She'll start getting ideas." Brian's smile widened into a full-fledged grin. "But," Jake pointed out, "you didn't know that it would turn out so well when you got married."

"Actually, I *was* sure," Brian said. He chuckled at Jake's uncomprehending look. "At least until Becky's and my last premarital counseling session with our pastor." Brian set down the spool of fly line. "I hadn't heard anything too surprising during the counseling sessions, so I was excited, confident, and more than a little eager to make it permanent. Then our pastor, who happens to be a fishing buddy of mine, looked straight at me and said, 'Just remember what you taught me, Brian: It's never the same river twice.' That," Brian admitted, "really cut me down to size."

"I've heard that before," Jake agreed. "No matter how often you fish a stretch of water and how well you think you know it, the fact that it's a dynamic, constantly changing creation means that the next time you go there, it'll be completely different. But what did he mean by it?"

"Basically, the same thing. Both a marriage and the two individuals that compose it are like a river. Two dynamic, constantly changing creations joined together by God to form a third. Just like a river has differing currents, there have been times when Becky or I have surged ahead in some area of our life and then had to wait, usually impatiently, for the other to catch up. Or one of us is down in the deep midstream water, working really hard, while the other is sunning in the shallows. But the part that got me was the realization that, just like a river after a big storm, you can wake up one day and find that the terrain you're so familiar and comfortable with has been completely uprooted."

Brian flipped open the woodstove's door and tossed in another log. "Happened to me a few months after we were married. I had been looking forward to a good, long time with just Becky before we had kids—all the fun we'd been having *plus* all the goodies of marriage—when, out of the blue, there in the middle of that crummy desert, she tells me she's pregnant. So much for my much anticipated long, cozy weekends away. Not to mention what it did to her research schedule."

"What did you do?" Jake asked.

"First, I pulled the mandatory husband stunt of staring slack jawed at her and saying, 'Are you *sure?*' Then, after being impaled upon the Look of Death, I took a long walk." Outside, a lark began its nightly exaltation. "That part of the world is little more than rocks, sand, and dirt. For someone as drawn to water as I am, it was pretty depressing. The farther I walked, and the more rocks, sand, and dirt I saw, the more depressed I got. Finally, I sat down on one of those rocks and explained to God, in no uncertain terms, how it wasn't supposed to be working out this way. I told God that I *wasn't* supposed to be stuck in this wretched sandpile and that if I had to be stuck here, then I *wasn't* supposed to be deprived of my wife's exclusive attentions and that if I had to be stuck here *and* deal with a pregnant wife, then it was especially unfair *to me* that she should be so upset about the impact her pregnancy was going to have on her research."

Shaking his head, Brian chuckled. "God let me have my say, and then he let me stew for a while. Finally, he reminded me of something he'd said a long time ago to a bunch of people stuck in a desert, just like I was, who were complaining to him, just like I was."

"What was that?"

"God had Ezekiel tell the Israelites—who, incidentally, had *much* better reasons for griping and moaning than I did—'I will make a covenant of peace with them and rid the land of wild beasts so that they may live in the desert and sleep in the forests in safety. I will bless them and the places surrounding my hill. I will send down showers in season; there will be showers of blessing.'" Brian grinned at Jake's understanding nod. "After I had thought about that for a while, I realized a few things. That although I may have to live in the desert for a while, I'd someday get to sleep in the forests again—" Brian gestured at the expansive, well-appointed cabin—"and that when it's right, 'in season' as Ezekiel puts it, 'there will be showers of blessing.'"

With a forefinger, Brian gently stroked the hackle of a fly he was tying. "Knowing my love for water, God phrased his answer in terms I could understand and identify with. He does that a lot, and it helps a lot. That gave me the strength I needed to help Becky work through it. And after we relaxed, the blessings started almost immediately. Without the restrictions imposed upon her by pregnancy, Becky would've been out digging instead of translating, and so she never would've come across the Haradi Document." Brian gestured again at their surroundings. "The income associated with that has helped us a great deal."

Brian shrugged. "What I'm trying to say is that you'll never know even *after* you try. All you can count on is that since you, your wife, and marriage itself are all God's idea, he's on your side. Pretty good odds if you ask me."

Jake nodded. "If God is for us, who can be against us?"

"Remembering one other thing helps a lot, too," Brian added.

"What's that?"

"Marriage is like casting a fly: The less you think about it and the more you relax, the farther, faster, and smoother it goes."

✧ ✧ ✧

An ice-haloed moon shone bleakly as Bill Estes pulled his squad car to the side of the road. He rolled down the window and squinted into the deepening night. The final part of his daily patrol was to drive up State Route 15 to his home in Rockwood, some fifteen miles north of Greenville. This took Estes past Mount Kineo, a spire of rock over seven hundred feet high that jutted out of the deep waters of Moosehead Lake.

The deputy's attention had been attracted by a flicker of light. Glimpsed out of the corner of his eye, it had appeared to come from Kineo's peak. As Estes squinted, he again had the briefest glimpse of a ruddy glow high on the mountain.

Estes pulled his binoculars from the glove compartment and got out of the car, keeping his eyes fixed on where he had last seen the light. Bracing his elbows against a rail fence, Estes carefully scanned the western side of the peninsula through the binoculars. The lights in the tents at the Hardscrabble Point campground could be seen clearly, strewn like sparks across the beach at the north end of the island. The rest of the Kineo massif was only darker black against the night sky. The deputy completed his search, then lowered the binoculars.

Get a grip, William, Estes thought as he returned to the squad car. *If there's an unauthorized fire up there, what are you going to do about it? It's three hours around the lake to the bridge to the island, and the whole place will have burned up by then, if it'd burn at all.*

The wind turned chill, and Estes rolled up his window. *Anyhow, it's probably only a bunch of frat kids from Orono up there on initiation, freezing their buns off and wishing they were home in their beds. Grab the police launch from the dock tomorrow and check it out the easy way.*

Estes drove on.

9

"They're back!" Anne called.

Rebecca and Lauren joined Anne as Brian pulled his Cessna up to the dock.

"Phew!" Anne protested as Jake held her against him. "It's certainly obvious that you've been outdoors! Didn't you catch any *live* fish?" She smiled up at him. "If I were big enough, I'd throw you in myself, just like you were going to do to me the day you got here." Laughing, Jake kissed her. "And your beard scratches, too," Anne added as she rested her head against Jake's shoulder, her hands on his back, feeling his muscles move as he stroked her hair. "Not that I mind."

"Come on, you two," Rebecca called to the men. "Anne and I will have lunch ready by the time you've cleaned up." She surveyed her husband critically. "Actually, from the looks of you, it'll probably be dinner."

"Jake's quite a fisherman," Brian told Anne over lunch. "Not at all like some of my other clients, who seem to think a fly rod is a deadly weapon. Jake watched, listened, and—" Brian slipped Jake an intent glance— "paid close attention to *all* my advice."

"Brian knows his stuff," Jake replied, returning Brian's look. "And he's got some *very* definite opinions."

"Did you get your pictures?" Rebecca asked.

Jake nodded enthusiastically. "Big Reed Pond is gorgeous. Brian flew us in just after dawn, when the mist was beginning to come off the water. By the time I got set up, the clumps of red maple that dot the edge of the pond were beginning to show through the fog like a string of bonfires."

"I had no idea Jake was so eloquent," Rebecca whispered to Anne.

"He is about *some* things," Anne replied acerbically. "When it comes to his work, his fishing, or that car of his, Jake can go on for hours."

"There's one shot," Jake finished, oblivious to Anne's comments, "with the fog, the maples, and a pair of loons that I think'll do nicely." Jake shook his head. "When the Good Lord made that place, he sure got it right."

"Jake's a very efficient photographer," Brian commented. "We were done by nine."

"So, *then* what did you do?" Rebecca asked, feigning a look of intense interest. "Care to take a guess, Anne?" Rebecca asked. She peered at her cousin. "Ready? All together now. You . . . went . . . FISHING!" the two women chorused.

"Sure did," Brian agreed cheerfully. "Jake and I put a scare into Big Reed's population of blueback char that'll last 'unto the third and to the fourth generation.'"

"Did you fly back out and stay at your camp?" Rebecca asked.

Brian's black curls swayed as he shook his head. "Nope. Dave Youland let us use one of his cabins."

"You would've loved it," Jake told Anne. "It was so quiet and peaceful, sitting on the porch watching the sun set along the lake. A cozy woodstove, the softly hissing gas lamps, and

then, when night fell, it would've been just you and me and—"
Jake paused, leaning close.

"Yes?" Anne asked expectantly.

"And about twenty thousand field mice."

"Oh, how *gross!*" Anne exclaimed. She shoved Jake away.

"Wasn't too bad after you got into your sleeping bag," Jake
went on, "as long as you didn't mind them running across your
face." He grinned at Anne, who glared playfully back at him.

"I put drain cleaner out before we left," Brian told Rebecca.

"You mean the cabin actually had plumbing?" Anne asked.
She looked reprovingly at Jake. "So why didn't you shower and
change before you came back and smeared fish guts all over my
best sweater?"

"The 'plumbing' is about thirty feet back in the woods,
Anne," Brian explained. "And to keep the vermin down, we mix
peanut butter, which mice love, with drain cleaner and leave it
out for them. The little beggars chow down on it and then keel
right over."

Anne's hands flew to her face. "You *don't!*"

"They only squeal a couple of times before they stop
twitching," Jake added.

Rebecca closed her eyes. "Gosh, Anne," she said quietly,
"aren't you *glad* they're back?"

"Chief," Mark Sewell asked cheerfully, "is it the lighting in
here, or are you looking a bit green?" Sewell and Shiloh Turk
were standing the afternoon watch in *Alameda*'s Combat Information Center.

Turk growled at the young lieutenant.

Mark grinned. "After three helpings of Cookie's chili for
lunch and two of those lethal cigars of yours for dessert, it's no
wonder you're out of sorts."

Goaded, Turk leaned back in his chair. "Kid," he said, the

rancor in his voice belied by his grin, "*you're* the one who's out of sorts. All that Bible reading and talks with the chaplain. What kinda fun is that?"

Mark propped his feet up on the chart table. He'd had this talk with his friend and mentor many times before. "It's interesting, it's fun, and it's good exercise for my mind."

Turk snorted. "Maybe so, but a book won't keep you warm at night." He ignored Mark's tolerant chuckle.

The master chief stared up at the overhead. "Did I ever tell you about the time back in '73 when me and two other guys from SEAL Team Two got liberty in Naples? No sooner had we hit shore than we found ourselves smack-dab in the middle of the Italian Nursing Society's annual convention." Turk gave a low whistle. "Talk about your intensive care—"

"Blackjack Flight, Spyglass Two." Both men sat up as the transmission from an E-2C Hawkeye reconnaissance aircraft came over the CIC's speakers. "Radar contact, bearing three-three-five. Vector tango-delta-two."

"Roger that, Spyglass," the commander of the squadron of F-14 Tomcats based aboard the USS *Paul Revere* replied. "Jericho Five, Blackjack Leader."

Mark put on his headset and flipped the microphone into place. The 233d Tactical Fighter Wing's code name was Jericho. As duty fire control officer, Mark was Jericho Five.

"Blackjack Lead, Jericho Five. Over," Mark replied.

"Unidentified radar contact. Request permission to prosecute." Like all sentries, the leader of Blackjack Flight had to request permission to leave his post.

"Permission granted."

"Then we'll go have ourselves a look-see. Blackjack Two, follow me," the flight commander ordered his wingman.

"Got anything?" Mark asked Turk.

The radarman peered at his screen. "Not really. Blackjack

Flight was patrolling at the extreme edge of our range to begin with, and now they're headed lickety-split due northwest."

"Blackjack Flight, vector bravo-alpha-three." The Hawkeye's intercept officer homed the F-14s in on their target.

"Visual," Blackjack Leader reported. "Bogies in sight. We have two MiG-29 Fulcrums showing Iraqi insignia. Closing at twelve o'clock high."

Mark grimaced. "Coming right at 'em," he muttered. "Blackjack Flight, to five." Mark ordered the two F-14s down to five thousand feet. Standard rules of engagement called for U.S. military aircraft in an intercept situation to first give their targets a wide berth.

"Staying with us," Blackjack Leader reported. "Just blew past us. Each bogie is armed with four Archers." Turk grunted. The AA-11 Archer was a deadly Soviet-made air-to-air missile. "They've jinked around and are coming in," Blackjack Leader added.

Perspiration dotted Mark's brow. The sharp, high-speed turn the Fulcrums had performed was considered a warlike maneuver. "Blackjack Flight, to two." Mark hoped his voice was calm as he ordered them down to two thousand feet.

"Not much room down there," Turk said quietly.

"They can outrun the Fulcrums."

"But they can't outrun an Archer."

"Heading two-eight-five," Blackjack Leader reported. "They've just jinked around on us for the third time."

Mark picked up a red phone. "Captain to CIC. On the double."

The CIC speakers crackled. "Keep tight, Two," Blackjack Leader ordered his wingman. "Don't want these boys to think we're a cheap date."

Commander Jerry Hall took the steps down from the bridge two at a time. "What you got, Mark?"

"They've come around on us again," Blackjack Leader reported as Mark quickly outlined the situation.

"Are they over international waters?" Hall asked.

"Blackjack Lead, feet wet?" Mark said into his microphone, asking if the flight was over water.

"Affirmative. They've just jinked around on us for the fifth time and are closing fast."

"Weapons free," Hall ordered. Mark repeated the command. Military law says that a commander "owns" all the weapons in his charge. Thus, no shots may be fired until the weapons are freed by the commanding officer.

A beeping tone indicated that the pilots of Blackjack Flight had just pressed the *MASTER ARM ON* buttons mounted on consoles near the pilots' left hands.

"Right in on us," Blackjack Leader reported. "Their noses are coming up—"

A shrill squeal interrupted the flight commander's report. Sewell, Turk, and Hall stiffened, recognizing the sound of the F-14's threat radar reporting a missile launch.

"MLD!" Blackjack Leader barked. "Two, break left!"

A series of sharp bangs erupted as the lead F-14 launched chaff containers. The containers would explode in midair, filling the sky with strips of reflective aluminized plastic in an attempt to distract the Archers.

"Blackjack Leader, report," Mark ordered.

Silence filled the CIC. As Mark began to repeat the order, the radio hiss was replaced with a thunderous roar.

Mark glanced nervously at Turk, only to find him smiling broadly. "Afterburners," Turk explained. "They're going after them."

"Closing," Blackjack Leader reported. The warbling tone of a hard-target radar lock-on echoed through the CIC.

"Fox one! Fox one!" two voices shouted together as the

weapons officers of both F-14s fired an AIM-7M Sparrow air-to-air missile at their attackers.

"Look at 'em go, Boss!" the young pilot of Blackjack Two said excitedly. "They've turned tail and are runnin' away!"

"Impact in three seconds," Blackjack Lead's weapons officer reported.

This isn't near as much fun as I always imagined it would be, Mark thought as he waited those three long seconds.

The voice of Blackjack Leader crackled through his headphones. "Two clean kills. One parachute sighted."

"Blackjack Flight, return to base," Mark ordered.

Jerry Hall pushed his cap back on his head. "Order search and rescue for that downed pilot, Mark, and then join me on deck. We'll take a cutter over to the *Revere.* I'm sure the admiral will want to know all about it."

Mark dispatched a Seahawk search-and-rescue helicopter to search for the Iraqi flyer, then turned to Turk. "Feeling better, Chief?"

Turk beamed. "I feel just *fine.*"

"Now just calm down, Harry," Roy Barnard said patiently. "You're not making any sense." The sheriff crossed his arms and waited for the small, heavyset man standing in front of him to stop waving his arms. Swinging gently above them was a faded sign reading:

BRUNSON'S PETTING ZOO
SODA—ICE CREAM—COLD BEER

With an effort Harry Brunson calmed himself down. "I'm telling you, Roy, it was that guy yesterday."

"What guy yesterday, Harry?"

"The weirdo. We usually get the kind of traffic you'd expect for this sorta place," Brunson explained. "Minivans full of kids, motor homes, those kind of folks. But this guy yesterday was somethin' else. As soon as he came up, I started to pull a six-pack outta the cooler, since I figured he couldn't be here for anything else. But no, he paid his admission and went on in." Brunson pulled a large bandanna out of a pocket and mopped his brow. "Since he looked like a refugee from one of those rock concerts they have down in Portland, I decided to keep an eye on him. So I had Dolores take over while I followed him around."

"Did he act strangely?"

"No, not at least until he came to Clementine. Then he jumped a foot. Thought at first a deerfly had got him. He must have spent the better part of twenty minutes wanderin' around Clemmie's pen looking at her. Then he lit outta here like the devil was after him."

"And it's Clementine who was allegedly stolen?"

"Ain't no 'allegedly' about it!" Brunson replied heatedly. "Just as the missus and me were getting ready for bed last night, Clemmie started bawling somethin' terrible. Sounded like she was trying to kick down her pen." The zookeeper frowned. "Well, we've had trouble with bears, y'know, so Big D grabbed the over 'n' under and took off lickety-split out the door. Sure enough, she saw a dark shape carrying off poor old Clemmie. Got off both barrels, but she missed. Says the sleeves of her nightgown got tangled up in the sights." Brunson looked disgusted.

Barnard closed his eyes. *Terrific*, he thought. *With Dolores and Old Man Petersen both blazing away at anything that moves, we're going to kill somebody yet.* "Probably was a bear," he decided. "Any sign of blood?"

"Nope. But that's not all," Brunson finished. "Right after that, Dolores heard a car revving its engine and peeling away up the road like the summer boys do. Big D said she could still smell the burned rubber this morning." He peered up at Barnard triumphantly. "Ain't no bear can drive like that. And if there is, I want it for the zoo."

"One more thing, Harry," Barnard said. "Who or what is a 'Clementine'? It would help to know what we're looking for."

Brunson stared at the sheriff. Then he relaxed. "Guess you wouldn't know, not havin' any young ones to bring around. Clementine's my star attraction. We keep her over in the part of the zoo we call the Funny Farm. None of the big zoos," he boasted proudly, "can say that they have a five-legged calf."

The sheriff barely kept a straight face. "OK, Harry. I'll tell Bill to be on the lookout for a stolen calf."

"A stolen *five-legged* calf."

"Right." *Thank heaven summer's almost over.* The sheriff's stomach growled. "And speaking of hot veal, I haven't had lunch yet. Bye, Harry. I'll let you know." Shaking his head, Barnard walked back to his squad car.

"Here you go, hon," Doris said as she exchanged Roy Barnard's empty plate for one laden with a slab of key lime pie. "Fresh this morning." Doris refilled his coffee cup, winked, and sauntered away.

"What's with her?" Barnard asked as Sandy Neill, cup of coffee in hand, slid into the booth next to him. "If Doris floats any higher, I'm going to have to cite her for flying without a license."

Sandy chuckled. "She's been seeing one of our guests pretty regularly for the past few days. Maybe you've noticed him—a tall foreigner."

Barnard looked up from his pie. "A foreigner? *I* haven't noticed one, but the Keefes sure have. If this boyfriend of Doris's is tall and skinny with a big nose, I want to have a talk with him right away."

The Lakeview's manager frowned, surprised by the intensity of her usually easygoing friend. "Professor Marduk's tall," she replied. "He's trim, but certainly not skinny. And I wish *my* nose looked as good as his. Why do you ask, Roy? Something going on?"

Barnard shrugged. "Some tall, big-nosed foreign guy in a skiff has been playing peekaboo with Becky Keefe, a guy with the same description nearly caved in George Willams's head with a fuel can, Bill thought he saw weird lights on top of Kineo last night, and Harry Brunson's in a royal snit because one of his star attractions has disappeared." The sheriff grimaced. "This is just too much excitement too late in the season to suit me. So when you see him, do me a favor and ask the good professor to drop by the station house, will you?"

❖ ❖ ❖

"Lunch is ready, everyone," Robin Hawkes called as he made his way through the knot of admirers surrounding the president in the Rose Garden. "The president will join you on the East Lawn shortly."

When the White House ushers had escorted the last of the visitors out of the Rose Garden, the president looked at his watch, then at his chief of staff. "What's up, Robin? Senator Rutherford is not going to be pleased that I cut short my photo op with the Rutabaga Grower's Council."

"There's been an incident, Mr. President," Hawkes replied. "You're needed in the Situation Room."

"What sort of 'incident,' Robin?" the president asked as he strode from the garden. "Someone trip on the front steps, or did some third-world upstart pip-squeak finally nuke their neighbor?"

"I'll let General Rodriguez explain," Hawkes answered.

The Situation Room, located in the sub-subbasement of the White House, was dominated by a massive, oval oak table. The baffled, shadowless fluorescent lighting seemed to expose and magnify the tiniest details of the room, bringing into stark clarity the fine grain that ran the table's length. The pads of paper that ringed the table glowed white, their blue lines all but invisible in the merciless light, the pencils arrayed along their tops bright yellow.

Barbara Waite, the secretary of state, rose as the president came in. chairman of the Joint Chiefs of Staff, General Jaime "Roddy" Rodriguez, came to attention. The president waved them both into their chairs as he sat down. Rodriguez remained standing.

"What's going on, Roddy?" the president asked.

"Sir," Rodriguez answered, staring straight ahead, "it is my duty to inform the commander in chief that U.S. forces have engaged in combat operations."

"Very well, I am now so informed. Now cut to the chase. And sit down, you're making me nervous."

The general sat down. "About two hours ago, sir, two F-14 Tomcats on routine BARCAP from the USS *Paul Revere* of our 233d Tactical Fighter Wing, stationed in the Strait of Hormuz, shot down two MiG-29 Fulcrums displaying insignia of the Iraqi Air Force."

"Just a second, Roddy," the president interjected. "What's a 'bar cap'? Something Daniel Boone wore?"

Barbara Waite smiled. The general did not. "BARCAP, sir," Rodriguez replied stiffly, "stands for Barrier Combat Air Patrol. It's the routine patrolling done around a flotilla stationed in unfriendly waters."

"Sorry, General. The joke wasn't worth the interruption. Please continue."

"The Tomcats, following standard rules of engagement, intercepted the Fulcrums. After warning off the Iraqi fighters and after several threatening maneuvers on the part of the Fulcrums, each of the F-14s fired a single AIM-7M Sparrow air-to-air missile, shooting down both MiG-29s."

"So the Iraqis made the first threatening move? We're quite sure of that?"

"Yes, sir. Quite sure." Rodriguez picked up a remote control. A grainy videotape began playing on a screen in front of them. "This is the gun camera tape from the lead F-14. Notice how the Iraqis keep turning back toward the F-14s every time they turn away. This is called jinking and is universally considered a threatening maneuver." The president clutched the arms of his chair as the supersonic aircraft rollercoasted across the sky. "While this was going on," Rodriguez continued, "the fighters received permission to shoot if they felt the situation warranted it. As you can see it did—right *here*. The thin trail of smoke is the exhaust from one of the Sparrows. And . . . detonation." Rodriguez smiled to himself as the civilians in the room winced at the sudden, lethal fireball. The screen went dark.

"Who gave the pilots permission to fire?" the secretary of state asked.

"As per standard operating procedure," Rodriguez replied, "weapons were released by authority of Jericho Five. That's the duty fire control officer."

Robin Hawkes looked up from his notes. "Do we know who was on duty at the time of the incident?"

"According to the information I have," Rodriguez replied, "it was a—" the chief of staff turned a page— "Lieutenant Mark Sewell."

"And this Lieutenant Sewell acted properly?" the president asked.

"Yes, sir. As did the pilots. All was done strictly according to accepted NATO rules of engagement."

Barbara Waite frowned. "Were there any survivors?"

Rodriguez nodded. "One. He was picked up by one of our search-and-rescue teams. The deployment of which, I might add, is also standard procedure."

Smiling, the president leaned back in his chair. "Good. Very good." He turned to his secretary of state. "Barbara, get that smarmy little Iraqi Ybrahim Ibn in here. I may have missed the barbecue on the East Lawn, but at least I'll get to roast *something* today."

Waite smiled at her old friend. "My, we *are* feisty today, aren't we?" The president sneezed, then wiped his streaming eyes with a handkerchief. "Ah," she added with a knowing smile, "I should have known. Been pressing the flesh again, eh?" Nodding grimly, the president stood up.

Trailing behind the president and Hawkes as they left the Situation Room, Roddy Rodriguez looked at Barbara Waite. "Just what did the president's sneezing explain?" he asked.

Waite smiled. "It explained why he's in a mood to rake Special Envoy Ibn over the coals. You see, he absolutely *hates* meaningless Rose Garden photo ops like the one Robin rescued him from today. They *always* put him in an evil mood. And heaven help the person he takes it out on."

"Why does he hate garden parties? Because he considers them a waste of time?"

"No," the secretary replied with a grin, "because he's allergic to roses."

Late afternoon sunlight stained the cedar paneling of Elliot French's living room a warm gold as he opened the small refrigerator under the bar and handed Randy Cavanaugh a beer. The house, nestled among the pines at the tip of Ames Point on Maine's North Haven Island, looked southeast across the Fox Islands Thorofare.

"Nice place, Boss," Randy observed as he watched the sailboats scurrying along the thoroughfare, bound for their evening berths. "But I don't think you flew me up here just to compliment Chris's architectural skills." French's wife, an architect, had spent her pregnancy designing and overseeing the construction of the vacation home.

"Right the first time," French replied. "We're here because this place is secure—the boys and girls over in the Technical Directorate installed a few things in the walls which see to that. We're also here because this morning, as Chris was getting out of the shower, just for grins I called out, 'Thar she blows!'" French grimaced. "*Big* mistake. A few minutes later, I decided that today was just the day to come over and close this place up for the winter." He paused. "I hope," the father-to-be added thoughtfully, "that it doesn't occur to her to have the locks changed while I'm gone."

When Randy had stopped laughing, the CIA's director of operations leaned against the bar. "Since you're leaving tomorrow, I thought you'd like to know what you're really going to be doing in Baghdad. You ready to go?"

Randy nodded. "Sure. I'll call Lee tonight. Then I'll wrap my cloak around my bottle of poison and toss it into my booby-trapped briefcase along with my dagger and decoder ring."

"How's it going with Lee?" French asked.

"Great. She's beautiful, smart, fun to be with, and utterly disarming," Randy replied. "Of course," he added reflectively, "'disarming' is a term that can be applied to nuclear weaponry, too."

Randy finished his beer. "As for what I'll be up to over there, the question has crossed my mind. It can't be to act as nursemaid to the ambassador—she's got a squad of marines to baby-sit her."

"You wouldn't talk about baby-sitting if you knew Lydia Doral the way I do," French replied seriously. "Let me know when you get back just who did the nursemaiding." He handed Randy a piece of paper. On it were written a date, a time, and an address. "This is what you're really going over there for. The address is that of an outdoor café near the embassy. Be there at the time and date shown. Order coffee, medium sweet. But order it in Russian." The DO frowned. "By the way, how *is* your Russian? You haven't had a chance to practice in almost a year now."

"*Spasibo, tovarisch. Ya horosho govoru po Ruski,*" Randy replied, his Russian accentless.

French nodded. "Good. When your bill comes, take the bill and leave without paying. On the back will be further instructions. Do what they say, when they say to do it. But remember," French cautioned, "leave the café without paying. If you don't, you'll find nothing waiting for you."

Randy shrugged. "OK, but why the *Mission Impossible* routine?"

French crossed the room. He unlocked a desk drawer and took out a file. "*This* is why." He handed Randy the folder.

Emblazoned on the folder's thick cover was SCI-SCIMITAR. Randy whistled. Sensitive Compartmented Information. In an attempt to control damage in the event of a leak or a turncoat selling secrets to the enemy, the CIA compartmented especially sensitive information, limiting access strictly to that part of the information the reader needed to know. Randy had heard of the SCIMITAR compartment before, but he had never seen a document so marked.

"Where's your gun, Boss?" Randy asked.

"Why?"

Randy gestured at the folder. "Don't you have to shoot me as soon as I read this?"

"As of this minute, you're cleared for it. Read."

Randy pulled open the Velcro tab holding the folder shut. Fastened to the inside of the front cover was a small LCD display. The display had a small solar cell below it. Each time the cell was exposed to light, a microcomputer embedded inside the display counted it.

Randy glanced at the display, which read *007*. *Wonder if that's the number of times this folder's been opened*, Randy thought, *or its owner*. Such tamperproof technology was used to guard only the most sensitive of information. "Boss, I think you'd better play it safe and shoot me now," Randy said as he started reading.

COVER NAME: SCHEHERAZADE
NAME: UNKNOWN
DOB: UNKNOWN
POB: UNKNOWN
OCCUPATION: UNCERTAIN (MAY INVOLVE TELECOMMUNICATIONS)

BACKGROUND:
On 17 April 1990 one Hafez Adid, an Iraqi national, presented a packet of papers to the chargé d'affaires at our embassy in Ankara, Turkey. Finding that the documents were in Russian, the chargé placed them in that night's diplomatic pouch for forwarding to Washington.

Upon translation and examination, the documents were found to detail the specifications and deployment of the SS-1 SCUD missiles recently sold to Iraq by the then Soviet Union. The information presented included the specific revision level of each missile, warhead size and type, and planned location of the underground bunker for each missile's mobile launcher.

The accuracy and veracity of the information was independently verified through National Technical Means.

Randy chuckled at the CIA's euphemism for spy satellites.

Thereafter, approximately every six weeks, Adid would appear at the embassy with new information. Adid's claim to be a merchant banker for Iraq's largest export company has been verified. To date, information provided by SCHEHERAZADE has included Iraqi troop movements, details of Iraqi covert activities in Israel and Saudi Arabia, and reports on clandestine imports by the Iraqi government. During Operation Desert Storm, SCHEHERAZADE provided particularly valuable intelligence concerning Iraqi troop placement and overall strength.

This asset is unusual in several respects. Both SCHEHERAZADE and Adid have refused any payment for the information provided. And while, like most of our valuable assets, SCHEHERAZADE's services were volunteered by the asset personally, none of the rationale, justification, or requests for remuneration which usually accompany such offers was made.

Nothing is known of SCHEHERAZADE other than the obvious fact that the asset has access to top secret information. Adid has consistently and steadfastly refused to answer any questions regarding SCHEHERAZADE. When pressed for details, SCHEHERAZADE refuses as well, claiming the value of information provided is verification enough.

That SCHEHERAZADE may be an especially clever source of disinformation planted by the Iraqis cannot be discounted. The value and accuracy of the information provided to date, however, would tend to contradict this. Nonetheless, ongoing, independent verification by

NTM and other means when possible is recommended.

It is further recommended that, because of this asset's strategic importance, SCHEHERA-ZADE be kept deep black and assigned SCI status. Compromising SCHEHERAZADE in any way would result in the loss of one of our most important Middle Eastern assets."

The report was signed by two CIA analysts.

Randy took a deep breath. "Deep black" was CIA jargon for the highest level of secrecy. *And the deeper the black*, he thought, *the deeper the associated danger.*

French handed Randy another SCIMITAR folder. "Now, read this."

When he was finished reading, Randy looked at his boss. "How do we transport stuff this hot?" *If what this says is true . . .*

"By hand," French replied. "It's much too sensitive to be transmitted by any other means. This Adid character delivers the typed information to your partner in crime, Gil Markham. Gil, as you well know, is currently our Ankara station chief." Randy grinned at the mention of his old friend and colleague. "Markham," French continued, "scans the typed sheets into a PCX file on his PC. To remove any trace of origin, he then uses a Company-developed optical-character-recognition program to turn the PCX image file into a vanilla ASCII textfile."

"The kind any word processor can read," Randy interjected.

"Right. He then uses a specially modified Lempel-Ziv encoding program to compress the file, stores it on a writable CD-ROM, and ships it to us via embassy courier."

Randy frowned. "But anyone who intercepted the CD-ROM could decompress it."

"Not without our software, they couldn't," the DO replied

with a grin. "Our program uses a standard 'lossy' compression technique—it throws away certain bytes in the file to be compressed which the program determines to be redundant."

"You really love this stuff, don't you?" Randy asked his boss. "If this is what moving into management does to you, I'll stay out in the field. This torture is a lot worse than anything the other side could think up."

French ignored him and went on. "Our program takes a standard GIF-format image file—I think it's of the Three Stooges—and determines which bytes of the GIF image the lossy compression algorithm is going to discard.

"After the compression is finished, our program inserts the bytes of the file Gil scanned into the empty spaces in the compressed GIF image, based on a twelve-digit onetime code that Gil enters at the beginning of the process. Since the spaces into which we insert our information are considered empty by standard decompression software, it'll ignore our stuff when it expands the file." French grinned. "The beauty of it is that without *both* the onetime code and our software, anyone who decompresses the file will end up with nothing but an old publicity still."

"The palimpsest theory," Randy observed. "Hide what you don't want found under something that you don't mind being found."

"Exactly," French agreed. "Rather than being obviously encrypted, the CD-ROM is outwardly innocent. And with a little bit of work, the CD-ROM yields something both innocuous and reasonable. This, we hope, would dissuade the interceptors from digging further."

"And I'm to meet with this SCHEHERAZADE," Randy said.

French nodded. "The last love letter Adid dropped off finally mentioned a price. In exchange for full details on the

Iraqi nuclear capability and the weapons recently acquired from Russia, SCHEHERAZADE wants to be extracted."

"So my job," Randy realized, "is to find SCHEHERA-ZADE and get him out of Iraq." French nodded again. "You got it, Boss," Randy agreed. "But why the code name SCHEHERAZADE?"

French shrugged. "Don't know, exactly. That was how this guy signed the first of his communiqués." The DO grinned. "But since the Scheherazade in the *Arabian Nights* told a thousand and one tales, we're hoping ours will, too."

10

"Mark four minutes," the soft, pleasant voice in Allison's headphones said. "Pass 5507 begins in four minutes."

Allison spent the minutes reviewing parameters of the satellite flyby. *Another pass down the Red Sea*, she realized. *Undoubtedly looking for amphibious terrorist camels. OK, we can do that.* Two lights came on at the top of her console, indicating that the CRYSTAL/KENNAN spy satellite had been ordered to switch on its infrared and mapping-radar sensors.

Radar first, Allison decided. *That'll show us everything on the surface, and maybe if I'm lucky I'll get to see the submarine races.* She grinned. *The last time I saw submarine races was from the backseat of a '74 Mustang.*

She took a light pen from its holder on the right side of the console and touched the tip of the light pen to several choices on the menu displayed on her screen. The choices lit up, and a pattern like rumpled cardboard appeared. Allison studied the patterns for a few moments. *No way*, she decided. *No sub races today. Too much surface traffic. Plus, it looks really choppy down there. Didn't NOAA post something about a big storm passing through?*

Allison switched over to the infrared scanner. *Now, that's more like it.* Two hundred miles below the spy satellite, the Red Sea, warmer than the cold desert sands surrounding it, glowed phosphorescent blue in the infrared image displayed on her console. Tiny dots of lighter blue moved across it. Allison touched one of the dots with her light pen, then she selected IR SIG from the menu.

Half a world away, the infrared scanner on board the CRYSTAL/KENNAN gathered data about the heat being generated by the ship Allison had selected. Via tight microwave beam, the spy satellite passed the information along to a MILSTAR military communications satellite in geostationary orbit above North America. With a short burst of krypton-argon laser light, the MILSTAR then relayed the information to the NSA communications facility at Fort Wayne.

A microcomputer embedded in Allison's console accepted the infrared data fed to it. The computer analyzed the data, then compared the result against a range of values stored in a relational database on the NSA's main computer down in the basement. Within milliseconds the dot was identified. "POSITIVE ID (PROB 98%): CG75 ALAMEDA USN" appeared at the bottom of the screen.

Allison smiled. *Ninety-eight percent probability. This sure beats the hardware back at my old job at the State Department. Let's see what else is around.* Touching a bright cluster of light at the left edge of the screen instantly brought up the annotation "CAIRO." Allison frowned. *Cairo. That's where that MacIntyre thing happened a couple of years ago. Never did see what Anne saw in him. He's good looking but awfully old for her, and not too bright. Or so it seemed.* A faint glimmer of light caught her eye. *Let's see what this thing can really do.*

Using the same sequence of commands, Allison gathered information on the smudge of light. She frowned at the result, then repeated the process. *I know you're telling me that you have a sixty-five percent probability*, she thought, *but I still don't believe you.*

"Thirty seconds until datapoint deacquisition," the synthesized voice whispered in her headphones. Allison grimaced. She had only thirty seconds until the target disappeared over the horizon. *That's what you get for daydreaming, girl,* she chided herself.

She tapped a menu item marked *SAR*, then tapped the target. The spy satellite's synthetic-aperture imaging radar took an electronic picture of the target. *We should be almost overhead by now,* Allison realized, *so we should get a good image.*

Allison stared at the image that appeared on the monitor. *Can't be. Makes no sense. What's one of* those *doing there?* She ran the image through each of the five image-enhancement algorithms available to her RS/6000. Each time, the probability of a positive identification grew.

Just as Allison touched her light pen to the rectangle marked *SAVE IMAGE*, her monitor went blank. "Target deacquisition at fifteen-twenty-three Zulu," the computerized voice announced. Allison thumped her console with the flat of her hand. Ignoring the sidelong glances surrounding her, she stared intently at the now-blank screen. *If it* was *there,* she reasoned, *it's still there. And if it's still there, then we need to get on top of it.*

Allison touched a button. "DDST," she said into the microphone attached to her headphones.

"Office of the deputy director for science and technology," a voice answered.

"Kirstoff at NSA," Allison replied curtly. "Put me through to the director, please."

"I'm sorry," the operator replied with professional sweetness. "The director is unavailable."

"Then page him!"

Thirty seconds later, Allison heard, "Yes?"

"Kirstoff at NSA, sir. I have a priority-tasking request for COMIREX."

"Very well. Call me in the morning. COMIREX meets at ten."

"It can't wait until then."

"Why not?"

"It's a tasking for the CRYSTAL/KENNAN."

The long breath from the other end of the line sounded like an exasperated sigh. "Very well. My office in twenty minutes."

◇ ◇ ◇

"For a place called the Roadkill Café," Anne commented as she finished her coffee, "the food was really quite good."

"It's a nice place to get away to," Rebecca agreed. "It's close and inexpensive." She glanced at the folk-music group standing on the low dais at the end of the crowded, brightly lit dining room. "And it's especially fun," she added, "to come when Offshore is playing." To scattered applause, the four-member group finished their rendition of "Tree of Life."

Anne looked at Jake. "Still, I can't believe you ate something called a Bye-Bye Bambi Burger."

"Great burger," Jake told her. "Nice and juicy." He stopped, made a face, then ran his tongue over his teeth.

"Need a toothpick?" Anne asked.

"Yeah," Jake replied. "I've got something stuck between my teeth."

"Piece of gristle?" Brian asked.

"No," Jake answered. "Feels more like antler."

Brian nodded sagely. "Figures, since this place's slogan is 'You kill it, we grill it.'" The two men laughed, enjoying Rebecca's and Anne's disgusted grimaces.

"Breakfasts are really good," Brian remarked. "Lots of food, cheap and hot. Plus, they're open hours before my slugabed wife is even awake, much less willing to get up and feed her starving husband."

"Look, buster," Rebecca retorted, leaning affectionately against Brian's shoulder, "if you want to get up at four in the morning to go stand up to your armpits in the middle of some freezing stream and use little hairy things to try and catch poor, unsuspecting fish, that's *your* problem. Lauri and I will get out of bed when we feel like it, have breakfast when we're good and ready, then we'll snuggle up by the woodstove while you're out there getting slowly covered with snow."

Brian laughed and tousled his wife's hair. He looked at his watch. "Speaking of Lauri, we'd better go. We told Doris we'd be home by ten."

As they rose to leave, a voice called out, "Annie! Annie Dryden!"

Anne turned toward the dais at the end of the room. Hillary Packard, Offshore's fiddle player, was waving. Anne smiled and waved back.

Jake's eyebrows shot up. "You know them?"

"Ladies and gentlemen," Packard announced, "we have with us tonight one of the best fiddle players in all of Down East." She gestured to Anne. "Annie Dryden, come on up!"

Anne laughed and nodded. Jake, Rebecca, and Brian sat back down as she made her way to the stage.

"All I've ever heard her play is Paganini and stuff like that," Jake commented. "So what's she going to play with them?" He didn't see Rebecca and Brian smile, then exchange surreptitious winks.

Packard presented Anne with her violin, then picked up a banjo. The toe of Anne's riding boot peeked out from under the ruffled hem of her skirt as she tapped her foot three times, then swung Offshore into a performance of "The Orange Blossom Special" that had the audience cheering and clapping.

Thunderous applause erupted the instant they finished.

Anne hugged Packard, returned her violin, and came back to the table. "Whew," Anne said, brushing her hair back from her high forehead, "I haven't done that sort of thing in a while."

Jake looked at her, dumbfounded. "I didn't know you could play like that. All I've ever heard you play is classical pieces."

Anne shrugged. "The only real difference between violin music and fiddle music is that it's considered bad form to tap your foot while playing Bach's 'Air on a G String.'"

"There's more to Anne than meets the eye, Jake," Rebecca said.

"And that's saying a lot," Brian added, "considering just how good-looking what meets the eye is." He stood up. "And now, Mr. MacIntyre, it's time to make the rest of the guys here insanely jealous by leaving with the two prettiest women in Piscataquis County." Brian held his hand out to his wife. "Let's go rescue Doris from our daughter's tender mercies."

Joshua Litchfield was not happy. At forty-two, dates were becoming rare enough that he was considering having his social life placed on the endangered species list. The covert field operations necessary for advancement in the CIA had cost him his first marriage, and the years of Washington backslapping and backstabbing necessary to be appointed the CIA's deputy director for science and technology had seemingly cost him the possibility of a second.

He leaned back in his swivel chair. *So much for my chances with Beth. Dumping her unceremoniously into a cab outside Maison Blanche was* not *how I expected the evening to end.*

Litchfield picked up a sterling silver dinner fork from his desk and began tapping its tines against his desk blotter. The fork had been recovered by the CIA salvage vessel *Glomar Explorer* from a Soviet attack submarine that had sunk off the Hawaiian Islands. An engraved hammer-and-sickle emblem was still visible on its handle. Next to the fork was another twisted piece of metal, this one from an RH-53D Sea Stallion helicopter. The rest of the helicopter still lay burned and ruined in the Iranian desert, a mute memorial to the failed 1980 mission to rescue the hostages held in the American Embassy in Tehran. Both artifacts served as constant reminders to Litchfield of covert technology at its best and worst.

I know how mad she was, he thought with a wince. *The question is, how mad will she stay?* Litchfield shrugged. *And all because some pimple-faced nerd with a bad haircut has probably interpreted a chocolate smudge on his screen as the start of World War III.* The DDST tossed the fork across his desk. *Well, if it isn't the start of WWIII, I'm certainly going to make him wish it was.*

"Come," Litchfield called as the knock sounded on his door. He looked up to see a stunning woman in his doorway. "May I help you?"

The woman nodded. "Allison Kirstoff, NSA."

Amazing, Litchfield thought. *She doesn't need a haircut, and there's not a pimple in sight.* "What've you got?"

Allison explained her mysterious contact.

The DDST held out a hand. "Let's see your data."

Allison took a deep breath. "I don't have any data. I got deacquisitioned before I could get a lock."

Litchfield's eyebrows inched toward his hairline. "And *this* is why we're here at—" he glanced at his watch— "nine thirty-seven on a Friday night?" *Maybe I'll let her off easy. Maybe I'll just have her shave her head and knit her hair into a sweater for my Labrador retriever.* "Be back here at eight tomorrow morning. With your supervisor." He turned away in dismissal.

"Sir," Allison began, "if you remember, I mentioned that this incident occurred on pass 5507 of CRYSTAL/KENNAN."

Litchfield turned back toward her. *She gets points for reminding me of something I'd forgotten.* "So?" *Let's see just how much else she knows.*

Allison hung on. "CRYSTAL/KENNAN has only one more pass over that area before it de-orbits and burns up. A pass at three-seventeen tomorrow afternoon."

The DDST nodded. "And you want me to convince COMIREX to retask CRYSTAL/KENNAN to overfly your *alleged* target." *Hold it*, Litchfield realized suddenly. *This target of hers just may have something to do with that dogfight over the Strait of Hormuz that was reported in this morning's NID.*

The NID was the *National Intelligence Daily*, the top-secret intelligence summary seen each day by no more than two hundred people in the country. COMIREX, the Committee on Imagery and Exploitation, was the interdepartmental government agency that decided just what America's multi-million-dollar spy satellites would snoop upon.

Lips white, Allison nodded. "Yes, sir."

"Even though you have no corroborating evidence whatsoever?" The DDST leaned forward intimidatingly, glaring at her. *Let's see if she sticks to her guns.*

"Yes, sir. I saw what I saw. If it was there, chances are it's still there."

Litchfield nodded sharply. "Very well. Be here at ten, not eight. You're going with me to COMIREX. And forget the supervisor."

❖ ❖ ❖

"Well, at least the place is still standing," Brian observed as he and Rebecca entered their living room. The front door closed behind them as Jake and Anne left for a walk along the lake.

Doris smiled at them from where she was curled up on the couch. "She was an absolute angel," Doris told them. "I checked on her just a little while ago. She was all snuggled up in the corner of her crib with her two little fingers in her mouth."

Brian looked around. "Since there's no blood visible, I

guess I'll believe it." He smiled at Doris as she stood up. "Thanks a bunch. We had a great time."

"Good," Doris replied. She glanced at her watch. "Thanks for getting home early. Now I've still got time for *my* date." She grinned at Rebecca as she crossed the living room.

"Doris Rodgers, you just wait!" Rebecca protested. "You're seeing someone? Who? Don't you dare leave without telling me who it is!"

"Tell you all about it tomorrow!" Doris called as she hurried out the front door.

"Well!" Rebecca huffed in mock exasperation. "Of all the nerve! To think that Doris is seeing someone and Sandy hasn't said a word about it!" She looked at Brian. "You know anything about this?" When Brian shook his head, Rebecca added, "I'll just go check on Lauri."

As she turned to go, Brian took her hand and swung her around. "Speaking of seeing someone," he said, smiling down at her, "I haven't seen much of you the last few days." Brian put his arms around his wife and pulled her to him. "And I'd like to see a lot more of you than I'm seeing right now."

Rebecca smiled. "First Lauri, then we'll see about seeing."

Instead of letting her go, Brian pressed Rebecca against him. "You heard Doris—Lauri's sound asleep." He kissed her thoroughly, smiling to himself as he felt her relax.

"OK," she whispered, "just this once."

Brian grinned. "What do you mean, *just once?*" he teased as he led her from the room.

Crummy paperwork, Bill Estes thought as the small police skiff nosed against the shingle beach of Kineo Cove. A mountain of government-mandated compliance and regulatory forms had delayed his departure to investigate the mysterious lights he had seen atop Mount Kineo the night before. *I wanted to get up there*

just at sunset and give those frat guys and their girlfriends the shock of their little lives. No chance of that now.

Estes cut the outboard motor. He jumped out of the skiff and pulled it farther up onto the crescent-shaped, driftwood-littered beach of Kineo Cove.

Estes made his way along the southwestern edge of the peninsula. Lights glowed in the bed-and-breakfast near the Mount Kineo Golf Course. He glanced briefly at the foreboding, dark-eyed hulk of the abandoned Kineo Lodge as he passed by, its ruined rafters thrust like tusks against the night-blue sky.

When he reached a small outcropping, Estes turned into the forest that lined Kineo's western shore. Three steps into the trees, the last remnants of light disappeared. *Good thing I've taken this hike about a thousand times,* the deputy thought as he took a flashlight from his jacket pocket.

An hour later, flashlight clenched in his teeth, Estes scrambled up a steep, rocky pitch. His foot slipped on a patch of moss, and he banged a knee against a rock. Stifling a curse, he lay prone against the hillside, waiting for both his breathing and the throbbing in his knee to subside. He checked his watch. *Eight-thirty. Terrific. My dinner's on a plate in the oven and Janis is putting the kids to bed. Great, just great. Whose idea was this, anyway?*

Suddenly, Estes could see the face of his watch as well as its luminescent hands. He froze. Quietly he switched off his flashlight and looked up the hillside. A flickering, ruddy light had appeared above him. It spilled over the crest of the slope on which he lay, bathing the trees in a weird, shifting glow. A strange, murmuring chant drifted down the hillside. *Gotcha!* he thought. *Time to put the fear into you boys for keeping me from my dinner.*

Estes inched his way up the hill. Just above him, the trail emptied onto a small plateau before continuing upward to the fire tower at Kineo's summit. The light seemed to be coming from the plateau, and the deputy grinned at the number of citations he was about to get to write. Preparing to come to his feet, Estes peered over the lip of the hill. *What the . . . ?* Riveted, he stared at the plateau. *If those are frat boys, I'm Peter Pan.*

From behind a protective screen of brush, Estes watched the bizarre scene before him. The flickering light that had attracted his attention came from torches stuck into notches carved into the trees that lined the plateau. A crackling bonfire in the clearing's center added its light. Arrayed around the clearing were four men clad in long, close-fitting brown tunics and black turbans. Each held a slender-spouted oil lamp, whose flame wavered as it was swung in front of him. The brown-robed men were chanting softly, swaying back and forth in time to the chant. To one side stood a tall man robed in white. A woven band of coarse yellow-and-orange material encircled his waist. On his head was a tall, shaggy black cap with a fringe that hung down, obscuring the upper part of his face. Motionless, his eyes closed, the man held something long and thin before him. It glittered in the firelight.

Estes could only see the back half of the plateau. As he inched his way forward, his eyes widened. The front half of the clearing was covered by an intricately woven, tasselled rug. Torchlight glinted from its elaborate brocade. A tall, candle-stick-shaped object sat close to the fire. It seemed to Estes to be made of a series of stacked copper balls and plates on a circular base and was topped with an ornate, stylized statue of a bird. Estes gazed at it in disbelief. Then his eyes flicked downward to the carpet in front of the candlestick. Beneath a heavily embroi-dered sheet, fastened to the carpet at its corners, something struggled mutely. *All right, gentlemen,* the lawman decided, *this party's over.*

Just as he began to get up, the chanting stopped. The four brown-robed men set down their lamps. Two took slender flutes from their belts while the other two picked up tambourines. They turned, forming a line behind the man in white, who took up the chant. Holding the slender object in front of him, the white-clad man began marching around the clearing. The polished wooden flutes gleamed in the torchlight as the men began to play a strange, repetitious melody punctuated by the tambourines.

Estes watched in amazement as the men marched around the clearing. As each passed close to the fire he swept his right hand through the flames, rubbed his right eyebrow, then brought the hand to his lips. With each trip around the fire the flutes rose in pitch and the staccato crash of the tambourines grew more rapid. The march of the brown-clad men became a frenzied, whirling dance.

The fringe on the leader's black hat squirmed grotesquely as he writhed. As the man approached the front of the clearing, Estes saw that what he held before him by its point was a long, narrow-bladed stiletto. The wavy edges of its blade glinted cold silver in the firelight. Estes, motionless, watched as the leader approached. The knife blade was engraved with strange, wavy inscriptions. Two rubies, bloody in the firelight, were set into the ends of the dagger's polliard, and the heavy gold grip was checkered with flashing gems.

Suddenly, just in front of Estes, the leader stopped. One hand left the knife's point and closed around its hilt. A huge emerald set into the dagger's pommel jutted from the man's clenched fist. The other hand joined the first, baring the blade's needlelike point. The white-robed man knelt facing Estes, the shrouded figure struggling beneath the sheet in front of him, the musicians arrayed in a semicircle behind him. The chanting grew louder. He slowly raised the dagger above his head. The sound of the flutes became a maniacal scream. Firelight glittered from the stiletto's serpentine blade. The ecstatic frenzy overcame the white-robed man, and he threw back his head. As the tasselled fringe of the man's black cap fell away, Estes started with recognition.

Head back, eyes closed, the robed man tensed. Then with savage ferocity he thrust the dagger down toward the small body struggling helplessly before him.

"*Freeze!*" Estes's bellow drowned out the shrieking instruments. The flutes stopped, and the dagger stopped just above the sacrifice's heaving chest. In an instant, the bizarre sacrificial rite became an equally weird tableau. "Police! Nobody move!" Revolver drawn, the deputy came to his feet. Then something heavy and hard crashed against the back of his skull, and Bill Estes crumpled to the ground.

11

Anne stretched as she came into the kitchen. She poured herself a cup of coffee, winked at Jake, then turned to help Rebecca with breakfast. Brian and Jake, seated at the breakfast table, were each immersed in a section of the *Portland Herald-Tribune*. Sunlight surged through the windows, glancing off copper pots and staining the countertops a honeyed gold. On the center island a riot of late-blooming asters overflowed a cut-glass vase.

"Missing someone, aren't we?" Anne asked as she began slicing thick slabs of raisin-hazelnut bread for the morning's French toast.

Rebecca glanced at the clock on the stove. "The later she sleeps, the better it usually works out," she replied. "But it would be best if she napped during our walk today, so I think I'll get her up." Rebecca dried her hands with a dish towel. "Put a little vanilla in the eggs for me, will you?" she asked Anne as she left the kitchen.

Brian got up and poured himself another cup of coffee. "Did Jake," he asked Anne, "get around to telling you about his run-in with a porcupine while he was on the way to the privy the other night?"

Anne arched her eyebrows and looked accusingly at Jake. "No," she replied. "It would appear that he conveniently left that part of your adventure out."

Brian laughed and shook his head. "You should've seen it. The best part was the expression on Jake's face when he realized that—"

A scream rang out, an explosion of sound that arced slowly from anguish to terror. Then another, more frantic than the first, resonated through the house and into the very marrow of all those within hearing.

"*Becky!*" Brian was through the kitchen door and gone.

Anne's eyes met Jake's as his newspaper fell to the floor. Jake came instantly to his feet, and they headed toward the door together.

Rebecca was backed into a corner of her daughter's bedroom, her screams now muted into rasping sobs. Brian stood in the center of the floor, fists clenched as if he were ready to strike.

An awful silence filled the room, broken only by ragged breathing. Jake's photographer's eye captured each element of the horrifying scene. The open window. The lace curtains billowing with gentle innocence on the morning breeze. A rag doll and crocheted blanket strewn across the floor. A red-nosed, overstuffed clown perched grinning on a toy chest. The silent, empty crib.

The morning sun sparkling on the long, wicked blade of a jeweled, ornately carved dagger embedded savagely in the cradle's headboard.

PART II

12

This would sure go down easier in shorts and a tank top, Randy Cavanaugh decided. The meager shade provided by the pavilion under which he stood was no match for the fierce desert sun reflecting off the tarmac of Baghdad International Airport. Lydia Doral sat in front of him, cool and serene in an ivory linen dress, a wide-brimmed straw hat, and white gloves. Seemingly oblivious to the interpreter who hovered nearby, she listened with apparent attentiveness to the Iraqi foreign minister's welcoming speech. Uncomfortable at being part of such a public spectacle, Randy leaned slightly to the left, trying to keep the foreign minister between himself and the cameras of Iraqi Television.

"Boss," the young man next to Randy whispered, "what's that coming in on final?"

Randy flicked his eyes toward the end of the runway. In the distance, blurred by the shimmering heat, a small, needle-nosed plane was on final approach, its swept-back wings gleaming in the intense sunlight. *I know I've seen one of those before*, Randy mused, *but where?* Then, just as it passed in front of him, the plane disappeared behind a row of hangars.

"Must be some honcho's private plane," the other agent observed. "He's got about half the Iraqi army for a welcoming escort." The two men watched as a dozen or more jeeps careened down the runway after the plane.

I wish I could've gotten a better look at that plane, Randy thought. He tried to sort out the enigma of the plane until Lydia Doral rose and it was time to go.

One member of the security phalanx surrounding the Iraqi foreign minister, a tall one-eyed man, watched Randy intently as he left.

The uniformed marine guard saluted smartly as the motorcade swept through the gates to the American Embassy compound. From the backseat of her limousine Doral surveyed the grounds, now a wasteland of dead trees and fallow flower beds.

As her car stopped before the embassy's weather-stained front steps, a middle-aged staff sergeant opened Doral's door. "Welcome to paradise, Mrs. Ambassador," the sergeant said as Doral got out.

"I am *not* here in an ambassadorial capacity," she began as she turned. "Furthermore—" Doral stopped. "Charlie!" she gasped. "Charlie Davenport!"

Randy watched as the burly marine enveloped Doral in a massive bear hug. "When I heard you was comin' here," the sergeant told her, "I got myself orders to head up this security detail of yours." Davenport gave a lopsided grin. "Don't worry, Mrs. Ambassador, I picked everyone of 'em myself. They're a tough bunch."

Doral beckoned to Randy, and the two men exchanged a knuckle-busting handshake. "Charlie headed my security details in both Egypt and South Africa," Doral explained. "I trust him completely." She turned to the marine. "Randy is my chief technical advisor on this mission."

Davenport's grin widened. "A spook, eh? Terrific. I get

some of my best laughs watchin' you guys work." The sergeant, a head shorter than Randy but as broad across the shoulders, sized the younger man up. "You been in the service, Cavanaugh?" he asked. "You look like you mighta been."

Randy shook his head. "No, Sarge, I'm afraid I missed out."

"No matter. Pay attention while you're here, and you might learn something." Randy found himself grinning at the old soldier's amiable ways.

"So far, Charlie," Doral said, "all I've seen are you and the gate guard. Where's everyone else?"

"Gettin' the best practice a jarhead can get, Mrs. Ambassador," Davenport replied. "Just come with me and see for yourself."

Davenport led them up the steps and into the embassy foyer. As he turned and swung open a set of massive double doors, Davenport bellowed, "Tenshun!" Ten men, covered in sweat and soapsuds, leaped to their feet. One lost his footing on the slick ballroom floor and sat down heavily.

"DeLong!" Davenport shouted at the hapless marine. "Ten laps around the compound, full kit, after you're done in here!" He turned to Doral. "Thought we should get this place spiffed up in case you wanted to throw a party or something. Besides," Davenport continued in a lower tone of voice, "they need something to keep 'em busy. But since there's no paint, I can't have 'em painting anything, so scrubbing's the next best thing. Carry on!" he shouted as they left the ballroom.

"Seriously, ma'am," Davenport continued as they walked the length of the marble-floored foyer, "I've got your quarters and office on the third floor cleaned up, but that's about it. The two-legged Iraqi mice that've been through here since we pulled out left nothing behind. The only toilet that we got— that's the one in your suite—I had to buy back from the Iraqi who was supposed to be our 'caretaker.'" He looked at Randy.

"As for you and your boys, there are cots in the conference room and a latrine out back." Davenport watched Randy closely.

"No problem, Sarge," Randy replied casually. "We've seen a lot worse than this."

Davenport nodded. "You know, I believe you have."

"This place is a security nightmare," Randy observed from the passenger's seat of the olive drab jeep. A hundred yards of formerly immaculate lawn, now rank with tall weeds, lay between the compound wall and the embassy. "You could hide a regiment in those weeds."

"That ain't the worst of it," Davenport said. "Check out this section of wall."

Davenport stopped the jeep next to a dilapidated section of compound wall. A marine slouched listlessly in the driver's seat of another jeep parked next to the pile of broken cinder block and mortar. "They've stolen most of this chunk of wall and all of the barbed wire that topped it," the sergeant pointed out.

"Any trouble, Hopkins?" Davenport asked.

The young marine corporal snorted derisively. "You kiddin'? They pass by and look in, then when they see me they jump a foot and scurry away like frightened rabbits." Hopkins mopped his brow with his uniform sleeve. "Sure wish they'd planted some of those trees closer to the wall," he added, looking wistfully at the tall eucalyptus trees that dotted the compound.

"Why do you think they planted 'em that way?" Davenport asked. When the corporal shrugged, Davenport looked at Randy.

"Belgian gates," Randy replied.

The sergeant beamed. "Smart boy!" He turned to the young marine. "Listen up, Hopkins!" Davenport growled. "You

146

just might learn something." The corporal looked expectantly at Randy.

"Those trees are acting as Belgian gates, an obstacle invented during World War II," Randy explained. "They're set just far enough apart to interfere with a helicopter's rotors without providing much cover for invaders on foot. The idea is to limit any rapid insertion of hostile types into the embassy compound."

"Remember that, Hopkins," Davenport ordered, "then maybe next time you won't get the duty sweatin' out here in the sun."

"The only problem with Belgians," Randy observed as they drove away, "is that they also effectively prevent rapid helicopter extraction of friendlies from within the compound." Randy watched the thin streams of smoke that drifted lazily upward from the teeming slums surrounding the embassy. "That's something I hope we *don't* have to do. You going to keep someone posted there all week, Sarge?" Randy asked.

Davenport shook his head. "Nah. Not unless one of them makes me mad. I plan to string the opening with wire and chop down all these weeds. Then I'll institute random patrols past the section." He grinned. "I put in a requisition this morning. I thought the quartermaster was gonna come unglued when he saw it."

"Why?" Randy wondered. "What did you ask for?"

"Six weed whackers, two spools of razor wire, and eight cases of Coors." Randy laughed, and Davenport went on. "But the best part was what I put down under Justification."

"What was that, Sarge?"

"'Items are needed for intensive, full-contact gardening.'"

❖   ❖   ❖

Andy Danver, Greenville's physician, came into the kitchen. Brian looked up from where he was sitting with Roy Barnard.

"I'm afraid I had to sedate Rebecca rather heavily, Brian,"

Danver said. "After a few hours' rest, we'll try bringing her out of it gradually." The doctor looked at Barnard. "Sorry, Roy. I know you need to talk to her. But you probably wouldn't get anything coherent out of her right now, anyway."

Worry etched Brian's strong features. Jake stood motionless, his arms folded, staring out over Moosehead Lake. Anne, her eyes puffy from crying, busied herself with the breakfast dishes.

Barnard listened to something for a moment, then spoke into his shoulder microphone. He turned back to Brian. "Headquarters in Augusta wants a recent picture of Lauren to start broadcasting to other agencies. Do you have one?"

Brian nodded numbly and made his way to his bedroom. Anger and grief racked him anew at the sight of his wife, pale and drawn, curled up beneath the sheet. Brian slid a picture from a silver frame, then crossed the room. He stood beside Rebecca for a moment, looking down at her in anguish, then bent over and gently kissed her. "It's going to be all right, love," he whispered. "It's going to be all right." Rebecca stirred, muttering faintly. "Sleep, hon," Brian said softly, the backs of his fingers caressing her cheek. "Sleep."

A silent war raged within Roy Barnard as he looked at the picture Brian had handed him. In it a baby girl, her hand clasping a pink-and-white rattle, smiled out at the world. A new tooth was a thin line of white against her pink gums, and a yellow ribbon was tied in a bow around a stray wisp of hair curling up from the top of her head. Roy's many roles—lawman, father of four, church elder, friend—battled within him. The professional lawman struggled with increasing force to remind the father in him that the perpetrators of this crime must be dealt with justly, according to the law. The church elder fought to remind the friend that vengeance was not his to exact.

He could not take the law into his own hands, no matter how much he was tempted to do so.

"Nice picture," Barnard commented. "Looks fairly recent."

Brian nodded. "Taken just a few days ago. Jake took a roll for us after Becky complained that we didn't have any pictures of Lauri."

"She was so happy that afternoon," Anne said tremulously. She bit her lip, fighting back tears. Then a wet glass slipped from her fingers, shattering in the sink with a report that made everyone jump. "I'm sorry," Anne sobbed as the men turned and looked at her. "I'm sorry!" She rushed from the room.

"Pat!"

At her husband's call, Pat Dryden looked up from the trellis of string beans she was tending. Joel stood on their back porch, holding a cordless phone. When Pat got up and started toward the house, Joel beckoned to her. Concerned, Pat started to hurry.

Pat rushed up onto the porch. "What is it?"

"It's Annie," Joel replied, handing his wife the phone.

Something in Joel's tone told Pat to skip the formalities. "Annie, what's wrong?" she asked her daughter. The color drained from her face as she listened.

"*No!*" Pat gasped. "Not Lauren!" She looked to Joel. He was standing beside her, rubbing his chin, his anguish evident. "Of course we're coming," Pat assured Anne. "We'll be there as soon as we can. How are Brian and Becky?" Pat closed her eyes at Anne's report. "All the more reason for us to come. We love you, honey. We'll be there soon."

Pat reached out to Joel, comforted by the reality of his arm beneath the denim work shirt. Joel covered Pat's hand with his. "Let's get packed, love," he said quietly. "I'll drive, you pray."

"Good job, Kisloff," Joshua Litchfield said as they walked down a plush-carpeted corridor. "Getting COMIREX to play ball isn't always the easiest thing to do."

Allison smiled. *Maybe not for you, Mr. Litchfield, but you're just another middle-aged man in a room full of middle-aged men. My only problem is that getting a man, or a roomful of men, to do what I want them to do is so easy it's boring.*

They reached the elevator at the end of the hallway. Feeling Litchfield's eyes on her, Allison turned.

The DDST was gazing at her intently. "We just stepped on a lot of toes to get the last pass of our last CRYSTAL/KENNAN. It's not that I especially mind stepping on toes, it's just that I want to know I'm going to get my money's worth." His eyes, the color of polished oak, bored into hers. "This had better be good. *Real* good."

She gazed back unflinchingly. "It will be."

❖ ❖ ❖

After giving Anne a big hug, Pat Dryden followed her daughter into Brian and Rebecca's kitchen. A congenial-looking man with wiry gray hair got up from the kitchen table. "Dr. Dryden?" he asked, offering his hand. "I'm Andy Danver."

"Call me Pat, please," Pat replied, shaking Danver's hand.

"Then it's Andy," Danver replied. The bright blue eyes clouded. "I'm so sorry about Lauren's abduction. There aren't too many youngsters in this town anymore, so caring for her has been a special treat. She's quite a little girl." He shook his head. "This sort of thing isn't supposed to happen in a place like this. L.A. or New York maybe, but not here. It's good that you could come so quickly," the doctor added, "since we haven't been able to contact Rebecca's parents."

Pat nodded. "My brother and his wife have been in Australia for almost a month now," she explained. "We have no way of reaching them for another two weeks."

"Anne said you had to sedate Becky," Pat continued as the two physicians sat down at the kitchen table. "She's your patient, of course, but I'd be more than willing to consult if you wish."

Danver nodded vigorously. "I was just about to ask. Given what Anne's told me about your experience in a psychiatric practice, your advice will be invaluable." The physician grinned. "I had the usual introductory course in psychiatry the med school faculty gives to those they've already tagged to be general practitioners. Nowadays my practice is limited to frostbite in winter and removing fishhooks in summer, with the occasional hunting accident thrown in for excitement." Danver gestured helplessly. "I'm somewhat out of my depth in situations like this."

"Tell me what happened."

"When I arrived about an hour after the kidnapping was discovered," Danver began, "Rebecca was displaying all the classic symptoms of hysteria. When she failed to respond to a mild sedative and became increasingly agitated, I administered five ccs of librium. This seems to be keeping her calm enough to function without knocking her out entirely."

Pat nodded approvingly. "Quite appropriate. I assume your intention is to taper her off the librium?" When Danver nodded, Pat went on. "Then what I'd recommend is . . ."

Anne left the corner where she had been standing and wandered out the kitchen door. The back porch framed a view of Moosehead Lake, its dark blue waters whipped by a brisk wind. Whitecaps, brilliant against the dark backdrop of forested islands, skated across its surface. Far overhead, an osprey searched for its lunch.

Anne headed for the ash tree where she, Rebecca, and Lauren had so recently had so much fun. She sank down onto the grass. There, surrounded only by the rush of wind and the far-off call of the osprey, Anne bowed her head.

Why, Lord? Why a baby? Why this baby? Why is such pain inflicted on such good, caring, loving people? Tears stained Anne's dress. *Did the Egyptian mothers ask this when you snatched their babies from them? Did the mothers of Bethlehem ask this as they watched Herod's soldiers put their baby boys to the sword? Did Mary ask this as she knelt in agony at the foot of the cross? I don't understand, Lord. Why does it have to hurt so much? Why did you allow this?*

I know I don't get to know, God, Anne admitted, *so please, help me to accept what the psalmist wrote so long ago: "How many are your works, O Lord! In wisdom you made them all." Help me to remember that Lauri, and Becky and Brian, and Jake, and I are all your creations, to do with as you please. But please, Lord, please do something else that David asked. Be a shield around Lauri, wherever she is, and Becky and Brian, too. Be their glory and the lifter of their heads.*

❖ ❖ ❖

Joel Dryden sat on the couch, looking over the sheriff's notes as Brian paced across the living room floor. Jake stood at the picture window, gazing out into the yard. When Roy Barnard began to speak, Joel turned his attention to the sheriff.

"Brian, listen," Barnard said intently. "Whoever they are, they can't get far. The word's gone out. Every floatplane around is up, buzzing every boat on the lake and any strange car they see. It looks like the Fly-In out there." Brian smiled grimly at Barnard's mention of the annual September aerial event. "I've notified the state troopers," the sheriff went on. "They've closed the border crossings into Canada and Nova Scotia. The ferry terminals and airports have been alerted, as well as every tollbooth along the turnpike." Barnard's voice grew quiet and hard. "They can't get away, Brian. They *won't.*"

"I'm going to see to that," Brian growled. As he began to

stride from the room, Barnard put his hands on Brian's shoulders.

"No, you're not," Barnard said with gentle implacability. "I won't permit you to take the law into your own hands. Not only is it illegal, it's stupid." Barnard returned Brian's glare with a frown. "Remember when we were hunting up in Aroostook County last October and that blizzard caught us?" Brian nodded. "Did *I* decide," the sheriff continued, "how we were going to get down off that mountain alive, or did I let *you* call the shots?" Brian's shoulders sagged. "I trusted you then," Barnard said earnestly, "you trust me now. OK?" Brian nodded again, and his friend clapped him on the back.

"So, what do we do?" Brian asked.

"We wait," Barnard replied. "Either we'll find the kidnappers, or they'll contact us." The sheriff spread his hands. "They obviously want some sort of ransom—they can't have any use for Lauren herself."

Joel looked up from the sheaf of notes. *That used to be true,* he thought grimly. *But not anymore. Not these days.*

"By the way, Brian," Barnard added. "That little white nightcap that Lauren was wearing. Who gave it to her? We just might want to talk to them."

Brian frowned. "A nightcap? I've never put her to bed with one, and I don't think Becky does. Lauri *hates* caps, hats, hoods—you name it. Rips them off faster than we can put them on. And I don't think she got anything like that as a present."

"Wait here." Barnard strode out of the room. He returned quickly, one fist wrapped around a scrap of white cloth. "This was in Lauren's crib," he explained, handing it to Brian.

Brian examined the small, close-fitting, fezlike cap. The white silk was embroidered intricately. A dozen small gold coins dangled from silken threads in a circular row halfway up the cap. "I've never seen this before," he said emphatically. "I've handled enough gold coins to know the real thing when I see it.

153

Besides, what mom in her right mind would put her kid to bed in something like this?"

The three men stared at one another. "What the hell is going on here?" Barnard muttered.

Joel stared at the sheriff over his reading glasses. "'Hell' just might be the operative word in this case, I'm afraid."

An FBI agent beckoned to the sheriff from the living-room door. She held up two sealed plastic bags covered with numbered labels.

As he joined the agent in the hall, Barnard saw that one bag contained the dagger that had been stuck into the crib. In another bag was a strip of parchment, covered in strange writing, that the dagger's point had pinned to the headboard.

"We're sending these to headquarters for analysis," the agent explained. "Need you to sign the transfer paperwork."

The sheriff inspected the bags. "Any idea what this is?" he asked, holding up the bag containing the strip of parchment.

"Beats me," the agent admitted. "It's a bunch of wavy lines. Must be some kind of writing."

Barnard looked sharply at the agent, then snapped his fingers. "Come with me," he ordered.

With the agent in tow, the sheriff marched outside and around to Lauren's bedroom window. Teams of agents and police were combing the area. Police photographers were methodically recording the scene. "Your comment about wavy lines reminded me of this," Barnard said, pointing at the windowsill. "You'll find more of it down in the boathouse, too."

The agent removed the strip of parchment from the bag. "Looks like the same kind of writing, if that's what it is," she observed. The agent beckoned to a photographer. "We'll get on it right away." As Barnard turned to leave, she held out the transfer paperwork.

"Any word as to my deputy's whereabouts?" Barnard asked as he initialed the documents.

"Not that I've heard."

"His wife said he didn't come home last night. That's just not like Bill." Barnard tried unsuccessfully to rub some of the tension out of the back of his neck, then shrugged and went back inside.

"We've completed the initial search of the area," one of the troopers informed him.

"Find anything?"

"Nothing. Except—" The trooper glanced at Brian, who was standing at the window silently watching the activity. The policeman took a deep breath. "In the bushes outside the victim's room."

"What did you find?" Barnard asked impatiently.

"Blood. Lots of blood."

13

Allison tried to ignore them as the satellite image built up on her screen. She knew they were back there, standing behind thick glass in the observation room, the same batch of middle-aged men she had talked to this morning at COMIREX, along with a few braid-heavy uniforms. It didn't help that the guard she had made friends with had excitedly told her that Elliot French, the CIA's director of operations, was going to be there.

Someone slipped into the chair of the console next to her. Allison glanced over at the new arrival, then winced. It was Fred, the CIA analyst she had so thoroughly snubbed the day before. *Well,* she thought, *all we can do is hope that what goes around doesn't come around this time. Besides, he deserved it. If he'd just spend a little more time looking at his screen instead of at my chest . . .*

On her right was an analyst from the Defense Intelligence Agency, the military counterpart to the CIA. So far, the DIA analyst, who wore both a navy commander's uniform and a wedding ring, had stared at nothing but his monitor.

"Target acquisition in thirty seconds," the computer voice intoned.

"Got it?" Allison asked as the image, a faint, light-blue smudge, appeared on her screen. "Screen coords minus two-eight-three by six-three-five."

"Got it," the CIA man answered.

"Affirmative," was the commander's laconic reply.

The three analysts began running the data from the smudge through their agency's computers. *Let's see*, Allison thought as her eyes flicked from the image to the data readouts on another screen, *localized, stationary, not too high in temperature. Now, if I can match its heat signature against something known . . .*

Allison typed a command. A few seconds later, her eyes went wide. *Yes!* she exulted. *I knew it!* "Positive ID," Allison reported. "Target is—"

"The natural gas burnoff at the al-Kafhar oil refinery in the Iraqi city of Basra," the CIA analyst interjected.

"What?" Allison blurted out. "No way. The heat signature exactly matches that of a Russian Kilo-class attack submarine's diesel engine!" She turned and stared incredulously at the CIA man.

"Roger that," the DIA analyst said. Allison swung around and smiled at him. He wasn't smiling back. "Confirm target signature consistent with refinery gas burnoff." The commander shrugged sympathetically.

"Wait!" Allison called. "Look at it in the 150-nanometer range!"

The image on her screen flickered and vanished. "Deacquisition of signal," the voice announced. "Asset de-orbit and reentry commencing."

The DIA analyst took off his headphones. Shaking his head slowly, he got up and left. From the corner of her eye Allison saw the CIA agent smiling at her. *He's gloating*, she realized. *The little twerp is gloating.* Confused shock dissipated her mounting rage.

An unfamiliar, acerbic voice appeared in her headphones. "Nice work, Josh. You used that last pass of our last aerial asset to conclusively prove that the Iranians still have oil fields." A snort of derision could be heard in the background.

A commanding voice cut through the muted snickers. "My office, Kirstoff. Now."

Allison closed her eyes.

❖ ❖ ❖

Roy Barnard knocked on the frame of Sandy Neill's office door, then stepped inside.

"Any news?" she asked, already seeing the answer in her old friend's eyes.

The sheriff grimaced. "No. The entire Bangor office of the FBI has turned out, and so far, all we have is circumstantial evidence and no suspect." Barnard looked at Sandy. "I'm afraid, however, that this is a business call. Have you seen Doris?"

Neill shook her head. "This is one of her days off. She's probably with that Egyptian, Professor Marduk. She's been spending almost all her free time with him recently." She gave Roy a pointed look as she shook her head. "Come to think of it, I haven't seen her all day."

"When she shows up, tell her I need to see her pronto, OK? She was the last person to see Lauren, and we *really* need to talk to her." The sheriff turned his head slightly to listen to his radio. He frowned, then picked up Sandy's phone and dialed.

"This is Barnard," he said when the phone was answered. His frown deepened as he listened. Then Barnard closed his eyes and leaned against Sandy's desk. "I'll be right there," he finished, then hung up.

"Roy, what is it? Did they find Lauren?"

"No, but they *did* find Bill. He's been missing, too, and Janis has been frantic. I didn't worry about it too much—Bill can take care of himself, and I haven't had time to give it more than a passing thought." The sheriff winced. "Guess I should've worried about it more. A group of hikers found him unconscious up near the summit of Mount Kineo. One of the hikers used their cellular phone to call 911. A medevac helicopter came in and took Bill to County General."

"How bad is it?" Sandy asked, feeling the pain and worry gather around her.

"They don't think he's going to make it." Barnard left quickly.

As the wail of the sheriff's siren faded into the distance, Sandy Neill buried her face in her hands.

Doris pulled up next to the sleek corporate jet. Mechanics scurried around the plane, removing hoses and closing access panels. A wind laden with the promise of rain swept the smell of jet fuel across the airfield.

The man Marduk had introduced to Doris as Dr. Sayed helped a woman out of the backseat. Doris stood next to Marduk, holding his hand.

Sayed spoke rapidly in a foreign language to Marduk, who nodded. "Doctor Sayed asks me to thank you again for the immense favor of driving them to Boston on such short notice," Marduk translated. "The news of the unexpected death of Mrs. Sayed's mother was a terrible blow to her, and the doctor is very grateful for your kindness in enabling them to return home as quickly as possible."

Doris nodded to the short, corpulent man. "Please extend my sympathies to Mrs. Sayed," Doris said, smiling compassionately at the anguished woman. The wind shifted, and the thin crying of the heavily swaddled infant she carried drifted to them.

Marduk spoke at length to the couple, who then boarded the plane. The tall man turned to Doris. He took her other hand in his and gazed down at her solemnly. "I must go, too," he told her.

Doris was stricken. "Please," she stammered. "Not now, not just when—"

Marduk silenced her with a kiss. "I must," he said softly, "even though there is nothing I want to do less than leave you. The Sayeds speak no English, and there are many stops between here and our home." Marduk smiled gently as Doris's eyes began to fill. "Surely you understand, my love. As leader of this expedition, I can do no less." Doris nodded. "And," he added, bringing her hands up and kissing them softly, "I will return soon. Very soon." The wind swirled around them as he gazed down at her. "For you."

Another gentle kiss, and he was up the ramp and gone. A mechanic pointed at Doris's car. Shaking the tears from her eyes, Doris got in and drove to the airport fence. From there she watched as the plane taxied onto the runway and then arrowed upward into the gathering clouds.

Doris started to wave, then stopped. *Bad luck to wave a plane out of sight, they say*, she thought. She watched, tears coursing down her cheeks, until the jet had disappeared. *Please*, she begged. *Please come back soon.* A gust of rain pattered against the windshield as Doris began the long drive back to Greenville.

❖   ❖   ❖

Allison waited, standing before Joshua Litchfield's desk like an errant schoolgirl. Her eyes flicked from the trophy marlin on one wall to the shelves of leather-bound antique books on another. Litchfield sat behind the mahogany desk, flipping casually through the pages of a red-trimmed folder.

"First in your class at Cal Tech," he observed. "Did your master's work at MIT, studying the adaptive feedback of neural networks under Seymour Papert. Professor Papert seems to think quite highly of you." He turned a page. "Promoted from the State Department to a real job at the NSA two years ago after a piece of analysis on your part enabled State to rescue an American citizen being held captive in Peru and exonerate an innocent man." Litchfield gazed at her sardonically. "I'm sure the fact that the rescued American happened to be Joel Dryden's daughter had no bearing whatsoever on your being awarded a position most people fight for ten years to get." Allison bristled at the implication.

The DDST adjusted his reading glasses and turned the page. "Granted compartmented, code-word clearance last year. Authorized to access the SCIF just last month." Another page. "Your evaluations include comments like 'brilliant synthetical and analytical capabilities,' and 'an extraordinary degree of technical competence.'" He glanced up at Allison, making sure she was paying attention. "And then there's this comment, which I find particularly apt: 'I'd gnaw my own leg off before I'd work with her again.'"

Allison blinked, wondering which of the many men she had socially dismembered might have written that.

Litchfield took off his glasses and set them on his desk. "All in all, a meteoric, fast-track career that should culminate in a directorship or a major research post." He tossed Allison's dossier onto his desk. "Until this, that is. In the case of a world-class bonehead stunt like this one, a track record like yours is more damning than redeeming."

He looked at her. To Allison, unnerved by her first professional failure, it seemed that the look in his eyes was rimmed with the hoarfrost of a midwinter night. "I must admit, Kirstoff," he continued, "that you sure know how to pick the high-visibility, big-potential, make-or-break opportunities. First the Dryden affair, and now—this." Litchfield leaned forward, arms crossed, riveting her with his gaze. "Only *this* time you fouled up. Royally." His eyes grew even colder. "You, the junior member of the SCIF staff, were a cabinet-level embarrassment to yourself, me, and the agency. More importantly, you single-handedly rendered worthless the last moments of an irreplaceable piece of equipment." Litchfield motioned slightly with one hand. "Well?"

Allison found herself without words. For the first time, she had encountered a man who was both her intellectual equal and impervious to her feminine charms. "I know I'm right," she insisted. *Then why*, she asked herself, *don't you sound like you are?*

The DDST's grizzled eyebrows began their ascent of his forehead. "Really? Both the CIA's top analyst and the navy commander from the DIA—who, incidentally, began his analysis career about the time you were born—disagreed with you. Furthermore, they agreed both on the actual nature of the target and on something else." Litchfield seemed to grow larger before her eyes. "They both agreed that you . . . were . . . *wrong.*"

Allison winced as he flung out the words. She felt her throat tightening. "I am *right!*" she barked back.

Litchfield stared back at her, unperturbed. "Not this time, sweetheart. And it's going to cost you." He gestured dismissively. "I'll probably have to take the hit for this little fiasco of yours, but at least if my head rolls, I'll have the privilege of first holding the door for yours."

Allison listened, dumbfounded. *It sounds like he's firing me.*

Litchfield took on an administrative air. "You got high marks in systems analysis at MIT. So, tomorrow, start looking at the NSA analysis algorithms and see if you can figure out why their results were so different from the CIA and DIA algorithms. That ought to keep you busy until you can find a position more commensurate with your limited abilities."

Stunned, Allison examined each of Litchfield's words. *He wants me to do* what? *Debug someone else's code? Like some third-rate contract programmer or a new hire fresh out of some technical school?* Allison jerked her head around. "I'll tell you why my results were different from those of that pimple-headed nerd and that navy fossil, *Mister* Litchfield," Allison spat out savagely. *"My results were different because I was using *my* code, not that antiquated, inefficient mass of spaghetti that you've been limping along on for so long. The algorithms *I* substituted are so far superior—"

"Stop!" Litchfield thundered. The sheer intensity of that blast brought Allison's tirade to a midsyllable halt. "Are you telling me, officially, that you used your own code in place of the officially approved NSA analysis program?"

"You bet I am! And my code—"

Litchfield's face lost all expression. "Allison Kirstoff, I hereby charge you with the following crimes: felony tampering with government property for your alteration of the NSA computer code, felony theft of government property for your unauthorized use of NSA computer time, copyright infringement in violation of subparagraph (c) (1) (ii) of the Rights in Technical Data and Computer Software clause in the DFARS, and felony destruction of government property for aiding and abetting the destruction of the CRYSTAL/KENNAN reconnaissance satellite. A charge of espionage shall be held in abeyance pending further investigation."

"Espionage? Why are you talking about espionage?" Allison's mind reeled. Espionage meant spying. And spying meant jail. He couldn't be serious. An unfamiliar surge of fear knotted Allison's stomach.

"Tomorrow, all NSA and State Department computers will undergo a complete scan to detect any additional viruses, Trojan horses, or back doors you may have introduced."

Viruses? Trojan horses? That's the kind of stuff disaffected teenage crackers do. Those are felonies! *What's going on here?* "Look, Litchfield, get somebody competent up here, and I'll explain the algorithms to them. And I mean somebody *competent*, not those two flunkies of yours."

Litchfield pressed a button on his intercom. His office

door opened, and a large man in a gray suit stepped in. "Your ID, please. And your SCIF access card."

Allison glared at him.

"Kirstoff, either you give them to me or Jenkins over there gets to take them from you."

One glance at Jenkins told Allison just how much he was looking forward to the prospect. *Well, at least I get to spoil someone else's day.* With shaking fingers Allison deposited her cherished cards on Litchfield's desk.

"Keep yourself available. Don't leave town, and notify NSA Security whenever you leave your apartment." One last burst of indignation on Allison's part was quelled by Litchfield's glare. "I'd have you arrested right now, but so far no damage can be conclusively connected to your activities." Shaken, Allison swallowed hard. The DDST turned to the agent by the door. "Jenkins, see her out of the building." Litchfield looked at Allison and shook his head slowly. "Get out of here."

Allison brought her fire-engine red SAAB 9000 Turbo to a squealing stop outside a brownstone overlooking the Potomac. She stormed up the marble steps and savagely speared the dead bolt with her key. The door banged open, narrowly missing a lithe Abyssinian cat waiting in the foyer. Kicking the front door shut, Allison stalked into her bedroom. Her daypack sailed across the room and crashed against the far wall. Sitting on the edge of her bed, she stared out at the dying remnants of a sunset.

All I've ever asked for is a chance. A fair chance to show what I can do and to do what I love to do. And all the men ever see are the hair and the legs and all the rest of it, and all the women ever see are the men looking at me instead of at them. And now this. Litchfield didn't even give me a chance to explain, a chance to show that I know what I'm doing. The last of the light in the room disappeared. *Jail. Arrested. He can't be serious, can he? If I didn't know better, I might think this was just a ploy to get me to sleep with him. I almost wish it was—I could deal with that.*

Salome, her Abyssinian, appeared in Allison's lap. Whiskers tickled her throat as the cat, purring contentedly, butted her head against her mistress's chin. Allison ran her fingernails down Salome's back and along her elegant tail. *You, my love, accept me for who I am. You expect only what you deserve and give all you have to give. Why can't anyone else act that way toward me?*

Worry and exhaustion enveloped her. Allison sank backward onto her bed. *Isn't there anyone who will accept me just for what I am and just the way I am?*

Then, spread-eagled in the darkness, eyes closed, fists clenched, Allison Kirstoff cried, hating each tear as it traced a searing path down her cheek.

14

Gil Markham smiled warmly as Hafez Adid came into his office. He came to his feet and shook hands with the young Iraqi. "Before we go, Hafez, I'll need to know everything about your partner. Name, address, hat size—I mean *everything.*" Markham eyed the young man sternly. "We're going to send someone in after your partner. But if, and only if, I'm satisfied that we've got everything we need to make a successful extraction." Markham started a small tape recorder. "Now, shoot."

Markham listened for twenty minutes, his eyes growing steadily wider. "I think that should do it," he said when Adid finished. Markham shut off the tape recorder, picked it up, and locked it in his wall safe. "Ready to go?" he asked. Adid nodded eagerly.

Markham took a manila envelope out of a desk drawer. "Here's your passport."

Adid took the small blue-and-silver folder. Opening it reverently, he leafed through its pages. Suddenly, his eyes widened. "It says here that I was naturalized in 1978, and that I live in Lima, Ohio!" He turned a page. "A Turkish visa that says I've been in Ankara for six days on business!" Adid looked wonderingly at Markham. "Tell me, my friend, how do you do these wonderful things?"

"Crayons, mostly." Markham grinned, then reached again into the folder. "Here's some business cards naming you as president of the import/export outfit you run in Ohio, a picture of your wife and kids, your plane tickets, and two hundred dollars cash."

Adid's face fell. "But, under our agreement, I was to receive—"

"This is just to get you to the States," Markham cut him off. "The people who meet you in America will have the rest of it." Markham smiled at the young man, liking him. "Trust me, my friend. Now, let's go. We have just enough time to get you to the airport."

The battered Volvo B100 rattled protestingly into life as Markham turned the key. Dented and rusting, it blended perfectly into the mongrel packs of cars that crowd the streets of Ankara. Markham edged the Volvo out into Ankara's notorious traffic and began the twenty-minute drive to Ensenbo'a Airport. Adid sat beside him. Markham smiled as he noticed how Adid frequently reached up and touched the packet of documents inside his jacket.

"What about Atal—I mean, Scheherazade?" Adid asked, looking over to see if Markham had noticed the slip.

Markham, his face impassive, kept his eyes on the traffic as he filed the bit of unsolicited information away. "All the information you gave me, including Scheherazade's request for extraction and asylum, has been passed along to my superiors in America." Markham looked over at the nervous young man next to him and smiled reassuringly. "Don't worry, my friend. You and Scheherazade will soon be reunited in America. You'll like Lima, Ohio. I grew up there and—"

The three seconds that Markham had spent looking at Adid instead of the street was enough for the decrepit flatbed truck to roll across in front of them. He stood on the brakes, and the Volvo came to a squealing stop just in front of the truck. Markham held down the Volvo's horn button as he leaned out his window, shaking his fist.

Suddenly Markham peered intently through the Volvo's windshield. Then, with a muttered curse, he shoved the Volvo into reverse and began backing up rapidly.

"What is it?" Adid asked.

"There's no one in the truck's cab," he barked, craning over his shoulder through the dusty rear window. "And there's no one on the street. We've been set up."

Markham reached down between the B100's bucket seats. "See any traffic cops around?" he asked.

Adid stared at him. "No, but why—"

Markham pulled up hard on the emergency brake. A cloud of white smoke erupted from beneath the squealing Volvo as Markham, spinning the wheel furiously, whipped the car into a bootlegger's reverse. The Volvo's rear end smashed into parked cars as it swung around. When they were facing the opposite direction, Markham released the brake. He jammed the car into first and floored it.

"That's why," Markham growled. He drove with one hand, fishing inside his jacket with the other. "There's a police station in the next block. If we can just make it—"

Thirty feet from the corner on which the police station stood, the intersection was suddenly filled with a pale-blue panel truck. "Down!" Markham shouted, shoving Adid forward as the Volvo careened toward the truck.

With a rending crash the Volvo smashed into the panel truck. Markham's head slammed into the steering wheel. He pulled his head back, shaking blood from his eyes as he looked up. Through the Volvo's cracked windshield he could see the rear doors of the panel truck shudder as someone inside pounded against them. A quick glance told him that the Volvo's fender had wedged the doors shut.

"Get out!" Markham thundered at Adid. "Now!" Head pounding, the agent threw himself against his door, which reluctantly swung open. Across from him, Adid pounded furiously on his unyielding door. As Markham rounded the back of the Volvo on his way to help Adid, a burst of gunfire erupted above his head. The doors of the panel truck flew open, revealing three masked men. The barrels of three Uzi submachine guns came up, and Gil Markham readied himself to die.

He stood motionless, feeling trapped in a sort of viscous slow motion, as the barrels of the Uzis centered on his heart. Then, just as slowly, they continued past him.

Suddenly a hailstorm of gunfire shattered the illusion. The Volvo's windshield vanished in a cloud of silvery sleet. Markham watched helplessly as Hafez Adid vanished beneath the onslaught of high-velocity bullets. With a bellow of incoherent rage, Markham brought up his Walther P5. Blinded by fury and blood, he began firing at the truck. One of the assassins doubled over and fell onto the pavement. The other two pulled the truck's doors closed as it sped off.

It wasn't me they wanted, Markham realized. *They could've killed me, too, but it wasn't me they were after.* He ran his hand over his forehead, and his fingers came away red and sticky. Figures began to pour out of the police station down the block. *Gotta get out of here. Can't be associated with this.*

Markham turned to run. He collapsed onto the pavement, the red smear on his pants revealing a leg wound he hadn't even felt. He crawled between two parked cars and into a fetid alley. Gasping with pain, he pulled himself upright. *Gotta do one more thing.* He braced himself against a wall. Using a two-handed grip, Markham pumped bullets into the Volvo's gas tank. On the fourth round the car erupted into a ball of orange-black flame and smoke. *Sorry, my friend*, Markham thought as the makeshift pyre enveloped Adid, *but it has to be this way. Too bad—now you'll never know there's lots better beer than San Miguel.* Markham turned and limped away, disappearing into the alley's gloom.

15

"No," Brian said to the reporter from the *Augusta-Kennebec Journal*, "I have no idea at all why anyone would want to take Lauri."

"What are you doing to find her, Sheriff?" the reporter asked Roy Barnard.

"Everything possible," Barnard replied firmly. "An all-points bulletin has been issued to every law-enforcement agency in New England, a volunteer from a missing-child foundation in northern California is flying in to oversee the distribution of five thousand posters throughout the state, and at my request, the FBI has joined in the search for Lauren."

The reporter turned a page in her notebook. "May I speak to Mrs. Keefe now?"

"Not yet," Pat said as she came into the kitchen. "Mrs. Keefe is under my care and is unavailable for comment."

"And you are?"

"Dr. Patricia Dryden."

The reporter made a note. "What's wrong with Mrs. Keefe, Doctor?"

Pat smiled. "Let's just say that Mrs. Keefe is currently in seclusion."

"When will she be available?"

"I'm not prepared to say."

The reporter closed her notebook and stuffed it into her oversized handbag. As she rose to go she turned to Brian. "Thanks for the interview. I really needed an exclusive."

"No problem," Brian replied. "It's the least I could do—your paper is the only one around that carries 'Calvin and Hobbes.'"

The reporter paused, her hand on the doorknob. "One last question. Do you think Lauren is still alive?"

Stricken, Brian stared at her. "I don't *think* so," he said at last, his voice intense and unwavering. "I *know* so."

"Becky's awake," Pat said when the reporter had gone. "Still groggy, but awake."

"Can I see her?" Brian asked eagerly.

Pat nodded, and Brian was on his feet. Pat touched Brian's arm as he strode past. "Remember what she's going through."

Rebecca lay listlessly against a stack of pillows, dark circles beneath her eyes. Brian ached inside at the pain etched into her face and then ached again when his smile was not returned. Sitting gently on the edge of their bed, Brian took Rebecca's hand and kissed it. "I love you," he told her, brushing Rebecca's bangs out of her eyes.

"Have they found her yet?" she whispered.

At Brian's solemn "No," she slumped against the pillows. Tears squeezed between tightly shut lids.

"It's just a matter of time, hon," Brian said reassuringly, stroking her hand. "They can't get far—there are more FBI agents than locals around here right now."

"I *should* have checked on her," Rebecca said, the weakness of her voice in no way diminishing the force of the self-accusation. "It's all my fault. If I had just done what I was supposed to, then Lauri wouldn't be . . . be . . . " Her whisper gave way to racking sobs.

Fighting back a feeling of overwhelming helplessness, Brian took a deep breath. "It's not your fault, hon," he told her with quiet conviction. "It's not your fault—it's not *anyone's* fault. It happened, and now it's up to us to trust God and do our level best to get her back."

"Shouldn't have let you talk me out of it," Rebecca murmured, shaking her head slightly. "Should've checked—shouldn't have let you—all my fault . . ."

Brian closed his eyes. "Love—"

Rebecca snatched her hand from her husband's. "Go away. Just leave me alone."

Pain skewered Brian's heart. "Becky, no—"

"Just leave me alone!" Sobbing, she buried her face in her pillow.

✧ ✧ ✧

Brian's face told Pat all she needed to know. "It'll be all right," she said gently as the distraught husband slumped into a kitchen chair. "Like you, she's terrified, but you have had people to talk to and things to take care of. All Becky's had is an endless, echoing litany of self-recrimination." Pat got a can of soda out of the refrigerator. She set it and a glass in front of Brian. "Now that she's awake I'll be able to talk to her, and so will Annie. Having someone to share her feelings with should help to begin the process of healing."

"She told me to get out." Brian morosely emptied the can into the glass.

Pat nodded sadly. "She hates herself right now, Brian. All she knows is that when her baby needed her the most, she wasn't there."

"But, it *wasn't her fault!*"

Pat sat down across the kitchen table and gazed at Brian intently. "That doesn't matter to her at all. She really is terrified. That she'll lose her baby, and that since losing her baby shows that she's a failure as a mother, you'll consider her a failure as a wife. Then she'll lose you, too."

Brian's fist closed around the empty soda can. "That makes no sense whatsoever!" The ball of aluminum clattered and bounced as he flung the crushed can angrily across the kitchen.

Pat looked at him compassionately. "Neither does stealing a baby girl from her crib in the middle of the night."

Brian got up. "I'll be outside."

"Brian." The authority in Pat's voice, instilled by years of a physician's self-discipline, stopped Brian in his tracks. "She needs you." Brian snorted contemptuously, but Pat's voice stayed unrelenting. "She needs your presence, your strength, your confidence, your reassurance." The steel in Pat's voice was replaced by soft encouragement. "She needs your love."

Randy got out of the decrepit taxi and handed the driver a hundred-dinar note. Dressed in a denim jacket, black T-shirt, jeans, and worn cowboy boots, Randy turned and made his way along Sadoun Street's refuse-strewn sidewalk. His Glock Model 19 9-mm pistol pressed reassuringly against his left side.

Across the street, Baghdad's souk bustled with activity. The breeze shifted, and Randy was enveloped in the aromas of saffron, cumin, and dry ancient dust. Mounds of henna and tumeric glowed ocher and gold in the late afternoon sun. A tinker, his back against a glaring portrait of Iraq's strongman leader, sat cross-legged in the dirt, hammering an ornate design into a brass platter. Next to him, a pack of curs fought viciously for scraps discarded by a butcher.

Should be at the end of this block, Randy decided, glancing at street numbers as he strode along. *Hope I don't get lost, since the nuts who run this country have outlawed maps. Of course, they've outlawed weather reports, too, for "security reasons."*

He stopped at the end of the block. Ahead, across a wide

boulevard, the muddy Tigris flowed sluggishly. A low, tiled wall skirted the street corner, forming a small patio dotted with tables. Randy looked up at the archway leading into the patio. Arabic writhed along the arch, and beneath the Arabic, the translation: Mom's Homestyle Café. *Well*, Randy thought as he walked in and sat down at the cleanest of the tables, *if this isn't the place, then maybe I can at least get a meatloaf sandwich.*

A flamboyant waiter scurried up. *"Ablan wa'salan,"* he said, welcoming Randy effusively. He took an order pad from a pocket of his stained and ragged apron. *"Aywah, habibi?"*

Randy waved away the menu. "Coffee, medium sweet," he said in Russian.

The waiter stared. Randy repeated his order. The man scurried away. Randy watched the waiter enter into an animated conversation with another man. *Terrific. They're probably out of meatloaf, too.*

Another patron entered, sat down at a table, and disappeared behind a newspaper. Randy's waiter went to the newcomer, while the man he had been talking to came over to Randy. "You want coffee?" he asked, his English atrocious.

"Coffee, medium sweet," Randy said in Russian for the third time. The new waiter frowned, then broke into a bucktoothed grin. He disappeared into the restaurant, and Randy relaxed.

A third man, tall and heavyset, emerged and headed toward him. Randy's ease evaporated when he saw no cup of coffee in the man's hands. The man glanced around nervously before speaking. "You ordered coffee?" he said softly in perfect Russian.

"Yes," Randy replied again in Russian. "Medium sweet." The man turned abruptly and went back into the kitchen. Randy shook his head. *Wonder if he's supposed to keep me busy while the rest of the jokers who run this place are out rounding up their relatives with baseball bats to come have a little chat with me.*

The man returned, bearing both a cup of coffee and a bill. Randy sipped experimentally, then smiled as he relished the flavor of strong, pure Arabian mocha. By the time a barge laden with bales of cotton had drifted by on the Tigris, Randy was finished. He stood, picked up the bill, and fished a wad of dinars out of his pocket. After leafing through the sheaf of notes, Randy surreptitiously folded the bill into the wad, stuck it back into his pocket, and left.

At a nearby table a single eye peered over the top of a newspaper. When Randy was out of sight, the man got up and strode into the kitchen.

The helicopter's rotor whickered softly behind him as Barnard strode up to the small plateau near Mount Kineo's summit. Unmindful of the superb view of Moosehead Lake that stretched out southward below, the sheriff turned to the FBI agent in charge of the investigation.

"Got anything?" Barnard asked.

The agent held up a sealed bag in each latex-gloved hand. Barnard peered at them. "You've got some blackened scraps of cloth in that one," he observed. "What's in the other? Looks like charred sticks."

"I wish they were sticks," the FBI man replied. He looked from the bag to the sheriff. "They're bones. Fresh, burned bones."

16

With cool hazel eyes Barbara Waite regarded Elliot French skeptically. "So you're telling me that half of the team you're trying to get out of Iraq is now dead?" the secretary of state asked. French nodded morosely. Waite looked at him sharply. "And you're absolutely certain our Ankara station chief can in no way be connected with the assassination?"

"Absolutely. The only people who saw Gil Markham were the shooters, and they're not about to come forward and finger him." French gestured casually. "Street killings are an everyday occurrence in Turkey, and Gil has enough connections in the Ankara City Police to make sure the case is investigated quickly and minimally."

The secretary thought for a moment. "Shouldn't we cut our losses?" Waite questioned. "Just let Doral do her thing and then hightail it out of there?"

French shook his head emphatically. "This makes it all the more imperative that we successfully extract the remaining asset."

Waite chuckled. "You're not going to refer to the twins as 'assets,' are you? Chris will have a fit if you start reading them

fairy tales and describe Hansel and Gretel as 'covert oper-
atives.'"

French grinned. "Actually," he went on, "this assassination really has very little bearing on the mission. Scheherazade
is the one we really want, and we were planning all along to
bring them out separately. The only question now is whether to
inform Cavanaugh of Adid's death."

"Does he need to know?"

"Strictly speaking, no. But I'd much rather have Cavanaugh find out from us instead of from Scheherazade. The boy's
a master of improvisation, but the more he has to go on, the
better he'll do."

Waite smiled. "Sounds like you think quite highly of him."

The CIA director of operations nodded. "I'm grooming
him for big things. Besides, Randy reminds me of my younger
days—the ones before I had to trade in my Tom Clancy novels
for *How to Get Your Baby to Sleep through the Night.*"

The secretary of state laughed. "Any news on the twins?"
Waite asked.

"Due any minute now," the father-to-be replied. "We're
all packed and ready to go." Just then, French's pager began
beeping stridently. He looked at the device, then at Waite.
"Uh-oh."

✧ ✧ ✧

The lights, hazy and indistinct, drifted toward him. They
looked like soft, glowing spheres floating in a misty sea. *It's true*,
he thought, wincing because thinking hurt. *Everything I've read
about angels coming to get you is true.*

The lights slowly solidified, arranging themselves into
parallel rows. Thoughts of his wife and family flickered through
his mind as the glowing shapes hovered overhead. *No time like
the present, as they say*, he thought. *'Specially when it's you doing the
calling, God.* A sense of peace engulfed him as he surrendered
himself to the beckoning lights.

Bill Estes's eyes opened, and the lights snapped into focus. In an instant the warm, inviting presences became cold, aloof banks of fluorescent light overhead. His sense of deep disappointment was interrupted by a gasp. Something squeezed his left hand. It hurt. With an effort Estes inched his head toward the sound.

Unwashed, stringy hair lay limply over the shoulders of her dirty sweatshirt. Her eyes were hollow and red, her lips dry, her face wan and without makeup. She had never looked better to him.

"Hi, hon," he rasped. *Thanks, God, for the glimpse of glory.* Feebly, the deputy sheriff smiled. *And thanks for a little while longer down here.*

Eyes wide, her lips moving in silent prayer, Janis Estes squeezed her husband's hand again.

Her squeeze still hurt, but Bill didn't mind.

Brian answered the door to find Doris Rodgers dabbing at her eyes with a lace-trimmed handkerchief, her ashen face stark against the pink of her uniform. "I just found out, Brian," she said, peering up at him through red-rimmed eyes. "I can't believe it."

In the living room, Doris rushed over to Rebecca. "Becky, I'm so sorry," she sobbed, flinging her arms around the younger woman. Overcome, the words poured forth. "Yesterday was my day off and I got back late and since I didn't start until lunch today I slept in and I only found out when Sandy told me and—"

Rigid, Rebecca pulled away from her friend. "You lied to me," she said, her voice a grating whisper.

Doris's torrent of words dried up instantly. "What?"

"You lied to me. You said my baby was safe."

Distress mingled with confusion on Doris's face. "Becky,

181

honey," Doris pleaded, "she *was* safe. Like I told you, I looked in on her just before you got home."

Rebecca stared, flinty-eyed, at Doris. "Because you lied to me, my baby's gone."

Tears streamed down Doris's face. "Please, Becky. Please don't even think that."

"You wanted her gone. You wanted her gone because you don't have a baby of your own."

Trembling, crying, Doris shook her head mutely.

Rebecca stood. "Get out of my house, liar!" she ordered. *"Get out!"*

Brian strode across the room. *"Becky!"* he thundered. *"Stop it!"* Rebecca whirled, shoved past him, and fled. The front door was flung wide, and Doris had disappeared.

"I'm telling you, Roy, it was no dream." Bill Estes stared at his boss, who was leaning back precariously in an armless hospital chair, his feet resting on the end of the deputy's bed.

"I agree," Roy Barnard replied. "Sounds more like a night-mare to me. Robes and turbans and candlesticks shaped like birds. It just doesn't make sense." Barnard held up a hand to ward off Bill's protest. "Now don't go having a stroke to match that concussion of yours."

Barnard took a pack of cigarettes from his shirt pocket, then realized where he was and hastily put them back. "It's not that I don't believe you, Bill, it's just that there's no hard evidence to back up your story. You got a good whack on the back of the head and spent the night unconscious on Kineo. Good thing that group of hikers found you. Guess I'll never make fun of their carrying cellular phones again," the sheriff admitted with a grin. "Then you spent the better part of a day and a half right here. When you weren't out cold, you were thrashing around, muttering about fires and knives—scared poor Janis half to death. And you yourself admit that you slipped at least once on the way up, so we can't rule that out as a cause. And while all this is important, there's no way yet to connect it with Lauren's kidnapping." The sheriff nodded encouragingly. "But you did ID that Marduk character clearly enough for me to go have a little chat with him." Barnard looked at Estes. "Now, if you were me, what would you do?"

The deputy started to shrug, then thought better of it. "I'd file it under 'possible assault with intent to kill,' put 'unknown' in the 'perpetrator' field on the report, and dismiss the rest as concussion-inspired ravings." Estes looked unhappy. "Didn't the search turn up *anything?*"

The sheriff studied his friend and coworker. *No way am I going to tell him about the burned bones we found up there. And I'm not going to tell him about the blood outside Lauren's window. Not yet. Not in his condition.* "Not much," Barnard replied. "That wicked big storm we had while you were out cold trashed the place real good. We found evidence of a fire, but kids have been having campfires up there for years. I turned the investigation over to the FBI forensics folks, who have packed the whole mess up and sent it off to the pathology lab at FBI Headquarters." The front legs of the sheriff's chair hit the floor. "Right now, Deputy, your job is to get back up to snuff. I'll take care of the rest of it."

Estes nodded resignedly, then snapped his fingers. "One more thing. I can't get that candlestick thing out of my mind." He took a spiral-bound notepad from his nightstand, tore off a sheet, and handed it to Barnard. "Here's a sketch I made before you got here."

Barnard took the drawing and stuck it in a pocket. As he got up to leave, a nurse came in. "This just arrived for you, Mr. Estes." She handed him an envelope and left.

Estes frowned at the handwriting on the outside of the envelope. "It's from Jack," he told Barnard. Jack Carver, the marina operator, had been Estes's friend and fishing buddy since high school.

Estes tore off one end of the envelope and upended it. A rearview mirror taken from the windshield of a small boat fell out, along with a piece of paper. Estes unfolded the note, read it, then burst into laughter. Wincing with the pain his outburst had caused him, Estes handed the note to Barnard. It read, "Thought this might come in handy in the future."

Brian stripped off his shirt and dropped it into the hamper. "Treating Doris that way was completely uncalled for," he said quietly. He could just see the top of his wife's head over the back of the armchair. She sat with her back to him, staring out the bay window that formed one corner of their bedroom.

He walked across the oak-planked floor and sat down on the window seat. Rebecca's profile was etched against the moonlit sky. *She looks so pale*, he thought worriedly. *I hope it's just the moonlight.* "It wasn't fair to accuse Doris."

Rebecca didn't look at him. "She was responsible for Lauri. It's her fault."

Frustrated, Brian shook his head. "For all we know, Lauri was taken after we got home. We just don't know. In any case, reminding Doris that she's single was a cruel and heartless thing to do."

"She deserved it."

Brian sighed. *I remember the night we moved into this place. I sat in that chair, holding her as we watched the moon rise. She was so happy, so excited. She was so much younger than she seems right now. And I felt like I was ten feet tall and could conquer the world.*

Is this what it comes to, Lord? he wondered. *Does it always have to end this way? Must everything fade and wither and become rusty and moth-eaten?* Brian sighed. *You may be a "lamp to my feet and a light for my path," Lord, but it sure feels right now like there's a washed-out bridge you didn't tell me about.*

Brian got up. "It's really gorgeous outside. Thought I'd take a walk—fresh air feels like a real good idea right now." He extended his hand hopefully. "Want to come along? We could use some alone time, hon. To talk and to pray."

Rebecca didn't move. "Don't wake me. I'll be asleep when you get back."

Brian turned away. "As always," he muttered angrily. He grabbed a shirt and stalked from the room.

17

The alarm signal thundering from the Klaxon blasted Mark Sewell from sleep. With reflexes honed in the deserts of Kuwait and Somalia, he was on his feet instantly.

"General quarters, general quarters," the speaker set into the overhead blared. "SAR teams man your boats."

Dodging seamen struggling into life jackets and helmets, Mark ran down the companionway. A feetfirst lunge down a gangway brought him to the doorway of the Combat Information Center. Shiloh Turk was already there, barefoot, his shirt-tail flapping. The nightwatch fire control officer, a young lieutenant junior grade, was staring at a radar screen.

Mark turned to the FCO. "Report, mister." The lieutenant looked at him, mute and ashen faced. "I said report, mister!" Mark rapped. "That's an order!"

The lieutenant took a deep breath. "Seven minutes ago," he reported, "the *Mayfield* blew up."

"Hostile action?" Mark asked, glancing at the radar screen. "BARCAP report any bogies?"

The young man shook his head. "No, sir. Nobody reported anything. One minute she's sailing along beside us, pretty as you please, and the next minute—*boom.*"

"You're relieved."

The lieutenant looked up at Mark, unable to hide his surprise and worry.

"It's OK," Mark reassured him. "I was due to relieve you in half an hour anyway. We'll plan on reviewing the Mark 7's data at eight bells." Mark gestured at Turk. "Besides, the chief here hasn't had a chance to shower yet. So go grab some chow before your appetite disappears completely."

"I'd prefer, sir," the lieutenant replied earnestly, "to join a search-and-rescue team. I've got buddies aboard the *Mayfield*."

"Very well," Mark agreed. "But be back here at eight bells." The lieutenant nodded and left. Mark switched on the high-resolution video camera mounted atop the *Alameda*'s mainmast. "Well, Chief," he suggested, "let's scope out the damage. Where is she now?"

Turk waited until the navigational radar had made a full sweep. "Bearing one-one-five and stationary," he replied.

Mark swung the camera around until a pillar of black smoke came into view. He tracked the camera down the column. Both men whistled as the FFG-class guided-missile frigate USS *Mayfield* came into view. Listing badly to starboard, the rear third of the frigate was submerged. Flames, steam, and more greasy smoke billowed from portholes and hatches. A covey of small boats circled the stricken ship, plucking its crew from the water. Helicopters hovered, lifting the injured up in baskets and then flitting away.

"Looks like she took one right in the fuel tanks," Mark observed. "One of those Silkworms we were talking about the other day?"

"Maybe," Turk agreed. "Or maybe some seaman third was smoking where he shouldn't have been. Hard to say."

Mark eyed the old sailor. "This *is* a first, Chief. Usually, your opinions are unassailable, vociferous, and profane."

Turk shook his head. "You haven't been in these waters

long enough," he replied seriously, "or you'd be as uncertain as I am."

"If it wasn't an accident, then what caused it?"

Turk shrugged. "There sure isn't a shortage of suspects. Coulda been a Silkworm—skimming along the wave tops like they do, they're hard enough for an *experienced* radarman to see, much less the pup who had the duty. Or it could have been a mine left over from the Yom Kippur War that suddenly popped out of the mud. Or it even could have been some crazy man named A-hab, wearing nothing but a turban and a death wish, who swam out to the *Mayfield*'s hull with twenty kilos of gelignite and pushed the button." The chief bit down on an unlit cigar. "Like I said, there ain't no shortage of suspects. So, sir, let's get to reviewing that data from the Mark 7."

Sewell began typing. "My thoughts exactly."

Commander Jerry Hall ran his fingers through his thinning, gray-blonde hair. "Let me get this straight, Mark," the captain of the *Alameda* said. "Nothing showed up on radar before the *Mayfield* went up?"

Mark nodded. "You can see it right here, Skipper," he added, pointing to the terminal set into the CIC central console. "Both the phased-array air search and the ISC Cardion surface radars are completely quiet until—" Mark's finger traced wild fluctuations in the radar's traces— "kablooie. There goes the *Mayfield*."

Mark looked at the young lieutenant JG who had been the duty fire control officer at the time of the incident. "You were right, Dennis," he said reassuringly. "One minute the *Mayfield* was making way nicely, and the next minute—*boom*."

"I need answers, gentlemen," Hall said firmly. "We're Jericho Five for this task force, and that means we're supposed to have an explanation for things like this." His gaze gathered in both Mark and Turk. "So far all you have to offer me is 'boom' and 'kablooie,' neither of which is going to make Admiral Pierce a happy man. And if I have to explain to him why that's the best we can do then *I* won't be happy either, if you catch my drift."

The two SEALs swapped a quick glance. "Only one thing to do, Skipper," Turk offered. "We'll go have us a look-see if it's all right with you."

Hall looked relieved. "I can't order you to go look, since you're on detached duty, but I was hoping you'd volunteer." He picked up a phone. "I'll order a launch immediately."

The chief held up a hand. "No need to rush, Skipper. It'll take us the rest of the afternoon to break out our gear. Besides . . ." Turk trailed off with a shrug.

Jerry Hall grinned. "That's right. I'd forgotten you commando types hate daylight. Very well, go Zulu 5 Oscar at five bells." Hall left the CIC.

"What's 'Zulu 5 Oscar'?" the lieutenant asked.

"Z/5/O," Turk replied, "means 'evade and escape.' We go do what we want to do, and the bad guys don't notice we're doing it to 'em."

"Sounds like fun," the lieutenant said. "Mind if I come along?"

"You've had BUD/S?" Mark asked skeptically, referring to the Basic Underwater Demolition/SEAL training both he and Turk had attended. *He sure isn't big enough to be a SEAL.*

"No," the lieutenant replied. "But I *am* SCUBA qualified."

"Coronado or Little Creek?" Turk asked, referring to the two Underwater Demolition Team training facilities in California and Virginia.

"Neither. I got my NAUI certification last year on leave."

"So you've got a civilian certification, eh?" Turk observed. The lieutenant nodded proudly. The old sailor scratched his chin thoughtfully. "Well, sonny boy, there's only one problem with you going along."

"What's that?"

"The *Mayfield* is sitting on a ledge in about a hundred feet of water. Right next to that ledge, the sea floor falls away to about three hundred feet."

"So?" the JG replied. "I've been down to a hundred feet before. What's the problem?"

"The problem is," Turk replied slowly, "that when your diapers get waterlogged and drag you right over that cliff and down to that three-hundred-foot bottom, who's going to go get you?" The master chief looked at Mark. "Let's gear up."

✧ ✧ ✧

"You all right, Mr. President?" Robin Hawkes asked.

"I'm fine, Robin," the president reassured his chief of staff. "I just dropped the phone." The president looked at the clock radio on his nightstand, squinting to bring the fluorescent-green digits into focus. *Three fifty-two. Well, they said the job included overtime.* "What's up?"

"There's been an incident in the Persian Gulf. More specifically, in the Strait of Hormuz."

"Who'd we shoot down this time?"

"I wish that was the problem. We've lost a ship."

"What do you mean 'we've lost a ship'?"

Hawkes took a deep breath. "At four-thirty in the morning, local time, the navy frigate USS *Mayfield* exploded, caught fire, and sank."

"Do we know who did this?"

"Not yet. Reports from the task force involved are still coming in."

Swearing, the president banged his fist against his nightstand. His glasses glinted in the light from the clock as they tumbled to the floor. Alarmed by the noise, his wife sat up in bed. "I want General Rodriguez and Admiral Harrison in the Situation Room in twenty minutes," he ordered into the telephone as he reached with the other hand to smooth his wife's hair. "That'll give me time to get dressed—and to find my glasses."

A marine guard in dress blues saluted, then opened the door as the president and Hawkes approached. "Let me get this perfectly straight before we go in, Robin," the president growled. "It took almost six hours after the *Mayfield* sank for me to be notified?"

Hawkes nodded grimly. "That's right. The Pentagon is staffed at night by junior officers, and, of course, each of them wanted to verify the report before sending it upstairs with their chop on it—"

The president cut him off with a wave of his hand. "I get the point. Well," he added as they entered the Situation Room, "despite all the generals and admirals in here, we're not the only ones who are going to be seeing stars, believe me."

General Roddy Rodriguez and Navy Chief of Staff Admiral Cornell Harrison stood as the president entered.

"Just exactly why, General," the president barked, "did it take six hours for news of this incident to reach me?" He didn't motion for the officers to sit down.

"Minimal off-hours staffing," Rodriguez replied calmly, "combined with a verified lack of overt hostile activity."

"You mean we're not under attack?" the president exclaimed. "A sunken warship sounds very much like an attack to me, General!"

"I mean we've detected no *overt* hostile action, Mr. President. Whether we are under attack or not remains to be seen."

The president frowned. Then he smiled and shook his head. "My apologies, gentlemen, for jumping to conclusions. Please, sit down." The president looked at Hawkes. "Robin, see if you can get some coffee and juice down here." Stifling a yawn, he sat down in his chair. "General, since you and Admiral Harrison have been at this a lot longer than I have, why don't you tell me what's going on."

18

"I'd say it's too early to tell, Mr. President," Lydia Doral reported. She and Randy Cavanaugh were sitting at her desk in the refurbished ambassador's quarters in the northwest corner of the embassy's top floor. On the desk in front of them, an ordinary speakerphone was plugged into a small box the size of a cellular phone. The box, a SATCOM unit, transmitted their conversation via tight microwave beam to a satellite in the MILSTAR worldwide military communications network.

"I've been monitoring Radio Baghdad since I received word of the incident," Doral went on. "The Iraqis are, of course, claiming full credit for the sinking, making it sound as if their beloved president personally ripped the *Mayfield*'s hull open with his bare hands. At the same time, however, Iraqi television is accusing us of intentionally sinking the *Mayfield.*"

Both Randy and Doral smiled at the president's disbelieving *"What?"*

"Their rationale, if such a word applies," the ambassador explained, "is that, in collusion with Israel, we're out to conquer the Middle East by poisoning the Persian Gulf with the *Mayfield*'s nuclear reactor, thus eliminating their fishing industry and starving the downtrodden masses."

A chorus of contemptuous snorts emanated faintly from the speakerphone as the Joint Chiefs expressed their opinion.

"Is contamination a possibility?" they heard the president ask.

"No, sir," Admiral Harrison replied. "It is not. All FFG-class vessels such as the *Mayfield* are powered by gas turbine engines. There was no fissionable material aboard the *Mayfield*."

"How about the locals, Randy?" Elliot French asked. "What's up with them?"

"I took a stroll along Abu Nawas Street a little while ago," Randy replied. "That's the fishmonger's street that runs along the Tigris," he explained, neglecting to add that the street was also notorious for its bars and brothels. "The locals are pretty excited about the *Mayfield*'s sinking. So excited, in fact, that they didn't even complain when Iraqi broadcasting cut in on the Arab Cup soccer finals to report the news. Normally, interrupting a soccer match would result in general insurrection."

"The people in the restaurant I hung out in," Randy added, "were still worked up about our shooting down those two Iraqi Air Force MiG-29s the other day. They were primed and ready for that swill the television was dishing out about nuclear contamination, and they lapped it up. I bugged out when the anti-American 'Death to the imperialist West!' slogans started. Things are definitely heating up," he concluded.

"Do you wish to be recalled, Mrs. Ambassador?" the president asked.

"Not at this time," Doral replied. "Not much notice was taken of our arrival, so we should be able to lay low here in the embassy compound. Besides," she added, "the trade talks are just beginning to make substantive progress."

"And Cavanaugh's 'appointment' isn't until tonight," they heard Elliot French add.

"Very well," the president agreed. "Carry on. We'll have a

contingent of DELTA Force staged in Kuwait, just in case."
The line went dead.

The ambassador steepled her long, manicured nails.
"How long would it take a quick-extraction force like DELTA
to get here from Kuwait?" she asked Randy.

"If they blaze right in and onto the roof," the CIA agent
replied, "about an hour."

As they watched through the office window, a man paused
in front of the compound gate. He spat copiously and flamboy-
antly on the embassy's driveway before continuing on.

"That might just turn out to be one *very* long hour,"
Randy said softly.

✧ ✧ ✧

A jagged Omani hilltop impaled the setting sun as the cutter
carrying Mark and Turk reached station above the *Mayfield*'s
grave. The frigate's twisted and blackened mainmast jutted
from the water.

Looks like the skeleton of a long-dead lighthouse, Mark thought
as he pulled the black neoprene hood of his wetsuit over his
head. He spit into his face mask, then rubbed the saliva around
to keep the glass from fogging up.

"Where're your tanks?" the yeoman conning the cutter
asked.

Mark held up a small apparatus. "Draeger Model Nines,"
he explained. "Bubbleless Aqua-Lungs. They're self-regenerat-
ing, so no gas escapes. That way, we don't leave a trail of bubbles
for the unfriendlies to wonder about." Mark snapped the unit
into a socket set in the bottom of his full-face mask. "Plus," he
added, "the Model Nine has a short-range underwater transmitter built in." Mark demonstrated by placing the mask
against his face and speaking. From the other end of the cutter
Turk nodded in response.

The yeoman shook his head. "You wouldn't catch me

down there at all, much less sucking on something that looks like a cross between a toilet paper tube and a pacifier."

The two SEALs put on pairs of waterproof Starlight night-vision goggles, then fitted their face masks carefully over them. The light-amplification goggles transformed the Arabian dusk into a bright green panorama.

"How ya gonna see down there?" the yeoman asked.

"Matches," Turk growled. "Lots and lots of matches. Now shut up." The chief looked at Mark, indicating his readiness with an upturned thumb.

Mark returned Turk's thumbs-up, grabbed his face mask, and rolled backwards into the waters of the Strait of Hormuz.

An initial flurry of bubbles was replaced by a calm sense of floating. Mark glanced at his depth indicator, then adjusted his buoyancy compensator slightly. He began a leisurely descent, watching as the numbers on the depth indicator increased.

At fifty feet he switched on the headlamp attached to his wetsuit's hood. Turk did the same. The two men looked down, watching as the deck of the *Mayfield* seemed to drift up toward them from the depths.

It looks like we're falling, Mark thought, *but it sure doesn't feel like we are. Wonder if I'll ever get used to it.*

They paused, level with the *Mayfield*'s port gunwale. Mark reached up and increased the sensitivity of his night-vision goggles. The sunken frigate snapped into phosphorescent green focus. She had slammed stern-first into the hard mud bottom, crumpling her fantail, then had settled almost upright. Knowing that the explosion had occurred toward the *Mayfield*'s stern, Mark waved Turk toward the rear of the ship. The two men swam energetically, fighting a current that was acting like a head wind.

Ninety feet down, they swam alongside the destroyed ship, drifting past buckled plates and twisted piping. Blackened and scorched fittings told the two men of the inferno that had raged within the ship.

"Wasn't no cherry bomb did this," Turk observed. The short-range communicator built into the heliox unit made his voice hollow and metallic in Mark's headphones.

"You're right there, Chief," Mark agreed. "Let's move on back toward the fireroom." Below him, eerie green in the goggles' artificial light, a sand shark worried a shapeless mass of flesh. Mark kicked his flippers, eager to move on.

"Check this out, Lieutenant," Turk called. He was in front of Mark, about fifty feet from the *Mayfield*'s stern.

Mark pulled up next to the chief. The frigate's slender stern was twisted, the steel plates torn open. "That hole must be twelve feet across," he observed. Mark held on to one of the jagged strips of steel, fighting the increasingly strong current. "You were right, Chief. Look how the plates are blown outward. Something must've happened in the fireroom. Maybe one of the gas turbines blew."

"Maybe, sir," Turk replied. "But maybe not. I've got an idea." He took a line of thin nylon rope from a hook on his belt. He clipped one end to a ring on his buoyancy compensator, then handed the coil to Mark. "Play this out for me, will you?" Turk began to swim toward the hole.

Mark held the rope firmly, jerking Turk up short. "Bottom time, Chief," he said firmly, emphasizing his statement with a gesture at his dive computer, a watchlike instrument strapped to his wrist. "At this depth and with this current, we're down here for a max of four minutes."

"Aye-aye, sir," Turk replied calmly. "Shouldn't take that long. Just humor me on this." Mark agreed. Turk had been diving since before Mark was born. The chief disappeared into the hole torn in the *Mayfield*'s side.

Mark hung suspended in the blackness, his eyes flicking between the coils of rope slipping from his gloved fingers and his dive computer. Small bits of detritus flushed by in the current, green snow in Mark's night-vision goggles. Visibility was quickly reduced to near zero.

"Two minutes," he called into the darkness. No response.

At one minute Mark tugged on the line. Thinking he felt an answering tug, he pulled again.

The rope went slack, sinking slowly toward the bottom.

Mark plunged into the gaping mouth of the hole. "Chief!" he shouted into his mouthpiece. "Chief! Report!"

The line lay slack on the frigate's deck. Mark shone his headlamp on the crater blasted into the *Mayfield*'s interior. The hole, clogged with a tangle of wires and pipes, disappeared into the depths of the ship.

Mark started violently as something brushed against the back of his neck. He spun around. An arm, pale and flaccid, dangled limply from a hatchway. A buzzing filled his ears, and Mark looked at his dive computer. Its red display, blinking angrily, read 00:00. Mark shut off the buzzing alarm with a savage punch. He knew he had only seconds to begin his ascent. He looked around the hold once more. No sign of Turk. Stress and oxygen deprivation combined to make his head feel as if it were about to explode.

Mark swam out of the ship, searching frantically for any sign of his vanished friend as he kicked for the surface.

❖ ❖ ❖

"So . . ." Jack Carver paused dramatically. Bill Estes and Roy Barnard leaned forward, eager for Carver to finish his latest story. ". . . just as this client of mine leans way over to scoop this big ol' togue up in his net, a humongous deerfly zips up and bites him right on the—"

Shouts and a metallic crash echoed through the half-open hospital room door. Barnard was on his feet and out of the room instantly, followed closely by Jack Carver. The two men dashed down the corridor toward the source of the commotion.

Carver and Barnard burst into the emergency room. A doctor shouted for restraints as she and an orderly attempted to wrestle a man back onto a gurney. A tray of instruments was scattered across the floor, interspersed with lengths of bloody gauze. The two men grabbed the writhing man's shoulders and held him down while the orderly pinioned his legs. The doctor quickly grabbed a syringe, filled it, and plunged it into the man's thigh. The thrashing ceased as the man went limp.

"I'm surprised he had that kind of fight in him," the doctor said, brushing her hair out of her eyes. "Get that turban off his head," she instructed a nurse. She turned back to Barnard. "Thanks for the help."

"What happened, Dr.—" Barnard peered at her name tag— "Linehan?"

"He literally dragged himself in here," Linehan replied, "which isn't surprising, considering that he's missing a big toe." Barnard glanced at the man's left foot, which was swollen and red. "The orderly got him onto the gurney while I was being paged. When I came in, he was sitting quietly. He just stared at me when I introduced myself. But as soon as I tried to lift his foot to examine the wound, he just went bonkers." The doctor shook her head. "Maybe he doesn't like blondes."

As the unconscious man stirred restlessly, his head flopped over toward the trio. Jack Carver stared at the man, then grabbed Barnard's arm. "Roy," he whispered, "that's him. The bird-watcher. The one Brian and Rebecca were complaining about."

The sheriff studied the man's face. "He matches the description George Williams gave me of the guy who clobbered him," Barnard told Carver. The sheriff waited until the doctor had finished making notes on a clipboard. "How is he?" Barnard asked.

"Not good," Linehan replied bluntly. "That wound of his has gone septic, and gangrene's setting in. Add to that dehydration and blood loss. I've got him started on a saline IV and massive doses of antibiotics." She shrugged. "That last little outburst of his really drained him. If we don't have to amputate that foot, and if renal failure doesn't set in, and if he doesn't get any shockier, then we just might save him."

Barnard nodded. "He's a suspect in an assault case, so I'm going to post a deputy outside his room. Call me when you know one way or the other, will you?"

The doctor looked at the sleeping man. "In twenty-four hours we'll know. One way or the other."

Nadia Sayed glared at the men gathered in the tiny Baghdad apartment. "We are *not* going anywhere tonight," she said sharply. "The baby is tired, and so am I." Nestled in Sayed's arms, the child stirred briefly and went back to sleep.

Ahmal Sayed shrugged off Darius Marduk's look of impatient disapproval. "My wife watched over our future *Kalifa* before she was spirited away by her infidel parents," he reminded Marduk, "and we brought her along to care for the child. Besides, *Pir*, we are in no hurry. There are preparations to be made, and we cannot anoint the child *Kalifa* until the next full moon, when the portents are correct."

Marduk nodded. "Very well, then. We will leave for Ain Sifni tomorrow."

A knock rattled the door at the base of the stairs that led up to the apartment. Frowning, Marduk strode across the room. He peered out the latticework window. Two men laden with packages stood in the cobblestone street below.

"That should be the food I ordered," Nadia Sayed said.

Marduk whirled. "You acted without consulting me?"

"The child will soon be hungry," Sayed replied, unperturbed. "I naturally assumed you would want only the best for our next living saint."

Mollified, Marduk jerked his head toward the door. Ahmal

returned with two men, one of whom put his parcel down on the rickety kitchen table, opened it, and began removing cans of condensed milk.

"See?" Nadia asked. "Real food for the child, not the spicy *ful* and lumpy *daal* you men would undoubtedly try and feed her." She shook her head. "Men have no idea how to care for a baby."

"And I have food for the rest of you," the other arrival said. They turned to find an assault rifle pointed at their heads. The first man pulled a pistol from his waistband and leveled it at them.

"What is the meaning of this?" Marduk demanded.

"An alert immigrations officer noticed the arrival this morning of an Iraqi child with suspiciously blue eyes," the man with the rifle told him. "My office was alerted, and you were trailed here. I have a use for the child. Give her to us, and we will leave."

"Never!" Marduk bellowed. "I will die before I will again lose our *Kalifa!*" As Marduk lunged toward the man, a burst from the rifle cut him in two.

The man gestured toward Ahmal Sayed. "Kill him," he ordered his companion. A shot thundered, and Sayed was thrown against the apartment wall.

"I don't want to kill you, too," the man told the terrified woman. "After all," he said with a sardonic grin, gesturing with the rifle at the crumpled bodies of her leader and her husband, "if *these* men were so incapable of caring for an infant, think of what would happen if someone like *me* tried to." He adjusted the patch that covered one eye. "We leave."

Flanked by the two men, a weeping Nadia Sayed carried the wailing baby down the stairs and into the night.

❖ ❖ ❖

"Looks like you're planning a big evening," Charlie Davenport commented from where he was sprawled in a chair in the embassy kitchen.

Randy finished sliding bullets into the magazine of his Glock Model 19. He slammed the magazine into place in the pistol's grip, cycled a round into the chamber, and flipped on the safety. The 9-mm pistol disappeared into the holster under Randy's worn leather jacket.

"I've got a date," Randy replied. "A blind date." He fished the piece of paper he had been given at the café out of his pocket, unfolded it, and handed it to Davenport.

"What kind of writing is this?" Davenport asked.

"Russian," Randy replied. "It says that someone will pick me up tonight at the embassy's back gate."

The marine sergeant peered at Randy. "Sure you want to go alone? I wouldn't go into Baghdad with less than a squad of marines during the *day*, much less at night."

Randy grinned at Davenport. "Who do you think needs a chaperone, Sarge? Me, or my date?" The grin faded into dead seriousness. "I've done this sort of thing before, and it isn't like the movies. When they say come alone, they *mean* come alone."

The walkie-talkie clipped to Davenport's belt squawked. Davenport listened, then looked at Randy. "Someone's here. To see you."

Dust rose behind them as Davenport brought the jeep to a shuddering stop in front of the embassy gates. A large, swarthy man stood just inside the gates, flanked by marines. Randy recognized him as the Russian-speaking waiter who had slipped him the note. At the sight of Randy the man pointed, then jerked his head toward a rusting panel truck parked outside the compound.

"If that's your idea of a date," Davenport muttered, "then you've been in the field *way* too long."

Randy nodded curtly to the man, then walked past him and through the gates. At the man's gesture, Randy got into the passenger's side of the truck. The man slid behind the wheel, and they departed in a cloud of sooty, diesel-scented smoke.

"Did you say something about a date, Sarge?" one marine asked as they watched the truck vanish into the gloom. "Think Cavanaugh's gonna get lucky?"

"Not that it's any business of yours, DeLong," Davenport growled, "but he'd better."

❖   ❖   ❖

The panel truck ground to a stop in the mouth of a narrow alleyway. Randy stepped out of the truck's cab, his boots squishing into two inches of mire. Lamb kebabs sizzled over an open fire as a woman stirred a pot of bubbling stew. Half-naked children shrieked as they chased each other down the lane. Music droned from somewhere inside one of the hovels that crowded the alleyway. Without looking back, the large man began walking.

They passed the entrance to a mosque. A quick glance inside showed Randy ranks of worshipers prostrate on mats arrayed on the ornately tiled floor. The man, with Randy close on his heels, went through a nondescript doorway into a darkened room. A knot of people, clustered around a blaring television at the far end of the room, ignored them.

Randy's guide crossed the room and opened another door. A rectangle of soft light fell over a worn Persian carpet. The man motioned for Randy to go in.

Cavanaugh shook his head. "No way, Ali Baba." He gestured to the man. "After you."

The man scowled. He motioned again, this time curtly. Something appeared in his hand. In the gloom, Randy was unable to make out what it was.

Doesn't look like a gun, Randy thought, *but it sure doesn't look like the keys to the city, either*. Randy stared at his guide, shrugged, and walked into the room. As his eyes adjusted to the light,

Randy realized that the room was a *salamlik*, the formal reception room in a Middle Eastern home.

The soft light came from a copper bowl suspended overhead by a trio of finely wrought chains. The polished interior of the bowl reflected the light from the single bulb back up and off the ceiling. An intricate latticework of designs carved into the bowl cast an intriguing pattern of light and shadow over the cream-colored walls of the oblong room. A three-legged brazier sat in a corner, its smoldering cone of incense filling the air with the faint perfume of sandalwood. Covering the floor, Randy noticed, was a priceless sixteenth-century Ardabil carpet. In its center was a medallion in earth tones, surrounded by a complex, sandy border, the rest covered with a floral pattern.

The carpet's pattern led Randy's eye to the far end of the room. Seated in the middle of an overstuffed, heavily brocaded pillow was a figure shrouded in black. Randy's guide spoke in rapid Arabic to the figure, who appeared to nod. The man left the room, closing the door behind him. Randy stood, waiting. He could feel eyes watching him from behind the shroud.

"You are the American?" the figure asked at last in flawless Russian. The voice was husky, muffled by the thick black cloth.

"*Da*," Randy replied. "Randy Cavanaugh."

The figure rose and stepped toward him. Randy tensed, realizing belatedly than anything from a derringer to an Uzi could be concealed beneath that billowing veil.

The specter stopped just in front of Randy. Suddenly, with a quick, sweeping motion the shroud was removed. As it crumpled into a pool of black on the carpet, Randy Cavanaugh found himself looking at the most beautiful woman he had ever seen.

"I," she said softly, "am Scheherazade."

19

She stood facing him, fists on hips, her head tilted slightly to one side. Thick, blue-black hair curved softly around her face and cascaded over her shoulders. Her small mouth, with lips pursed as she studied Randy, gave way to high, aristocratic cheekbones and startlingly blue eyes. The woman who called herself Scheherazade was dressed in whipcord riding breeches tucked into leather boots. A wide leather belt held her sleeveless linen blouse against her narrow waist, showing off her figure to her advantage.

Suddenly, it all makes sense, Randy realized. *I'd forgotten that the Scheherazade in the Arabian Nights was a woman.* His eyes went to the pile of cloth on the floor. "A chador."

The woman's mouth relaxed slightly. Her eyebrows formed a gentle arc. "So, you are not unacquainted with our ways."

Randy smiled. "Quite familiar, actually. And," he added, gesturing toward her riding outfit, "given a choice, I prefer what you have on."

With a sudden, vicious kick she sent the chador sailing across the room. "So do I," she replied, her conversational tone in stark contrast to the hatred in her eyes. "And that is why you are here."

Scheherazade clapped her hands. The door opened and Randy's guide entered, bearing a tray. He set it in the middle of the carpet, bowed slightly to Scheherazade, and left.

"Sit," she invited Randy. "Sit and eat with me while I explain." Scheherazade sank gracefully, sitting cross-legged beside the tray. Randy followed with somewhat more difficulty.

The tray was laden with mounds of honeyed dates, a rice pilaf tinted with saffron and laced with sultanas and pistachio nutmeats, a bowl of the vegetable stew called *molokiya*, and squares of *basbousa*, an intensely sweet dessert.

Scheherazade scooped some pilaf into a bowl, covered it with *molokiya*, and handed it to Randy. He waited while she served herself, then accepted the silver spoon she handed him. *Antique Georgian sterling*, Randy realized as he hefted the spoon. *And that's the Romanoff crest on the handle.* Randy glanced down at the priceless carpet on which they were eating. *Table manners, chum*, he chided himself, *or you're gonna get the dry-cleaning bill to end all dry-cleaning bills.*

After a few bites Randy waved his spoon toward the crumpled chador. "I take it you're not overly fond of the traditional Islamic woman's garb."

"*Pigs!*" she muttered. "Men! They claim women are inherently immodest, while they swagger around like camels in heat. They require us to remain docilely at home while they go down to the mosque and give the *Khatib* a few dollars to 'marry' them for the afternoon—to a girl no older than their granddaughters. *That,*" she said, pointing imperiously at the chador, "symbolizes perfectly all that is wrong with Iraq!"

Wincing, Randy scratched the back of his neck while he waited to see if the diatribe would continue. *Terrific. I come all the way to Iraq and end up having a clandestine dinner with the president of the Baghdad chapter of NOW.* When it was clear she was finished, Randy looked at her. "I already told you that I prefer your current outfit," he said, his eyes not leaving hers.

"Now, what's your real name? It can't be Scheherazade, since you don't sound like the harem type to me."

At the word "harem" her eyes flashed a deeper blue for an instant. Then she relaxed, and "Scheherazade" suddenly seemed to Randy much smaller and younger than she had a moment before.

"Ataliya," she said. "Ataliya Marakova." She looked at Randy. "You are not surprised at my name?"

Randy shrugged. "Why should I be? All this has about used up my quota of surprise for the evening." His gesture included both her and the room. "Besides," he added with a grin, "it suits your accent." Marakova's glittering smile quickened Randy's pulse. "How is it," he asked, "that you came to learn Russian? It's not, I imagine, part of the average Iraqi schoolgirl's curriculum."

Marakova toyed with her pilaf for a moment before answering. "My father was Russian, a Soviet military liaison. My mother was of royal blood. As a cousin to King Faisal II, she was an Iraqi princess.

"Mother was seventeen when she met my father at an embassy ball." A poignant smile flickered briefly across her heart-shaped face. "She told me many times how handsome and dashing Father looked in his scarlet Cossack dress uniform. They fell in love that night, and King Faisal granted them permission to be wed on Mother's eighteenth birthday. Then King Faisal was assassinated two months after the wedding.

"Mother bore my father two sons. At Mother's insistence Pyotr and Grigor were given Russian names, just as I was when I arrived five years later. We were happy—Father's influence with the Revolutionary Command Council that took Faisal's place grew as Iraq's need for Soviet weaponry grew, and Mother's family was still both wealthy and powerful.

"Then came the war with Iran. Father saw it coming. He also foresaw the outcome. When neither the Revolutionary

Command Council nor the dictator who had just taken power would listen to him, Father took Mother and me to his home in St. Petersburg. Pyotr and Grigor, to whom Iraq was home, stayed to fight the Iranians." A long, desolate look told Randy the fate of Marakova's brothers.

"We stayed in Russia the whole eight years of that horrible war. I grew up there, and I consider Russia my home. I learned my Russian at St. Petersburg State University, where I took a degree in macroeconomics." Randy listened, captivated by her eyes and voice. "I loved it there!" she told him, her radiant exuberance stirring him. "We went to church at the Cathedral of Saint Isaac, and on Saturday nights Father would take us to the opera or to see the Kirov Ballet. I often spent a whole day at the Hermitage Museum."

The joy in Marakova's voice evaporated. "Then, after the war was over, we left St. Petersburg. The Soviet presence in Iraq had diminished during the war with Iran, so Moscow posted my father back to Baghdad with orders to restore their former influence.

"There was nothing to come back to. The beast who now rules this country despised my father for leaving at the start of the war, even though Father had warned him repeatedly. And he detested my mother's royal blood. Mother returned to find her family either dead or destitute, victims of the Revolutionary Command Council.

"Shortly after we returned, Father disappeared." Marakova spread her hands helplessly. "He simply *disappeared*. They told my mother that he had requested to return to Russia. But Father never went anywhere without Mother. They had been inseparable since that night they met at the ball." Her icy tone chilled the room. "We never found out what happened to him, but I know who gave the order to have him killed."

Randy watched as the young woman across from him seemed to wilt. "Mother had to go to work to support us. It wasn't easy for a princess who had never been forced to work before." Marakova's voice became the merest of whispers. "Mother was still beautiful. She never told me what she had to do to get me my job at the Ministry of Economics, but I think I know. The men I work for have asked me for the same thing often enough."

"But," Randy asked, "if men run the show, how have you managed to get your hands on such sensitive information?"

"I see the information because *I* am the only one competent to deal with it!" Marakova snorted contemptuously. "My office is full of men. Some of them sit with their backs to their office walls, staring at the door, terrified of assassination. Others spend the day puffing placidly on their hookahs. Those who actually *do* anything are busy trying to embezzle enough money so they can flee the country." She offered Randy a honeyed date.

"Slowly, over the years, I've assumed certain duties—things no one else could do. When our Russian translator was killed, I took over. And when our economist fled the country, I took over his job, too." Scorn clouded her azure eyes. "Since I won't sleep with them, they put up with me because I do their jobs for them."

Randy's eyes held hers as he took one of the dates. "Why are you spying for us?"

"Do you not yet understand?" He winced at the scintillating force of her glare. "Instead of the homeland I remembered so fondly, I returned to find a country of butchers and lechers who all bow obsequiously to a madman." She toyed with the nap of the carpet, bleakly sweeping it with a polished fingernail. "There is nothing for me here. Instead of *Anna Karenina*, there is the Koran—if women were permitted to read it. Instead of the cathedral choir on Sunday mornings, there are the muezzins braying their calls to prayer at all hours." Marakova im-

paled the chador with a glance. "And instead of cillm and mbls,
there is *that.*"

Randy took a deep breath. "Right." *This woman's got
enough attitude for a regiment of marines*, he thought. "What part
does Hafez Adid play in all this?"

Marakova brushed her hair away from her face with her
fingers. A smile crept to the corners of her mouth. "Haffie and
I met when my office started doing business with his bank," she
explained, suddenly shy.

Randy blinked at the abrupt change of demeanor.
"Haffie?"

"Hafez. After we had worked together a few times, he
asked me out. Since he was so different from the men I worked
with, I accepted. Over coffee I found out that he had been
educated at Cambridge and that as a courier for the government bank he is permitted to travel freely. I also found out that
his father had been a general in the army. The war with Iran
ended in a stalemate, and our illustrious president had General
Adid, a true war hero, executed as a scapegoat. When we found
out that both of our fathers had been murdered by those in
power, we decided I should become 'Scheherazade.'" Marakova
smiled. "He wants to marry me."

"Do you want to marry him?" Randy asked, not sure if he
wanted to hear her answer.

She tilted her head to one side, considering. "Perhaps.
Someday." The sparkle in her eyes became a steely glint. "But
not until we have avenged his father and my parents."

"Your parents? Your mother is dead, too?"

"She died last month. Of sorrow." Marakova's hands collapsed into small, white-knuckled fists. "They broke her body,
then her spirit, then her heart." Resolve emanated from her
small, slender frame. "And now that I've broken the men who
broke her, I want to leave Iraq forever." She gazed intently at
Randy, her indigo eyes probing deeply into his. "With you."

20

"It should have occurred to me that someone using the code name SCHEHERAZADE would be a woman," Elliot French admitted, "but I've been a little distracted recently." Lydia Doral and Randy, sitting in the ambassador's conference room, heard French chuckle over the phone. "It's twins, Lydia. Twin girls."

"Wonderful!" Doral exulted. "Congratulations! Everyone doing fine, I assume?"

"All the women in my life are doing great," French replied. "And," he added with a relieved sigh, "at the moment they're *all* sound asleep."

Doral smiled knowingly. "Names?"

"Juliana Kincaid, after Chris's mother. And, if you don't mind, we've named her sister Lydia Marie. We'd like you be her godmother."

Oblivious to the fact that she was talking to a speakerphone, Lydia Marie Doral bowed gracefully. "Of course I will," she said quietly. "I am honored."

"Back to business," French continued briskly. "Randy, all the documents you'll need to extract Marakova will arrive by special courier before your covert mission ends. We'll get her off an Air France flight and have her met in Paris." French paused. "You should know, Randy, that there was a shootout in Ankara. Gil Markham was taking Hafez Adid to the airport. Gil's fine, but Adid's dead. I think it'd be wisest not to tell Marakova yet, but I thought you needed to know."

Randy nodded, staring out over the Baghdad skyline. "I agree, Boss. She doesn't need to know. Not yet, at least."

Lydia Doral watched the young CIA agent. *For someone who's just received information that makes his mission much more difficult*, she thought, *he almost seems pleased. . . .*

"I don't think you'll get much out of him," Jamie Linehan said as she opened the hospital room door.

Roy Barnard looked at the physician. "Why? You said on the phone that he was conscious."

"He is," Linehan agreed as they went in. "But he doesn't appear to speak any English."

The man's eyes fixed on Barnard, then widened as he saw the sheriff's badge and gun. After a few queries, Barnard gave up. "He speaks English, all right," Barnard countered. "He's been asking enough questions around here this week. But it seems that he's suddenly forgotten how." The sheriff glanced at Linehan. "Any ID on him?"

"None. The labels in his clothes, however, appear to be in Arabic."

Barnard took out his notepad. "I'll get someone in here who speaks that kind of stuff. Anything special about his wound?" the sheriff asked. "Any sign of violence?"

Linehan shook her head. "I know it wasn't shot off, and I know it wasn't torn off. Wound is too clean for that. Might have been chopped off—I cleaned bits of canvas out of the incision."

"So he was wearing shoes? He wasn't when I saw him in the emergency room."

Linehan consulted the man's chart. "Nor was he when he came in. But there's a good chance he was wearing canvas shoes when he was injured." She looked at Barnard. "His toe could've been bitten off—there's a line like teeth marks along the top of his foot. I'd show it to you, but right now it's important the foot be immobilized." The doctor frowned thoughtfully. "But it'd take a lot of pressure to sever the big toe joint. Anything around here that could bite a man's toe off?"

"Sure," Barnard replied. "Lots of critters. Wolverines, badgers, wolves, maybe even a fox. But most of them wouldn't stop at your toe."

Dr. Linehan shuddered. "I'm from California—doing two years back here to pay off my student loans. Where I come from, the only thing that might bite your toe is an overly aggressive panhandler. The bugs back here are bad enough, much less the notion of things that go chomp in the night."

"You're sure he got chomped in the night?" Barnard asked.

Linehan nodded. "Definitely. From the state of the wound when he was admitted, I'd say he was injured about thirty-six hours before he showed up here. Gangrene was starting to set in. That would place the time of injury between midnight and six A.M. two nights ago."

That's the night Lauren was kidnapped and Bill was clobbered, the sheriff realized. *Everybody sure was busy stirring up trouble that night.* "Thanks, Doc," Barnard said. "You've been a lot of help. I'll be back with someone who hopefully will be able to interrogate him." Barnard winked at Jamie Linehan. "Now, you stay out of the woods, hear?"

"No, sir," Mark replied. "I saw no evidence of hostile activity. All indications point to some kind of fire-room explosion." Across the briefing room table a middle-aged, avuncular man winced. A furrowed brow and dark circles framed eyes dulled from sleeplessness.

I wouldn't look my best, either, if I'd just had my ship blown out from under me, Mark thought sympathetically as he looked at Captain Derek Connaught, commander of the sunken frigate *Mayfield.*

Admiral Thomas Pierce, commandant of the 233d Tactical Fighter Wing, spoke up from his seat at the end of the table. "Thank you, Lieutenant Sewell. The information you have provided is most valuable." The admiral looked at his junior officer. "I understand that it was obtained voluntarily and at great personal risk. An entry so noting will be placed in your current fitness report."

"Thank you, but, Admiral . . . "

The old sailor's eyes narrowed at Mark's hesitation. "Yes, mister?" he barked. "What is it?"

Mark stared straight ahead. "Sir, I'd like permission to go back down there."

"Permission denied," the admiral replied curtly. His tone softened. "Mr. Sewell, it's been almost twenty-four hours since Chief Turk disappeared. The SAR teams found no trace of him. Further searching would be pointless."

"I understand that, sir," Mark replied, his iron discipline throttling his pain. "But Chief Turk must've noticed something I missed—something that necessitated his swimming into the *Mayfield*'s interior. If I could just go back down there, I could probably find out what it was."

"Perhaps you could," Pierce agreed, "but our hydrologists report that the current you encountered has increased in strength, making diving excessively risky." The admiral grimaced. "It's going to be hard enough for me to explain to COMSPECNAVWAR how I managed to lose *one* of their best men, much less *two*. When the forensics team arrives here from Newport News, diving conditions permitting, I shall expect you

214

to escort them to the wreck. That is all." The steel returned to the admiral's voice. "Dismissed, Lieutenant."

Resting his chin on his fists, Mark leaned on the teakwood rail. Below him a petrel skittered across the water in search of dinner, its dance seemingly timed to the rap music that boomed from somewhere near the *Alameda's* bow. The setting sun had turned the surface of the sea bloodred again.

Well, Shiloh my friend, Mark thought as he watched the petrel, *you know now, don't you? No more frequent, raucous, and profane denials that God really cares about us and is involved in our lives. You've met him face-to-face, you know him now, and I bet you've finally found a superior officer you'd take that stogie out of your mouth for.* Mark laughed quietly, remembering how Turk was a legend in the fleet for talking to everyone from stokers to admirals with the butt of his cheap cigar dangling from the corner of his mouth.

He looked up. High in the indigo sky, Venus rode on the shoulder of a crescent moon. *There was a seaman's prayer on the wall of our church in Hyannisport, Lord. Something about "for those in peril on the sea." I wish I could remember it. I'd offer it to you on his behalf, if I could.* Mark smiled again. *Shiloh, you'd laugh yourself silly if you knew that I was praying for you. You always did.* The petrel flew off, a flickering silhouette against the moon's arc. Mark watched it disappear into the night. *Now that you know the truth, my friend, I wonder if you're still laughing.*

Another elbow appeared on the railing. Mark looked over to see Gary Faust, *Alameda's* executive officer, watching the flickering lights wink into life in the back of the ubiquitous fishing dhows. Both men were natives of Boston, and both were thirty-two. Faust was a "mustang," an enlisted sailor whose intelligence and drive had propelled him upwards through the ranks. While Mark was a head taller and thirty pounds heavier than the sparrowlike Faust, both shared a complete fearlessness and an innate ability to earn the unconditional trust of the men they commanded. The XO dug a cigarette out of his uniform pocket. He smiled at Mark's disapproving grimace as he lit up.

"Nice goin', middie," Faust remarked affably. The executive officer, who had finished high school via navy correspondence courses, enjoyed teasing Mark, who had been captain of cadets his senior year at Annapolis.

"If it's broken, I'll fix it," Mark replied. "And if we've run aground, I'm off duty."

Faust grinned. "I mean getting an attaboy from old Iron Pants Pierce back there in the debriefing. *Much* harder to do than merely keeping the ship on course. Rumor has it that even Mrs. Pierce salutes him."

Mark looked bleak. "Yeah. Thanks." Ten miles away, headlights moved along the coastal road that ran from Oman to the United Arab Emirates.

"Never lost a man before, have you?"

"Not until now."

Faust rolled up the sleeves of his tan shirt. "I have. Once. Remember Grenada?"

"Sure. We followed the invasion's progress in my Game Theory seminar at the War College."

"Is that so? Well, while you were playing games, I was gettin' shot at." The levity evaporated from Faust's voice. "It was at the end of the op. A signalman and I were taking some commo gear ashore in an LBS. This guy was so excited, I considered cutting the engine, throwing him overboard with a line in his teeth, and having him tow us ashore. Seems he had proposed to his girl that morning, and she had accepted. They carried it live on *Good Morning, America*. Never seen someone so happy.

"No sooner had we hit the beach than there was this tremendous *whump!* and I was flying through the air. When I picked myself up, I found that the signalman was gone, and I don't mean that he ran away. Seems the Grenadians had mined the beach during the night. All that was left of a signalman third-class and a groom-to-be was a fine red mist hanging in the air." Faust shook his head. "In one instant you go from seeing yourself as a great leader of men to thinking you're the Great World-Class Foul-Up." Faust shook his head, suddenly weary. "Now I know what it must be like for a parent to lose a kid." The XO flicked his cigarette butt into the water. "Written the letter yet?" Faust asked, referring to the inevitable task of writing to Turk's next of kin.

"Don't have to," Mark replied. "Under the 'relatives' entry in his fitrep, it said, 'None known.'"

"You're lucky," Faust told him. "Nothing worse than sitting with a pen in one hand and a personnel file in the other, trying to think of words that'll help someone whose world has just turned to dust." He nudged Mark. "There is one letter you'll need to write, though."

"Really? Who to?" Mark asked, surprised.

"The company that makes those stogies of his. They'll probably have to lay off an entire shift." Faust turned toward the hatchway. "I've got the duty," he explained. "See you later."

A *dhow*, sails drooping limply, drifted up below Mark. Beyond it, two bobbing trails of phosphorescence marked the passage of a pair of dolphins. Remembering the trick Turk had taught him, Mark called to the fisherman standing at the *dhow*'s tiller. The fisherman, his kaftan ragged and dirty, and his face shrouded in the depths of a red-and-black kaffiyeh, caught the quarter Mark tossed him. The man scooped a large fish from a bucket on deck and slapped it on the water, then tossed it high into the air. Two dolphins converged on it, and the depths exploded in a watery shower.

"*Shukran,*" Mark called to the man.

"You're welcome, Lieutenant," the fisherman replied.

Mark turned to leave, then stopped. *Wait a minute. It's too dark for him to see my lieutenant's bars. . . .* He leaned over the *Alameda's* railing. "Hey, you down there!"

The fisherman was leaning close to the fire crackling in the *dhow's* stern. As Mark called to him, he whipped the kaffiyeh from his head.

A grinning Shiloh Turk looked up at Mark. "Thanks for the quarter, sir."

Half an hour later, showered and changed, Turk joined Mark, Gary Faust, and Jerry Hall in the captain's cabin.

"Welcome back, Chief," Hall said, his relief evident on his face. "By the way," Hall added, "the smoking lamp is lit."

Turk grinned at Mark and took out a cigar. He bit off the end, put it in his pocket, and lit up.

"You can put that butt in here," Faust offered, holding out a trash can.

"No thanks, sir," Turk replied. He took the cigar end out of his pocket. "You see, when I get about a hundred of these, I roll 'em up like this—" The chief rolled the end into a ball. "Then I sell 'em to Cookie, and the next night we have his famous meatball stew for dinner."

After the groans had subsided, Hall asked, "What took you so long to get back? And why the insistence that you meet with just the three of us, in my cabin?"

The master chief, now all business, leaned forward intently. "You've told them what it was like down there?" he asked Mark. At Mark's nod, Turk went on. "The current on the other side of the *Mayfield* was even stronger than what the lieutenant described," Turk explained. "After I exited the ship the line connecting me to the lieutenant got tangled in some wreckage, forcing me to cut myself free. Once I was loose, I was literally swept away. By the time I surfaced I was well behind the last of our ships."

"But we searched for miles around the dive site," Faust protested.

Turk nodded. "I know, sir. I saw you. But I didn't have any signaling gear."

Mark winced at the omission. *What was that Gary said?* he wondered. *"You go from seeing yourself as a great leader of men to thinking you're the Great World-Class Foul-Up."*

"Anyway," the chief continued, "I came up near a *dhow*. They let me come aboard, but since all I had to offer them was a wet suit and a used-up air tank, they weren't particularly interested in going out of their way to bring me back. So I cut 'em a deal—I helped 'em fish in exchange for a day's rest in their village and a ride back tonight."

Hall nodded. "That explains your being seriously out of uniform. But how did you lose contact with the lieute—"

"Hold it!" Mark exclaimed. "Chief, you just said that the current *on the other side* of the *Mayfield* swept you away. That means you—"

"Swam clean through the *Mayfield*. Yes, sir, so I did." Blue smoke curled overhead as Turk puffed in satisfaction. "And on the side I exited from, the *Mayfield*'s plates were buckled *inward*."

Mark picked up the thread. "That means that something went clear through the *Mayfield*." He looked at Turk. "One of those Silkworms?"

The chief shook his head. "Nothing short of a MiG can get close to a frigate. They've got a Mark 75 three-inch gun mounted amidships. Puts out eighty-five rounds a minute, controlled by an SWG-1 Harpoon weapons-direction system." Turk smiled grimly. "You don't have to aim it much—you just wave it around until you hit your target. No Silkworm could have come close. Besides, the *Stark* took two Exocets in the port side back in '87 and didn't sink."

He ground out his cigar. "Toughest part of my little side

trip wasn't getting back to the surface," Turk confessed. "It was the day and a half in that village with no stogies." He grinned at Jerry Hall. "Put me in for a medal for that, will you, Skip?" Jerry Hall laughed and made a show of jotting down a note.

"Could it have been a mine?" the executive officer asked.

"Maybe," Turk agreed, "but it'd have to have been bigger than any mine *I've* ever seen." The ship's bell chimed, announcing the changing of the watch. "I was stationed aboard the *Samuel B. Roberts*, a frigate identical to the *Mayfield*," the master chief went on, "back in April of '88 when she hit a mine. Later, we figured the mine contained around two hundred fifty pounds of high explosive. Anyway, the blast tore a hole nine feet across in her starboard engine room and ripped a twenty-foot gash in her starboard side. Gear bolted down in the bilges was blown clear through the main deck."

"Sounds like what happened to the *Mayfield*," Faust pointed out.

"Agreed, sir. But with one slight difference—the *Roberts*, like the *Stark*, didn't sink. The *'Field*, however, went down like she was suckerpunched. No mine or antiship missile coulda blown a hole clear through her."

"Only one thing can blast clear through that much steel," Hall observed. "A shaped-charge torpedo."

"Aye aye, sir." Turk agreed quietly. "And that's why I wanted this little talk to be private. Wouldn't do to let the crew know that somewhere out there is a submarine full of people who don't like us very much at all."

As one, all four men looked toward the picture window that formed one wall of the captain's cabin. Beyond it lay only blackness.

✧ ✧ ✧

"Lemonade, Roddy?" the president asked. "Find a chair—Robin will be up in a minute."

General Rodriguez sat down in a nail-studded wing chair

as the president, wearing a polo shirt, jeans, and a worn cardigan, fetched two tumblers of lemonade from a bar set into the wall of his private study on the second floor of the White House.

He's like this leather, Rodriguez thought as he idly stroked the arm of the chair. *Smooth and supple to look at, but you don't know how strong and resilient it's going to be until you put it to the test.* The president handed him a glass, then sat down in a well-used Eames chair. *No time like the present to find out,* Rodriguez decided. The study door opened, and Robin Hawkes came in.

Rodriguez waited until Hawkes had arranged his lanky frame on a side chair. "We've just received information from our task force in the Strait of Hormuz that the frigate *Mayfield* was almost certainly sunk by hostile action."

The president leaned forward, frowning. "What sort of information, General?" Hawkes showed no sign of having heard Rodriguez.

"Two navy SEAL divers inspected the wreck. They found a hole almost four meters across blown clear through the *Mayfield.* No internal explosion could have caused that sort of damage."

"Then what did?" Hawkes asked.

"Based on the SEALs' report, Admiral Pierce's staff has narrowed down the cause of the blast to two possibilities: a torpedo or a suicide mission."

The president's eyes narrowed. "A suicide mission, Roddy?"

"Yes, sir. The Gulf fleet is constantly surrounded by small fishing vessels. Mostly Omani fisherman just trying to make a living—they stay out of our way, and we stay out of theirs. It'd be easy enough for a bunch of Tangoes to commandeer one of the boats, load it with high explosives, sail out next to one of our ships, and push the button."

"'Tangoes'?" Robin Hawkes repeated.

Rodriguez smiled. "Sorry. Tango is the military call sign for the letter *T*, which in turn is short for terrorist. The bad guys."

"So what you're telling me, Roddy," the president replied slowly, "is that we've either got some locals on land who are sending us floating car bombs, or we've got somebody in a submarine who's decided to play Captain Nemo on us." Rodriguez nodded gravely.

Hawkes frowned. "Captain Nemo?"

"Jules Verne," the president replied. *"Twenty Thousand Leagues under the Sea.* Nemo went around blowing up warships in an effort to end war."

"Orders, Mr. President?" Rodriguez asked.

The president smiled humorlessly. "Two radically different threats from two radically different quarters, and I'm the one to give the orders. Makes me wonder why I worked so hard to win those preelection debates last year." Roddy didn't miss the commander in chief's acid look. "You, I assume, have a plan?"

"Yes, sir. Put the 233d Tactical Fighter Wing, as well as our forces in Kuwait, on modified alert. Step up antisubmarine warfare, and order all civilian vessels to stay a thousand yards away from our ships."

The president nodded. "Very well, General. Make it so."

"One more thing, sir," Rodriguez added. *Time to test his leather.* "We need to begin developing options, as well."

The president held Rodriguez's eye. "By *options*, I assume you mean *retaliation?"*

"Yes, sir."

"Very well, General. Let me know what you come up with." The president paused. "And when you figure out what sank the *Mayfield*, do one more thing."

"What's that, sir?"

"Hang a lantern or two in the steeple of the Old North Church."

Rodriguez smiled. "Longfellow, Mr. President?"

"'The Midnight Ride of Paul Revere.' One if by land, two if by sea."

"That's not the line that's got me worried about what might happen if a war starts in the Gulf, Mr. President."

"Oh?

"'Hardly a man is now alive.'"

Brian watched as the deputy Roy Barnard had posted waved the sedan to a halt. After a brief exchange, it moved up the drive toward the house. *Mustn't be more reporters if he's letting them through*, Brian decided. He went out to meet the arrival.

A large man in a gray suit and a crew cut emerged from the rear of the vehicle. He held out a small parcel wrapped in brown paper. "Package for Mr. Joel Dryden."

"I'll sign for it," Brian offered.

The man smiled. "No signature's necessary, Mr. Keefe." He got back into the sedan. Brian took the parcel inside as the car and its mysterious courier drove off.

Brian found Joel in the family room. "This just came for you," he said, handing the package to Joel. "By courier."

Joel removed the paper to find an ordinary videocassette. Stuck to its protective cardboard sleeve was a note:

> **Joel—**
> **The NSA folks out at Fort Meade just pulled this off a COMSAT satellite downlink. I thought you should see it before it hits the nightly news—it concerns what you called me about.**
> **Elliot**

"Who's Elliot?" Brian asked.

"A friend of mine in Washington," Joel replied. He didn't add that French was the director of operations for the CIA. *With Elliot's budget in the shape it's in*, Joel thought, *he'd only spring for a special courier if it was something really important.* Joel tried to keep his sudden surprise and worry from his face. *Which, in Elliot's line of work, means that it's* really *bad news.*

Pat, Anne, and Rebecca came in as Joel hit the VCR's play button.

"Who was at—" Rebecca stopped as the screen came to life with a fuzzy picture of a map of the Middle East and a blare of tinny music. Rebecca frowned. "What on earth? That's the news from Baghdad. We watched it when we were over there. We'd invite some local friends over for dinner, and they'd translate it for us."

On the screen, a sloe-eyed woman looked up from a sheaf of papers. "Our top story tonight," an English voice-over said, "comes to us from the port city of Basra. We go there live." The picture faded to a close-up of an olive-skinned man holding a microphone. Behind him a latticework of brightly lit towers and pipes disappeared into the night sky.

"We are here at the al-Kafhar oil refinery near Basra," the man began, "to report on an act which demonstrates that even within America, there are those who stand in solidarity with us against the oppressive policies of the Great Satan's colonialist overlords." Slowly, the camera began to pull back. "Two Americans sympathetic to our cause," the reporter continued, "have made a voluntary gesture of support for the Iraqi people."

A heavily veiled woman came into view. As the camera zoomed in on what she was holding, Rebecca's hands flew to her face.

"These heroic Americans have volunteered their only child as a human shield here at al-Kafhar, joining with every

224

Iraqi in their defiance of the death-bringing imperialist military."

As the small face in the woman's arms came into focus, Rebecca sank to her knees by the screen. "It can't be," she gasped, her voice a ragged whisper. "It can't be my Lauri."

The reporter smiled. "A personal message of thanks to the American couple from our illustrious president is expected shortly."

Rebecca reached out to the screen. "Oh, God," she sobbed. "Oh, God, they've got my baby." Her fingertips caressed the blurry image of her daughter's face.

Joel pulled a cellular phone from his pocket and began dialing. Pat glanced at her daughter, curled up in the protection of Jake's arms, then watched Rebecca intently.

Brian stood slowly, his eyes never leaving the spot on the now-blank screen where his child's face had appeared. He slipped his hands under his wife's arms, pulling her up against him. Slowly, Brian turned Rebecca around. "Look at me, Becky," he whispered. "Becky, honey . . ."

Rebecca stared at Brian as if she didn't recognize him, her face a taut, thin-stretched mask of pain. Then, suddenly and silently, she collapsed.

21

As Lydia Doral watched from the window, the jeep full of marines pulled up in front of the gates guarding the embassy compound. The MP insignia stencilled on the side of the jeep glowed white in the glare of the arc lamps. Through the closed window, Doral could hear the chanting roar of the swelling mob.

The intercom on the desk in the ambassador's office buzzed. "Line one, Mrs. Doral."

Doral picked up the phone. She waited, accustomed to the protocol that required that she come on the line before the president. A glance out the window showed the marines sitting quietly in their jeep. Fists were thrust through the bars of the gate and shaken at them. It seemed to Doral that the mob's roar had increased in volume.

"Good evening, Mrs. Doral," the familiar voice said. "Any news?"

"Only bad, Mr. President," Doral replied. "The foreign minister went public immediately with our assertion that our warship was sunk by hostile force. Broadcast it on the evening news."

The president swore. "And the reaction?"

"Right now, I'd say there are several hundred Iraqi nationals outside the front gate letting us know in no uncertain terms just how displeased they are with us."

"Is the foreign minister stalling?" the president asked. "Trying to get us to up our ante?"

Doral thought for a minute before answering. "I'd say not, Mr. President. 'Stonewalling' would be closer to it. Never before in my diplomatic career have I met with such unyielding intransigence."

"Are you in any danger?"

"I don't think so. I've seen it before; they're showing their flag and burning ours. They'll get tired soon and go home for the night."

"Take no risks," the president ordered.

Doral laughed quietly. "Don't worry. I can't afford to be taken hostage. My grandson's birthday is coming up, and I still have an entire bed of columbine to plant." The satellite link made the president's chuckle sound hollow. "I'll report again after tomorrow's round of so-called negotiations."

Lydia waited until the line went dead, then hung up. From the doorway she surveyed the office. The furniture was dusty and flyspecked. Doral watched as a large cockroach scuttled across the portrait of the Iraqi president that had been glued to one wall. *And for this I came out of retirement*, she thought morosely as she switched off the lights.

In the Oval Office, the president leaned on his desk. "What's the security situation like over there, General?"

Roddy Rodriguez grimaced. "Not good, sir. We've got a task force steaming northward in the Persian Gulf, but it's still more than a day away from being able to reach them if things get dicey."

"Then there's a chance she and the marines could be taken hostage?"

Rodriguez shrugged. "There's always that chance. But I've known Lydia Doral for years. I was her security chief when she was first posted to Johannesburg." He smiled mirthlessly. "If the Iraqis take her hostage, they're in for the surprise of a lifetime."

✧ ✧ ✧

"Then you have no idea whatsoever, Brian," Elliot French asked, "why anyone would want to kidnap Lauren and take her to Iraq?"

"No, sir," Brian said to the speakerphone in Rebecca's office. "No idea at all."

"Did you make any enemies while you and your wife were over there?"

Brian shook his head. "None that I know of. Becky could charm the socks off a snake, and I mostly just hung around and helped with the digging."

"What's being done to get her back, Elliot?" Joel asked.

"We've filed an official protest through the American Interests Section of the Iraqi embassy in Paris, demanding Lauren's immediate return. Ambassador Wainwright reports that the Iraqi ambassador seemed truly shocked by the news." French paused. "The Iraqi's confusion just might be genuine," he added, "since there's no plausible reason for Iraq to attempt to antagonize us on a level like this. Especially when we've got Lydia Doral's diplomatic mission in country."

Joel's brow furrowed at the mention of his old friend. "Keep us posted, Elliot. And thanks for the tape."

"Least I could do," French replied. "By the way, Brian, I've asked the FBI to post a detail at your home. Once that tape hits the evening news shows, the reporters are going to be thicker than black flies in May."

"That's it?" Brian protested. "All you're going to do is complain to some politician in *France?*"

"That's all we can do right now, Brian," French explained patiently. Brian muttered something uncomplimentary about bureaucrats. "You're right, Brian. I *am* a bureaucrat," the CIA chief went on. "Just ask Joel what I think of the paper pushing and deal making I have to do. But I'm also a father. Have been for just about twenty-seven hours now. Twin girls—and already I can't imagine what I'd do if I lost one of them. So I can imagine how you feel. And I promise you I'll do my level best to get Lauren back."

When French had hung up, Joel turned to Brian, who sat silently, punching his palm with a fist. "You've got the nation's top spy on your side, Brian," Joel chided gently. "That's not a bad start."

❖ ❖ ❖

The last light of evening crept through the beveled window-panes of the tall French doors that opened onto a secluded, master-bedroom deck. Rebecca stirred, and Pat looked up from the magazine she was reading. Anne came in, a glass of juice in each hand. She sat down quietly beside her mother.

Rebecca's eyes fluttered open. When she saw the two women, she turned away, winding the sheet around her tightly clenched fists.

"It's all right, dear," Pat said gently, smoothing the cover-let. "We understand."

"How could you possibly understand?" Rebecca cried. Her voice was an anguished whisper. "Your daughter is right here with you!"

"One of them is," Pat replied quietly.

"What do you mean, 'one of them is'?" Rebecca asked. She raised a tear-mottled face to look at her aunt.

"When Annie was almost three," Pat explained, "I gave birth to her baby sister, Deborah Joan."

"Debby," Anne said.

Pat nodded, her smile distant. "One morning, when Debby was about Lauren's age, she didn't stir at her usual time, so I went in to check on her. She was tucked into the corner of her crib, clutching her blanket, with her round little bottom sticking up. But as soon as I saw her, I knew." Pat watched as a loon, her nestling snuggled between her wings, drifted by on the lake's placid, darkening waters. "We call it SIDS now; back then we called it crib death."

"What did you do?" Rebecca asked.

"I picked her up and took her into my bedroom."

"You didn't call emergency?"

Pat smiled gently. "I am a physician, dear. I'm licensed to certify deaths." Rebecca dropped her eyes as Pat went on. "After a while, Joel came in to see what was taking so long. He found me rocking Debby in our old rocking chair. When he realized what had happened, Joel took Annie next door. Then he came back, picked both of us up, and sat down with us in the rocker. We talked and sang to Debby for a while, and we asked God to make a lap as big as all creation for her to crawl into. Then I held her as Joel drove us to the hospital." Pat toyed with a button on her sweater before continuing. "She's buried in the churchyard near our summer home in Trenton. When I go there, I pick some flowers along the way. Then I sit next to her grave in the shade of the tall, white steeple. I tell her that I love her and that I miss her. And I tell her one more thing."

Rebecca swallowed. "What's that?"

"That I'll see her again someday."

"Brian!"

Jake's shout brought Brian out the back door of his kitchen. Jake was standing next to the road outside Lauren's bedroom window. "What's up?" Brian asked.

"I was taking the trash out," Jake explained, "when I saw

something thrashing around in the weeds here. At first I thought it might be an animal caught in one of your traps."

"One of *my* traps?" Brian replied, frowning.

Jake nodded. "You called Roy Barnard and asked him to set some out before we went up to Big Reed. Remember?"

Brian nodded wearily. "Right. Seems like forever ago."

"What I found," Jake went on, "was a possum worrying at something caught in the trap." Jake parted the grass with the toe of his boot, and Brian's eyes went wide.

Jamie Linehan wrinkled her nose. "Where did you find it?" she asked, looking with distaste at the object lying in the stainless-steel dish on the examining table.

"Friend of Brian Keefe's found it in a trap outside Lauren Keefe's bedroom," Roy Barnard answered. "Can't be Lauren's—it's too big." The sheriff looked at the young doctor. "So, what I want to know is, can you prove this big toe belongs to our silent suspect in that room down the hall?"

"It's pretty far gone," Linehan replied, "but it shouldn't be a problem. There's enough blood and tissue left to do both a blood-typing and a DNA match. We'll need blood and tissue samples from the patient, however. And that means court or-ders and all sorts of stuff."

Barnard smiled. "You just leave that 'all sorts of stuff' up to me."

"And my client understands that he may refuse to answer any question?" the court-appointed attorney asked.

Mahamet Fahrad, an Arabic-speaking FBI agent with a cherubic face and iron eyes, looked up from his bedside chair. "He does. I've informed him of his Miranda rights."

"And you wish to show my client something?"

Fahrad nodded. Barnard stepped up to the bed. Holding

the bowl in front of the patient, the sheriff whipped off the covering cloth.

The attorney gasped at the sight of the decomposed toe. The bedridden man moaned, then covered his face with his hands. Fahrad bombarded him with a torrent of Arabic. Still moaning, the man nodded slowly.

"What did you say?" the attorney demanded.

"I asked him if it was his toe," Fahrad replied. "And I told him where we found it. I also told him that we have permission to take samples of his tissue and blood to prove the toe is his."

The attorney looked at the writhing man. "Is that why he's so upset?"

Fahrad nodded. "Among certain Middle Eastern nomad tribes, if someone obtains a specimen of your hair, teeth, blood, flesh, or bone, they can use sorcery to exert complete control over you. He's terrified and thus completely willing to confess."

"That's coercion!" the attorney protested.

The FBI man shrugged. "I told him the truth." Fahrad smiled mirthlessly. "You're from the ACLU. *You* tell *me* when telling the truth is coercion." He pointed to the small tape recorder sitting on the table. "Get an independent translation if you want." Fahrad barked at the man, who lowered his hands, then looked up as the TV over his bed flickered into life. Barnard and Fahrad studied the man intently as he watched the Iraqi news broadcast.

"Well?" Fahrad demanded in Arabic when the broadcast was over. "Who are those people?"

"I swear, *habibi*, that I don't know!"

"Liar! Keep lying to me, and I will tell the white infidel woman doctor to take your tissue sample with a carving knife! Now, tell me your name and the names of all your accomplices!"

The man blanched. "I swear to you, *habibi*, by the blood of Allah, that I am not lying! My name is Ali Hassad. I came here with my *Pir*, Darius Marduk, and his *cawal*, Ahmal Sayed. We brought along the *cawal*'s wife to care for our *Kalifa*. They are not the people you just showed me—I don't know who those people are."

"Marduk?" Barnard interjected. "Did he say 'Marduk'?"

Fahrad nodded. He glared at Ali Hassad. "Where are your companions?"

Hassad shook his head bleakly. "I don't know that, either. After we got our *Kalifa* back, I stepped in that cursed trap. The car ride was a nightmare from *Sheitan*. I passed out in a hotel room, and when I woke up I dragged myself here." He closed his eyes and resumed moaning.

Fahrad recounted the conversation to the two men.

Barnard looked at the attorney. "Marduk is the name of one of the other suspects, and this character was seen scoping out the Keefe home a few days before the kidnapping. Any questions?"

The public defender shook his head. "And to think I moved here from New York City to get away from this sort of thing."

Fahrad frowned. "He referred to the Keefe girl as 'our *Kalifa*.'"

"That isn't Arabic for 'little girl' or 'baby,' is it?" Barnard asked.

The agent shook his head. "It's a title, but I'm not sure just what it means. I'll ask him why he's using it in reference to the Keefe girl."

In response to Fahrad's question, Ali Hassad curled up, shaking his head vigorously.

"We're not going to get anything else out of him today," Fahrad decided. He stood, turning to Barnard. "I'm staying at the Lakeview Inn, room five, if you need me before tomorrow."

The sheriff flipped open his notebook and jotted the information down. He frowned, then pulled a piece of paper out of the notebook. "Ask him if he knows what this is. It was the last thing my deputy saw the other night just before someone tried to rearrange his brains."

Fahrad held out the paper and spoke sharply to Ali Hassad. Hassad's eyes became glittering slits, then snapped wide open as his head shot forward. The cords stood out in his neck, and he began to scream. *"Melek Taous! Melek Taous! Yezidis! Ahkbar Yezidis!"*

The shrieks cut off suddenly as Ali Hassad collapsed against his pillows.

✧   ✧   ✧

FBI Senior Agent Kyle Watkins smoothed back his hair in frustration. *Why don't the clues ever fit together nice and neat, the way they do in the Sam Spade movies?* he wondered. "OK, people," he said to those assembled in the Keefes' living room. "Let's go over all this again. Maybe this time it'll all hang together, though I'm not betting the ranch on it."

Watkins gestured at the objects arrayed on the living-room table. "First off, the eyewitness reports: According to Sandy Neill, manager of the Lakeview Inn, a suspect named Darius Marduk wouldn't eat anything green and went berserk at the prospect of staying in a blue room. Another suspect, one Ali Hassad, allegedly almost killed a shopkeeper named George Williams for no apparent reason. Someone named Harry Brunson is missing a five-legged calf. And, to top it all off, there's Bill Estes's account of that ceremony he witnessed up on Mount Kineo." Watkins shook his head. "Now for the hard evidence, which, of course, throws considerable light on this case." Joel smiled at the sarcasm evident in the agent's voice.

"The one piece of good news I have," Watkins reported, "is that those burned bones Sheriff Barnard found up on Kineo turned out to be from that missing five-legged calf. Why anyone would want to sacrifice a freak cow is beyond me, but at least we've tracked that one down."

Roy Barnard smiled wryly. "Harry's going to have a stroke when he hears this."

Watkins picked up a report with the FBI seal in the letterhead. "The blood outside the victim's window, thank God, turns out not to be from Lauren. We compared it against the frozen samples taken when you brought her home and got a complete negative. We think the blood comes from a suspect by the name of Ali Hassad, but we're waiting for the pathology lab results before we can be sure. But that still leaves plenty of other pieces to play with." Watkins gestured at a glossy photograph. "Deputy Sheriff Estes has positively identified the dagger found embedded in the headboard as the one he saw used during the Kineo ceremony. The microscopic traces of blood found on the dagger's blade—" Watkins held up a restraining hand as Brian started. "Sorry, Mr. Keefe," he apologized. "The reason you hadn't heard about that is because the blood is not of human origin. We don't know exactly where this blood came from yet, but we're fairly sure it's from that dead calf." Brian sank back in relief.

"And those scratches on Lauren's windowsill turned out not to be scratches at all," Watkins continued. "As Sheriff Barnard noticed, they're the same as what's on that strip of parchment. Our Analytical Division folks have discovered that they both are, in fact, carefully written Arabic."

"Why on earth would there be Arabic on Lauri's bedroom window?" Anne wondered.

"Beats me, Miss Dryden," Watkins confessed. "The translation of the writing on the windowsill reads, 'Herein sleeps our beloved Kalifa.' Watkins grimaced. "Who or what a *Kalifa* is we still don't know."

"By the way," Barnard interjected, "the guy in the hospital used that same term. He got real worked up over it when we asked him about it."

Watkins jotted something in his notebook. "And what's

written on that piece of parchment the dagger pinned down," he went on, "is the same kind of Arabic. Our philological department has managed to translate it, too. Turns out it's a verse from the Koran." Watkins looked at Brian. "You're not Muslims, are you?" Brian shook his head.

"What does the verse say?" Joel asked.

The FBI agent checked his notes. "According to this, the verse is from the Koran ii 256. It says, 'God, there is no god but He, the living, the self-subsistent. Slumber takes Him not, nor sleep. His is what is in the heavens and what is in the earth—' Then there's a section that's blurred and unreadable," Watkins reported, "but the strip finishes with, 'His throne extends over the heavens and the earth, and it tires Him not to guard them both, for He is high and grand.'"

"Sounds like Psalm 121," Pat observed. She looked at Brian. "Has Rebecca ever studied the Koran as a part of her linguistics work?"

Brian stared at Pat. "You think *Becky* put it there?"

Pat smiled reassuringly. "Of course not, Brian. But if Becky's familiar with the Koran, then perhaps I can use that knowledge to get her involved in deciphering this verse. Right now she needs something external—something to focus on outside herself."

Watkins held up a scrap of parchment. "Next, there's the paper Sheriff Barnard found in the boathouse. It's authentic parchment, with stylized drawings on it of a lion, a snake, a hatchet, a man, and something resembling some sort of brush." The FBI agent looked at Brian. "You have no idea when this might have been tacked up in your boathouse?"

"None whatsoever," Brian replied. "I keep that place locked." He snapped his fingers. "But Becky *did* tell me that Bill Estes had found it open during that big thunderstorm we had a while ago. She teased me to no end about leaving my precious boathouse unlocked."

Anne shivered. *So we really did see someone out there.* She stuck her hands into the jacket she had borrowed from Rebecca. Anne frowned, pulled out one of her hands, and opened it. "Here," she told Watkins after examining her discovery, "you may as well add these to your collection." Anne dropped the small clay balls she and Rebecca had found into the agent's outstretched hand.

Watkins stared at the balls. "What on earth are *these?*"

Anne recounted how she and Rebecca had found them set in a notch cut into the giant tree by the lake.

"Any ideas, Brian?" Watkins asked.

Brian took one of the balls and rolled it around in his hand. "None. That's not a custom I've ever heard of, and there's no clay even vaguely like this anywhere around here."

The FBI agent set the balls on the table. "Lastly," Watkins finished with a sigh, "we have the only statement made by the one suspect we have in custody. It is, and I quote, *'Melek Taous! Melek Taous! Yezidis! Ahkbar Yezidis!'*" The FBI man shook his head. "Anyone who can tell me what that means can have my badge."

The room was steeped in thoughtful, depressed silence until Joel sat up. "You might want to reconsider that offer of your badge, Kyle," Joel remarked. "I think I've got just the person."

22

Kyle Watkins strode into the Keefes' kitchen. "Somebody at the checkpoint to see you, Mr. Dryden." He grinned. "Emphasis on the 'body.'"

Joel followed the agent out of the house and down the driveway. "Any ID?" he asked.

The agent shook his head. "Refused to show us any. But since she knew your name, I figured I'd come get you."

A fire-engine red SAAB 9000 Turbo was stopped on the far side of the barrier. The other agent manning the checkpoint stood next to the car, staring intently into the driver's window. As they neared the roadblock, a waterfall of copper-gold hair cascaded out of the window, followed by an oval, animated face.

"Joel!" the woman called, then broke into a glittering smile.

"Let her through, Kyle," Joel instructed. "I know her."

Watkins spoke into his walkie-talkie, and the other FBI man pulled the barrier aside. "Hey, Mr. Dryden," Watkins said enviously, "think if I asked her out she'd smile at me that way?"

Joel looked the tall, muscular FBI agent over. "It's worth a try," he replied, grinning slightly. "How about if I introduce you?"

Watkins grinned. "Would you? Thanks."

The SAAB sprayed gravel as it skidded to a stop just in front of them. The driver's door opened, and Watkins's eyes widened as a pair of long, slender legs unfolded themselves from the SAAB's interior. The legs were followed by a rounded torso and an alert face, all caped in the thick hair that fell well below her narrow waist.

"I came as quick as I could," the driver told Joel, bestowing upon him another of her dazzling smiles.

Joel nodded his thanks, then motioned to the FBI agent. "Kyle Watkins, this is Allison Kirstoff."

Allison's smile disappeared as she surveyed Watkins coolly from behind her sunglasses. She said nothing.

"Sorry about holding you up back there, Miss Kirstoff," Watkins began lamely. "If you had just shown us some ID, we could have let you through."

"Are you an FBI agent?" Allison asked.

Watkins nodded proudly. "Yes, ma'am. Seven years now."

Allison took off her sunglasses. She peered up at the agent, her expression one of impressed innocence. "Really? Wow, a real FBI agent."

The smile she gave him quickened both Watkins's pulse and his confidence. "You live in D.C.?" he asked. "Then maybe," he added in response to Allison's nod, "when this is over we could go out sometime."

Allison's smile warmed. "Could we see FBI Headquarters? I've *always* wanted to see that."

Watkins grinned. "Sure. I'll give you a *personal* tour." He winked. "Just give me your phone number, and I'll call you."

"Great!" Allison beamed. Watkins jotted the number she gave him down in his notebook. "But I sometimes work late," she cautioned, "so only call after midnight, OK?" Watkins nodded enthusiastically.

"Bye!" Allison called over her shoulder as she left with

Joel. "I can't wait to find out what you think of the message on my answering machine!"

Once inside, Joel waited until Allison's mutterings about "cretinous, narcissistic, pinheaded dorks" had subsided.

"About that phone number, Allison . . . ," Joel began.

Allison looked at him, her face the picture of innocence. "He asked for a phone number, and I gave him one."

"But that number happens to be—" Joel folded his arms and waited.

Allison nodded. "The FBI director's private emergency line. The one in his bedroom."

"And you told poor Watkins to call after midnight."

She smiled sweetly. "That self-centered lump of testosterone-soaked muscle deserved it."

Joel returned her level gaze, trying hard not to laugh. "I'm going to have to tell him, you know. He's a good agent."

Allison wrinkled her nose. "Oh, all right. Go ahead and spoil it. But," she added with a laugh, "I *would* like to have known just what he thought of my 'answering machine.'"

Joel brought Allison into the Keefes' living room. From the sofa across the room, where she sat curled beneath a comforter, Rebecca watched Allison's entrance. As she did so, a strand of unwashed hair fell across her face. Rebecca started to brush it aside. Then she stopped, rubbing it between her fingers, noticing as she did so how the light scintillated from Allison's thick, rust-colored mane.

Rebecca's eyes flicked to her husband, watching as Brian rose and crossed the room to shake Allison's hand.

"Thanks for coming all this way to help us, Ms. Kirstoff," Rebecca said after introductions had been made. "Please forgive me for being—" she pushed a strand of hair behind her ear—"unprepared to receive you."

Allison shrugged dismissively. "Call me Ali—everyone

else does. Everyone except Joel, that is," she added with a smile. Allison looked compassionately at Rebecca. "And don't worry about how you look, for heaven's sake, especially considering what you must be going through. Hope I can help—my sister's got a little boy about Lauren's age. Besides, it's a lot . . ." She hesitated and glanced quickly at Joel. "It's a lot prettier up here right now than it is down in D.C."

Brian returned with two nylon flight bags. Allison pointed. "That one can go in my room." She looked at Rebecca. "Is there someplace I could set up my stuff? A window facing northeast would really help."

Rebecca nodded. "My study has a northern exposure."

The oak-plank floor of the rectangular room was dotted with hooked rugs. Cedar wainscoting topped by wall-mounted bookshelves covered three sides of Rebecca's study while through the northern wall's windows Burnt Jacket Mountain loomed large from across an expanse of Moosehead Lake.

Rebecca watched as the young, trim woman surveyed the room. *She notices everything*, Rebecca observed. *She certainly noticed Brian.*

Allison walked across the room. "Wow," she breathed, peering closely at a large stone tablet mounted in brackets on the wall. Engraved on the tablet was a tall figure dressed in ornate, flowing robes. Human but for a pair of long, pointed wings and a crested, hook-beaked eagle's head, the figure was picking fruit from a flowering vine and depositing it in a basket it carried. "Assyrian, isn't it?" Allison asked.

Rebecca nodded. "It's a genius, which isn't, in this context, what you might think," she explained. "It's—"

"The singular form of *genii*," Allison interjected, still staring at the bas-relief, "who didn't really come out of lamps but were the servants of the Assyrian gods." She turned to Rebecca. "Sort of like angels."

"Sort of, but not exactly." Rebecca eyed Allison. "You

242

know quite a bit about Assyrian archaeology." *For someone who looks like she spends most of her time by the pool, almost wearing a bikini.*

Allison shrugged. "Knowing about stuff is my job. When Joel asked the—asked the people I work for to let me come up and help find Lauren, your name rang a bell." She smiled at Rebecca. "You weren't hard to find. The name of Dr. Rebecca Sewell Keefe, B.A., M.A., Ph.D., whose postdoctoral dissertation on her deciphering of the Haradi Document earned her a National Science Foundation Fellowship, is all over the literature. So I decided to do a little reading before I met you."

Allison set her flight bag on the antique banker's desk that dominated the center of Rebecca's study. "This is *gorgeous,*" she exclaimed, running her fingertips over the wood. She looked at Rebecca wistfully and suddenly seemed very young. "Wish I had some nice things like this for my apartment." Her gaze shifted to the computer on Rebecca's desk. "And a Macintosh Quadra 950. Cool." Rebecca watched her, fascinated by her sudden shifts from analyst to young woman to computer nerd. "Is it OK if I work here?" Allison asked. When Rebecca nodded, Allison began to unpack her equipment.

Brian, Jake, and Joel came in.

"They can smell it, you know," Allison said as she continued to unpack.

"Smell what?" Rebecca asked.

"New hardware," Allison replied. "Just like sharks smell blood." Allison ignored Joel's chuckle. "Whenever I break out something new, they start showing up. It never fails." She caught Rebecca's eye. "Works a whole lot better for me than perfume." They watched as Allison assembled the items she had unpacked.

"High-resolution, flat-square, Field Emission Display color screen," Allison explained as she snapped what looked to

Rebecca like an oversized Etch-A-Sketch into a stand that held it at a forty-five degree angle.

"Bet you can't say that again," Brian joked. Rebecca couldn't see the look Allison gave Brian, but she could see the effect it had on her husband.

Allison attached a small box to the base of the stand. "RISC-based hundred-and-fifty megahertz symmetrical multi-processor with 512 meg of memory. PCMCIA IV gigabyte hard drive, PCI bus, and VESA-compliant local-bus hi-res video."

Rebecca saw Jake and Joel nod judiciously. Brian, however, seemed to be staring harder at the young analyst than at the computer she was assembling.

"CD-ROM?" Joel asked.

"You kidding?" Allison replied scornfully. "I'd need a roomful of those things to hold a fraction of the data I process. Nope," she added proudly, "I brought along something *much* better." She reached into her flight bag.

"Looks like a miniature satellite dish," Brian observed as Allison set the last piece of equipment on the desk.

"That's exactly what it is," Allison replied approvingly. "This is the production model of the prototype that Jake trashed in Tibet last year." She laughed teasingly as Jake winced at the memory of losing fifty thousand dollars' worth of government property. "You didn't have to pay for it, did you?" she asked.

Jake shrugged. "I never got a bill. Not yet, at least." He looked pointedly at Joel.

Joel chuckled. "Let's just say that money recovered from a certain senator who was convicted of misappropriation of federal funds was used to pay the bill of a certain taxpayer who was operating at his government's behest."

Allison peered at Joel. "Good trick, a reallocation like that. Just the kind of thing my checking account could use. I'll have to see if I can figure how you pulled it off." Joel smiled at her benignly. Allison gestured at the workstation. "Anyway, this is what I need a north-facing window for. I just point this satellite dish at a—" She glanced at Joel, who shook his head. "Well," Allison backtracked, "let's just say it's a way for E.T. to phone home. This'll get me access to the databases I use to figure things out." The analyst picked up the PC's power cord and looked around. Then she rummaged around in her flight bag's pockets. "Darn! All the outlets are being used, and I must have forgotten the extension cord I usually bring along. You wouldn't happen to have one?" she asked Brian.

"You bet!" Brian replied. "Got a power strip down in the boathouse." Rebecca frowned as she watched her husband stride from the room. A minute later he stuck his head around the door frame. "Pat and Anne request your assistance *tout de suite*," he told Joel and Jake. The three men left together.

Allison pointed to a picture in an ornate silver frame sitting on Rebecca's desk. In it Brian sat cross-legged on a beach, holding an infant in his lap. "Is that Lauren?"

Rebecca picked up the picture and ran her fingers over the glass that separated her from the image of her baby daughter. Tears filled her eyes as she looked at Allison and nodded. Allison followed as Rebecca, still clutching the picture, walked over and sat down on the love seat beneath the picture window.

"I know this is hard," Allison began, "but I need to find out a few things."

Rebecca closed her eyes. "I've been over it time and again with the police. I have no idea who would want to do something like this to us."

"I know," Allison replied. "I've read the state police and FBI reports. They haven't got a clue." Allison's tone of voice caused Rebecca to wonder briefly if Allison meant their lack of evidence or because they were men. "That's why Joel arranged for me to come up," Allison continued. "Part of my job is to take seemingly unrelated pieces of information and fit them together into a coherent whole."

"You must like jigsaw puzzles," Rebecca observed.

Allison grimaced. "Hate them. If I ever get another jigsaw puzzle for Christmas, I'll throw up." She paused. "But at least you asked. One of the guys I used to work with tried to score points by giving me a jigsaw of a picture of *himself*. In a very small swimsuit, no less."

"You can't be serious," Rebecca replied.

Allison shrugged. "Men are creeps. I'm getting used to it."

Rebecca stared at Allison. "Well," she said at last, "it sure sounds like that one was. But they're not *all* creeps. Some of them, like Brian and Jake, do quite well when provided with the proper incentives."

Allison smiled briefly. "Maybe you're right. But I haven't met many guys like Brian, I'll admit."

Rebecca shifted uneasily. On the one hand, Allison was a potential rival for Brian's attention, but she also might be a newfound friend, given the right circumstances. Rebecca wasn't sure which would win out—the rival or the friend.

"Anyway," Allison continued, "it might help if you told me stuff you haven't told the feds." She thought for a moment, then pointed across the room. "That carving on the wall of the genius. Tell me about it?"

Rebecca frowned. "You already know where it came from. What else would you like to know?"

"How did you get it?" Allison asked. "Museum-quality artifacts like that one don't come from Wal-Mart."

"It was a gift," Rebecca replied. "When the Oxford folks I was working with found out that Brian and I were newlyweds, they got the governmental overseer's permission to present us with that carving as a wedding present. It's a representation of the genius who protects the home, and the picking of fruit from the vine and the placing of it in the basket is supposed to ensure an abundance of food." Rebecca spread her hands. "Brian and I certainly don't believe in pagan gods, but we could hardly refuse such a thoughtful gift." Suddenly Rebecca wondered just how good an idea that had been.

"I'll get it!" Jake called in response to the doorbell. Leaving the others in the kitchen, he answered the door. Standing on the front porch was a blonde, wavy-haired man. The navy blazer he was wearing had a logo on the breast pocket. Behind him stood a man enmeshed in video equipment.

"Morning, Mr. Keefe," the man said with a toothy smile. "Biff Richardson, HSN."

Jake frowned. "HS *what?*"

"You know," Richardson said heartily. "HSN—the Headline/Shopping Network. Surely you've heard our motto: First we tell, and then we sell." Jake's disbelieving stare dimmed the smile. "Don't blame me," the anchorman protested. "It was one of those mergers. Anyway," Richardson pressed on, "Mr. Keefe, HSN is prepared to offer you *one thousand dollars* for an exclusive feature on your daughter's kidnapping by the Iraqis. Terrible tragedy, by the way," the newsman added offhandedly. "My sincere condolences. So, how about it?"

"How did you get past the roadblock?" Jake asked.

"What roadblock?"

Jake looked down the driveway. It was, indeed, empty. A glance at his watch told Jake that it was time for the shift change in guards, which usually left the post unoccupied for a few minutes. *Wonder if this weasel hid in the woods all day, waiting for them to leave?* "How did you find out whose child was kidnapped?" Jake demanded to know.

"A journalist *never* reveals his sources," Richardson announced piously.

Jake nodded. "Oh, I see. Well, even though I, too, am a

journalist of sorts," he added conspiratorially, "I'll reveal one thing to you."

Richardson beamed. "Great!" He turned to the man behind him. "Roll it, Fred!" A microphone appeared. "Is there anything you'd like to say, Mr. Keefe," Richardson intoned solemnly, "to your daughter's abductors?"

Jake held up a hand. "First, I'll reveal to you that I'm not Mr. Keefe."

Richardson swore. "Cut it, Fred!" He glared at Jake. "Just who are you, then?"

"A family friend. The Keefes are currently unavailable."

"Oh. Well, forget that offer."

As Richardson turned to go Jake said, "Wait!"

"Yeah?" the anchorman snapped. "We're not interested in you, fella."

"I might be able to get you what you need."

Richardson straightened up. "I'll tell you how much you'll get after I see what you've got. Roll it, Fred!" The mike came up again. "We're talking with—what'd you say your name was?"

"Jake MacIntyre."

"Right. From the top, Fred. We're talking with Jack MacIntyre, a family friend of the Keefes."

"Let me show you the crime scene," Jake offered, pointing the way. "I think you can still see some blood."

An officious Richardson nodded importantly. As he turned, Jake grabbed his elbow in a grip he had learned during his Special Forces training. The newsman froze, his eyeballs protruding slightly. Jake frog-marched Richardson over to the HSN van, followed by the astounded Fred. Throwing open the door with his free hand, Jake shoved the anchorman inside.

"I told you I'd get you what you needed," Jake growled. "And what you need is a lot smaller mouth and a bunch fewer teeth, both of which I'm sorely tempted to give you right now."

Richardson blanched. "But," Jake added, "since I'm sure there's no shortage of guys eager to perform some impromptu dentistry on you, I'll leave it up to one of them." Jake slammed the van door. "However, if you or any other newsman so much as drives by here, I'll provide you with a live, on-air, *very* up-close-and-personal exclusive. You get me?"

Richardson, rubbing his elbow, nodded vigorously. "Let's go, Fred," he croaked.

Jake turned to the cameraman and snapped his fingers. "The tape, Fred." Behind him, Jake could hear Richardson resume swearing. Fred pulled the videocassette out of the camera and tossed it to Jake, who caught it and then jerked his head toward the road. "Now beat it."

Gravel flew as the van tore down the drive. On his way inside, Jake peeled the tape out of the cassette, wadded it up, and threw it in the trash.

"Thanks for helping me fix this," Allison said from her seat behind Rebecca's desk. "I'm back on-line now."

Brian finished tightening the two small screws that connected Allison's monitor cable to her PC. "No problem," he replied. "Those cable connectors can be hard to reach, and I've got long arms." He smiled as he brandished his screwdriver. "I may not know near as much about computers as Becky does, but when you're a bush pilot, you've got to know how to use one of these. Sometimes I think Becky married me just to fix things for her."

"Must be fun, flying around the wilderness like you do," Allison said. *At least out there,* she thought, *if a hairy, ugly, old wolf doesn't stop pestering you and go away when you tell him to, you can shoot him.*

Brian nodded. "It can be, at times. But there are also times when you've got to get a fuel line unclogged before the blizzard the Weather Service didn't tell you about sets in, or you arrive at your pickup spot and find no clients to be seen. Usually that means that they decided to spend an extra day at the really good fishing spot they discovered just upstream. But you don't know that, so you use up all your profits flying search and rescue until they stumble out of the woods."

"Are you worried when that happens?" Allison asked.

"Sure," Brian responded. "Who wouldn't be? But the worry isn't the toughest part of it."

"What is? Finding them?"

Brian shook his head. "Nope. What's toughest on me is refraining from beating the living daylights out of them for being so stupid." He grinned at Allison's delighted laughter. "Any luck?" he asked.

"My search for 'Yezidis' has turned up two matches, so far," Allison replied. "Unfortunately, they're both at the library at Stanford University out in California."

"Why unfortunately?" Brian asked. "From what I hear, Stanford's a top-flight school."

"It is," Allison agreed. "I'd like to teach there someday. But the library's World-Wide-Web homepage is still under construction, so I can't get all the information about 'Yezidis' right away. I know it's from a book by someone named Austen H. Layard, but that's *all* I know at the moment. I sent the folks at Stanford e-mail, and they said they'd have the rest of the reference and the text of the book on the Web tomorrow. We'll see then."

Allison looked up from her screen to see Brian holding the picture of him and Lauren that sat on Rebecca's desk. "Brian?" she said quietly.

Brian tore his eyes away from the picture of his baby daughter. "Sorry, Allison," he apologized. "I tuned out right after you started in with the technospeak." He frowned at her. "Is that what you talk about on dates?"

What I wouldn't give, Allison thought with a sigh, *just once, to go out with somebody willing to talk with me. Not to me, but with me.* "I don't go out much," she replied simply. She looked up at Brian's tired, forlorn face. "You really miss Lauren, don't you?"

"More than I can tell you," he replied quietly. "More than I ever imagined I could." Brian settled down on a corner of Rebecca's desk. "Like most men, I imagined that the only changes in my life after I was married would be that I'd have someone to cook for me, clean up after me, and show up at bedtime for me." Brian chuckled at Allison's disgusted expression. "I can see you already know just how wrong I was. Becky's a strong-willed woman, and she's had teachers like her mom and her Aunt Pat to help her understand when to recognize that her husband was in charge and when to, as they put it, show me the error of my ways." Allison noted Brian's grimace at the painful memory.

"As you can imagine," he went on, "during the first few months of our marriage, my ways had considerably more errors than I was prepared for. At times it was pretty rough, especially since we were stuck together in a nine-by-twelve tent surrounded by desert." Brian's gaze followed a floatplane landing on the lake. "Actually, being stranded like that turned out to be a blessing, since out of sheer boredom if nothing else, we were forced to talk about our problems."

Brian glanced again at the picture of his daughter. "But what really brought it home for me was when I found out I was going to be a father." He laughed. "I was working a jackhammer, breaking up some rubble to be carted away, when I saw Becky running across the site toward me. By the time I finished the cut I was working on, she was standing right next to me, waving her arms. Becky was saying something, but there was no way I could hear her. I shut off the jackhammer just in time to hear the tail end of what she was hollering at me. That meant that, much to our chagrin, a loudly shouted, 'I'm pregnant!' was heard all over the dig."

Brian's chuckle faded. "But it wasn't until that night, with Becky snuggled up next to me, that it truly became real. I started thinking about what it means, from God's perspective, to become 'one flesh' and how God chose to have the expression of that union be the means by which he performs his most wondrous act of creation." He smiled sadly at his daughter's picture. "I feel like Lauri's a piece of me. A piece that's missing. I don't feel complete without her." Brian swallowed and looked away.

Allison sat quietly. *My operating mode,* she realized, *since I was old enough to need to need one, has always been that those men who weren't wolves were pigs and that I've always wished they'd feed on each other instead of trying to feed on me. But, there's something different about Joel, Jake, and now Brian.* Allison shrugged to herself. *Face it, girl, there just might be "more things under heaven and earth than are dreamt of in your philosophy."*

She got up and rested her hand on Brian's broad shoulders. "Don't worry," she said, filled with a compassion she never thought she'd have for a man. "We're smarter than they are, whoever *they* are. We'll have Lauren back in no time." Brian looked at her and smiled.

Rebecca walked out of Lauren's room. She had been sitting in the rocking chair where she had nursed her baby. The voices drifting from her study caused her to stop in the doorway. Rebecca watched for a moment, then silently turned away.

23

"Good luck, Cavanaugh," Charlie Davenport said as Randy came into the embassy communications room.

"Should be a piece of cake, Sarge," Randy replied. "Sent word to her yesterday through the waiter at the café, so she'd better be packed and ready to go. I'll be back here with Ataliya just about the time her papers arrive in the diplomatic pouch. We put the finishing touches on them, take her to the airport, and ship Scheherazade stateside."

Davenport smiled at the alliteration. "Sounds OK." He pulled something from a desk drawer. "But just in case that piece of cake's a little stale, take this." He tossed a small, black object to Randy.

The CIA agent caught the device and examined it. "What is it?" Randy asked. "Looks like a cross between a cellular phone and a hand warmer."

"SATCOM unit," Davenport replied. "New model. Made by Motorola. With it you can bounce a signal off of one of the MILSTAR geostationary communications satellites. Talk to anywhere from here to Timbuktu."

"I've used them before," Randy replied, "though not quite

like this one." He stuck the device, the size of a deck of cards, into a back pocket. "Might come in handy at that," Randy admitted. "Never know when you might get a craving for pizza." Randy waved jauntily. "Later, Sarge."

✧ ✧ ✧

The sergeant's radio crackled. Charlie Davenport unclipped the radio from his belt. He pressed the transmit switch. "Davenport."

"Harris, Sarge," the marine on guard at the front gate replied. "It's getting pretty tense out here."

"Any trouble?" Davenport asked.

"Not yet," the young sentry replied. "But I've got a couple dozen guys outside the gate here, and I'll bet you a nickel every one of them is bad-mouthing my mother."

"Need reinforcements?"

"Nah. They're mostly just waving and shouting."

Davenport went to the office window. He could see Harris and another marine sitting in the jeep. Muted Arabic curses reached his ears. The sergeant frowned. *This is beginning to smell real bad*, he thought. He keyed the radio again. "Harris, lock and load. And make sure they see what you're doing."

Davenport watched as the two marines stood and ostentatiously ratcheted rounds into the chambers of their M16s. The crowd backed away a step, but it seemed to Davenport that the fervor of their cursing increased. "Hang tight, Harris," Davenport advised. "Keep in touch."

"Roger, Sarge. Wilco."

Davenport started to turn away from the window, then stopped. *Hold it. DeLong should have reported in first this watch.* The order in which the sentries were to check in was changed every six hours.

Davenport glanced at a roster on his desk, then at his wristwatch. His frown deepened. "DeLong, report," the sergeant said into his radio. He waited, then repeated the order.

Silence. He rushed out the door of the communications room. "Harris, can you see DeLong and Foster?" Davenport asked as he trotted toward his jeep.

"Not through the underbrush," Harris replied. "We'll go check if you want, but we've kinda got our hands full here."

Davenport cursed the unkempt foliage as he approached his jeep. "Stay put, Harris," he ordered. As he started the jeep he suddenly remembered that the gap in the compound wall that DeLong and Foster were guarding was the closest approach to the stairs leading to the ambassador's private entrance. Tires smoked as Davenport floored the accelerator and aimed the jeep toward the outpost.

In Scheherazade's *salamlik*, Ataliya Marakova stood before Randy once again. A black leather Eisenhower jacket had been added to her outfit, and a chador dangled limply from one hand.

Randy glanced at the small valise on the floor beside her. "Where's the rest of your luggage?" he asked.

"That is all of it," Marakova replied curtly. "Aside from a few family mementos, I wish to leave everything behind."

"Always have liked a girl who traveled light," Randy said admiringly. "It's so much easier that way to duck out the back door when someone's trying to kick down the front."

"Besides," Marakova went on, apparently ignoring him. "The terms Hafez dictated will secure me a most comfortable life in America." Eyes gold-flecked like polished lapis lazuli gazed at him. "Will Hafez be waiting for me?"

Randy swallowed, grimaced, and scratched the back of his neck. *Baaad timing, lady.* "Not exactly," he prevaricated. "You see, there's been a minor complication. . . ."

"Hafez is dead, isn't he?"

The directness of the question, and the coolness with which it was asked, caught Randy off guard. He studied her for a long time before nodding.

"In Ankara?"

"Yes," Randy replied. "They were ambushed on their way to the airport."

"I'm not surprised," she said. Her gaze went beyond him. "I told Haffie repeatedly that he was being too brazen in Turkey, that he was taking too many chances. But he loved the intrigue and the secrecy. Hafez loved playing the spy, and he knows now what my father taught me long ago: It's not a game at all." Her slight smile was unreadable. "Poor Haffie. Now he, too, shall have to be one of the things I leave behind." Marakova disappeared beneath the *chadoor*. "We go." She picked up her valise and marched toward the door without looking back.

Man, Randy thought as he followed her. *I sure wouldn't want to get "Dear Johnned" by this lady.*

Davenport stopped the jeep beside the gap in the wall. In a jeep next to his, one marine lay sprawled. Blood dripped from the face of a second marine, who was working feverishly on the injured man.

Davenport strode over. He examined the motionless sentry, then put his hand on the man's shoulder.

"Forget it, DeLong. Foster's had it."

"But, Sarge—"

"Forget it, I said," Davenport ordered, a snap in his voice. "Now, report."

DeLong wiped his face with the back of his hand, turning his forehead into a scarlet smear. "Six of 'em came over the wall, firing. Out of nowhere. They each had a Kalashnikov with a hush puppy on it. By the time we could even get our weapons up, Jack was hit, and I musta caught a ricochet. When I came to, they were gone. They took our weapons, smashed the radio, and shot out the tires." DeLong wiped the blood from his eyes. "These weren't your ordinary amateur-night yahoos, Sarge. These guys know what they're doing."

Davenport spoke into his jeep's radio. "Security alert—perimeter breach. All personnel to the ambassador's quarters. Weapons loaded—safeties off." A buzzer began sounding inside the embassy.

The sergeant tore a strip of bandage from a roll DeLong had been using. "Patch yourself up with this," he ordered. "You OK?"

"Fine, Sarge. It's just a scratch."

Which may just cost you an eye, Davenport thought grimly. He slid into the driver's seat of his jeep. "Get in," he ordered. "We're going where the action is."

"We're comin' up the stairs now," Davenport said into his portable radio. "So all you jarheads just hold your fire."

The two marines entered the hallway on the top floor of the embassy that led to the ambassador's private residence. As Davenport had expected, a knot of marines was clustered around the open door that led to Lydia Doral's apartment. "Report!" Davenport ordered as he trotted up, DeLong close behind.

Lance Corporal Jeremy Witt, his M16 at the ready, shrugged. "See for yourself, Sarge." The marines parted, and Charlie Davenport walked into the room.

Lydia Doral sat calmly on her living-room couch, two men on either side of her. A man wearing a bulky vest sat in a chair, with another man standing beside him.

"You all right, ma'am?" Davenport asked.

"Just fine, Sergeant," Doral replied.

Davenport nodded. *Her calling me "sergeant" means that this is a formal occasion.* His practiced eyes swept the room. The six men watched him, alert but not eager, their weapons trained on him. Each man's head was swathed in a *kaffiyeh* patterned in a distinctive red and blue. All Davenport could see were eleven glittering eyes.

The standing man spoke, his voice muffled by the *kaffiyeh*. "You are the head of security?"

Davenport nodded. "I am. And who are you? You are trespassing illegally on the sovereign territory of the United States of America." *Since Mrs. Doral's not an ambassador this time, that's not exactly true, but let's see if ol' raghead here knows that. . . .*

"Since this is not an ambassadorial mission, what you say is a lie," the terrorist commander replied. "Indeed, it is the Great Satan who trespasses illegally upon the sovereign soil of Iraq."

"Save the lecture for your fellow garden-club members, buddy," Davenport barked. "What do you want?"

"Since Mrs. Doral has an active role in the carrying out of your government's policies, it has been decided that she shall be transported to a location where she will be even more deeply affected by those policies." The commander gestured, and all the other terrorists stood. Two of them brought Doral to her feet. "Now," the commander explained, "we leave."

Davenport didn't move. "I think you just might have a little trouble doing that." From behind him came the sound of rounds being chambered into twelve M16s.

"We shall have no trouble whatsoever," the commander replied. Despite the *kaffiyeh*, Davenport could tell he was smiling. The commander barked in Arabic, and the man in the bulky vest raised his hand. In it was a switch, which the man pressed.

"The vest contains twelve kilos of Semtex," the commander explained. Davenport's jaw clenched; he recognized the readily available, lethal Czechoslovakian plastic explosive. "If he now lets go of the switch for any reason, it explodes. And so ends the life of the diplomat you're sworn to protect."

Davenport shook his head. "No way. You're not leaving here."

The commander spoke again in Arabic. The man raised

his hand. As his fist came up Davenport could see the plunger in the switch begin to rise.

"Stop!" Davenport shouted.

The commander nodded. The man lowered his hand.

Davenport looked at his old friend. "Ma'am?"

"I'll be all right, Sergeant. You have a job to do, too." Davenport thought of all the times they had worked together and laughed together. *I wonder if I'll ever have the guts to tell her she's braver than I am.*

"Yes, ma'am. I do." He finished the message with his eyes, then turned to his men. "Let them through."

From the apartment window Charlie Davenport watched, shaking with anger, as the van carrying Lydia Doral vanished through the embassy gates.

✧ ✧ ✧

"It would be best if we travel to the embassy separately," Marakova whispered as she and Randy emerged from the alleyway that led to her home.

"Why?" Randy asked, careful not to look at her as he spoke. "I'd hate to lose you now," he added, wondering as he did so just what he meant by that.

"The insecure pigs who surround us would go insane with rage if they saw me with a foreign man," Marakova explained. "So I will meet you at the embassy's front gate. What will happen to me then?" she asked, sounding much younger.

Randy grinned. "Scheherazade, in traditional Iraqi women's dress, will be escorted into the embassy. A few hours later Ataliya Marakova, dressed in the latest in Western fashion, will leave the embassy in an official car."

"What *Western fashion?*" Marakova interrupted.

"When I told Mrs. Doral that you and she were about the same size, she offered you free run of her wardrobe. Then," Randy went on, "using our diplomatic passports, you and I will—"

259

"*Used* clothes?"

Randy snorted in exasperation. "Look, honey, take it up with Mrs. Doral, OK? I'm just the footman in this little operation." *Ah, for the good old Cold War days when the only people I had to deal with were big, ugly guys in bad suits who were merely trying to kill me.*

"Do I get to choose my footman?" Marakova snapped.

"No. Now flag down this cab and take it to the embassy. I'll be right behind you."

With seeming disinterest Randy strolled away. When the cab containing Marakova had pulled away, Randy quickly hailed a cab of his own and sped after her.

"Now what, Sarge?" Greg DeLong asked.

Davenport turned away from the window. "Now we get on the horn to the States and let them know what just happened. And they are going to throw an absolute fit when they find out." The sergeant led his men downstairs. "DeLong, Carter," Davenport ordered, "take my jeep and patrol the perimeter. If you hear anything louder than a camel's sneeze, report in." Davenport went into the communications room. He flipped the send switch on the SATCOM transmitter. "Magic Lamp, Magic Lamp, this is Aladdin. Over."

Five minutes later Davenport had finished reporting. *It's gonna be a long night for the powers that be,* he thought. *Meanwhile, we've got our own behinds to watch out for.*

His walkie-talkie came to life. "Sarge!" DeLong shouted. "Major breakthrough at the main gate. Hundreds of 'em, some armed. They're headed for your position."

"Fall back and join up with us," Davenport ordered. "Move!" He hit the SATCOM's send switch. "Magic Lamp, Aladdin. We are under attack. Repeat, we are under attack. Request emergency evac." Davenport waited, swearing impatiently, then nodded at the response. "Roger that," he replied.

"We'll be ready." Davenport threw down the microphone and ran from the room.

DeLong and Carter burst through the front doors just as Davenport arrived. "Everybody upstairs," the sergeant ordered. "We've got a little time to kill." At the top of the stairs Davenport looked at two of his men. "Witt, you and Sanchez stay here. Nobody, and I mean *nobody*, comes up these stairs. If you need help, just holler."

"You got it, Sarge," the corporal agreed. "We know how you hate to have your beauty sleep disturbed."

Grinning, Davenport turned to the rest of his squad. "Everybody take a window. Stay low, and don't shoot first. But if they open fire, let 'em have it." He checked his watch. "We've got another fifty-seven minutes before the cavalry arrives, so just hang loose."

The beeping of his portable SATCOM unit interrupted Davenport's uneasy pacing. He pulled the small transceiver from his pocket. "Magic Lamp, this is Aladdin," he answered. Davenport stopped. "Oh, it's you, Cavanaugh. Forgot I gave you one of these things. Where are you?"

"Scheherazade and I are right across the street from the main entrance. What'd you do, Sarge? Hang up a banner announcing Today Only—Free Visas?"

Davenport recounted Doral's kidnapping to Randy. "So we've been in this Arab version of a Mexican standoff for fifty minutes now," the sergeant finished. "Lots of milling around and shouting, but no shots fired. So far. We expect evac in five or ten minutes. You see any way you can join up with us?"

"Negative on that, Sarge," Cavanaugh replied. "There's too many of them, and more are arriving all the time. Hold on—hear that?"

"Sure do. Almost as loud as my kid's stereo. What is it?"

"It's a sound truck," Randy told him. "Just pulled up

outside the front gate. It's getting them worked up into a real lather. Hang on a sec—"

Davenport peered cautiously out a front window. With each wave of sound, the mob was swept into a greater frenzy.

"No wonder they're getting all heated up," Cavanaugh continued. "Scheherazade says the truck is announcing that the 'Great Satan' has just begun a massive invasion of Iraq."

"They must've detected the choppers coming to get us," Davenport replied.

"They're also ordering the immediate deaths of the infidels holed up inside the imperialist stronghold. I think," Randy added, "that means you."

From somewhere in the mob a shot rang out, followed instantly by a barrage of gunfire from the embassy windows. "No kiddin' that means us," Davenport replied. "Fall back! Everyone onto the roof!"

"The mob is storming the building!" Cavanaugh's voice crackled. "I can see the gates starting to give way!"

"Roger! Going up!" Davenport yelled into the transceiver. "Check with you later—I hope."

He waved his men up the stairs that led to the embassy roof. "DeLong! Sanchez!" he ordered. "Lob a grenade at the first face you see at the bottom of the stairs, then join up with us." He glanced at his watch. "The last bus should be here in four minutes, so don't be late."

Once on the roof, Davenport switched frequencies on his SATCOM transceiver. "Flying Carpet, this is Aladdin. Do you read? Over."

The pilot of the lead UH-60 Blackhawk helicopter responded. "Read you five-by-five, Aladdin. Our ETA is three minutes. Have your men split into two groups, one at each end of the building. We'll be fast-roping you out."

"You do the ropes, and we'll have no problem with the *fast*," Davenport answered.

A tremendous explosion shook the building, knocking Davenport down. Witt and Sanchez came pelting through the rooftop door, followed by a cloud of dust.

"Witt!" Davenport yelled as he scrambled to his feet. "One minute! Get your men to the far end of the roof. We're fast-roping, so get rid of your junk." As the corporal gathered his men, Davenport and his squad trotted to the roof's other end. Helmets and ammunition belts were tossed into piles.

"There they are!" someone shouted.

Davenport could see two dark shapes screaming toward them from the southwest. He thumbed his transceiver. "We're outta here, Cavanaugh! Good luck!"

The Blackhawks flashed into place overhead. Three thick ropes uncoiled downward from each helicopter's cargo door. Davenport pointed upward with a shouted *"Go!"* Two men swarmed up each of the six ropes.

Shots rang out. Davenport whirled. Armed men were boiling through the rooftop door. The sergeant laid down a covering fire, watching his platoon. When the last man had disappeared into the far chopper, Davenport whirled his arm in a circle, signaling the pilots to leave. Still firing, he grabbed a rope with one arm as it snaked away, and the chopper jerked him upward and off the roof.

"Grab the rope!" Greg DeLong shouted to the other marines inside the Blackhawk. "Heave!" Other marines joined him, pulling on the rope. Davenport dropped his now-empty rifle and climbed upward.

From above, Greg DeLong saw Davenport jerk suddenly. He saw a dark red stain appear between the sergeant's shoulders.

"He's hit!" DeLong screamed. "Somebody belay me!" Hands tightened around DeLong's web belt.

DeLong leaned out of the speeding Blackhawk. He could

feel the rope sliding upward beneath him. Charlie Davenport had stopped climbing. DeLong reached down. "Grab my hand, Sarge!"

Davenport clung to the rope. He shook his head.

DeLong stretched, buffeted by the wind. "Hang on, Sarge!" The rope inched along beneath his belly. DeLong's straining fingertips touched Davenport's knuckles. Davenport started to open his hand, reaching upward.

Then, suddenly, the empty rope trailed limply in the Blackhawk's slipstream.

✧   ✧   ✧

Watching from a doorway across the street, Randy Cavanaugh closed his eyes and turned away.

"Did you know him?" Marakova asked Randy quietly, watching him.

"Not well enough," Randy replied. A window in the embassy burst outward, followed by a gout of flame. A knot of people rushed past them, toward the compound, shouting and waving their fists. Randy turned up the collar of his jacket and pulled down the brim of his hat. "It'd be a real good idea to be someplace other than here," he observed. "Got any ideas?"

"I have a cousin who owns a butcher shop not far from here," Marakova told him. "We will be safe there for a while. Follow me."

Moments later Randy said, "If I'd known the stench was going to be this thick, I'd have brought my machete."

An unfrosted bulb glared down on a stained wooden table. "Give him fifty dinar," Marakova ordered. "He's not that close of a cousin." Randy fished a bill out of a pocket. He handed it to the butcher. Bill and man both disappeared.

"Hope he puts that in his Get Some Refrigeration in Here Pronto fund."

Ataliya Marakova's lithe form appeared from beneath the chador. "How much money do you have left?" she asked.

Randy threw the rest of his wad of bills onto the table. Marakova added the money she took out of a jacket pocket. She counted it, then frowned and shook her head. "It is not enough."

"Not enough for what?" Randy wondered. "Not a pound of this guy's hamburger, I hope."

"If we had twice this much," Marakova explained, "we could buy our way across the border. You would be yet another rich American businessman taking yet another young Iraqi girl off to be his mistress. The guard would leer lustfully at me, wink crudely at you, take the money, and wave us through." Her expression told Randy exactly what Marakova thought of that particular form of commerce. "As it is, we only have enough for one."

With a sudden, radiant smile she brought her eyes up to his. "But you have your diplomatic passport, no?" she asked happily. "You can use it to leave, and I can buy my way through with this."

"Just one small problem with that," Randy replied grimly. Marakova's eyebrows raised in question. "My diplomatic passport, along with the papers we had prepared for you, is going up in flames right now as the embassy burns down around it."

Frost rimmed Marakova's smile. "You mean you don't have it with you?"

"Nope. On a short, completely unofficial trip like picking you up, something identifying me as an American diplomat would be a definite liability if I got caught."

Silence, broken only by the unceasing drone of flies, settled over them. Marakova stared at the tabletop, then laughed quietly. "How appropriate is the name I picked for myself," she told Randy. "One of the one thousand and one tales my namesake, the legendary queen of Samarkand, told her husband, King Schariar, was about a young man who discovers a wonderful flying carpet. In the story, he uses it to escape from danger and imprisonment." The blue in Marakova's eyes deepened. "I am in the prison, I am surrounded by the danger, and I have the young man. All I lack is the carpet on which to fly away."

Randy frowned. "Fly away . . . ," he murmured as he rubbed his chin. "A flying carpet . . ."

The sudden crash of Randy's fist against the tabletop caused Marakova to jump. She looked up to find Randy grinning jubilantly. "*Yes!*" he shouted. "That's it!" He leaped to his feet. "C'mon! Let's go!"

Blinking in confusion, Marakova came to her feet. Randy came around the table. "Scheherazade, you're as clever as your namesake."

"But what did I do?"

"You merely caused me to come up with *the* way to get us out of here." He smiled down at her. "You know, for an inspiration as brilliant as that, I've half a mind to kiss you."

Ataliya Marakova lifted her face to his and closed her eyes.

24

Commander Ed Nila of the Defense Intelligence Agency stared at Joshua Litchfield. "How can you deny what's right in front of your eyes?" he demanded, gesturing sharply at the sheaf of documents scattered across the desk of the deputy director of science and technology. "I dragged it all the way up here to tell you that one of your analysts is right after all, so why are you telling me that she's *still* wrong?"

Litchfield leaned back in his chair. "Tell me again how you arrived at this conclusion," he asked, gazing at Nila over steepled fingertips.

The naval officer took a deep breath. "Once more from the top, then, and this time I hope it takes." He reached for a folder. "Just after I got back from our little meeting up here, I saw a DIA report about the sinking of the *Mayfield*. It says that the forensics team that examined the wreck confirmed absolutely what those two SEALs had said. Namely, that the *Mayfield* was sunk by a torpedo. Where there are torpedoes, there are usually submarines. Since I had just helped prove that there *wasn't* a submarine where one obviously had to be, I got out the tapes of that satellite pass your analyst and I worked on."

Nila opened another folder. "This time, I did what she suggested. I ran it through a 150-nanometer filter and, bingo, one submarine." He pointed at a radar image. "The Iraqis are clever—they were using the flare from the gas burnoff at the al-Kafhar oil refinery to mask the heat from the sub's boilers. But, just as your analyst suspected, the filter erased the burnoff and left the sub sitting there plain as day." Nila tossed the folder to Litchfield. "The data's all there if you want to review it."

Litchfield shook his head. "No need to, Commander. Your analysis is quite remarkable. I'll see to it that a commendation is placed in your file."

Nila stood. "It isn't *my* analysis, Litchfield. It's that hot-shot analyst of yours. *She's* the one who deserves the commendation, not me." He started to go, then turned. "Is she around? I'd like to talk with her. That 150-nanometer idea was inspired."

"She's been reassigned."

Nila shook his head. "Too bad. Well, tell her for me that if she ever wants to enlist, I have a great job waiting for her."

When Nila had left, Litchfield picked up the phone. "The president, please," he intoned. "This is the DDST. Tell him I have urgent new information."

"Excuse me?"

Kyle Watkins looked up from the paperwork strewn across a vacant desk in the Piscataquis County Sheriff's Office. The woman addressing him was tall and thin, her gray-blonde hair swept in a tight bun. Lines of worried exhaustion creased the corners of her eyes.

"Are you in charge of finding Lauren Keefe?"

The FBI agent shrugged. "I hope that's the way it turns out. And you are?"

"Doris Rodgers."

Watkins nodded. "You baby-sat the Keefe girl the night

she was taken." He looked at Doris closely. "Before you tell me anything, take a moment to decide if you want to tell it to an attorney first."

Doris frowned. "Whatever would I need a lawyer for?" She sat down. "I just found out from my friend Sandy Neill that you want to talk to Darius Marduk. Well, I'm afraid you can't."

"And why not?" Watkins inquired.

"Because he's gone home," Doris replied. "You know, back to Egypt."

Watkins looked confused. "Egypt? Why do you think he's gone to Egypt?"

Doris stared at him. "Because that where's he's from. He told me all about Egypt."

"How well do you know Mr. Marduk?"

"We're . . . friends," Doris replied, not meeting the agent's eyes.

"And you know for certain he's left the country?"

"Sure do. Took him to the airport in Boston myself."

Watkins's tone sharpened. "When was this?"

Doris swallowed, unnerved by the sudden change in Watkins's questioning. "The morning after I sat Lauri. Why? Surely you don't think that Darius—"

The FBI man held up a hand. Watkins took several grainy, black-and-white photos from a folder and set them before Doris. "Are any of these Darius Marduk?"

"That one is," Doris answered immediately, pointing to the middle photo. "Of course, he doesn't have a mustache in that picture, and he's a little heavier now, but I'd recognize him—"

Watkins cut her off again. "That is a photo of one Suliman al-Hassim, a well-known religious terrorist operating out of northern Iraq. He's our prime suspect in the kidnapping of Lauren Keefe."

Doris blinked rapidly. "What are you telling me?" she

asked sharply. "That's a picture of Darius, not some Sillyman whatever-his-name-is. And he's from Egypt, not Iraq." A mixture of uncertainty and betrayal crept across Doris's face. Tears began to course down her cheeks.

Watkins got a tape recorder and a box of tissues from a desk drawer. "Miss Rodgers, you need to tell me all about your relationship with al-Hassim. Right now."

❖ ❖ ❖

"And so it was only *after* I got back from Boston that I found out about Lauren," Doris finished.

"And they left in a private jet?"

"That's right, D-Darius and some friends of his and their little baby—" Suddenly horrified, Doris gaped across the desk at Kyle Watkins. "Surely you don't think that little baby that woman was carrying was Lauri?"

Watkins nodded. "Yes, ma'am. That's exactly what I think."

Racked with sobs, Doris looked away. "Please, may I go now?"

"I'm afraid not."

"*What?*" Doris gasped, her voice a tattered whisper.

"By your own admission, you aided and abetted Suliman al-Hassim and his companions in their illegal abduction of Lauren Keefe, a violation of the Lindbergh Act." Kyle Watkins suddenly seemed very large as he rose to loom over her. "Doris Rodgers, you are under arrest."

❖ ❖ ❖

I don't like it when he paces, Robin Hawkes thought as he watched the president from his chair in the Situation Room. *He comes up with the rashest notions when he paces.*

"General," the president addressed the chairman of the Joint Chiefs, "how long would it take to mount an attack on Iraq?"

"What kind of attack did you have in mind, Mr. Presi-

dent?" Roddy Rodriguez asked. "Preparations for a full, land-
and air-based assault would take several months, at least."

"I was thinking more of the so-called surgical strike," the
president replied. "Take out the sub that sunk the *Mayfield*. It's
hidden by some oil field, isn't it?" When Rodriguez nodded, the
president went on. "Wouldn't hurt to take out the oil refinery,
too, while we're at it."

The general didn't hesitate. "We have the assets already in
place, Mr. President. The 233d Tactical Fighter Wing. F-14
Tomcats from the carrier *Paul Revere* have the range and fire-
power to make the strike on Basra."

"The *Mayfield* was part of that wing, wasn't it?"

"Yes, sir."

"Then we'll let them avenge their own. Get it started,
General."

"Very well, Mr. President." Rodriguez picked up a phone.

Elliot French took a deep breath. "Mr. President, there's
something I think you should know."

"Yes, Elliot?"

"We have unconfirmed reports that the infant child of an
American couple is being held at Basra."

"You mean that Iraqi TV clip that was plastered all over
the network news the other night?"

"That's the one." The CIA director of operations looked
at his boss. "It might be wise to verify the report before ordering the air strike."

"Elliot has a point, sir," Robin Hawkes added. "We'll catch
a lot of flak unless we can plausibly deny the Iraqi's claim."

"Can we verify this in a reasonable time frame, Elliot?" the
president asked.

"We can. Randy Cavanaugh, the agent in Baghdad with
Ambassador Doral, could be redeployed to Basra to check it
out."

"Could he pull off a stunt like that?" the president asked skeptically.

"Start checking under your bed, Mr. President," French replied with a grin. "Just in case I order Cavanaugh to hide under it."

The president folded his arms and stared at the floor. "Very well," he said after a moment. "I'll delay the air strike for seventy-two hours." The president looked at Roddy Rodriguez, who nodded. "If the child's presence in Basra is not confirmed by then, we go. *But,*" he added, "if that sub so much as budges, we attack right then, child or no child, agent or no agent. Am I understood?"

"Perfectly, Mr. President," French replied. "But allow me to suggest that it might be a good idea to start hoping that the parents of America will understand just as perfectly."

The secure phone in the middle of the Situation Room table chimed. Robin Hawkes answered it, then handed it to the president. He listened for a moment then leaned forward, resting his weight on one arm. "Are you absolutely certain?" he asked. "Iraqi radio is announcing it?" The table vibrated as the president's fist slammed against it. "Very well, keep me informed."

The president hung up, then turned to the others. "We have just received a confirmed report that our embassy in Baghdad has been looted and burned. The military personnel were evacuated by helicopter, incurring casualties while doing so, and are currently being debriefed aboard the *Paul Revere*. With two notable exceptions, the civilian staffers were all turned over unharmed to the Swiss embassy."

"And those 'two notable exceptions,'" Hawkes ventured, "are Ambassador Doral and—"

"Randy Cavanaugh," French finished.

"You're both right, I'm sorry to say," the president affirmed. He turned to Rodriguez. "What's the minimum amount of time necessary before we're ready to strike, General?"

"Thirty-six hours, sir," the chairman replied. "It'll take us that long to develop a battle plan and rules of engagement, and to get the recon data to the 233d."

The president nodded. "Do it." He looked at his chief of staff. "Robin, call the Speaker, and the Senate majority and minority leaders. Tell them what we're going to do and that General Rodriguez and I will brief them tomorrow morning at eight. I'll want a national TV feed tomorrow, just as the strike is beginning."

The president's face hardened. "And, Robin, get the Iraqi envoy in here. *Now.* When I see that smarmy little liar Ybrahim Ibn, I'm going to—" With an effort, the president stopped himself. "Never mind what I'm going to do, since my wife says I shouldn't talk like that. Just get him in here." Hawkes hurried from the room.

Without pausing, the president turned to French. "No, I haven't forgotten about the alleged hostage, Elliot."

"Alleged?" French burst out. "There's nothing 'alleged' about Lauren Keefe's disappearance!"

"Agreed," the president replied. "I'm not disputing that the girl is missing. But even you must admit that all we have is a brief shot of *some* baby in front of *some* place that looks like an oil refinery. According to the Iraqis, it's al-Kafhar and it's this Keefe girl, but when did we start believing *them?*" He gazed out over the South Lawn. "Plus, when word of the abduction of our envoy gets out, we'll be expected to react proactively and aggressively."

"Just give me—"

The president cut him off. "The asset you planned to send to find out about the child is now nowhere to be found, and we can't afford the time to get another operative in place." He sighed. "I'm not any happier about it than you are, Elliot.

Nonetheless, in thirty-six hours, baby or no baby, the al-Kafhar oil refinery ceases to exist."

Scheherazade's black chador was a fluttering shadow beside him as Randy strode along the cracked, filth-encrusted sidewalk. Eyes peered warily at him from the interior of a windowless wreck of a car jammed against the curb. A string of low-wattage lightbulbs dangling precariously across the street some distance ahead provided the only illumination. The air was redolent with the acrid tang of smoke from dung-fueled fires.

"Where are we going?" Randy asked. To their right, a tiled wall covered with peeling prorevolution posters gave way to an iron-spike fence with only blackness beyond.

"To a cousin of mine. He is a cabdriver; he will give us a ride." Cloaked as she was in the black chador, it seemed to Randy that her voice came from nowhere.

"Why didn't we just grab a cab outside that aromatic butcher shop?"

"Because those cabdrivers that aren't secret police report to the secret police."

Randy looked at her skeptically. "And your cousin isn't in the secret police?"

"No. He is an informant."

"Then what makes you think he isn't just going to drop us off at police headquarters, collect the reward, *and* demand that I tip him for the cab ride on top of it?"

"Because he is my cousin," was the enigmatic reply.

Flickering light bathed them as they rounded a corner. Ahead, forms writhed in front of a crackling bonfire. Shouts and shots punctuated the night. A loudspeaker blared impassioned Arabic.

"What's going on? Randy asked.

Marakova listened. "They are celebrating the banishment of the imperialist dogs and their infidel schemes of subjugation from the sacred soil of Iraq," she translated. "That means you," Marakova added with a laugh.

"I think I'd already figured that one out," Randy replied, grinning.

"If we stay on the sidewalk and show no interest, we should be able to pass by unmolested."

They walked, hugging the wall. Randy kept his face averted, as if talking to Marakova. As they were passing the bonfire, they heard someone running up behind them. Randy whirled, fists ready. Their pursuer careened past them, snatching Randy's hat from his head as he passed.

"Hey!" Randy shouted. He began to give chase.

"Stop!" Marakova snapped. "He is drunk. Ignore him and keep walking."

The drunk slammed into a light pole, then disappeared. The impact rattled a dead streetlight fastened to the pole. It snapped into life, bathing Randy in its glare. The crowd, attracted by Randy's shout, stared at him. Cries went up, fingers pointed at his blonde curls and white skin. Marakova began shouting back in heated Arabic.

Randy walked on calmly as the crowd closed in menacingly. "How much farther to the cabstand?" he whispered.

"Just a few more houses," Marakova replied.

The horde following them stopped at the perimeter of the circle of street light. Randy casually reached inside his jacket, closing his hand on his pistol.

"Almost. My cousin's house is just—"

The shot spun Randy around. He crumpled at Marakova's feet, his face a bloody mask in the harsh streetlight.

25

"Elliot, that's completely unacceptable!" Joel exclaimed into his cellular phone as he paced the length of the back porch. A brewing thunderstorm clattered dead leaves against the storm windows and then hurled them away. "No, I'm not shooting the messenger. Sorry. Just tell Robin Hawkes for me that I'll be calling him to see when I can try and talk his boss out of this madness." Joel nodded as he listened. "Thanks, Elliot. I know you're doing all you can. Love to Chris and the twins, and remember that when *they* sleep, *you* sleep." Joel grinned at French's reply.

Brian and Jake came in, stripping off the gloves they had been wearing to put up the storm windows. "Looks like we got done just in time," Brian commented as the wind banged the porch door shut behind them.

"You two round up everybody and meet me in the family room," Joel ordered.

"What's up?" Jake asked, disturbed by the look on Joel's face.

"Trouble."

From one end of a cushion-strewn love seat, Pat watched her husband. *Last time he looked like that*, she thought, *was when he was about to tell me that he was going into the Peruvian jungle to fight Rafael Cienfuegos.*

They waited as Joel, standing before them, hands in the pockets of his windbreaker, watched the gathering storm ruffle the waters of Moosehead Lake. Just as he was about to begin, Rebecca appeared in the doorway.

"I woke up and couldn't find anybody," she explained, her eyes still puffy from sleep. Brian opened one arm, and Rebecca padded across the room and snuggled down against him.

Joel glanced at Pat, who responded with a tiny shrug. "Are you all right, honey?" she asked Rebecca.

Rebecca nodded. "I'm all right," she responded. "I really am. I just needed some time to—to adjust." Joel glanced again at Pat, who again shrugged.

"Elliot French, the man who sent us the videotape, just called with some disturbing news." Allison Kirstoff looked up in sharp concern. "It seems that our former embassy in Baghdad has been overrun and Lydia Doral, a special envoy, taken hostage."

Joel took a deep breath. "Elliot also told me that it's been verified by his Department of Science and Technology that the USS *Mayfield* was sunk by an attack submarine." Joel looked pointedly at the shocked and infuriated Allison. "It's also been been verified that this sub is based at the al-Kafhar oil refinery, near the port city of Basra. Elliot called," Joel told them, "to warn me that in less than thirty-six hours an air strike will be launched against the sub and the refinery that serves as its base."

"Wait a minute," Brian exclaimed. "Al-Kafhar is where that Iraqi newscaster said Lauri's being held as a human shield!"

Joel nodded somberly. "That's why Elliot called."

Rebecca clung to Brian. "But why would the Iraqis come *here*," she asked quietly, "and take *my* baby to use that way?"

From across the room Pat watched the overwhelmed young mother closely.

"Becky, we just don't know," Joel replied compassionately. "We don't know how she got there. We don't even know for sure that she's in Iraq—"

"That was *my* Lauri on that videotape!" Rebecca stated adamantly.

"I agree," Joel responded. "And Elliot asked me to tell you that the president's aware of the situation. If any hard evidence arises, proving Lauren's presence at the al-Kafhar oil refinery, he'll call off the attack immediately."

"That's it?" Brian asked. "All he's going to do is sit on his hands and wait for somebody to tell him something?" He pounded a fist against his leg. "Isn't he going to send anybody in first to look for her?"

"That wasn't discussed as an option," Joel replied. He sat down next to his wife. "Rebecca seems to be taking the news pretty calmly," he whispered.

"That's what's got me worried," Pat whispered back. "I'd be happier with hysterics."

✦ ✦ ✦

Brian looked at his wife for a long time, then got up. From the middle of his living room he watched as gusts heralding an approaching storm ruffled the surface of Moosehead Lake. Fists clenched, he stared out at the onrushing turbulence as if to ward it off by sheer willpower alone.

"That's it," Brian said quietly. "That's enough. Enough reporters. Enough large guys in cheap suits. Enough politicians." Brian looked pointedly at Pat. "Enough talk."

Pat returned Brian's gaze. "Right now, talk is the best approach," she replied. "Let Joel's friends talk to the Iraqis while you talk to the reporters."

Rebecca Keefe looked up at her husband. "And to me, too," she said quietly.

Silence gathered as Brian stood motionless. Bursts of rain-drops clattered against the picture window.

A distant thunderclap echoed the sudden crack of Brian's fist against his palm. He looked at his wife. *"Emshee."* Rebecca went white. Brian turned to Jake. "Time for some CQB. You with me?"

Jake got up and nodded curtly to Brian. The two men strode from the room.

Pat came over and sat down next to the trembling Rebecca. "What did he say to you?"

Rebecca stared at the door. *"Emshee,"* she replied. "It's one of the few Arabic words Brian learned while we were overseas. He used to yell it at camel drivers. A rough translation is 'get on with it!'" Worry etched itself more deeply into her face.

"And what did Brian say to Jake, Daddy?" Anne asked.

"CQB. It's a military abbreviation for 'close-quarters battle.'" Joel smiled grimly. "Sounds like he and Jake are planning on taking the fight to the enemy."

Rainwater streamed from Joel's slicker as he hung it up on a peg by the boathouse door. The door to Brian's gun safe was open, and he and Jake were sorting through a pile of weapons scattered along a counter.

"Forget it," Joel said flatly. "There's no way you can get to Iraq in time." As Brian turned to glare at him, Joel went on. "At least, not without help."

"What do you mean?" Brian asked.

Joel sat down on a stool. "I agree with what you want to do and I believe there are biblical precedents for going to rescue our wives and families. Plus, Jake and I have done it once already." Jake nodded. Joel had, after all, helped Jake rescue Anne from the grasp of Peruvian terrorists. Joel glanced at Brian. "You've told me before how hard it is for you to walk away from a fight, Brian. That's why I wanted to let you know that I think you're doing the right thing."

"Walking away *is* tough," Brian admitted. "Always has been, though I've learned to do it when necessary." Brian's face hardened. "But now someone has stolen something I've been entrusted with. Something very precious to me. I'm not walking away." Brian stared at his massive, white-knuckled fist. "And neither are they."

"That's why," Joel continued, "I've just finished spending some time on the phone with some friends of mine, calling in almost all the favors I have left. You two will fly to Bangor—"

"Not in this weather, we won't," Brian interjected as a gust shook the boathouse.

"By tomorrow morning, according to the National Weather Service, the storm will have cleared. You'll be met in Bangor by a Grumman C-20D military jet. Ten hours later, at our air base in Turkey, you'll switch to a carrier onboard-delivery helicopter, which an hour later will deposit you on the flight deck of the aircraft carrier *Paul Revere*. That'll give you just six hours to get organized, get in, get Lauren, and get out. Think you can pull it off?" Joel grinned at the younger men's expressions, wishing he were twenty years younger. "Once you're onboard the *Revere*, you're on your own. Almost."

"Almost?" Jake echoed.

"Mark Sewell's going along for the ride," Joel replied, watching Brian.

"*Yes!*" Brian exulted. "Becky's younger brother, remember?" Brian said to Jake. "He became a SEAL just about the time I retired. He's rough, tough, and has got the stuff." Brian grinned. "We've got it wired, now."

Joel got up. "Then get that gear stowed and come on up to the house. You two have some good-byes to say."

Commander Jerry Hall, captain of the *Alameda*, pushed his hat

JON HENDERSON

back on his head. Lieutenant Commander Gary Faust, Hall's executive officer, studied his friend's expression. "Push your hat back any farther, and your bald spot'll start showing," Faust warned. It was widely known aboard the *Alameda* that the farther Hall's hat was back on his head, the more worried he was.

"At this rate, I'll tear it out before it'll fall out," Hall replied sourly. He handed his XO the flimsy sheet of paper he was holding. "The *Revere* just received this ROCKET. They had to wake Admiral Pierce up to sign for it. So, naturally, he had me come fetch it personally. Tell me what you make of it."

Faust glanced at the sheet of paper containing the ROCKET—navy parlance for an urgent message—that had been transmitted to the carrier from a military communications satellite.

Z143405ZSEP
PRI: XRAYDELTA
FM: COMNAVSPECWARGRUTWO
TO: CVN21 PAUL REVERE
//R09533//

1. LT MARK SEWELL AND MCPO SHILOH TURK OF CG75 ALAMEDA ARE IMMEDIATELY DETACHED AND REASSIGNED TO TAD OF INDEFINITE DURATION AND UNSPECIFIED NATURE.

2. EXPECT ADDITIONAL VIP OPS PERSONNEL VIA COD AT 2330 ZULU.

3. YOUR COMMAND TO PROVIDE OPS PERSONNEL WITH ANY AND ALL REQUESTED SUPPORT.

282

OPORDS FOLLOW.

RADM MENDEZ SEND

Faust read the ROCKET again. "What I make of it," the XO said slowly, "is that Admiral Mendez is sending off one of our junior officers and our senior petty officer on some sort of TAD." The executive officer grinned. "Usually, TAD means some sort of temporary additional duty like escorting visiting congressmen on their boondoggles. That's why it's also referred to as 'traveling around drunk.' Maybe they've gotten lucky."

Hall scowled. "Not this time. No congressman in his right mind—if there was such a thing—would come *here* to party. Anyway, look at this." The skipper handed Faust a thick envelope. "Here's the OPORDS the ROCKET said would follow. Arrived via courier on the *Revere's* flight deck an hour ago."

The XO looked at the packet of operational orders, then hastily handed it back. It was labeled EYES ONLY and followed by Sewell's and Turk's names. The envelope was bordered in fluorescent-blue tape and heavily sealed. Faust looked at Hall in disbelief. "These two are being given orders that we're not cleared to see?"

The *Alameda's* skipper nodded grimly. "And that's not all. The worst part is that Old Man Pierce on the *Revere* doesn't know what's in here, either. He's just been told the same thing we have: Give these two anything they ask for. And when an admiral doesn't get to know something that a lieutenant *does* get to know, that makes the admiral one unhappy camper." Hall sighed. "Best get Sewell in here. Maybe these orders authorize him to tell us *something.*" He shook his head, causing his hat to wobble precariously on the back edge of his bald spot.

"Don't worry, Skipper," Faust said affably as he reached for the intercom. "There's always toupees."

He's pretty cool for a lieutenant reading top secret material, Hall decided as he watched Mark Sewell. *Why do I get the feeling he's done this sort of thing before?*

Mark finished reading. He put the orders back into their envelope, then looked at his commanding officer. "Here's what I *can* tell you, Skipper," he said calmly. "Turk and I will transfer to the *Revere* immediately. If all goes well, we'll be back within twenty-four hours."

"That's all you can tell me?"

Mark shrugged. "Sorry, sir."

Hall grimaced with frustration. "Why Turk, *if* I may ask?"

The young lieutenant looked nonplussed. "Can't say, Skip. Let's just say he's the best man for the job. Now, if you'll excuse me, I'm supposed to brief the admiral." Mark saluted and left.

Hall turned his attention to the two personnel files on his desk. Sewell's was slender compared to the thirty-year record of the veteran Turk. *I don't get it,* Hall thought. *One's a master chief who came up the hard way, the other's a fair-haired Annapolis grad. Turk was promoted to noncom about the time Sewell was born.* The commander leafed through the dossiers, then stared out at the azure waters of the Persian Gulf. *The only thing they've got in common is that they're both SEALs, they've both been through the underwater demolition school, and they've both spent a lot of time working as instructors in amphibious warfare.*

Hall leaned back in his chair, suddenly realizing what that combination of talent, training, and experience meant. *So I've got a couple of covert special-forces types aboard. And now they've been ordered out somewhere. Probably after someone.* He looked out at the coastline of Iran, some thirty miles away. *Whoever you are, it's time to start being* real *nervous.*

Unhappy with the paucity of information provided him by this very junior officer, Admiral Thomas Pierce glared across the polished expanse of his rosewood desk. "And what will your operations task force require of me, Lieutenant?" he asked testily.

"I'll know better after the rest of the personnel arrive," Mark replied. "We'll have a shopping list for you in the morning, Admiral."

"Can you at least tell me who will be arriving aboard *my* ship?"

"I think I can tell you that, sir." Mark smiled. "My brother-in-law and a friend of his."

Brian stared at his reflection in the bathroom mirror. Creases had appeared in his brow, and his robust, tanned face was now tired and pale. Brian dried himself off, went into the bedroom, and pulled on his clothes. On the far side of the bed, Rebecca was a small, huddled shape beneath the covers. Massaging his temples, Brian suppressed his overwhelming fatigue. Concern for his wife washed over him as he crossed the room.

"You asleep, Beck?" he asked as he sat next to her.

"Go away."

Brian rubbed his forehead as he wondered what to do. "Becky, honey, I'm worried about you. I'm leaving in a few hours, and it's important to me that we talk before I go."

"I'm fine. Just leave me alone." She turned her face from his.

"You're *not* fine, hon. I understand. I know how you feel." He spread his hands helplessly. "Is there anything I can do?" One hand drifted down and gently smoothed her bangs.

Rebecca's nails bit deep into Brian's wrist as she flung his hand away. A blizzard of covers enveloped him briefly, then she was on her knees, facing him, her face inches from his.

"Stop it!" she shrieked. "Stop it!"

"What?" Brian stammered as he reeled back. Drops of

blood from his wrist begin to pattern the white linen sheets. "What did I do?"

"You touched me!" Rebecca screamed. "You *touched* me!" Brian watched her pale blue eyes widen as they filled with an irrational fear. "And every time you touch me that way, you touch me other ways, and then I end up having babies that I can't take care of!" Her nightshirt rose and fell as she stared at him. "I'm not going to let that happen again to me. I'm not!"

Brian recoiled beneath each word's hammer blow. "Beck," he pleaded, "it's not like that. It's not like that at all." He reached again for her, then thought better of it. Brian watched, incredulous, as his beautiful wife became something cornered and feral.

"Keep away from me, I said!"

Then something else entered Rebecca's eyes. She tilted her head to one side as she watched him. "You want another baby?" she asked, her voice cunning. "Then go find that Kirstoff woman. *She's* been paying enough attention to you." Hysteria tinged her harsh, ragged tones. "Maybe if you touch *her* the way you touch *me*, she'll give you a baby that won't get taken away!"

Shocked and scared, Brian fought for words. "Beck, honey, why are you saying this? You can't possibly think that—"

"I've seen the way you look at her! I've seen how much time you spend together! I know what you want, *and you're not getting it from me!*" Crying hysterically, Rebecca pointed at their bedroom door. "Now get out! Go to her, go anywhere, I don't care! Just get out!" Sobs racked her as she flung herself facedown onto her pillow.

Rage born of exhaustion, fear, worry, and pride flooded Brian at the unjust accusation. His look of concern was swept away by one of fury. "Have it your way!" he thundered, coming to his feet. "I wouldn't *want* to touch whatever it is you've become, anyway!" With an echoing boom, he slammed his fist into the thick, oaken door of the armoire. Flinging wide their bedroom door, he stormed away.

Pat and Joel were standing in the hall outside. Brian glanced at Pat, jerked his head toward the bedroom, then brushed past them. A distant crash sounded as the kitchen door slammed open. Pat rushed into the bedroom. Moments later, through the hall window, Joel saw a light come on down in the boathouse.

A glance told Joel that Pat, her hand on Rebecca's shaking back, didn't need his help. He walked down the hall and tapped lightly on Anne's door. "It's Dad, honey. Get Jake and meet me in the living room. We've got some praying to do."

He stood quietly, watching and listening. Ahead of him, low on the horizon, Arcturus gleamed from behind the swaying tree-tops. A nighthawk flew by overhead, searching for dinner. Water lapped softly at the pilings below.

"It's not your fault, Brian."

He turned. Pat walked toward him, along the boathouse deck, her hands in the pockets of her cardigan. She joined him at the railing at the end of the deck, her psychiatrist's eyes searching his face.

"Is Becky all right?" Brian asked anxiously.

Pat nodded. "She'll be fine, eventually. I've sedated her—sleep is what she needs most right now."

"What happened?"

Pat thought a moment before replying. "You, better than anyone, know just how driven and perfectionistic Rebecca is."

Brian grinned. "In grad school, a ninety-nine on an exam was the equivalent of a scarlet letter."

"All her life," Pat agreed, "to be the best has been the only option. Plus, Rebecca will eagerly take on new challenges, but never at the expense of the ones she's already pursuing."

"You're right," Brian agreed. "Some of our biggest fights have been about her slowing down a little."

Pat nodded. "Graduate school, writing a doctoral dissertation, your marriage, her NSF grant, then whisking off with her new husband for a year of fieldwork." Pat ticked off the points on her fingers. "One thing right after another." She paused, then looked at Brian. "Lauren was a surprise, wasn't she?"

Brian nodded sheepishly.

"I thought so," Pat said, smiling her understanding. "So it suddenly became necessary to finish her research early, pack up, come home, and write up her expedition while taking up the domestic life with her new husband and even newer daughter."

"But she didn't seem to mind," Brian replied plaintively.

"She doesn't. The higher Rebecca's plate is piled, the happier she is. But do you notice what's missing from her plate?" In response to Brian's frown, Pat added, "Failure. Rebecca has never tasted the 'bread of adversity and the water of affliction,' which Isaiah tells us God permits into our lives." Pat sighed. "My brother and his wife never permitted Rebecca the small failures that strengthen us for the large failures that inevitably come our way, and now it's caught up to her."

"But all that stuff about me and Allison—" Brian closed his eyes and looked away. "Why?"

Pat touched his hand compassionately. "She doesn't mean it, Brian. She doesn't even know she said it. She feels she's failed you as a wife and Lauri as a mother, and in her frantic despair, she lashed out against the only available threat."

Brian's eyes widened. "Becky feels threatened by Allison? I don't get it."

Pat smiled. "Allison is young, beautiful, accomplished, and hasn't had happen to her the things that having a baby does to a woman's body. Right now she's at her best, Rebecca's at her worst, and Allison is spending time with you in Rebecca's home.

From Rebecca's point of view, Allison has succeeded at everything and failed at nothing." Pat pulled the cardigan closer around her. "Since Rebecca can't train her maternal ferocity on those who have her baby, she picked the only target in sight."

Pat put her hands on Brian's shoulders. "She wasn't attacking you, Brian, and she wasn't really attacking Allison. She was punishing herself." Pat continued to watch him. "And remember, none of this is your fault."

Brian smiled a rueful thanks, then shook his head. "It's *all* my fault. If only I had been—"

"If only you had been *what*, Brian? Here instead of out with a client, doing your job, providing for your wife and child?" Pat softened the rebuke with a compassionate smile. "My point is, Brian, that only by sheer happenstance could either of you have changed anything. It's *not* your fault."

Pat felt the railing vibrate as Brian slammed his fist against it. "It's just not supposed to work this way!" he growled.

"Remember your wedding vows, Brian?" Pat asked. Brian stared at her in confusion. "Doesn't surprise me that you might be a little vague about them," Pat went on, "since Rebecca's dress *was* rather low cut." The young husband's pain was softened briefly by a rueful smile. "I know you remember the 'for better or for worse' part," Pat added, having achieved the desired effect, "but did you ever stop to consider that *every* couple has to go through the *worse?*"

Brian shook his head and sighed.

"And," Pat finished gently, "since God knew that you two were going to go through this, he also knows how to see you through this."

Brian turned once more toward the lake. As a family of loons swam across the moon's rippled reflection, he whispered, "'For I know the plans I have for you,' declares the Lord, 'plans to prosper you and not to harm you, plans to give you hope and a future.'"

289

His shoulders sagged, and Brian bowed his head. "That's so hard to believe right now. I love both of them so much, and I feel so helpless. I need to be here with Becky *and* off rescuing Lauren. I don't know what to do."

"The Israelites held captive in Babylon undoubtedly felt the same way," Pat agreed. "But don't forget what God had Jeremiah tell them to do."

Brian thought for a moment, then nodded. "'Call upon me and come and pray to me, and I will listen to you. You will seek me and find me when you seek me with all your heart.'"

Pat turned. "Joel, Jake, and Annie are doing that right now. Let's join them." When he didn't move, Pat said, "Brian?"

"I just remembered what God said next," Brian told her, still staring out over the lake. "He makes a promise. Jeremiah wrote, '"I will be found by you," declares the Lord, "and will bring you back from captivity."'" He turned to Pat. "Let's go join the others."

❖ ❖ ❖

A wall of gray mist lapped against the bedroom window. Tired and disheveled, Brian stood next to his bed, watching his wife sleep. "I've got to go now, Beck," he said quietly. "But I'll be back, with Lauri, just as soon as I can." He went to one knee, his face inches from hers. "No matter what happens, my love," he whispered, "remember that I love you very much." Brian kissed Rebecca's cheek, then gently smoothed her bangs. Rebecca muttered something, but Brian couldn't make out what it was.

Jake was latching shut the cargo-bay door in the tail of Brian's Cessna as Brian came down onto the dock. "Are we going to be able to take off in this?" Jake asked.

Brian nodded. "Landing's the problem when it's like this, not taking off. But I just checked the weather radio and Bangor's clear, so we're set."

"The flight crew of the C-20D will have a packet of

intelligence reports for you," Joel informed them, "and we'll be pumping more intel to the *Paul Revere* right up until you jump off." He reached up and clapped both men on the shoulder. "Good luck."

"*You,*" Brian declared as he taxied the Cessna out into the middle of Moosehead Lake, "are going to be the one to read those intel dumps Joel said would be waiting for us, because *I* am going to sleep all the way to Turkey." Brian stretched as best he could in the close confines of the plane's cabin. "Just how does Joel arrange all this?" Brian asked. "I thought he was retired."

"It's easier to retire from the Mafia than it is from the CIA," Jake retorted. "Besides, Joel's having the time of his life. He has access to all the really hot intelligence, he's consulted with by presidents, and he knows that since he's supposedly retired, he can tell them all to go jump in the lake anytime he wants. Not a bad life."

"I noticed Anne wasn't up to see you off," Brian observed tactfully.

"So she wasn't," Jake agreed. "We sat up way late last night. Didn't talk much, just sat. That's a switch," Jake added thoughtfully. "The last time I took off, to Tibet, she unloaded all over me. Whether it's a good switch or not, I just don't know. Finally she got up, said, 'Please come back,' and went to bed." Jake shook his head. "I promised I would."

26

Despite his best efforts to ignore it, the buzzing persisted, driving him from the blessed refuge of sleep. Honkings, clatters, bangings, and shouts intruded. A pervasive, sticky heat surrounded him. He tossed uncomfortably on the lumpy mattress, causing a shower of pain-filled sparks to rocket through his skull. At last Randy Cavanaugh's eyes flickered open.

He found himself staring up at a cracked and mildewed ceiling, barely visible in the light that filtered through the heavily shuttered window. Randy lifted his hand to his right temple, from which the pain seemed to radiate like a sea urchin's spines. The buzzing increased as he did so, and Randy watched a cloud of flies dart away. He winced as he touched a furrow gouged into his skull. *Feels like the Grand Canyon,* he decided. *Complete with little mule trains.*

"We have no bandages," Marakova said from somewhere off in the gloom. "I am sorry. I have washed your wound as best I could."

"At the risk of being trite," Randy rasped, "where am I?"

"At the house of my cousin the cabdriver," Marakova replied. "He drove by, on his way home, just as you were shot.

When he saw me waving, he stopped. He thought you were dead and wanted to leave you, but I insisted on bringing you here."

"Smart move. Much appreciated." Randy tried to look at his watch, but it was missing. "How long have I been out?"

"All night and all morning." Marakova moved, and a straw brushed Randy's lips. "Drink this. It will help the pain."

Randy eagerly finished the container of tart, cool liquid. The thunder in his head began to ebb. Smooth fingertips rested gently on his brow, and he slept.

Good job, Stanford University Library! Allison thought approvingly. *You got me those Mosaic files I asked you for.* Spattered with leafy shade from the ash tree overhead, Allison's PC satellite dish sat on the grass next to her like a high-tech toadstool. *OK,* she decided as her fingers flew over the keyboard, *let's see what we've got here.*

Twenty minutes later Allison looked up. *This is way too weird,* she realized. *I've looked at it every way I can, and no matter how I analyze the data, it still adds up to the same thing.* A shiver ran through her as she surveyed the sunny, peaceful central Maine woods. *Talk about spooky. Even if Stephen King does live somewhere around here, this is still entirely too strange for me.* Allison gathered up her hardware and hurried toward the house.

❖ ❖ ❖

Anne came up the steps onto the back porch. Joel glanced at her, then put down the copy of *The Cruise of the Talking Fish* he was reading. As she approached, he shaded his eyes and made a show of surveying the horizon. "Looks like a storm's rolling in," he said thoughtfully. Anne stopped and glared at him, and Joel motioned to the other end of the glider. "Care to talk about it?" he asked. "A little thunder to go along with that green-eyed lightning you inherited from your mother?"

294

Anne plopped down on the far end of the glider, crossed her arms, and stared stonily out at Moosehead Lake. After a long silence Joel said softly, "Talk. A verb. To articulate something in words; to speak of or discuss."

"Oh, stop it, Daddy!" Anne said irritably. "You know what I'm mad about."

"Well," Joel reflected, "I suppose that's better than when your mother says, 'You're supposed to know what I'm mad about.'"

"That man is absolutely impossible! But *you* wouldn't understand," she added waspishly.

Joel watched his daughter, wishing that she didn't have to hurt so much and knowing that she needed to. "Try me," he said gently. "I just might understand, since I've been on the receiving end of both those comments more than a few times before."

"How could he do such a thing?" Anne fumed. "How could he just go off like that?"

Joel frowned. "I thought the two of you talked it over before he and Brian left."

"We did."

"And . . . ?"

"And he went anyway!"

Joel sighed. *I thought it would get easier as she got older.* "And now you're angry and hurt because Jake didn't do what you wanted him to do."

Anne looked at her father, her eyelashes laden with tears. "You make it sound so petty and childish."

Joel smiled fondly at her. "It's neither of those, love. It's a perfectly normal reaction to a tough situation."

Anne tried unsuccessfully to hide a smile. "You sound just like Mama when she's talking to one of her clients."

Joel didn't bother to hide his grin. "That's what happens when you sleep with a psychiatrist for almost thirty years." He propped his feet up on the porch rail. "But, in a way, I think you're getting what you do want. You just don't realize it."

Anne peered at him suspiciously.

"Let's turn your problem on its head," Joel suggested. "Suppose that, instead of trying to convince Jake to stay, you'd had to talk him into going along with Brian. Would that have been preferable?"

"Not when you put it that way," Anne admitted. "That sounds so craven."

"But I thought you wanted him on the sidelines; safe, comfortable, and readily available to you." Anne huffed in frustration. "Do you want to marry Jake?" Joel asked.

Anne toyed unconsciously with the ring on her left hand. "You know I do, Daddy."

"Jake's the kind of man your mother and I have always hoped and prayed you'd meet. Someone who will live in pain for the rest of his life because he chose to run back into Vietcong machine gun fire to retrieve one of his men. Someone who risked his life in Peru to rescue a woman he barely knew."

Anne bit her lip. "Me."

"Someone who does whatever it takes to get back a baby girl." Joel looked at his daughter. "If you're going to marry a *man*, love, this sort of thing goes with the territory. At least if Jake MacIntyre is the man in question."

Anne gave her father a sideways glance. "Don't you start with that 'a man's gotta do what a man's gotta do' stuff."

Joel laughed. "OK, I won't. My John Wayne accent isn't all that good. But it's still true. And I think you really *are* getting the kind of man you want."

"Jake *is* special," Anne agreed. She leaned against her father and rested her head on his shoulder. "I just worry so much about him."

Joel patted her hand. "That means you're keeping your end of the bargain."

Allison came up onto the porch. "Sorry to intrude, but could I borrow your dad for a few minutes?" she asked Anne.

Joel got up. "I agree, honey—Jake's really something." He winked at his only child. "It's not every man who's equally handy with both dishes *and* dynamite."

"Is he gone?" Rebecca asked.

"Yes," Pat replied from her bedside. "He and Jake took off this morning. Brian told me to tell you that he loves you and that he'll be back. With Lauren."

The young wife and mother stared out beyond Pat at a scarlet clump of sugar maple standing like a beacon on the lake's wooded shore. "I'm glad he's gone," she said quietly, "and I hate him for leaving."

Pat sighed, saddened once again by the seemingly limitless variety of pain with which a soul can be afflicted. "He couldn't stay, you know," Pat said gently. "Brian would have hated and doubted himself for the rest of his life if he hadn't tried to rescue Lauren." When Rebecca ignored her, Pat went on. "But there's another reason he had to leave, too."

Rebecca turned. "What's that?"

Pat caught and held her eyes. "He came in to say goodbye—to tell you that he loves you and that he'd be back. Brian wanted to leave here with a part of you, and instead he had all that was left of his home snatched away from him." Wishing she didn't have to but knowing it was necessary, Pat sharpened her tone. "Instead of taking with him your thoughts and prayers and encouragement and love, Brian left here feeling unwanted, unneeded, and unwelcome."

Welling tears matted Rebecca's long eyelashes as she stared fixedly out over the lake.

Pat allowed the silence to gather for a time. She watched Rebecca struggle, feeling for her, knowing her torment. Then

Pat added, seemingly as an afterthought, "I haven't finished my story about Debby, by the way."

Rebecca's eyes shifted a fraction in Pat's direction.

"After the memorial service, we dropped Annie off to stay with you and your family, and Joel took me to our home in the White Mountains of Vermont. Then he went away."

Rebecca's eyes widened. "He left you? At a time like that?"

Pat smiled, grateful that she had been able to engage Rebecca. "No, he didn't leave me. Joel went away in exactly the fashion that every wife wishes her husband would once in a while. Reassuringly nearby, but without making demands of any sort. Joel stayed close enough so I knew he was there and could be secure in the knowledge I was being taken care of, yet he left me to work it out alone if I so chose."

"I wish Brian would do that," Rebecca whispered.

"He tried, honey," Pat said softly. "He begged you to let him."

Tears darkened the rumpled sheets. Rebecca raised her reddened eyes. "What did you do?"

"For a week I sat in a chair Joel put in a sunny corner and searched Scripture for the answer I knew would be there. And when my reading proved seemingly fruitless and the anger welled up, I went for long, solitary, desperate walks. I sat silently for hours watching the light on the mountains, and in the middle of a flower-filled meadow, I threw back my head, flung out my arms, and screamed out my rage and despair that my God had let this happen to me." Pat smiled. "One day a blinding thunderstorm swept in while I was out walking. Joel came out and found me. He brought my rain gear along, but he didn't offer it to me. Nor did he say a word to me on that long, cold, soggy hike home. Still, I knew he was right behind me all the way."

Pat wrapped her sweater close around her. "Then," she continued, "the answer came. As we're guaranteed it will. It happened while I was reading about another woman who lost her baby."

"Who was that?" Rebecca asked.

"Hannah. A woman afflicted by two trials we've been spared: childlessness and the incessant abuse of a co-wife who was, to put it mildly, nasty. The Bible says that 'this went on year after year. Whenever Hannah went up to the house of the Lord, her rival provoked her till she wept and would not eat.' Her husband, Elkanah, tried to comfort her but was as insensitive to Hannah's inner turmoil as most men are." Pat was rewarded with a small, tenuous smile. "Even Hannah's prayers for a son were criticized," Pat went on. "They were so fervent that the high priest accused her of being drunk. Nonetheless, Hannah promised God that if she was given a son, she would dedicate his life to serving the Lord. God honored her prayer, and in due time Hannah gave birth to Samuel."

The two women watched as a hummingbird, on its way south for the oncoming winter, sipped the last of the nectar from the honeysuckle vine that framed the bedroom window.

"Sitting there that morning," Pat said, "I read about how Hannah kept her promise." She took Rebecca's Bible from her nightstand and opened it. "'After he was weaned, she took the boy with her, young as he was, along with a three-year-old bull, an ephah of flour and a skin of wine, and brought him to the house of the Lord at Shiloh. When they had slaughtered the bull, they brought the boy to Eli, and she said to him, "As surely as you live, my lord, I am the woman who stood here beside you praying to the Lord. I prayed for this child, and the Lord has granted me what I asked of him. So now I give him to the Lord. For his whole life he will be given over to the Lord."'" Pat paused, alone for a moment in her thoughts.

"It doesn't say what Hannah did," Pat went on, "but I sat for a long time that morning and thought about what I would have done if I had been her. I would have scrubbed Samuel until he was squeaky clean, dressed him in his very best clothes, and packed a bag of the foods he was learning to eat. Then, on the way to the temple, I would have told him over and over how much I loved him."

Pat set the Bible in her lap. "And then I tried to imagine how Hannah felt as she walked away from the temple, leaving her just-weaned baby boy in the arms of a big, insensitive lout of a man."

Rebecca smiled. "What did you imagine then?" Rebecca asked.

Pat shook her head. "I didn't imagine. I did what I was sure another woman had done, long ago, when she had just lost her precious child. I cried. I cried until it hurt too much to cry any more, and then I cried until I was done. Finally, after sitting there for a long, long time, I remembered the last thing Hannah did."

Rebecca tried to speak. Then, trembling, she just looked questioningly at Pat.

"Hannah praised the Lord," Pat told her. "In one of the most beautiful prayers there is, she sings of the glory, might, and majesty of God."

Pat took Rebecca's hand. "You and I had our babies taken away from us, honey. And there are few things harder to endure than that. But imagine how much harder it must have been for Hannah, who could have easily ignored her promise and kept her baby, to hand Samuel over and walk away, wondering if she'd ever see him again. And yet, amid all the pain, she found it within herself to praise God so beautifully."

Pat Dryden smiled fondly at her only niece. "It was then I realized, just like Hannah did with Samuel, that Debby had never really been mine in the first place. I was truly able to place her in God's hands. And say good-bye."

Rebecca took the Bible from Pat's lap. Pat watched as, her

lips moving silently, her tears wrinkling the thin paper, Rebecca read.

The young mother lifted her face to the hills that surrounded her home. "'My heart rejoices in the Lord,'" she whispered. "'There is no one holy like the Lord; there is no one besides you; there is no Rock like our God.'" With infinite slowness Rebecca closed the Bible.

Then, from deep within Rebecca Sewell Keefe, the long, racking, cleansing sobs poured forth.

27

"Hi!" Allison said brightly as Rebecca, showered and dressed, came into her study. "Glad you're feeling better."

Rebecca paused just inside the doorway. "Does Allison know what I said about her and Brian?" she asked Pat softly.

Pat shook her head. "Only Brian knows what you actually said, and all I know of it is what he told me."

Relieved, Rebecca went over and sat down next to Allison. "Haven't been much of a hostess, have I?" she asked.

Eyes on her PC screen, Allison waved dismissively. "You've got a wok for my stir-fry and a fridge full of Diet Coke, so it's been perfect."

"After spending time in Thailand and Korea, I thought I was accustomed to spicy food," Joel interjected as he joined them, "but Allison's concoctions have shown me new dimensions in pain. Just get some of her recipes, Rebecca, and you'll be able to cut your heating bill in half this winter." Joel sat down on the other side of Allison.

"And you've shown up just when I needed you," Allison told Rebecca. She gestured at her screen. "Look at this."

Rebecca, Pat, and Joel peered at the screen. Displayed on

it was an image of a large copper object. Two brass spheres were stacked on the object's base. These spheres supported a small brass dish that rested, in turn, beneath three more spheres. The object was topped by a cast impression of a highly stylized bird with an upturned tail and scimitarlike beak.

"What is it?" Rebecca asked. "It looks like some sort of candlestick maker's nightmare."

"That," Allison announced triumphantly, "is the *Melek Taous.*"

"The *what?*" Rebecca asked.

"The *Melek Taous.* That's one of the phrases that guy they caught said. Since we didn't know how to spell it, I started phonetically, using a 'wolf-fence' search algorithm, and *bingo*, out it popped."

Rebecca stared at Allison blankly. "What guy they caught?"

"It appears that Sheriff Barnard has caught one of the accomplices in Lauren's kidnapping," Joel explained. Rebecca listened intently as he recounted the incidents at the hospital.

"Fine," Rebecca said when Joel was finished. "Some creep shouts the name of something that looks like it came out of the clearance bin down at the local five-and-dime. What does that have to do with Lauri?"

"A lot, I think," Allison replied. "Talking about Assyria the way we did threw me off for a while, until I remembered that Assyria is an ancient name for—"

Rebecca paled. "Northern Iraq," she said quietly. "I should have made the connection with the video sooner," she added bleakly. "I should have—" Rebecca bit her lip, closed her eyes, and turned away.

Pat's hand squeezed Rebecca's shoulders. "You had other things to worry about, dear," she said with quiet firmness. "Things you were completely entitled to worry about. We've made the connection now, and that's what's important." Rebecca dabbed at her eyes with a tissue. She reached up and grasped Pat's hand.

Allison watched Rebecca uncertainly. She glanced at Pat, who nodded. "I found out something else," Allison added invitingly. When she had Rebecca's attention, she went on. "I found out what *Yezidis* is. Who they are, actually," she clarified, "since it's some sort of religion."

Rebecca thought for a long moment. "I remember hearing the term when we were over there," she said. "I didn't think much about it at the time since I was so absorbed in my work, but I seem to recall it was the name of a band of troublemakers."

Allison nodded. "You're not kidding. The Yezidis have been terrorizing northern Iraq for thousands of years." She clicked her mouse, and the title page of a book appeared on her screen. "They were first mentioned in the West in a book called *Nineveh and Its Remains*, by Austen H. Layard." Allison grinned. "It's been fun reading up about this Layard guy. Seems he was one of the first of the English 'gentlemen explorers.' When he was twenty-two he just packed in his job at a law office and headed out. Layard was fluent in Persian and Arabic, and a skilled navigator and geographer. For years he financed his campaigns by spying for the British ambassador in Turkey on both the Arabs and the Turks. Wish I could meet someone like that," she added thoughtfully. "Anyway," Allison finished, "when Layard got home, he wrote this book, which became a runaway best-seller."

"It's remained the seminal work on Nineveh," Rebecca confirmed. "I've never studied it since it contains nothing important about Assyrian languages, but it was required reading for the archaeology folks."

"The Yezidis are a *weird* bunch," Allison remarked. "I'm glad I wasn't reading this stuff late at night alone. Listen to this." Allison began reading from her computer screen. "'The Yezidis recognize one Supreme Being; but, as far as I could learn, they do not offer up any direct prayer or sacrifice to him.' But," Allison added, "Layard goes on to say, 'The name of the Evil Spirit is, however, never mentioned; and any allusion to it by others so vexes and irritates them, that it is said that they have put to death persons who have wantonly outraged their feelings by its use. So far is their dread of offending the Evil principle carried, that they carefully avoid every expression which may resemble in sound the name of Satan, or the Arabic word for 'accursed.' When they speak of the Devil, they do so with reverence, as *Melek el Kout*, the mighty angel.'"

"Sounds like the Israelites and the names they invented in order to avoid using the name of God," Joel observed.

"Maybe so," Allison agreed, "but these guys are even stranger than some of the televangelists I see on the public-access channels late at night. Listen to this: 'They believe Satan to be the chief of the Angelic host, now suffering punishment for his rebellion against the divine will; but still all-powerful, and to be restored hereafter to his high place in the celestial hierarchy. He must be conciliated and reverenced, they say; for as now he has the means of doing evil to mankind, so will he hereafter have the power of rewarding them. Next to Satan, but inferior to him in might and wisdom, are seven archangels who exercise a great influence over the world;—they are Gabriel, Michail, Raphail, Azaril, Dedrail, Azrapheel, and Shemkeel. Christ, according to them, was also a great angel who had taken the form of a man. He did not die on the cross, but ascended to heaven.'" Joel sighed and shook his head. "'They hold the Old Testament in great reverence,'" Allison read on, "'and believe in the cosmogony of the Bible. They do not reject the New Testament, nor the Koran; but they consider them less entitled to their veneration.'" Allison punched a couple of keys. "Layard also mentions that the Yezidis expect the second coming of Christ and that they baptize in water."

✦ ✦ ✦

The doorbell rang. Joel answered it, brought Roy Barnard and Bill Estes into the living room, and introduced Allison.

"Joel says you might have some answers for us," Barnard said, pulling up a chair.

"I think so," Allison replied. "And I'm hoping you have some for me." She looked at Barnard. "Joel says you've been having problems with a couple of things that have happened."

Barnard grinned wryly. "*Problems* isn't the word for it. Bill's positively identified this Marduk character as the 'high priest' in that oddball ceremony up on Mount Kineo, which makes us think he was involved in the rest of the strange goings-on."

Rebecca sat up. "What?" she exclaimed, staring at Barnard in disbelief. "Are you saying that Professor Marduk is involved in Lauren's kidnapping?"

"It looks that way, I'm afraid," the sheriff replied solemnly.

"But," the young mother stammered, "how could he be? He was so charming and kind the afternoon he was here." Sudden realization swept all the color from Rebecca's face. Eyes wide, she sank slowly back against the couch.

Barnard watched Rebecca for a moment, then turned back to Allison. "We're also looking for a motive as to why the guy we've got in custody attacked poor George Williams. Any help you can give us would be much appreciated."

Allison recounted to them Layard's descriptions. "Do you think the attacker is a Yezidi?" she asked when she had finished.

"Based on what you just told us, he sure acts like one," Barnard replied. "All he does is rave about 'Yezidis' and 'Melek Taous.'"

"He must be one of them," Allison confirmed. She pointed at her screen, showing the two lawmen the image of the candlestick she had shown the others earlier.

"That's what was up on Kineo!" Estes exclaimed.

307

Allison nodded. "That's the Melek Taous. A symbol central to their religion." She began typing. "As for the assault, did you say the shopkeeper's name was *George?*"

"That's right," Estes agreed. "George Williams. This creep went into George's store, and when George introduced himself, the nut whanged him upside the head with a can of kerosene."

"*Bingo!*" Allison said triumphantly. "A. H. Layard, the world authority on the Yezidis, says that 'the name of *Goorgis* (George) is, however, objectionable; and is never, I believe, given to a Yezidi.' Since the guy you've got in jail sounds like he's completely out to lunch, it follows that he went ballistic when Williams introduced himself."

The sheriff scratched his head. "Well, we'll probably never get it to stand up in court, but it should be good enough as probable cause to get his public defender off our backs and allow us to keep him in custody."

Allison grinned at Barnard. "Got any more?"

"Try this one," Barnard replied challengingly. "Doris Rodgers says that Darius Marduk always picked the lettuce out of his salad, and that he went nuts when they showed him his room at the Lakeview Inn."

"Was the room blue?" Allison asked.

Barnard's shoulders sagged. "OK. You win. How'd you know?"

"Layard mentions that they never eat lettuce, and some other green vegetables, which explains the salad. And he also says that the color blue is an abomination and is never worn in dress or used in their houses."

Barnard stood up. "That's enough," he exclaimed, his disgust evident. "We've got enough circumstantial evidence now to link Marduk with the crime." He motioned to Estes. "C'mon, Bill. All this ought to be enough for us to convince the FBI that Doris really was an unwitting accomplice and to release her." The sheriff put on his hat, then tipped it to Allison. "Thanks very much, Ms. Kirstoff," he said courteously. "You've been an immense help." He looked compassionately at Rebecca. "Brian'll get her back. I know he will."

Allison followed Barnard out into the hall. "Thanks, Sheriff," she said quietly.

Barnard frowned. "You're the one who deserves the thanks, not me."

Allison looked away. "You do, too. Most sheriffs, especially small-town sheriffs, would've taken one look at me and either asked me out for a sandwich or asked me to fix them one. But you asked questions, listened, and accepted my expertise. That doesn't happen very often, and it means a lot to me when it does."

Barnard smiled understandingly. "Two reasons for that, Ms. Kirstoff. First, you came recommended by Joel Dryden, who carries a lot of weight around here. Second, I've got four daughters. Two are out of college—one's a deputy district attorney down in Portland, and the other is the Hancock County Coroner. Both are cute little bits of things, and both come home and tell their hard-boiled, veteran sheriff daddy stories that make *me* shudder." Barnard winked. "Believe me, I've been well trained." Another tip of the hat, and he was gone.

Maybe all the good ones are *taken,* Allison thought, *but it's sure nice to meet one of them, anyway.*

After Allison had returned, Rebecca looked at her. "I'm still not clear about what all this has to do with Lauri's being taken."

"Everything," Allison replied. "I'm ninety-nine percent sure they took her. But, to be completely sure, and to figure out *why* they took her, I need your help."

"Anything," Rebecca promised earnestly.

"OK, then," Allison said. "First, some questions that are going to seem kind of off the wall." Without taking her eyes from the screen Allison asked, "You said that Lauren was born over there, right?"

"That's right. In an American missionary field hospital."

"In some place called Ain Sifni?"

"Ain Sifni is a village a few miles from the Nineveh excavation site," Rebecca confirmed.

"Was some sort of festival going on while you were there?"

Rebecca frowned. "Now that you mention it, yes," she said after a moment. "When I got back into good enough shape to care about such things, I asked the missionary couple about it. They said they were frustrated because it was some sort of religious observation that none of the locals would explain to them. Why?"

Allison held up a hand. "Did the locals display a lot of interest in Lauren? Even more than might usually be expressed in a foreign child?"

"They sure did," Rebecca replied. "There was a steady stream of them coming in to see her. Almost drove me crazy. Some of them even knelt down beside us and prayed over her. It didn't worry me, since Brian was there and I knew that the missionaries had some converts."

Allison stared intently at her screen. "That cap Brian said they found in Lauren's crib. Is it," she asked, "a white silk cap with gold coins sewn to it?"

"Why, yes," Rebecca replied with some astonishment. "How did you know?"

Allison merely frowned. "Was there a large white building nearby?"

"Yes," Rebecca answered, her voice now tinged with worry. "Right next door to the hospital. The festival seemed to center around whatever was going on inside the building. The missionaries didn't know what it was—they'd never been allowed inside."

"Did the building have a spire on it?"

Suddenly cold, Rebecca wrapped herself up in her sweater. "Yes, it did. A tall, white one. I liked it because it shaded the hospital in the afternoons."

"In talking to the Yezidi leaders," Allison explained, "Layard found out how they choose a new spiritual leader. He reports that on a certain day, when the Yezidi shamans have determined that the portents are correct, the child born closest to the hidden tomb of Sheikh Adi, the founder of the sect, is taken from its parents. This child is then raised by the Yezidis to become their next *kalifa*, or spiritual leader."

"Even if the allegedly 'anointed' child turns out to be a girl?" Joel asked.

Allison nodded. "When talking about the Yezidi spiritual offices, Layard says that they 'descend to females,' who are then treated with the same respect and consideration as the men." Allison took a sip of Diet Coke. "Also," she added, "Layard talks about how a white silk cap adorned with gold coins is placed on the child's head as an indication of divinity." Allison frowned. "The cap Sheriff Barnard found must've fallen off unnoticed after they'd put it on Lauren's head."

Allison found herself grimacing at her reconstruction. "And," she finished, "as for that Koran verse they found pinned to Lauren's crib, it's called the *Ayat el Courci*, or 'Throne Verse.' According to Layard, the *Ayat el Courci* is inscribed on the wall of the Yezidi leader's throne room."

"So," Joel reasoned, "if the Yezidis intend for Lauren to be their next spiritual leader, then it makes a perverse sort of sense that they'd announce that by leaving this verse behind."

Allison nodded in agreement, then turned back to her computer. "Layard then goes on to say that, at a time again decreed by the Yezidi shamans, the future *kalifa* must be transported to the tomb of Sheikh Adi and baptized in the water that flows from a spring located inside the tomb, which they believe to be sacred. Clay balls inscribed with the Arabic for 'kalifa' are presented to those attending the ceremony. They are believed to be powerful talismans." Allison paused. "Clay balls," she added, "just like the ones Anne and Rebecca found."

"I might add, however," Allison said, "that Layard, good Protestant Englishman that he was, wasn't too certain about the wisdom of all this. When his Yezidi hosts asked him to name a Yezidi child, Layard reports he was 'naturally anxious to ascertain the amount of responsibility I might incur, in standing godfather to a devil-worshiping baby.'"

Rebecca gasped. "So what you're telling me," she replied slowly, "is that just because my daughter happened to be born in a certain spot at a certain time, the members of an ancient Mesopotamian devil-worshiping cult have tracked her down, kidnapped her, and taken her back to Iraq to raise her as their next spiritual leader."

"I'm afraid so."

Rebecca got up. Without a word she crossed her den and lifted the bas-relief of the Assyrian genius from its place on the wall. Her face set, she turned and threw open the outside door. Joel started to follow her, but stopped at the touch of Pat's hand on his forearm.

Pat shook her head gently. "She needs to do this."

Rebecca marched resolutely to the end of the dock. She stared at the carving for a long time, her lips working. Then, with all her strength, she flung the bas-relief out into the deep waters of Moosehead Lake. When the ripples had disappeared, Rebecca started back toward the house.

28

"Randy! Wake up!" Marakova's voice shattered Randy's much needed sleep. He groaned, then swung his feet over the edge of the bed and sat up.

"This had better be good," he muttered, rubbing his face with his hands. *No wonder the shrinks compare sleep to falling,* he thought blearily. *In both cases, it's that sudden stop at the end that really fouls things up.* Randy's eyes opened and focused on a belt buckle. His gaze traveled upward, over Marakova's crossed arms, to her intense, clearly worried gaze. *Great,* Randy thought wearily, *if this cross between Jezebel and Genghis Khan is worried, then we're in deep trouble.* "What's up?"

Marakova sank into a chair next to the bed. "A friend of mine in the Information Ministry called. He told me that he had overheard part of an intercepted BBC World Service news report. He said that, according to the BBC, America has announced that they are going to attack Iraq."

Randy sat up suddenly, then wished he hadn't. "When?"

Marakova shrugged. "He didn't know. That was the part of the newscast he didn't hear."

"Why did your friend take the risk of telling you this?" Randy asked. "Does he know I'm here?"

"No!" Marakova replied emphatically. "Do I look so foolish?" Her voice hardened. "Because of my foreign heritage, I am considered potentially unreliable. People so considered are rounded up and imprisoned when anything out of the ordinary occurs." Marakova looked away. "Before the last war, a cousin of mine was taken away to a Republican Guard prison. She died—eventually. My friend called to give me time to escape before the Republican Guard comes after me." Randy caught a whisper of musky perfume as she leaned close. "You must escape, too. If they find you, they will kill you. Horribly."

Randy stood experimentally. "Well," he said after a moment. "I've felt worse. But usually after I've had a lot more fun than I've had the past couple of days."

Marakova studied his tired face. "Are you well enough?"

He looked down at the suddenly small woman standing next to him. "I'd better be," he replied with a grin. "I don't want to wave to the folks back home through the TV camera mounted in the business end of a half-ton smart bomb."

Marakova handed him a bowl of hot, mahogany-colored liquid. "This is made from *qat* leaves," she explained. "We use it here as you use coffee."

Randy sipped experimentally. "Yuck," he said, grimacing. "If this is your idea of coffee, then don't take me to one of your espresso joints." Making a show of holding his nose, Randy finished the *qat*.

Marakova tugged on Randy's hand. "We must leave. Now."

The rusted-out Trabant clattered to a stop. "This is as far as I go," Marakova's cousin declared firmly. The grimy glass front of Sadaam International Airport stretched away behind the car. Ahead, a sagging chain-link fence topped with barbed wire cordoned off the airfield. The smell of jet fuel hung heavily in the stagnant, late-evening air.

Randy and Marakova got out of the Trabant. A hand appeared from where the driver's side window should have been. With a muttered, "Keep the change, Abdul," Randy stuck the agreed-upon hundred dinar note into Marakova's cousin's hand. The hand vanished, and the car rattled away.

"Now what?" Marakova asked.

Randy stood thinking. *Let's see. . . . If the reviewing platform was over* there, *then that should put what I'm looking for right about* there. He nodded, then turned to Marakova. "Ready to board your flying carpet, princess?" he asked with an exaggerated bow.

"Certainly," Marakova replied. "But how?"

"First," Randy ordered, "it's time to lose the chador." Instantly the garment crumpled to the ground. Randy grinned as Marakova ground her heel into the cloth one last time.

Randy pointed. "See that sentry box by the gate down there?" Marakova nodded. Her eyes grew wide as Randy explained what they were going to do. "Got it?" Randy asked. She nodded again. *I know better than to ask if she thinks she's up to it,* Randy told himself. *This woman's got nerves of steel.* "One last thing," Randy finished.

"Yes?"

He glanced at her blouse. "Undoing a button or two would really help." Marakova drew herself up like a she-cobra preparing to strike. "Save it, honey," Randy commanded. "The whole point of your part of this little op is to make sure that the poor chump standing watch in that guardhouse down there is a whole lot more interested in *you* than he is in *me*." Randy grinned. "You've spent enough time rattling on to me about what pigs men are. I figure you should welcome this perfect opportunity to gather a little more empirical evidence in support of your theory."

Marakova's glare melted into a grimace. She nodded curtly, then turned her back.

"Ready?" Randy asked.

"Ready."

"Let's do it."

❖ ❖ ❖

She appeared suddenly in the pool of light cast by the goose-neck lamp mounted to the front of the guardhouse. The guard's eyes came up from his magazine, followed an instant later by the rest of his head. He stared as she walked slowly by, the light seeming to flow over her.

Please, Allah, he whispered in his mind as he ogled her, *please let this be a houri, one of the perennially beautiful, young, and virgin maidens who dwell in paradise and whom you send to reward true believers with sensual pleasures beyond our imaginings.* Breathing hard, he watched her approach. *Even if it means my death, please, Allah, let her be mine.* An incandescent smile took away what remained of his breath.

Then the woman swayed into the gloom, and the guard saw the overnight case she was carrying. He shook his head. *As always, it is another who is to sample the fruits of paradise tonight.* He stepped out of the guardhouse. "Excuse me," he called. "But I need to see your pass."

The woman whirled. Only her face reappeared in the cone of light, its smile replaced by a basilisk glare. "Are you talking to *me?*" she hissed venomously. Just as the sentry began to reply, she spat a stream of Arabic invective at him.

The guard flinched at the scalding insults. "Please, *habibi,*" he stammered, "I need to see your pass." *This is no houri; this is a desert sirocco in female form.*

"I need no *pass,*" she hissed. "At this very minute General Akif himself waits to whisk me off to a weekend in Tangiers." Her eyes, black in the dim yellow light, threw sparks. "Surely when the general arrived, you didn't check to see if *he* had a pass." The woman turned contemptuously on her heel.

I know every general who keeps a plane here, the guard

316

realized, *and there is no General Akif among them.* The sentry stepped out of the guardhouse with a shouted, "Halt!" As he strode after her, the edge of a hand flashed in the lamplight.

Marakova returned to where Randy was standing. "Did you kill him?" she asked.

"No," Randy replied, wincing as Marakova nudged the guard's inert form none too gently with the pointed toe of her riding boot. "But he'll have a very sore neck for a few days, if that's any comfort to you." He pointed toward a hangar. "And now, Princess Jasmine, your flying carpet awaits."

Marakova stared at him. "Princess *who?*"

Randy chuckled. "Never mind—you'll find out when you get to America. Let's go."

They trotted across the tarmac toward a row of tall, corrugated-iron buildings. A narrow band of light revealed that the first of the hangar doors was ajar. Beckoning for Marakova to follow, Randy headed toward it.

Randy pressed his face to the opening and surveyed the brightly lit interior.

"Well?" Marakova asked.

"Empty," Randy replied. "Let's try the next one."

"Don't you know where this 'magic carpet' of yours is?" Marakova asked as they jogged the length of the first hangar.

"Not exactly," Randy admitted. "But I do know where it should be." *Assuming it stopped here in the first place. And assuming it hasn't been flown back out or moved somewhere.* At the edge of the hangar he stopped and peered cautiously around the corner of the building. The road between the hangars was empty, and they dashed across to the next building.

"Locked," Randy muttered after tugging repeatedly on the hangar door. He turned to Marakova. "Let's work our way around and see if there's a back door. Sometimes there are offices in the rear—"

The wail of a siren cut him off. Both Randy and Marakova looked over their shoulders. Headlights were converging on the sentry box. "Looks like the changing of the guard isn't going too smoothly tonight," Randy noted. "C'mon!" Grabbing Marakova's hand, Randy dashed toward the third hangar.

When the door of the third hangar refused to open, Randy drew his pistol. *Always have wanted to shoot a lock off*, Randy noted. *Of course, in real life the bullet probably ricochets and kills you.* As his finger tightened on the trigger, Randy suddenly found himself enveloped in a rectangle of light. He whirled, bringing his pistol up.

Marakova stood behind him, holding open a small door set into the large hangar door. Harsh light from the hangar's arc lamps washed over her. "I don't think that shooting the lock off will be necessary," she observed calmly. "Besides, it can be quite dangerous."

"Thanks," Randy said, lowering the pistol. "Remind me to kiss you again sometime. Soon." He eyed Marakova wryly. "May I call you 'Mata,' or would you prefer 'Ms. Hari'?"

Ignoring Marakova's puzzled look, Randy stepped into the hangar. His shouted "*Yes!*" brought Marakova in behind him. "There it is!" Randy exulted, pointing. "There's our ticket out of here."

It sat in the center of the hangar, gleaming white, red and blue stripes racing back from its needle nose to the V-shaped tail. Uniformed mechanics bustled about, disconnecting hoses, still unaware of Randy's and Marakova's entrance.

"I saw it land during the ceremony the government held to welcome the diplomatic mission," Randy explained, grinning at the sleek aircraft. "It's a BD-10, manufactured by the Bede Aircraft Corporation of Saint Louis, Missouri."

"That is the personal aircraft of the thug who runs this country," Marakova added, ignoring Randy's aeronautical embellishments. "I cannot tell you how many times on TV I have seen that pig's repulsive face sneering down at the camera from this aircraft. While he *claims* to be a master pilot," she added waspishly, "it is common knowledge that all the flying is done by the 'bodyguard' in the backseat."

"Whatever," Randy answered. "Where you fly it from is irrelevant. The important thing is that it can get us out of here."

Marakova's look was plainly skeptical. "You can fly this?"

"Sure I can," Randy replied, radiating a confidence he didn't feel. "Cut my teeth in one." *Actually, almost* broke *my teeth in one*, Randy admitted to himself. *A fifteen-minute demo ride in one of these with a wild man at the controls is* not *my idea of a thorough check ride.* "They've finished preflighting it," Randy pointed out, "which means that the 'pig' himself will probably be here soon. If we're going to get out of Dodge in this little honey we should do it—" shouts went up as the mechanics, finished with the exacting job of readying the aircraft for flight, finally noticed them— "now!" Randy looked around frantically, then slammed his fist against a large red plate set into the hangar wall. With a motorized throb the hangar door began to inch its way open. Randy grabbed Marakova by the wrist and pelted toward the jet.

Randy raised the pistol he was still holding in his other hand. The sound of the shot echoed deafeningly around the hangar, and the ground crew scattered as glass from the shot-out light crashed down. A door at the back of the hangar flew open, and a man in an army uniform looked out. Randy snapped off a shot in his direction, and the man disappeared.

Its canopy raised, the little jet sat no more than five feet high. "Get in the back!" Randy ordered. He started around the back of the plane, firing shots at random into the hangar walls, thus keeping the ground crew occupied as he performed the most cursory of preflight inspections. A cardboard oval blocked the air intake on the jet's nose. Randy grabbed the long red ribbon that dangled down from the oval, pulled it out, and threw it aside. *Ready to go*, he thought as he came full circle around the plane.

Marakova still stood there, hands on hips, glaring at him.

"I told you to get in!" Randy barked. Soldiers began pouring out of the door at the back of the hangar. Randy fired over Marakova's head at them, smiling grimly as she flinched.

"I will *not* ride in the personal plaything of the cretinous lecher who had my family killed!"

Randy fired twice more, then holstered his weapon. "Last time a date of mine behaved like this, she walked home," Randy said threateningly. "But, since that's not a option this time, I'll have to do *this.*"

Randy swept Marakova into his arms. As she beat ineffectually against his chest, he lifted the protesting woman up and dumped her unceremoniously into the back of the BD-10.

A shot whistled past his head. *It'll only take one of those into this little honey to put us out of action*, Randy realized as he slithered into the pilot's seat. After two more quick shots the pistol clicked on an empty chamber. Randy threw the useless weapon away.

A commotion from behind him caused Randy to look around. Marakova had righted herself and was trying to get out. Randy shook his head in disgust. "Mind your fingers!" he called loudly as he flicked a switch on the control panel. Randy watched as Marakova snatched her fingers out from between the frame and the rapidly closing canopy just in time. He grinned as the descending Plexiglas bubble rapped her smartly on the top of her head.

"Buckle up," he commanded. "This is where the ride starts to get fun." Randy turned his attention to the instrument panel. "OK, sweetheart," he muttered. "Time to warm you up." His hands flew over the instrument panel. "Flaps thirty . . . preheaters to on . . . altitude preselect to auto . . . reset AOA/TVSI/AS." Randy's eyes swept over the instruments. Satisfied, he reached down with his right hand and flipped a covered switch. "Igniters—on!"

A whispering roar filled the aircraft as the General Electric J-85 engine came up to speed. Randy eyed the half-open hangar door as it ground open with agonizing slowness. *Just a couple of feet more.* He heard shots, muffled by the canopy. A quick glance revealed the soldiers racing the length of the hangar, toward the BD-10's tail. Randy stood on the brakes and shoved the throttle forward. The protesting aircraft quivered as the jet's thundering exhaust created a hurricane that filled the hangar, scattering the soldiers. *Time to go,* Randy decided. He released the brakes, and the sleek jetliner shot forward.

Randy held his breath and threaded the BD-10 through the hangar door's needle eye. As he brought the jet out onto the airfield, he glanced behind him. Marakova sat quietly, staring stonily out through the canopy, her arms folded across the restraining harness that held her to her seat. A flare of brilliant light snapped Randy's attention back around. Rows of headlights had suddenly appeared, blocking their path, growing ever brighter as the jet rushed toward them.

Randy jammed down hard on the left rudder pedal. The BD-10's nose wheeled around in an arc, and the faces of frightened soldiers swept past. The shuddering aircraft bucked violently as a wingtip nicked the roof of a jeep. *Hope we can live without whatever used to be there*, Randy thought as he fought to straighten out the jet.

"Do you always fly this way?" Marakova asked.

"This is nothing," Randy retorted. The aircraft shot off the tarmac and bounced across a median strip. "Just wait until we're airborne."

Randy swung the BD-10 back around to the right, centering the plane's nose on the runway. From the corner of his eye he could see the jeeps they had just avoided speeding toward them. He slammed the throttle home, and the jet leaped forward.

"Put on that headset beside you," Randy asked Marakova, "and tell me what the tower is saying about all this." The airspeed indicator crept toward takeoff speed. *Let's move it*, Randy urged the sleek jet.

Marakova's voice came from behind him. "Unauthorized takeoff . . . stop immediately . . . under arrest . . ."

"Good," Randy replied. "That means they've noticed us and will wave off any incoming aircraft." *I hope.*

Randy looked behind him. The jeeps had swung onto the runway in pursuit of the stolen jet. Machine-gunners were standing in the back of two of the jeeps. "Remember, boys," he muttered, "shooting big holes in your beloved leader's pet plane will *not* get you put on the fast track to promotion." Randy hauled back on the controls. *Nonetheless*, he admitted, *about now they're going to realize that they can't catch us.* He felt the plane's nose start to come up. *They also see we're taking off. Which means they're going to—*

Randy felt the BD-10 leave the runway. Instantly, he swung the controls hard over, throwing the BD-10 into a tight turn. Marakova gasped as the nimble little plane stood on one wing thirty feet above the ground. Red streaks from tracer bullets rushed past them in the opposite direction as they fled, climbing into the night.

29

The landing officer brought his luminescent paddles together and sharply down, signalling the Sikorsky SeaKing to land. As the helicopter settled to the *Paul Revere*'s deck, a crewman inside slid the cabin door open. "Last stop, gentlemen. Sporting goods, ladies lingerie, unfriendly natives. Hope you enjoyed the ride."

Jake and Brian shouldered their duffels and jumped out into the still, dry air of the Arabian night. In front of them a man wearing a helmet, his face a ghastly orange in the light of the hooded flashlight he was waving, was directing them toward a rectangle of light on the far side of the flight deck. A small cyclone laden with the pungent aromas of jet fuel and hot metal whipped up around them as the SeaKing lifted off into the night.

As the pair trotted across the deck, a figure stepped out of the lit hatchway. Brian waved. "My brother-in-law, Mark," he told Jake.

Mark nodded without smiling. There was no traditional SEAL greeting of punching each other's shoulders while swapping friendly insults. "I've got about four hundred friends onboard the *Alameda* who are chomping at the bit to help you get her back," Mark told Brian.

"They know about it?" Brian asked.

"You bet we do," Mark replied grimly. "It's been page-one news in the *Stars and Stripes* since the Iraqi announcement. What my shipmates don't know is that the two of you are here."

Brian shrugged. "Tell your friends thanks, but the four of us will manage."

Mark frowned. "The four of you?"

"Yeah. Jake, me—," Brian opened his jacket to reveal a gleaming stainless steel .357 tucked into a shoulder holster— "and Smith & Wesson." He zipped up his jacket.

"C'mon down to the goat locker," Mark suggested. "You can meet the last member of our little dance troupe."

"The goat locker?" Jake asked as he struggled to keep up with Mark and Brian as the two sped effortlessly down the near vertical gangways that led into the *Paul Revere*'s depths.

"The noncommissioned officer's galley and mess," Mark explained over his shoulder. "You only have to see one to know why they're called that. I tried to get Turk to wait for us in the officers wardroom, but he'd have none of it. So, off to the goat locker we go."

Shiloh Turk came to his feet as the three men entered the mess room. He threw Brian a casual salute, then stuck out his hand. "Welcome aboard, Commander. Good to see you again. And don't worry. When we're done with 'em, those ragheads are gonna be sorry they ever set eyes on your little girl."

"Thanks, Chief. And thanks for letting us tag along on your little sight-seeing tour."

Turk surveyed Jake appraisingly. "This the army guy?"

"His name's Jake MacIntyre, Chief."

Turk's gray eyes bored into Jake, who stared back with unwavering intensity. "The lieutenant says you were an officer." Disgust crept into Turk's eyes. "What outfit?"

Jake didn't move. "One-oh-one Airborne."

"Ranger?"

Jake nodded.

'Nam?"

Another nod.

"You see action?" Turk asked. "Or were you one of those prissy office boys?"

"I led patrols out of Chau Doc, Chief," Jake said quietly. "Every night. Two tours."

Turk relaxed slightly. He pulled a scarred K-BAR knife from its scabbard. Challenging Jake with his eyes, the chief inclined his head toward a dartboard mounted on the far wall of the mess room.

Jake smiled and shook his head. Turk's eyebrows shot up. "Thanks for the loan," Jake said softly, "but I prefer to roll my own."

In a single motion a wicked, gleaming bowie knife appeared in Jake's hand and was sent humming toward the dartboard. Before the three could turn to watch its flight, the eight-inch blade sliced into the target with such force that the board split in two. The knife ricocheted off the steel bulkhead and clattered against the deck.

Turk nodded approvingly. "You'll do." He bunched a massive fist to give Jake a friendly punch.

"Careful which shoulder you punch him in," Brian warned.

"Why's that?"

"One of them stopped a VC bullet."

The master chief shrugged disparagingly. "So? Just like a ranger to be too slow, too stupid, or too noisy to avoid gettin' popped." Turk grinned sardonically at Jake's glare.

"Jake took the bullet while making a pickup on one of his men," Mark said seriously. "They gave him a Silver Star for it."

"So you don't miss pickups, Army?" Approval glinted in Turk's combat-hardened eyes.

"Never have," Jake replied seriously. "Never will."

Turk's approval turned to respect. "I can work with a decorated ranger," the seaman decided. He stuck out his hand. "You may be army, MacIntyre, but you're one I'd be willing to have at my side during a scramble." He grinned. "Well, gentlemen, shall we get ready to hop-and-pop?" Turk motioned toward the door. "Let's go downstairs. Just wait till you see the toys that got delivered today."

✧ ✧ ✧

"Cripes, check this stuff out," the young sailor exclaimed. He was helping the chief quartermaster's mate unpack a large crate that a cargo jet had deposited on the *Paul Revere*'s flight deck earlier in the day. "No wonder we had to use the elevator to get it down belowdecks." The seaman held up a machine gun, its long snout deadly even through layers of wrapping. "Ain't seen one of these before," he said wonderingly.

"And no wonder," the other quartermaster replied scornfully. "That's a Heckler & Koch MP5. One of them costs the navy the same as about four of us. *Not* the kind of weapon issued to a cannon-fodder rating like you—"

"Tenhut!" Shiloh Turk's bellow echoed through the cargo bay. The master chief stormed up to the two rigid sailors. "Who opened this crate?"

"I did, Chief," the chief quartermaster replied, staring straight ahead. He knew better than to look at Turk. If one chief was dressing down another in front of an enlisted man, then something was *really* wrong.

"By whose authority?" Turk didn't bother with the quivering enlisted man.

"Standard operating procedure, Chief. All incoming cargo is to be inspected." The quartermaster didn't think the old "standard operating procedure" dodge was going to work this time. He was right.

Turk grabbed the H&K from the seaman's nerveless fingers and ripped it from its shrink-wrap cocoon. "And all incoming weapons are to be test fired before being put into service," he barked. "That's also SOP." The master chief fingered the barrel and glared at the terrified seaman. "Now, which one of you two dip-dunks should I try it out on first?"

Mark came into view, strolling casually across the hangar deck. "Think that'll really be necessary, Chief?" he asked calmly, having apparently accidentally stumbled across the altercation.

"If they aren't smart enough to read shipping labels," Turk growled, pointing to the EYES ONLY—LT. M. SEWELL stencilled on the crate, "then we'd be doing the navy a favor if we wax 'em."

"You have a point," Mark agreed. "What's your name, sailor," he asked the seaman. "so we can notify your next of kin."

"O'Connor, sir." The young man's eyes never left the machine-gun's barrel.

"Where you from, O'Connor?"

"San Diego, sir."

"Navy family?"

"Yes, sir."

Mark nodded sagely. "Then they're probably used to deaths in the family. You married?"

"Yes, sir. Four months now."

The lieutenant paused. "That'd mean a young widow. And it is tough these days to live on a survivor's pension." Mark made a show of reconsidering. "Think you can keep your mouth shut about this crate, O'Connor?"

"Yes, sir!"

"San Diego's a nice, warm place. You ever been stationed in Alaska, O'Connor?"

"No, sir."

"There's an icebreaker base up there, in the Aleutians, where it gets down to a hundred below at night. During the day, you go sunbathing when it gets above freezing. Guys I know who've been stationed there say that you get to like boiled blubber for breakfast—after eight or ten years." Mark stared at O'Connor. "Get my drift, sailor?"

"Aye aye, sir!"

Mark eyed the chief quartermaster's mate. "How about this one?" he asked Turk.

"Meet me in the goat locker at eight bells, Hopkins," Turk growled. The quartermaster suppressed a wince.

Mark nodded to Turk. "Dismissed!" Turk said, and the two sailors disappeared.

Laughing, Mark leaned against the crate. "I thought those two were going have to clean up after themselves. Shame to have to set them up like that."

Turk shrugged. "Yeah, it was," he agreed. "But it sure put the fear into them. And by the end of the watch, the whole crew will know that we're crazy, even for SEALs. They'll also know to give hangar twelve, its contents, and its band of psychos a wide berth." The old chief looked at his commanding officer. "It'll give us the operating room we're going to need."

"I know," Mark agreed. "But it was still a dirty trick."

"This was nothing, sir," Turk said quietly. "Not compared to the tricks we're going to have to play on the Iraqis if we're to get your niece and that lady ambassador away from them in one piece."

❖ ❖ ❖

Brian shook his head theatrically as they unpacked their gear. "I checked with the airlines, Mark, and all flights into Al Bahrah International Airport are booked solid. So, how *are* we getting into the petroleum paradise of Basra?"

Mark grinned. "Anxious to get on with the rowing, bro?" Brian nodded eagerly.

"We're going to row to Basra?" Jake asked. "I know this is a naval op, but isn't that a bit much?"

Mark and Brian laughed. "Something my dad taught me," Brian explained. "First time we went out fishing. I hadn't learned how to swim yet, and even though I was wearing a life jacket, I was still terrified of the water. So I asked him what we would do if the boat sprang a leak. He said, 'Pray real hard and row like mad for the shore.'" Brian smiled at the memory. "His other favorite phrase was, 'You do your best, and leave God the rest.' I eventually learned just what that means, and Becky and I have been trying with varying degrees of success to impress it on this hotheaded young relative of ours." Brian looked expectantly at Mark.

"Whenever a problem comes along," Mark replied, "part of the solution is up to you, and part is up to God." Mark grinned. "The trick is, for any given problem, figuring out which part is whose. Like now."

"The same rules apply now," Brian replied seriously. "My part is to do the very best I can to get Lauri back. If I fail, then if I'm still alive, when I get back my part will be to take care of Becky." Brian looked at Jake, who nodded his understanding. "Other than what I have to do to rescue my daughter, dealing with her kidnappers is not my job." Brian hefted a pistol and sighted along its barrel. "The rest of the solution, no matter how it turns out, is always up to God."

Brian eyed each of the men around him. "Enough talk." He turned to Mark. "If we're going to be rowing soon, why don't you show us what we've got in the way of oars?"

"Right this way, gentlemen," Mark replied. He waved them over to where they had laid their equipment on a counter that ran the length of the hangar wall. "First off, just to let you know that we've spared no expense on this airborne mission, these are our parachutes."

Mark grinned at Turk as he returned from the goat locker. Turk shook his head in reply and muttered something about young punk officers that can't tell a canopy from a canapé.

"Suppose *you* tell Brian and Jake what we're going to be using, Chief," Mark asked.

Turk pointed at one of the large, backpacklike objects. "This is your Precision Aerodynamics Mark VII 'Accuracy' model RW canopy. Specially modified for use by the SEALs, it features a higher-than-normal aspect ratio and a wing loading of point-five-oh."

"Point-five-oh is kind of low, isn't it, Chief?" Jake asked.

Turk shrugged. "Depends on what you want to accomplish. If you're out to float around, hobnobbing with the beautiful people and enjoying the breeze, then you're right, it is. But if your objective is to get down quickly and precisely to where the action is, then this is the job for you." Turk surveyed Jake coolly. "What do you normally jump with?"

"A Paradactyl. I find it the easiest to keep my class D current with."

"Touché, MacIntyre. Class D is the best a civilian can get. You must know what you're talking about. How about you, Commander?" the chief asked Brian.

Brian shrugged. "Before I retired, I jumped with a Para-Commander Competition. But it's been a while." He winked at Jake. "The skydiving in Iraq is even worse than the fishing."

"If you used a Competition, you should have no problem," Turk promised him. He waved at an assortment of gear piled next to the parachute packs. "Gloves, helmets, tiger-stripe camouflage jumpsuits, Cochran jump boots, digital altimeters, Dytter 'dirt alerts,' we've got it all." The master chief grinned. "And as for ordnance, this is where we're going to get *real* dangerous."

Mark took over. "Dangerous, yes," he agreed. "But due to the presence of noncombatants, we're going to maintain a low degree of lethality."

Brian winced at the description of his daughter as a non-combatant. "You sound like you're briefing the Joint Chiefs," he snapped. "Can we just cut to the chase?"

Mark nodded understandingly. "Sure thing. Sounds like it's time for some strain relief." He reached into a cardboard carton sitting on the counter and pulled out a cylinder the size of a soup can. Then he pulled a pin from one end and threw the cylinder across the hangar.

With a startled oath Turk lunged behind one of the hangar's workbenches. Brian and Jake were close behind him.

Mark counted "three . . . four . . . *five!*" As he knelt beside them there was a loud bang followed by a rapid pattering sound that filled the hangar.

Feeling something bounce off his knee, Brian looked down. He picked up a rubber ball about the size of a grape. As the men stood they could see dozens of the balls scattered across the hangar floor.

"M-452 Sting Ball Grenade," Mark explained. "Designed to disorient and disable without killing."

"I can testify to the 'sting' part," Jake remarked, rubbing his arm where one of the balls had caught him.

"Same idea as rubber bullets," Mark went on, "but in grenade format." He reached into another carton, then grinned as the other three men hit the deck again. "No demo of this one. This is the M-485 Multi-Flash. When detonated it expels twelve firecracker-sized submunitions that detonate over a period of several seconds. Lots of boom, lots of flash; maximum disorientation with minimum injuries."

Brian squeezed the sting ball he was holding. "I don't like the idea of one of these catching Lauri in the eye," he said, looking at the rapidly blackening bruise on Jake's arm.

"Understood," Mark agreed. "The fireworks are just to get us to Lauri and the ambassador. Once there, we get selective." Mark pulled aside a cloth. Lying on the counter were four pistols and two rifles. "Heckler & Koch P-9S," he said, picking up one of the pistols.

"How about our Smith & Wessons?" Brian asked.

Turk shook his head. "Can't put a hush puppy on 'em. And if we're going to get the ladies out of there nice and quietlike, we're gonna need our silencers."

"And," Mark added, "we'll have these." He picked up one of the rifles.

"Is that a Gale McMillian?" Jake asked.

Mark nodded. "Model 86. Just in case we need to reach out and touch someone."

Brian hefted one of the gleaming rifles. He peered through its night sight, then looked at his brother-in-law. "So much for 'a low degree of lethality.'"

"The low lethality is intended for *our* side," Mark replied quietly. "Not necessarily for theirs."

30

The ragged outskirts of Baghdad flashed by below them as Randy eased the BD-10 up into the indigo sky. *That's the problem with clouds*, Randy thought as he scanned the crystalline evening sky. *There's never one around when you need one.*

"Where are we going?" Marakova asked from the BD-10's backseat.

"Good question," Randy replied. "Due east will get us out of Iraq the quickest, but the Iranians hate Americans even more than the Iraqis do—if that's possible—so I don't think we'll go that way." Randy thought for a minute. "Did your friend say what kind of attack we were going to launch?"

"No. Just that you—we were going to attack."

Randy grinned at the emendation, and the little jet sped on in silence. "We're going south," he decided at last. "The attack will probably come from our air force bases in Turkey. Plus, they've been shooting down anything larger than a gnat in the no-fly zone up there recently. Add to that the fact that Kuwait City has an international airport with a runway even *I* can't miss, and it means that we go south."

"And if the attack comes from the south?" Marakova asked.

"Then I fly while you blow the pilot kisses," Randy retorted. "Got your safety harness fastened?" he asked, changing the subject.

"No," Marakova replied petulantly. "It is uncomfortable."

"Fasten it. I might have to do some fancy flying."

"No!"

Randy jerked the stick over hard. Instantly, the BD-10 whipped around its axis in a snap roll. There was a gasp and squeal of fright from the backseat. "Got it fastened?" he repeated. A torrent of Russian and Arabic invective filled his headphones, followed by the click of a safety harness snapping shut. Randy grinned as he pointed the jet toward Kuwait.

✧ ✧ ✧

The briefing was held in the *Paul Revere*'s wardroom. Admiral Pierce sat off to one side, his face an unhappy mixture of relief at finally being briefed and annoyance that a major operation had been put in the care of a junior-grade officer.

Jake suppressed a grin at the look on Pierce's face. *He's working for a lieutenant, an enlisted man, and two retirees, one of whom isn't even ex-navy. Bet the old man's about to bust a gut.*

From the front of the wardroom Mark gestured at a large map of Iraq resting on an easel. "Our target is Basra," he said, pointing at a city at Iraq's southern tip. "A large port city and petrochemical refining center. We plastered it pretty good during the Gulf War, but enough refineries have come back on line to enable Iraq to begin smuggling large quantities of high-grade oil past our blockade."

"Or so the smart boys in Intelligence claim," Admiral Pierce grumped.

Mark continued the briefing without comment. *Wise move,* Jake decided. *Admiral baiting is a sport that can get out of hand real fast.* "Our objective is here," Mark explained. He removed the map of Iraq to reveal a high-altitude, high-resolution photograph. On it an area near a waterway was circled in red. "The al-Kafhar refinery. It's located right on the Shatt al Arab, the waterway that connects Basra to the Persian Gulf." He pointed to a circled area on the map. "Infrared imaging from one of our recon satellites has confirmed this area here to be the base of the sub that sank the *Mayfield*." Mark turned from the photo. "Thanks to the Iraqis' little infomercial, we know that Lauren Keefe is being held there." The admiral's eyes flicked to Brian. "We also know," Mark added, "that as of yesterday, ambassador Doral was there, too."

"Are we sure of that?" Pierce asked.

"The smart boys in Intelligence are," Mark replied, looking steadily at the admiral.

The lieutenant flipped the photo over. On the other side was a grainy enlargement, a view looking straight down. "This was taken by one of our U-2 spy planes," Mark explained. In the photo three people were walking from a car to a building. "The person in the middle has been positively identified to be the ambassador."

Pierce's executive officer, silent until now, leaned forward with an expression of interest. "How'd the NRO spooks manage that?" he asked, referring to the National Reconnaissance Office, the supersecret government agency in charge of interpreting photos from spy planes and satellites.

"I asked the same question of the Defense Intelligence Agency agent who briefed me," Mark replied. "She got all stone-faced and said, 'That's classified, mister.'" The handsome young officer grinned. "Later on, over coffee, she loosened up a bit and told me the NRO's image-processing computers had enhanced the photo. They could make out a mole in the right spot on ambassador Doral's cheek and read the initials embossed on her handbag." Everyone in the room blinked in disbelief.

"How do you propose to approach the objective, Lieutenant?" Pierce asked.

"By air, sir. We plan on parachuting into the area."

Pierce frowned. "You won't be approaching by water? The target *is* close to a waterway, and you *are* all SEALs." Pierce, a blue-water sailor who had made his mark aboard battleships, still felt uncomfortable with the notion of aerial combat.

"Mr. MacIntyre was an army ranger, Admiral," Mark replied. The admiral shifted uncomfortably at the tactful reminder. "That's one reason why an airborne approach is ideal." Mark looked at Jake. "While in the service, Mr. MacIntyre received at least as much jump training as SEALs do, and he's kept his parachutist's license current."

Brian, sitting next to Jake, leaned over. "Does Anne know," he whispered, "that instead of spending time with her, you spend it throwing yourself out of airplanes?"

Jake shook his head.

Brian grinned. "I didn't think so."

"How about an approach by boat?" The executive officer suggested. "We could drop you off right at the mouth of the Shatt al Arab."

Mark shook his head. "Not enough time between our deployment and the air strike. In order not to blow the air strike's advantage of surprise, we have to move at the last minute. That gives us enough time to get in or get out by water, but not both."

"Move up your deployment?" the XO asked.

"That'd put us into daylight," Mark replied affably, "and you know how much SEALs hate daytime ops."

Mark turned back to the easel. He reversed the photo again, back to the view of the refinery area. "What we propose to do is this: Parachute onto this island *here*, just offshore from the refinery. Move by inflatable boat across the Rooka Channel to the objective, secure the area and rescue the hostages, then escape by boat down the Shatt al Arab." He looked at Pierce. "That's where you'll come in, Admiral. We'll need a SEAL

Tactical Assault Boat to sneak as far up the waterway as it dares. The sooner it retrieves us the happier we'll all be."

Pierce beamed, happy that at least some part of this operation was going to be nautical. "We'll be there, mister. Sure that island's uninhabited?"

"If it isn't, Admiral," Turk rumbled, "it will be shortly after we arrive."

"Then you find American women unattractive?" Marakova was asking.

"Not at all," Randy replied warily. "As a matter of fact, I'm dating one right now whom I find very attractive." *And who quizzes me just as incessantly about my love life as you do.* Lights appeared over the horizon. "Got any idea where that is?" Randy asked, grateful to be able to change the subject.

Marakova peered over the left wing. "That is Nasiriyah, an unimportant village containing little more than peasants and camels," she replied dismissively. "Now, tell me about this American girlfriend of yours. Does she have—"

Something that sounded like a thunderclap caught the little jet and threw it end over end through the cloudless sky. Randy fought the controls, his eyes fixed on the instruments. Red lights blinked angrily on the panel in front of him. He sucked in his breath with a sharp hiss as the plane's gyrations slammed his wounded head against the canopy. *Ignore it, Cavanaugh,* he told himself. *It'll hurt a lot more to crash.*

The altimeter flickered down toward zero. Randy levelled the plane, then whipped it over to right side up. A quick glance ahead revealed an onrushing line of hills. *Max power—now!* Randy slammed the throttle against the stop and hauled back on the controls. The agile little plane darted upward, just clearing the ridge.

"What happened?" Marakova asked

"Someone issued either the peasants or the camels in that

unimportant village of yours un antiaircraft gun," Randy replied, breathing hard. "If they had fired an instant later, we'd be
toast." He surveyed his instrument panel. "As it is, they may
have done their job anyway."

"Meaning?"

"Meaning that, at the rate the hole in our starboard-wing
fuel tank is leaking gas, we may not get to Kuwait at all, much
less to the airport. I had intended to swing around into Saudi
Arabia and approach Kuwait City from the west, but that's out
now."

"So what are we going to do?"

"Head straight south. Straight into the no-fly zone. By the
way," Randy added with a mischievous grin, "feel free to unbuckle your safety harness any time."

"Be serious," she replied, obviously miffed. "Is there anything I can do to help?"

"Yeah. Think small and unobtrusive. Try and look like a
gnat."

❖ ❖ ❖

Back down in hangar 12, Jake, Brian, and Turk found chairs as
Mark put up the photo of the Middle East he had used to brief
the admiral. "We'll helicopter from the *Revere* to Al Bahrah, in
Kuwait. From there a C-130 Hercules will take us north, across
the border, to just short of Basra."

"Fighter escort?" Brian asked.

"Won't need it," Mark replied. "Basra is within the southern no-fly zone. For some time now we've been making life very
unpleasant for any Iraqi aircraft that showed up in the area, and
we're stepping it up in anticipation of the air strike. But just in
case there are any Iraqi antiaircraft batteries still functioning,
we'll have a EA-6B Prowler electronic-countermeasures aircraft along. The kind of stuff they broadcast gums up an
antiaircraft battery's radar something fierce." Mark pointed at

the refinery. "When we're ten miles from our objective, out we go. You had much HALO experience?" he asked Jake.

"High-altitude, low-opening jumps?" Jake replied. "Some. Depends on how high."

"Forty thousand. I'd like to go higher, but we'd need pressure suits."

All three men winced. "Cold up there," Brian commented.

"Around twenty degrees," Mark replied. "I've heard you call that swimming weather. So," he added with a grin, "wear your mukluks."

"Air's kinda thin, too," Jake added.

Mark grinned. "Last time I checked, we were going to be carrying oxygen." He drew a line northeast across the photo. "To make sure we fool the radar, we're going to max-track most of the way."

Jake's eyebrows shot up. He was familiar with the concept of a free-falling skydiver arching his body and falling headfirst at a steep angle. This turned the skydiver's body into an airfoil. The resulting lift allowed them to cover considerable horizontal distances.

"Makes sense," Brian agreed. "Maximum free fall means minimum target," he stated pedantically. "That's what we pounded into their pointy little heads when we were teaching at COMPHIBTRALANT."

Mark nodded. "If we do it right, we'll be exposed to radar for no more than four minutes. Plus, since the only metal we'll be carrying will be our weapons, we should be really hard to see on a radar screen."

"How much distance do you think we can cover by max-tracking?" Jake asked.

"I'm hoping for at least five ground miles," Mark answered. "If we can manage that much, once we open our chutes at two thousand we should be inside the radar picket that surrounds Basra. Then, given a descent rate of four feet per second and a ground speed of thirty miles per hour, we should cover the remaining five miles in about ten minutes. Fourteen minutes elapsed time from out the door to touchdown. Any questions?"

"Why not come in faster and steeper, and then open lower?" Brian asked. "Floating around up there for ten minutes doesn't sound real appealing."

Mark pointed at the photograph. "Accuracy. When we drop into the ocean, a few yards one way or the other doesn't matter. But this island is about ten yards wide by a hundred long. Too small to even get up a good game of touch football on. That means we give ourselves more time to set up our approaches." He looked at the others. "On this mission, a few yards could mean the difference between the island and the deck of an Iraqi gunboat.

"Once down," Mark continued, "we take an inflatable boat across the Rooka Channel to the refinery. There we split up. Turk and I go after Ambassador Doral while you and Jake fetch Lauren. We meet up back at the boat, then make our way down the Shatt al Arab to where the STAB will be waiting. That'll be the toughest part, because we're going to have to scream down the channel flat out in order to clear the area before the Airedales show up." Brian grinned at Mark's usage of the affectionate nickname for naval aviators. "Still," Mark added, "the whole op should take no more than two hours, tops. What could possibly go wrong?" A shadow crossed his face, and he got to his feet. "Almost time for jump-off. Let's gear up."

Concentrating as he was on keeping the wounded plane level and monitoring the fuel leak, the sudden burst of Arabic in his headphones startled Randy. "Who's that?" he asked Marakova.

Marakova listened. "It's not an Iraqi, it's . . . an American!" Randy could hear the astonishment in her voice. "She says that we have violated the no-fly zone and that we are to turn around or be shot down. Who is this person?"

"The controller aboard an AWACS radar plane," Randy replied tersely. "Sent out here to do just what they're doing." With a gloved thumb, Randy depressed the transmit button on his control stick. "We are a private, civilian aircraft," he reported. "We are experiencing a malfunction and are calling Mayday, repeat Mayday." *I'd call getting shot up by a bunch of camel herders a malfunction*, Randy decided.

"Aircraft calling, squawk two-two-zero and ident," the AWACS ordered.

"No can do, sweetheart," Randy replied. "Transponders are not a real hot item over here in the Middle East, and if this plane had one, it's all shot up now, anyway."

"Then say your call letters." Randy could hear the tension in the controller's voice.

"Don't have any of those, either. Look," Randy added, speaking rapidly. "I'm Randy Cavanaugh, part of the diplomatic mission to Baghdad that got attacked the other day. I was kidnapped, but I got loose and stole this plane."

"You really expect me to believe that?" the controller asked scornfully.

"No," Randy admitted. "But it's the truth. If you'll just get on the horn to Washington—"

"Unidentified aircraft," the controller rapped, her voice suddenly hard, "we've just identified your heat signature as a *jet* aircraft. So enough of the 'private, civilian aircraft' nonsense, buddy-boy. If you don't turn your tail around *now*, I'm vectoring in the F-4s."

"Look. Just call—"

"Break off! *Now!*"

Randy lifted his thumb from the transmit button. *Talk about hard to deal with.* "It doesn't look good," he told Marakova.

"The AWACS is calling in a couple of F-4 Phantoms. Our only hope is these guys give us the once-over before they shoot."

"We cannot outrun them?" Marakova asked.

"Not a chance. F-4s can fly faster straight up than we can straight down." *A fact which may be demonstrated in about five minutes.*

With exhaustion threatening to overwhelm him, Randy stretched as best he could in the cramped cabin. As he reached up to adjust his shoulder harness, he ran the back of his hand along something hard.

"*Yes!*" Randy's shout rang throughout the cockpit.

"What is it?" Marakova asked anxiously.

"Something that just might get us out of here in one piece," Randy replied. Grinning, he pulled the SATCOM transceiver Charlie Davenport had given him out of a jacket pocket.

❖ ❖ ❖

Marakova sat quietly, listening as Randy spoke fervently into the SATCOM radio. Much of what he said was unintelligible, so she turned her attention outside. The moon had risen, and the desert sweeping by below was bathed in a bright gray-blue light, striped by the inky shadows of the crescent-shaped dunes. A valley dotted with ruddy sparks revealed the encampment of a band of nomads. Marakova was struck by the contrast between their primitive campfires and the lethal, high-tech fire that Randy said would soon consume them.

They look like the cooking fires of Baghdad, Marakova thought as the camp disappeared behind her. *It was on nights like this that Hafez and I would go up to the little park on top of Touar Hill. We'd spread out a blanket, drink some wine, and watch the city lights, blending into the shadows with all the other couples around us.* Frowning, Marakova gazed up at the stars. *Why do I not miss you, Hafez? We were so close and you loved me so much, yet I have felt nothing since I received the news of your death.* She watched Randy's animated face, lit by the red glow from the instrument panel and reflected in the Plexiglas of the canopy. *And why is it that the thought of this man dying—this man whom I barely know, who refuses me the obeisance every other man has afforded me, and who infuriates me in ways I thought unimaginable—why is it that the thought of his death terrifies me?* A curl of Randy's blonde hair had strayed from beneath his helmet. Tenderly, Marakova reached up with a fingertip and smoothed it into place.

"This is Lieutenant General Richard Gillespie, commander of the Joint Special Operations Command Center at Fort Bragg, North Carolina," the voice coming from the SATCOM unit told Randy. "Now, for the last time, identify yourself!"

"It *is* going to be for the last time if I have to keep this up, General," Randy replied, trying to keep the tension out of his voice, "because in about two minutes a couple of your F-4 Phantoms are going to arrive looking for something to shoot down, and I'm in no condition to play aerial tag with a pair of hotshot fighter jocks. Now, how about a hand?"

"I'll need time to verify your cock-and-bull story."

"Is ninety seconds enough?" Randy rapped. He took a deep breath, then launched a last, desperate gambit. "Look, General, if we get vaporized up here, you're *never* going to find out how I got this unit, are you? Now either I'm telling the truth and you're about to shoot down an American citizen escaping from his kidnappers, or I'm lying and you're about to shoot down a high-tech spy the DIA will *really* want to interrogate."

Silence. A new rivulet of sweat coursed down Randy's back for each passing second. "Any second now," he told Marakova softly. "I'm sorry it turned out this way. I did the best I could."

"I know you did, Randy," she replied with equal gentleness. "Thank you for my few hours of freedom."

Like the specter of the Lilith rising out of the desert sands,

343

the dark shape settled in silently beside the small plane. Randy felt it before he saw it, a blackness against the sand and stars. Startled, Randy looked to his left, then prepared to throw the plane into a last, frantic maneuver to escape certain death.

"Don't move, buddy," the voice said on the frequency the AWACS had used. "My wingman's on your tail, so if you so much as twitch you're history."

Randy could see the moonlight glinting off of the F-4's canopy, not more than forty feet from where he sat. "No problem, friend," he assured the Phantom's pilot.

"Switch on your cabin light so we can see who you are," the fighter pilot ordered. Bright red light flooded the BD-10's cabin.

Marakova took off her helmet and shook her hair out. Then, slowly, she turned and gazed imperiously at the F-4's crew.

"Man, oh man!" the pilot exclaimed. The Phantom edged a few feet closer to the BD-10. "How come I never get a backseater who looks like that?"

"Because you're married," another voice replied. Marakova could see the man riding backseat in the Phantom staring at her. "And, as of right now," he said slowly, "I, too, am willing to seriously consider the notion."

"If you two are finished," the AWACS controller said with some asperity, "I need to vector you in to Al Bahrah air base in Kuwait."

"Expedite our approach as much as you can," Randy asked. "I'm just about running on fumes up here."

"Roger that," the controller acknowledged. "Wilco." Her tone changed. "Never have received orders straight from a stateside general before, Cavanaugh. Nice job. See you on the ground."

"Do you know her?" Marakova asked.

Randy grinned. "No," he replied, relishing her sudden interest. "But from the sound of her, I might like to."

With the F-4s flanking him, Randy brought the BD-10 in over the Kuwaiti oil fields to a perfect landing. Jeeps packed with MPs swarmed around them as he brought the jet to a stop. Rifles glinted in the beams of headlights.

Randy opened the jet's canopy. Slowly and stiffly he climbed out, hands in the air. Then he turned and encircled Marakova's waist with his hands. He swung her up and out of the aircraft, bringing her down to stand beside him in the headlights' glare. A chorus of long, appreciative wolf whistles arose from the darkness. Unsure how to react, Marakova turned and looked up at Randy.

Randy grinned down at her. "Welcome to America."

31

Jake shifted uncomfortably in his hard bucket seat. The C-130's red lighting made the dark-green tiger-stripe camouflage jumpsuit appear jet black. "I feel like a wet seal in this," he told Brian, gesturing at the jumpsuit's slick, shiny neoprene surface.

"Hopefully, this stuff will keep you from becoming a wet seal, or worse," Brian replied. "We got the idea from watching the bobsledders at the Olympics. The smooth surface minimizes air resistance enough so, if you do everything else right, you end up on target instead of crashing through someone's bedroom roof."

The army loadmaster, seated near the hatch at the rear of the C-130, pressed his headset to his ears. "Five minutes!"

The four jumpers, two on each side of the C-130's center row of seats, made their final preparations. Jake put on his night-vision goggles, then strapped on his jump helmet. A quick check revealed that his Colt .45 was secured in place. Jake glanced over at Brian, who was sitting with bowed head and folded hands. When Brian looked up, Jake asked, "Just what sort of prayer do *you* say when you're about to step out of a plane eight miles up?"

Brian smiled. "This time, all I asked was that I'd find the one I love and bring her back safely to one I love even more."

Jake nodded. "Amen to that." As he bowed his head, Jake's fingers went to where the jumpsuit covered the breast pocket of his shirt. In that pocket was a small photo of an auburn-haired woman, smiling at him from a beach that just now seemed very far away.

The loadmaster's cry of "Two minutes!" opened Jake's eyes. "On your feet!" the army master sergeant shouted.

The four men got up. "Pin check!" Mark ordered.

Brian turned his back. Jake quickly checked Brian's canopy releases, rip cord, and canopy release handle, reminded Brian to check his instruments, then slapped Brian smartly on the shoulder.

Jake turned. He felt Brian check him, then Brian's gentle tap on his shoulder. "Thanks for remembering," Jake said with a grin.

"On my signal," Mark called, "start your timers. Three . . . two . . . one . . . Hack!" The four men stabbed the buttons on their watches that started the countdown. "Beacons on!" Mark ordered. Brian and Mark, as the lead jumpers, switched on tiny, light-emitting diodes attached to the back of their helmets. When seen through the light-amplification goggles, the flashing light would serve as a brilliant beacon for Jake and Turk to follow.

"One minute!" the loadmaster called.

"One minute!" four voices chorused in acknowledgment. A light over the hatch at the rear of the plane switched from red to blinking green.

The army sergeant spoke into his microphone, then looked at the man sitting across from him. "Navy," he announced with a smart salute, "your door!"

The navy jumpmaster returned the salute as he got up. "Oxygen!" he shouted. He and the sergeant both buttoned up their heavy, fleece-lined jumpsuits and slipped portable oxygen masks over their faces. Behind them, the four jumpers slid their small oxygen/communication units into place.

The Hercules tilted up slightly as the pilot slowed it to the jump speed of 130 knots. The jumpmaster stabbed a button, and a howling, icy wind filled the fuselage as the ramp at the back of the plane came down. Jake shivered as the C-130's meager heat vanished. Frost crystals sprouted on the windows.

After securing his lifeline to a stanchion, the jumpmaster walked out onto the ramp. "Ramp clear!" the jumpmaster announced as he reappeared.

"Lights off!" Mark ordered. The sergeant hit a switch, and the plane was plunged into blackness. "Goggles on!" The flashing green light over the hatchway became a shining beacon as Jake switched on his night-vision goggles.

"Thirty seconds!" the jumpmaster announced, his voice loud in Jake's earphones. "Jumpers, man the door!"

Mark, Turk, Brian, and Jake moved into position at the edge of the ramp. Mark grabbed the door frame with both hands, his knees flexed, ready to go.

Turk's laconic voice filled their ears. "See you on the ground, gentlemen."

"Save some bad guys for us, Chief," Brian replied.

Wonder if they feel as relaxed as they sound, Jake thought enviously. *Have to remember to ask Brian which is worse—waiting to drop or waiting to get married.* Jake grinned into the darkness. *Either way you're dressed up funny, and—*

The light overhead stopped flashing.

"Green light!" the jumpmaster shouted. *"Go! Go! Go!"*

Jake trotted forward as, one by one, his friends disappeared. Then, with a slap on the shoulder from the jumpmaster, Jake ran down the ramp and hurled himself into the night.

A wind like an iced razor sliced along Jake's exposed cheeks as he plummeted through the night. Hands at his sides and feet together, Jake arched his back. This brought him into the airfoil-like max-track position, necessary if they wanted to cover the ten ground miles between them and the island in the Rooka Channel.

"Everyone make it out?" Mark asked, his voice tinny in Jake's headphones. Through his night-vision goggles Jake could see Mark's helmet beacon about a hundred feet in front of him. Brian's was closer and brighter. Somewhere between them, Jake knew, was Shiloh Turk. "Turn right to zero-one-eight," Mark ordered after the others had checked in.

Jake pivoted forward. He was now falling face downward, at a sixty-degree angle to the ground. Below him was only darkness. *Never have had a sense of falling during night jumps*, Jake thought as he fell. *But the ground's just as hard as during the day, Mac, so stay awake.* He dropped his right shoulder, letting the tearing wind pull him around until the lighted dial of the digital compass strapped to his left wrist read 018. Seeing that he was still in a straight line with the two beacons, Jake relaxed.

"Through angels thirty-eight," Mark announced. "One ground mile covered. How're you doing, Chief?" he asked Turk.

"Just fine, sir," Turk replied. "Except there's not enough air up here to keep my cigar lit."

A fuzzy clump of lights appeared in Jake's vision. "That our target up there?" he asked.

"You got it," Mark replied. "That's the al-Kafhar oil refinery. We're going to come right in along the river, pull at two thousand, and drop right onto the island that's just across the channel from the refinery. And remember," Mark cautioned, "if you miss, make sure you miss left. *Way* left. We can always join up if we're all on land, but if you're in the Shatt al Arab or on the other side of it, you're on your own. Through thirty-five thousand now, seven miles to go."

"Jericho Five, this is Papa Bravo," another voice announced. "Victor X-ray Three Five." The voice cut off abruptly.

"Oh, great," Mark muttered. "That was our Prowler countermeasures plane. 'Vic-X-3-5' means they've been challenged by Iraqi aircraft and are scurrying for cover."

"Which means no protection from antiaircraft fire," Brian added.

"That's right," Mark agreed. "They shouldn't be able to detect us, but everybody think small anyway. And, Chief," Mark added, "douse that stogie. Through twenty-five thousand, six miles. I show terminal velocity."

Jake glanced at a readout on the instrument panel clipped to the top of the emergency chute strapped to his waist. His airspeed indicator read 137. *These days it's hard to get my MG to go that fast*, Jake realized with a grin. With his eyes fixed on Brian's blinking beacon, Jake sailed on through the darkness. The thickening air buffeted him, making it harder to maintain the max-track position.

"Through ten," Mark reported. "Everyone got the river?" The three others acknowledged their sighting of the thin ribbon of rippling water that was their guideline. "We pull in two minutes, on my signal. Unlimber your weapons as soon as your chute's deployed, and be prepared to hit the ground running."

"Just who you remindin', sonny boy?" Turk said. "Everyone else up here is *dry* behind the ears."

Their chorus of chuckles was interrupted by a sudden flare of illumination from the refinery. "Searchlights!" Mark exclaimed. "They must be tracking us on radar."

"Goggles up," Turk added. "Don't want to stare at no searchlight through these little honeys."

Jake reached up and pulled his night-vision glasses up onto his forehead. Although his jump goggles were untinted, it was still quite difficult to make out Brian's beacon against the onrushing welter of refinery lights. *Stay loose and stay on track*, Jake reminded himself.

"Five thousand. Pull in one."

"They're trackin' us," Turk observed as the searchlights began to swing their way. Lights on the ground began to rush away behind them with increasing speed.

"Stay together," Mark cautioned. "Three thousand. Prepare to pull."

Jake brought his gloved fingers up to the rip cord mounted on his left shoulder. Just as they closed around the steel D-ring of the canopy release handle, sudden fireworks appeared in the sky ahead of him.

"Flak!" someone shouted.

Flaming flowers blossomed all around Jake. Then a giant, invisible hand slammed into him and sent him sprawling through the air. Jake tumbled helplessly, falling toward the onrushing ground.

"Pull, Jake! Pull!" Brian's voice was loud and insistent in Jake's ears.

Jake shook his head to clear it, but the voice persisted. Then the jumble of spinning lights and darkness snapped into focus. Jake pulled savagely down with his right hand, triggering his rip cord. He felt his parasail deploy from the pack on his back. With a quick glance at the altimeter at his waist, Jake saw 1100 flash by.

There was no upward jerk. No slowing as the parasail unfurled. Still in free fall, Jake looked up. The refinery lights revealed tattered ribbons of nylon streaming away into the darkness. *That burst of flak got my chute*, Jake realized.

Reflexes conditioned by countless hours of training took over. Jake brought both hands up to his shoulders. Pain seared through his shoulder as he raised his right hand. *It got me, too*, he winced. He triggered the emergency releases with his thumbs and felt his main parasail let go. In the same motion his left hand went to the emergency parachute strapped to his stomach. Jake tugged on its release with all his strength. After a brief heart-stopping moment, he saw it unfurl.

The emergency parachute snapped open. Jake was tugged upward once, twice. Then he slammed into the unyielding ground.

Jake's nose tickled. *Funny*, he thought vaguely. *Didn't think we'd need to sneeze in heaven.* The tickling intensified, and Jake forced open one eye.

Another eye, small and beady, stared back at his. This eye surmounted a long, whiffling snout, at the end of which were curved, buck teeth and the whiskers that were tickling Jake's nose.

Jake closed his eye. *I can't be dead*, he realized. *There may be sneezing in heaven, but there sure aren't going to be any rats.* He dragged his hand out of the pool of slime in which it rested and batted at the rat, who scurried away.

"Jake, you there?" Brian's whispering was urgent and worried.

Jake rolled over. His head swam as he sat up, and he rubbed his forehead with his slimy hand. "Still with you," he told Brian. "Barely." Jake stared at the compass on his wrist until it came into focus. "Bearing zero-one-five, relative to you."

"Distance?" Brian asked.

"No clue," Jake admitted. He pulled down his night-vision goggles and looked around. "Just look for the city dump. But," he added, "mind the rats."

Jake clambered to his feet and began stripping off his jump gear. As he removed his helmet he caught a flash of motion from the corner of his eye. Jake crouched and spun, pulling out his Colt .45. "Brian?" he whispered. No reply. Jake called again, then reached up to where his headset's microphone should be. *You're off to a great start, Mac,* Jake berated himself as he realized that his headset was still inside the helmet he had taken off. *Now, just make sure you didn't leave what's left of your brains in the helmet, too.* Jake pulled the headset out of the helmet and put it on. "Brian?"

"Over here," Brian called, loudly enough to be heard without the radio. Jake turned again as Brian rose from behind a mound of bald tires heaped at the base of the hill on which Jake crouched. Brian walked toward him, shaking his head. "While you've been doing your little dance up here, nicely silhouetted against the lights of Basra, I could have been shooting at you."

Jake looked over his shoulder at the illuminated skyline. "Haven't done this sort of thing in a while." *And I was a whole lot younger the last time I did.*

"You OK?" Brian asked.

"Sure," Jake replied. "Feeling like I've been thrown down several flights of stairs is my normal operating mode these days. Check my shoulder, will you?"

Brian trained a small, red-lensed flashlight on Jake's left shoulder. "Nasty," he told Jake, "but the bleeding's stopped. Think you can use it?"

"Just as long as I don't have to bowl. Where are we?"

"On the far side of Basra from the refinery. I followed you down as best I could after you were hit, keeping one eye on you, one eye on Mark and Turk, one eye on the ground, and one eye on the bad guys. Mark and Turk landed smack-dab on the island, which is a good thing, since they have all the gear we need to get out of Fun City. While I was looking for you, they made it across the Rooka Channel, found the compound where the ambassador and Lauri are being held, and are waiting outside for us."

"How long did all this take?"

"Seventeen minutes," Brian replied. "Check your countdown timer—you'll see that we have fifty-three minutes left before our friends in the F-14s and F/A-18s arrive and light up the joint." Brian pointed toward the lights. "We've got about a mile to go to join up with Mark and Turk, so let's get a move on."

The dump was bordered by a road leading toward Basra. Brian and Jake trotted along it, watching for potholes that could snap an ankle, listening for any approaching vehicles.

"Fifty minutes and counting," Mark's calm voice said in their earphones. "Where are you?"

"About a half-mile outside Basra," Brian replied. "Give us five minutes to get to the city and fifteen to make it to where you—"

"Truck!" Jake hissed. The two men threw themselves into a muck-filled ditch as a truck came around a corner. They watched, screened by reeds, as the truck made its way slowly along the road. Soldiers lined both sides of the back of the truck, sweeping the sides of the road with flashlights as they drove along. Jake and Brian slid back down into the ditch. They hugged the miry bottom, motionless. The truck ground past them with agonizing slowness, the lights passing inches over them. When the truck could no longer be heard, they crawled back up to the edge of the road.

"We're later than we were a few minutes ago," Brian told Mark. "They're looking for us. Hard."

"Makes sense," Mark agreed. "They must've seen you and Jake come down, and missed us. That explains why it was so easy for us to get on station. Thanks for the diversion."

"Any time," Brian replied affably as he ran. "I set out decoys for my clients at home, so why not here, too?"

A single, pathetic streetlight marked the city limits of Basra. As Jake turned to skirt the town, Brian held up a hand. "No time. Our objective is straight across town and through the refinery. It's straight-line time." Brian pulled down a small, deadly Heckler & Koch MP5 submachine gun from where it was slung over his shoulder. "I'm on point. Let's go."

They trotted through the deserted streets of Basra, surrounded by dark, shuttered doors and the blank facades of rude masonry walls. At each intersection hung a single, bare bulb, swinging wildly in the wind. Down a side street, Bruce Springsteen's "Pink Cadillac" boomed from behind a shuttered window. A dog trotted across the street in front of them, saw them coming, and slunk away.

"Where is everybody?" Jake wondered.

"If you knew that the United States was going to blow up your town in forty minutes," Brian retorted, "where would *you* be?"

"This is not good," Brian told Mark eight minutes later. "The entrance to the refinery is guarded. There's a hundred yards of open space between us and the gate, and it's both well lit and well fenced. I can take the guard out from here, but it'll mean starting the fireworks early."

"How many of 'em are there?" Turk asked.

"I see one."

"Then I'll have the red carpet out for you boys in just a minute."

Crouched in the shadow of a building, Brian and Jake watched and waited tensely. Suddenly, for no apparent reason, the sentry collapsed. From the bushes on the far side of the fence a red light began blinking. Jake and Brian ran toward it.

"Welcome to the al-Kafhar oil refinery, gentlemen," Turk announced as he stepped out of the bushes. "I'm afraid the bar is closed for the evening, but there's still plenty of time to rock 'n' roll." One glance at the silencer on the end of the wicked-looking sniper rifle Turk carried told the two men what had happened to the sentry. "The lieutenant's over this way," Turk added as he melted into the undergrowth.

Mark grinned at them when they arrived, his teeth white

against the eerie green of his camouflage-painted face. He pointed to a pair of low buildings sitting across an access road. "The latest intel we've got says the ambassador's in the building on the right, and Lauren's in the one on the left." Mark looked at his brother-in-law. "Any preference as to who you go get?" he asked jokingly.

"Problem is," Mark went on, "we don't know just where in the buildings they are or who else is in there with them. So keep it quick and quiet for as long as you can. But, if you hear shots, turn it loose. Our inflatable is on the shore about a quarter-mile due east of here, right at the end of this road." The navy officer looked at each of his commandos in turn. "See you back on our beautiful island paradise, boys." Mark checked his watch. "We've got just thirty minutes, so let's do it to it." Turk gave them a thumbs-up, then slapped Jake on the shoulder.

"Turk pick the wrong shoulder?" Brian asked as they ran toward their building. Jake nodded grimly.

The building was a low, oblong structure, its windows screened by bushes. Jake and Brian trotted to the far end of the building, away from the road. Two concrete steps led up to a door in the building's end. A window set into the door threw a patch of yellow light onto the stony ground.

The two men crouched next to the steps, invisible in the deep shadow. Motioning for Jake to wait, Brian knelt on the edge of the top step and slowly raised his head until he could peek through the corner of the window. "We've got a hallway running the length of the building, with doors on either side," Brian reported as he knelt back down. "No one in sight. You take the right set of doors, and I'll take the left."

Brian reached up with a black-gloved hand. The doorknob turned. Brian and Jake slithered through the barely open door. As Jake came to his feet in the hallway the wind blew the door shut with a resounding bang. Both men froze, guns ready. Nothing.

Jake opened his first doorway. Darkness. The beam of a mini-flashlight he pulled from a pocket revealed rows of dusty filing cabinets. Jake worked his way down the hall, opposite Brian, every nerve taut, eyes constantly searching. An empty bedroom, more storage, a dank and vile-smelling toilet. Just as Jake began to open the fifth door, shots rang out in the distance.

"Contact! Contact! Everybody go!" Mark's voice rapped in Jake's headphones. Their surprise gone, Jake opened the door with a booted foot. The door crashed against the wall. Behind a desk across the room, a uniformed man was coming to his feet.

"Freeze!" Jake shouted. The man's hand moved. Jake's Colt .45 roared, and a crater appeared in the wall next to the man's head. "Move again," Jake warned, "and I won't miss."

"What is the meaning of this?" the man demanded. More shots sounded in the background.

"Set your gun on the table," Jake ordered. The man complied, slowly, his eyes never leaving Jake's. Jake jerked his head toward the hallway. "This way." Hands up, the man crossed the room. Jake followed him into the hall. Brian was nowhere in sight.

"Brian?" Jake said into his radio, his Colt pressed against the small of his captive's back.

"Two doors down," Brian replied tersely. "I could use a hand." Jake prodded the man down the hall. Using him as a shield, Jake stepped into the room.

Brian was backed into a corner by the door, his submachine gun at the ready. Diagonally across the brightly lit room from him was a tall, one-eyed man, equally cornered. Thrust out in front of him was a large-caliber handgun. Next to him a woman, her eyes large with fright, sat on the edge of a rumpled bed.

"Good timing," Brian said, his eyes riveted on the man. "This Iraqi standoff was getting kind of tense."

"Tell him to drop it," Jake said to his captive.

"*You* tell him," the man retorted. "He speaks better English than I do."

Jake repeated his demand. The man grimaced, then threw the pistol onto the bed. "Over there, next to him," Jake ordered, giving his prisoner a shove. The short, fat man trotted across the room to stand next to the one-eyed man, who glared at him.

"I'm looking for a baby girl," Brian said, "and I haven't got a lot of time. Do either of you know where she is?" The short man started to speak, but was silenced by a burst of Arabic from the one-eyed man.

"Look, chump," Brian thundered, "in about twenty minutes this place is history. I'm either leaving here with my daughter or I'm going up with it, and if *I* go up, *you* go up." Brian raised the muzzle of his MP5 menacingly.

The short man's eyes went wide. "The air strike? It is for real?" His face twisted as he looked up at the one-eyed man. "You lied to us! You told us it was all American propaganda!" The man stared at an open suitcase on the bed next to the woman. "But," he shouted at the man, "you were leaving! It *is* true!"

The one-eyed man smiled sardonically. "Of course it is true, you pathetic fool. And when word gets out that American warplanes have killed both an American baby *and* her father, how much sweeter my victory, posthumous though it may be, will taste to our illustrious president."

"Nineteen minutes, Brian," Jake said quietly. "You keep looking. I'll stay here."

Shaking with rage, Brian took a step forward. "Where's my daughter?"

The man raised one, glittering eye. "That, Mr. Keefe, you shall never know."

The woman's head came up. "Keeve?" she said, her thickly accented voice tremulous with fear. "Keeve *habibi*?"

Brian's eyes snapped to her. "Who are you?"

The short man showered her with Arabic, which was cut off when the one-eyed man slammed him against the wall.

The woman smiled. "Bree-an," she said, now calm. "Bree-an Keeve, *habibi.*" Quiet triumph suffused her as she looked up at the darkly furious one-eyed man. Then she opened the heavy shawl she had wrapped around her. There, nestled on her lap, was Lauren Keefe.

✧ ✧ ✧

"Save the snuggles for later," Jake cautioned as Brian hugged his daughter. "We've got to get out of here."

Brian backed across the room as the fat man struggled to his feet. "You now have eighteen minutes to get as far away from here as you can," Brian told them. "Heading west would be a really good idea."

"Why are you telling me this?" the one-eyed man asked disdainfully. "If you think to torture me before you kill me, then you have failed."

"I'm not going to kill you," Brian replied.

The one-eyed man frowned. "No? Why not? I would if I were you. Instantly."

"Because I've got a friend who has far worse in store for you than mere death. Someone who is fully entitled to *kharab wa-turab.*" The one-eyed man blanched at the finality in Brian's stare.

The fat man, seeing them distracted by the exchange, sprang. With surprising speed he grabbed the gun from where the one-eyed man had tossed it onto the bed. He whirled, the gun spoke, and the one-eyed man was thrown backward. The fat man tossed the gun down and raised his hands. "He was a general in the Republican Guard," the fat man explained. "The president's closest henchman." He looked contemptuously at the figure slumped in the corner of the room. "He was hated."

Brian stared at the one-eyed man. "You've just found out,

sooner than you expected, that I'm right, haven't you?" he said quietly.

"What was that you said to him?" Jake asked, gazing at the now-pathetic body.

"*Kharab wa-turab*," Brian replied. "The ancient Middle Eastern belief in the right to lay waste to someone who has wronged you and refuses to atone for the crime. The right to extract a blood price." Brian lowered the MP5. "The right to vengeance."

Brian turned to Jake. "Here," he said, handing Lauren to Jake. "Hang on to her for a sec." Brian pulled a floppy mass of denim out of his backpack.

"What's that?" Jake asked as Brian slung it in front of him and adjusted buckles and straps.

"Vital piece of gear for any search-and-rescue mission," Brian replied, taking Lauren back. "Every SEAL should carry one. Brought it all the way from the States." Brian inserted his daughter into the sling and zipped it up. "It's called a Snugli."

"Team Two, report," Mark's voice came through their earphones.

"Two clear," Brian replied. "You?"

"We're outside, waiting for you," Mark told them. "Let's move it—the last bus is about to leave."

Brian saluted the fat man. "*Jusqu'au boutiste*, my friend," he said.

The little man laughed. "And you go right to the edge, too, *habibi*," he replied, returning the salute.

Brian then turned to the woman. "*Shukran, shukran.* Thank you very much."

The fat man listened, then laughed. "Her name is Nadia Sayed. She says that she would have spoken up sooner, but she did not recognize you in your funny face paint." Brian grinned, remembering that the camouflage paint had turned his face

Martian green. "She says that you are welcome," the fat man translated, "and she wishes Lauren a long and happy life."

Nadia came over and kissed the top of Lauren's head. "*Salaam aleikum*, Laureen," she whispered. *Peace be unto you.*

"To do 'a long and happy life' we need to get out of here *now*," Brian said. He looked at the fat man. "There's a truck out on the road. Head west, as fast as you can." The man nodded, and he and Nadia Sayed hurried from the room.

❖ ❖ ❖

Brian and Jake ran out the other door. Three figures were waiting for them on the road. Mark waved them on, and Jake and Brian caught up with them as they started down the road.

"All right!" Mark exulted, looking as he ran at his niece, huddled against Brian's chest. "We're two for two, so let's go home."

"How're you doin', ma'am?" Turk asked.

"Fine, Chief," Lydia Doral replied. "Just fine. Never again will I curse those early morning jogs around the mall that my husband drags me off on." She gestured at her filthy silk suit. "Not that I'm exactly dressed for—"

Both Turk and Mark cut her off with an upraised hand. Jake heard the terse report in his headset, too. "Jericho Five, Jericho Five, this is STAB-one. We've struck a mine and have to abort. We cannot, repeat, cannot make rendezvous. Go to Plan Bravo. I say again, go to Plan Bravo." The transmission cut off.

"Sounds ominous," Brian remarked.

"It *is* ominous," Mark confirmed. "The SEAL Tactical Assault Boat that was supposed to be waiting for us isn't going to make it."

"What do we do now?" Lydia Doral asked calmly.

"We go to our fallback extraction plan," Mark replied. "It's a whole lot riskier, but it's the only chance we've got." The towering machinery of the refinery began to thin out as they neared the river. "Now," he went on, "as soon as we're across the channel we—"

"Stop!" From his point position ten feet ahead of them, Turk held up a hand. "Everyone into the bushes," he ordered. "Meet me in those trees up ahead." Those behind darted into the foliage, then crept up and joined him.

From the copse of scraggly trees at the edge of the river's shore, they could see the inflatable boat, tantalizingly close. They could also see, on either side of the boat, a jeep full of soldiers, and the heavy machine guns mounted in the back of each jeep. They waited tensely as Mark and Turk exchanged whispers and gestures.

"Here's the plan," Mark said at last. "The chief and I are going to lay down a diversion. As soon as it pops, everybody head for the boat. Brian, you and Jake get the women over to the island. The chief and I will cover you, then follow as soon as it's secure." Mark looked at Brian. "You ever deploy a Fulton SRS?"

Brian nodded. "Once or twice. I should be OK if they haven't changed it." His grin was a white line in the darkness. "I take it that this is Plan B?"

"Sure is," Mark confirmed. "The SRS is out on the island, right where we left it when we dropped in. I hope. If it isn't, we start swimming." Mark paused. "And, Brian, if it's time to go and we aren't there, you *go*. That's an order."

"Aye aye, sir," Brian replied with mock officiousness. "But be there. Remember, *I'm* the one who'll have to explain it to your sister if I lose you."

Mark punched Brian in the arm. "Later, bro. Duck and cover until it pops." He and Turk melted into the blackness.

"Turn your backs and shield your eyes," Brian ordered. He turned, hunched down, and folded his arms over Lauren's head.

A minute later, two sharp concussions rocked them. A flash of white light seared Jake's optic nerve even through his tightly shut eyelids. He heard something ricochet off a tree trunk, then it smacked painfully into his cheek.

"Up!" Brian shouted. "Go! To the boat!"

They broke out of the trees and raced down the shore. Ahead of them Iraqi soldiers were rolling on the ground, howling in agony. "They used the sting-ball grenades," Brian shouted.

Mark and Turk were a hundred feet on either side of them, racing toward them along the water's edge. Jake, Brian, and Lydia Doral ran toward the boat, dodging helpless, writhing soldiers. Brian put out a hand, steadying Doral as she stumbled on the rocky beach. Brian and Jake, guns ready, watched for any threat from the Iraqis.

They reached the boat, and Brian and Jake shoved it into the water. They helped Doral in, then jumped in after her. Behind them, in the rear of one of the jeeps, a soldier pulled himself to his feet. He grabbed the grip of his machine gun. Slowly, its barrel swung around toward the trio in the boat.

"Oh, no ya don't, raghead!" Shiloh Turk roared as he ran. The stainless-steel barrel of his sawed-off shotgun came up. It thundered, and the soldier disappeared.

Brian tossed Jake a paddle. "Dig!" he shouted. An Iraqi officer came to his feet, shouting orders. Jake's wounded shoulder screamed as he dug the paddle into the water. Bullets began whistling overhead as the raft slowly made its way into the channel.

With a sharp *whee!* a bullet ricocheted off the water. "Down!" Brian ordered Lydia Doral, who hunkered down in the middle of the raft. Behind them, Mark and Turk stopped, twenty feet on either side of the two jeeps. Turk's shotgun started roaring as Mark laid down the other half of a deadly cross fire.

The machine gun on the other jeep erupted, and a bullet snatched the paddle from Jake's hands. Another tore through the fabric of the boat. Air hissed, and the boat listed violently to the right.

"Can you swim?" Jake asked Doral. In reply, the ambassador rolled over the boat's side and began swimming strongly for the island.

As the boat sank beneath them, Jake helped Brian unbuckle the Snugli. Holding it and its squalling occupant out ahead of him, keeping his body between his daughter and the metallic death behind them, Brian began to swim for the island. Jake swam after him, each stroke sending agony searing through his shoulder.

Despite the bullets slapping into the water around him, Jake slowed as he was consumed by exhaustion. His useless right arm trailed in the water. Jake winced as a machine-gun round, not quite all its energy spent in the water, slammed into his calf.

"C'mon, Jake," Brian shouted. "Turk'll never let you hear the end of it if you don't beat him out of the water." A flash from the shore illuminated the barren, oblong hump of rock that was their destination. They saw Lydia Doral pull herself up onto the island, scramble across the meager rise in its middle, and disappear behind the other side. The concussion from the explosion surged through the water around them.

"Smart woman," Brian observed. "Too bad we don't get to do the same."

An eternity later Jake felt wet rock beneath his fingers. He scrabbled for footing, then hauled himself onto dry land.

Brian was right beside him. "Stay here and watch for Mark and Turk," Brian ordered after looking Jake over. "Be our defensive perimeter while I start setting up the SRS." Brian handed Jake his submachine gun. He vanished over the island's spine.

✧   ✧   ✧

"Mrs. Doral?" Brian whispered.

"Over here." Doral's face was a pale oval against the black waters.

Brian handed her the Snugli. "Keep an eye on her for me, will you? There are a few things that need doing if we're going to get out of here." Brian could see the ambassador smile as she took the terrified Lauren out of the carrier.

"Of all my diplomatic duties," Doral said as she held Lauren to her, "this is both the strangest and the most pleasant."

Brian trotted to the center of the island. He pulled down his night-vision goggles. One of the jeeps on the shore was ablaze, and its flames illuminated the island clearly. Brian ran toward a pile of equipment at the island's southern end. He jerked a backpack from the pile, opened it, and began pulling out its contents.

A few minutes later Brian returned to Doral's side. "I'll hold her while you get into this," he offered. Taking Lauren, he handed Doral a heavy, hooded coverall identical to the one he had put on. Brian zipped the sleeping Lauren into the Snugli, then zipped his extra-large coverall up over her.

Doral held it up. "Well," she said, examining it critically, "olive drab isn't one of my colors, but I'll manage." She pulled it on and zipped it up, tucking her hair under the hood. Brian took her over and snapped her suit to the cord.

The ambassador's eyebrows shot up at Brian's description of what would happen. "Well," she said dryly, "it can't be worse than the express elevators at the United Nations."

Jake watched the rippled waters, backlit by the burning jeep. A staccato burst of shots ripped through the night. *Probably just ammo cooking off inside that jeep*, Jake decided. He squinted across the channel. *I can't see anybody moving. Including*, he realized, *Mark and Turk.*

Jake looked upriver, then back down toward the Persian Gulf. Nothing. He shifted painfully, trying to ease his shoulder.

With silent swiftness, two dark shapes appeared on either side of him. Black silhouettes against the night sky, firelight glinting from the cold steel they held. Jake jumped as a green face, black circles around its eyes, turned toward him.

"Relax, Army," Shiloh Turk grunted. "We left all the bill collectors back on the opposite shore."

Mark pulled a small metal box from a pocket. "Chariot, Chariot, this is Jericho Five. Do you read? Over."

"Jericho Five, Chariot," came the reply. "It's about time you boys checked in." Mark grinned at the rich, drawling Southern contralto. "My ETA is six minutes," the pilot reported. "And y'all better be ready to go, 'cause I won't get more 'n one pass at this."

"Roger, Chariot," Mark affirmed. "We'll be ready." He glanced at his wrist compass. "Your approach vector is one-eight-three." Mark nodded at the pilot's acknowledgment. "Five out." He looked at Turk. "Chief, you and Jake keep your eyes peeled for Tangoes. If it moves, blow it away. I'll be helping Brian with the SRS."

"You got it, boss," Turk replied, his grin vicious in the dying firelight.

"What's an SRS, Chief?" Jake asked, his eyes scanning the shore.

"You never used one in the rangers?" Turk asked incredulously, then stopped, listening to something out in the night. After a tense moment he went on. "An SRS is a Fulton Skyhook Recovery System. It's a long, thick cord with clips on it. We dress in these cute little bunny suits, clip the harnesses built into the suits onto the cord, and then send one end of the cord up on the end of a tethered helium balloon. Then that Southern belle will bring the Grumman C-2A Greyhound she's herding in at about two hundred feet, going like all get-out. She snags the tether, the boys in the Greyhound's cargo bay clamp a winch onto the cord, and up we go. And I do mean *up*." Turk grinned at Jake. "You ever been bungee jumpin'?"

"Was going to go, once," Jake admitted, "but Anne threw a fit when she found out about it."

"Anne your wife?"

"No!" Jake replied hastily. "At least," he added after a pause, "not yet."

Turk nodded approvingly. "Keep her guessing. There's a whole lot more interesting things to do with your life than settle down and start having kids."

"Maybe so, Chief," Jake replied. "But I must admit I'm starting to wonder."

❖ ❖ ❖

"Three minutes," the pilot of the Greyhound announced. "I'm turning on final approach. Got your strobes out yet?"

"Not yet," Mark replied. "Laying them out now. Look for them at one minute out."

"Roger that. Y'all just make sure I can see 'em."

Mark switched frequencies. "Jake! Chief! Come get suited up!" The two men trotted over and zipped themselves into their coveralls. "Two minutes," Mark told them. "At one minute I'll switch on the approach strobes, beat it back here, and get clipped on. Then we're outta here, mission accomplished." He grinned at the lump beneath Brian's suit.

Mark checked his watch. "Time to get those strobes lit up. Everybody else clip on. Brian, send up the balloon."

Mark ran to the north end of the island. Two rows of flashing lights began to appear as he laid out and switched on the small strobe lights.

Brian picked up the cord and jerked the cover off a small package at its end. With a cracking hiss, a three-foot balloon rapidly inflated. Brian switched on a small, bright-red strobe light at the balloon's base. He released the balloon, and it shot up into the night.

Turk also picked up a section of cord. "OK, Army," he told Jake. "To clip on, you just take this and attach it—"

With a growling roar, a boat swept around a bend in the river downstream from the island. A searchlight snapped on, bathing the island in painfully bright light. Heavy gunfire began raking the southern end of the rock.

"Gunboat!" Turk shouted. He flung down the cord and raced toward the southern end of the island. Jake was right beside him, unslinging Brian's MP5 submachine gun as he ran.

They went to their knees at the water's edge. Jake slammed home the MP5's trigger, sweeping a deadly hail of bullets along the gunboat's waterline. Turk braced his shotgun against a hip as he pumped off round after round at the approaching warship.

"Fifty seconds out," the Greyhound's pilot announced. "I've picked up your strobes and your balloon. Guide me in— what in thunder is going on down there?" she asked, surprised.

"Firefight!" Mark shouted as he raced back toward the others. "Chariot, go around!"

"No can do, Five. In about two minutes this is going to be one *serious* no-fly zone. Forty seconds—I'm looking for your wands."

Mark skidded to a stop beside Brian and Doral. "Turk! Jake!" he shouted. "Break off!" Mark snapped himself to the cord, then pulled two plastic sticks from a pocket. He bent them, shook them, and the cryoluminescent wands flared into green-glowing life. Holding them over his head, Mark began waving the rescue plane in.

Turk fired once more. The searchlight went out. Flinging down their weapons, he and Jake ran pell-mell for the others.

"Thirty seconds. Wands sighted. Prepare for pickup."

Fifty feet. Forty. Thirty. The two men ran side by side. Twenty feet.

A shot rang out, and Turk crashed to the ground. Without breaking stride Jake reached down. Strong fingers closed around olive cloth. His shoulder screaming, Jake dragged Turk along. Ten feet.

"Twenty seconds." Jake could hear the Greyhound's two turboprop engines, coming in low from the north. Red and green running lights appeared. Mark crossed the wands over his head and then threw them down.

"Ten seconds—brace yourselves."

"MacIntyre," Turk thundered. "Let me go!" They were there.

"Not on your life!" Jake gritted his teeth and hauled Turk up. Brian reached over and snapped Turk to the cord. He reached, straining for Jake's clip, but it was too far away.

"Like I told you, Chief," Jake rasped, "I always make my pickups!"

Jake wrapped one arm around the cord. The Greyhound flashed in over the end of the island. Jake tried desperately to clip himself on as he was swept up into the night.

"You on, Jake?" Mark shouted.

"Not yet. The propwash is throwing me around." Jake tried to wrap his feet around the cord, but the galelike propwash snatched it away. The refinery lights dwindled away rapidly below them.

Once more, Jake tried to bring the clip on his suit up to the clip on the cord. Once more, he failed. The strength began to ebb from his ravaged shoulders and arms. "Can't hold on," he grated. "Slipping."

"C'mon, Jake," Brian said quietly. "C'mon!"

Jake's right arm fell useless to his side. The hurricane generated by the Greyhound's propellers flung him sideways.

Jake looked down, preparing himself for his fall into the inky abyss looming below.

A sharp pain raced through the top of his head. Jake felt himself pulled slowly and inexorably upward. The clip on the cord appeared. Jake fumbled once, twice. Then, with a last, supreme effort, metal clipped to metal.

"I'm on!" Jake shouted. The pain in his head ceased. Jake looked up to see Shiloh Turk reaching down, his fingers firmly entwined in Jake's hair. "Doesn't look to me like you're slipping," Turk told him. "Looks like you did OK, even for an army type. Good thing the wind kicked you up to where I could latch onto ya." He grinned down at Jake. "Don't forget, Ranger— SEALs make their pickups, too." Above them, the Greyhound's cargo bay grew steadily closer.

A deafening roar swept past them, followed by a buffeting shock wave. "There they are!" Brian shouted. They looked up to see a line of glowing afterburners flash by overhead. The five watched as the F-14 Tomcats and F/A-18 Hornets closed in on their target.

Quickly, Jake reached inside his coverall and unzipped a waterproof pocket. He took out his small battered Leica. Then, as the al-Kafhar oil refinery vanished in a series of brilliant, multicolored explosions, Jake began taking pictures.

32

"It's all right," Pat told Rebecca soothingly. "Annie was just as terrified of the candle on her first birthday cake." The roaring fire in the huge fieldstone fireplace cast a cheery glow over those assembled in the Keefes' family room and locked out the icy grip of a late-February Maine winter. "Annie and I will start cutting the cake," Pat offered, "while you calm her down."

"This is delicious," Ataliya Marakova commented, taking another sip from her steaming mug. "What did you say it's called?"

"Mulled cider," Elliot French replied. "Made from apples grown right in the French family orchards. It's got cinnamon, and cloves, and . . . " French faltered. "Chris could tell you what's in it," he added, "but she's off somewhere feeding the twins." French sighed. "Seems like she's *always* off somewhere feeding the twins."

Joel pulled up a chair. "How are you adjusting to life in the United States, Ataliya?"

Her radiant smile warmed the room another few degrees. "It's wonderful! I love Boston! Dr. Stafford, my Ph.D. advisor at Harvard, is simply amazing. And Randy took me out the other night for something called scrod." The woman once known as Scheherazade laughed. "Randy practically had to force me to taste it, but it turned out to be the most wonderful fish!" She cast a long glance across the room at Randy, who was deep in animated conversation with Lydia Doral and Allison.

French grew serious. "Based on your reports, along with those of Randy and Brian, we finally established just who the one-eyed man was."

Marakova looked sharply at him. "Kailim al-Murah?"

French nodded. "The late and very unlamented chief confidant and hitman of Iraq's illustrious president. I'm sorry," he added. "If we had known, we might have been able to save your partner from that team of assassins al-Murah sent into Turkey."

Marakova shrugged eloquently. "Hafez led the life he wanted to lead." Another long look at Randy banished the shadow that crossed her face.

"Too bad," Roy Barnard mumbled to Brian through a mouthful of birthday cake, "that Bill couldn't make it."

"Oh, he made it," Brian replied. "Just long enough to find out that Jack Carter had talked Mark's friend Shiloh Turk into going ice fishing up off Doughnut Cove."

Barnard frowned. "Turk was shot during the rescue, wasn't he?"

Brian nodded. "He spent a month or so recovering at Bethesda. Last month, when Mark got back from the Persian Gulf, he found out that Turk was still in the States, so he asked us if he could invite Turk up. For a tough old master chief," Brian added with a grin, "Turk plays one mean game of patty-cake. Anyway," Brian continued, "Bill, Jack, and Turk high-tailed it out of here like nothing else." Brian chuckled. "Ice fishing sounded real good to Jake, too. He had his parka on and was halfway out the door when Anne put her foot down. Right on his." Brian grinned. "Jake's beginning to realize that it's almost over. He's starting to hear the fat lady sing, and he's just noticed that she's singing at his wedding."

"When's Mark getting here?" Barnard asked, laughing.

"Any minute now," Brian replied. "He wrangled some leave, and a friend of mine offered to pick him up in Bangor."

"I've got a charter for you next week, by the way," Barnard added.

"Hunting trip?"

"Nope. News crew wants you to fly them around so they can get some aerial shots."

Brian grimaced. "Not again. I thought we were done with that."

Barnard grinned. "This one's special. It's one of those true-life shows. It'd be a favor to Bill and me."

Brian frowned at the sheriff. Then he smiled as he suddenly understood. *"True American Crime Stories?"*

"The very same," Barnard replied proudly. "We're going to be on next month."

Rebecca brought the coffee into the family room. Anne followed, carrying a tray of cups. Just inside the doorway Rebecca stopped, then nudged Anne. "Check *this* out," she whispered to Anne. "I asked him to watch Lauri while I went and got the coffee."

Anne followed Rebecca's eyes to the hearth rug in front of the fireplace. There a grinning Jake was stretched out, chin in his hands, playing peekaboo with a chortling Lauren.

"My, oh, my," Anne said softly. "If Job could only see this, he'd know he was right when he said that God 'performs wonders that cannot be fathomed, miracles that cannot be counted.'"

Rebecca smiled as she watched Anne's eyes shine with far more than the firelight.

✧ ✧ ✧

"So there I was," Allison was saying, "demo-ing this new, hyperexpensive space-imaging system to a bunch of stuffed shirts, including the director of the CIA and the president. So, after giving this long and incredibly simplistic explanation, the jerk I was working for signaled me to turn it on. I did, and what's the first thing this umpteen-gazillion-dollar system displayed? A ratty old glove left over from the Gemini space program back in the sixties. There it was, still sailing along in low-earth orbit." Her impish grin widened. "Well, I thought both my supervisor and the director were going to have strokes right on the spot. Plus, the fact I, lowly technician that I was, thought it was hysterically funny didn't help matters at all." Allison finished her cider. "Finally, the president looked at the glove for the longest time. Then he looked right at me and said—"

The whining roar of a turboprop engine cut her off. Everyone looked out to where a Cessna similar to Brian's was coming to a stop on the ice next to the Keefe dock. They watched as a waiting Brian secured the plane and the passenger door opened.

"So, anyway," Allison went on, still watching what was going on outside, "the president says to me—who's that?"

Randy frowned at Allison's nonsequitur. "Why," he asked, "did the president say 'who's that' when he was looking at a *glove?*"

"No, no," Allison replied. "Who's *that?*" she asked, pointing out the family-room window.

A young man was making his way along the path up to the house. Blonde curls peeked out from beneath a black watch cap. A peacoat was slung over one shoulder. A deep-indigo ribbed SEAL commando sweater hugged his broad shoulders, swept along his torso, and tucked into the trim waist of his tight jeans. White teeth flashed as he called out a greeting.

"Who, him?" Randy asked. "That's Mark Sewell, Rebecca's brother." He turned back to Allison. "Now, what did the president *really* say?"

Eyes still on the new arrival, Allison got up. With a brief "Excuse me," she hurried from the room.

Randy frowned. "Where'd she go?"

Amusement danced in Lydia Doral's eyes. "Right off the deep end, I'd say," she replied.

Mark dropped his duffel bag in a corner and threw his coat on top of it. He gave his sister a hug and relieved Rebecca of her daughter. Gripping her diapered bottom, Mark held Lauren easily at arm's length. Both laughed as they made faces at one another.

A coppery swirl caught Mark's attention. His eyes refocused from the very young woman he was holding to the somewhat older one standing behind her. "Hi," Mark said easily. "You must be Allison. Becky said you might be able to make it. I'm Becky's brother, Mark."

Allison smiled. "It's really cold out there," she replied, tilting her head toward the picture window. "Would you like something warm?"

Mark's saw the challenge in her eyes. His grin deepened as he wondered just what sort of gauntlet she was throwing down. "Sure," he replied slowly. "What do you suggest?" Without taking his eyes off Allison, Mark handed Lauren back to Rebecca.

"C'mon, sweetheart," Rebecca huffed to Lauren. "Let's go feed you. We know when we're not wanted."

Standing next to her husband, Pat watched Allison and Mark's spirited conversation. "What do you think of this development?" she asked.

Joel grinned down at her. "'How the mighty have fallen.'"

The house was dark and quiet at last. Brian, his hands behind his back, stood by the picture window, watching the gentle, blanketing snowfall. He relaxed in the knowledge that all was well, his guests secure, his family safe. With a small smile, Brian picked a teddy bear up off the floor and put it on the window seat. Then he crossed the room and stoked the dying fire into tiny flames that danced among the coals.

Rebecca, in her nightgown and slippers, came in and stood beside her husband. Lauren, sleepy and sucking on two fingers, lay swaddled in her mother's arms. "Why did you have me get her up?" Rebecca asked.

"To see this," Brian replied quietly. "To be with us for this." From his pocket he took out the long, thin strip of parchment on which was written the Yezidi Throne Verse. In its center was a small hole, from the needle-point of the dagger that had pinned the scroll to the headboard of Lauren's crib.

Brian wadded up the strip, crushing it in his massive fist. *"But if serving the Lord seems undesirable to you,"* Brian quoted as he tossed the ball of parchment into the fire, *"then choose for yourselves this day whom you will serve, whether the gods your forefathers served beyond the River, or the gods of the Amorites, in whose land you are living. But as for me and my household, we will serve the Lord."* Brian put his arm around his wife and daughter and drew them close.

Three figures, silhouetted by the fire, watched as the scroll vanished forever into the consuming flames.

THE END